MW01517822

Leader of the Pack
By Leighann Phoenix

Cover Design: Leighann Phoenix
Leader of the Pack © 2008 Leighann Phoenix
eXcessica publishing
All rights reserved

To the brave, belong all things.

-Celtic Creed

Chapter 1

Smoke thickened as the night wore on. Aislinn
moved from one person to the next along the crowded
bar, filling drink orders. She took the job a month ago,
when she arrived in town. Her scummy boss, Derrick,
was more than happy to hire her. He recently lost a bar
tender, and Aislinn was above average in appearance,
even if she didn't think so. When Aislinn applied to
the job Derrick didn't even asked if she could mix
drinks. He figured he could teach that. She wasn't a
super model, but she was attractive in a strange way,
and she was better than moving Kelly up. The patrons
liked her where they could reach her.

Aislinn hated the place. She learned relatively
quickly to keep space between herself and Derrick, the
ass. He tended to grab her and make lewd comments.
He even attacked her once, but she managed to get
away. Unfortunately, she needed the job. She needed
the money. That was the only reason she kept working
after that. One would think that after she decked him
he would stay out of her way, but Derrick just kept
trying. Aislinn thanked the stars that currently he was
at the far end of the bar talking with some regulars.
With Luke tending bar between them, that was about
the right distance tonight.

The other people she worked with were mostly
nice. Kelly was really the only bitch and that was
because Aislinn got the job Kelly wanted. In this

place, the best spot to be was behind the bar. Then the only person who could grab you was Derrick. Anywhere else and you were fair game for all the jerks who came in the place. Kelly thought that she did her time and deserved the bartender job. When Derrick gave it to Aislinn, he made Kelly a permanent enemy for her.

Aislinn approached the new guy who sat down at the bar near the wall. He was impressive. His presence caused most of the other patrons to make more than enough room for him, resulting in an unnatural amount of space at that end of the bar. Aislinn was perfectly happy to have a short lull in the number of people she had to deal with.

The man was pretty big, even sitting on the stool. He had black hair, brown-black eyes, and tanned skin. He looked hard muscled even under the black leather duster he was wearing. But the strangest thing was this ageless appearance to him. At first look she might have said he was in his late twenties/early thirties. Then, at second glance, he looked almost 100. Whether that was normal for him or because he just had the worst day of his life was up for grabs. "What can I get you?"

The guy looked up at her as if he only just realized that he was in a bar. Aislinn waited and when he didn't respond she asked again. "What can I get you?"

Cullen stared appraisingly at the girl speaking to him. She had an odd scent. It was hard to make out between the rancid smell of the bar, the smoke from the people around him soaking into everything, and some awful perfume she seemed to have bathed in. But there was something to it that caught his attention. She was attractive, but she wasn't remarkable in any way. She had brown hair, blue eyes, pale skin, and medium build. She wasn't his type. *I would probably break her*; he thought and grinned at himself. Besides she wasn't what he was here for. The last thing he wanted was a woman tonight. No matter how intriguing her scent was.

"If you're not ready to order I can come back in a couple," Aislinn offered at his silence and the annoyed, confused look on his face as he stared at her.

"Guinness."

Aislinn nodded, poured the beer and placed it in front of him. No sooner had she waited on the next person but he was pushing his glass toward her again. She gave him another. Then another. At first she was concerned. He didn't look very friendly and adding drunk to not very friendly usually didn't end well. But he kept to himself, paid for each glass as he indicated his need for a refill, and didn't do anything to bother her or anyone else. He just stared at his glass and drank. Something about him that she couldn't quite put her finger on kept everyone else away.

Aislinn really wasn't sure what kept drawing her attention back to him. His smell, for one thing, disturbed her. Since she had escaped her previous life, her sense of smell seemed more pronounced, sharper. After everything she'd been through to this point she kept her own council. That included not telling anyone that she could determine who she was talking to even with her eyes closed if she'd ever met the person before. Smells bothered her very easily. When she got out into the big wide world, she started layering on perfumes to mask the smells around her. But tonight his smell was getting through her defenses. He smelled foul or dead. At least that was the only way she could describe it. She didn't know what could possibly make that odor. Every time the air shifted she nearly flinched at the awful reek that overpowered even the rancid beer in this place. *God why did I decide bartending was a good idea,* she thought to herself.

Cullen was still sitting there drinking as the place was getting ready to close. He watched the girl who had been serving him all night walked up to him as she cleared the bar. "Hey, buddy, do you need me to call you a cab or something?"

"Cullen," he said before he knew that he had said it.

"What?" Aislinn stopped what she was doing and started reaching for a phone. "Is there someone I can call for you," she reiterated.

"My name. Cullen. Not 'buddy'. And no, I don't need a ride. I'll walk." He started to get up only to realize that he drank more than he originally thought. *It's been a long time since I managed to get drunk,* he thought with a measure of amusement. *Well that's what I came here to do wasn't it?* He sat back down on the bar stool.

Aislinn sighed and looked over at one of the other girls. Nikki just shrugged. "All right, Cullen," she said haltingly. "Look, we're closing. You're too drunk to move. You've got to have a friend somewhere who'll come get you."

He looked up at her and grinned with wry amusement. "Yeah," he said, "a whole *pack.*"

Normally a guy who said something like that and looked at her that way would have scared the crap out of her. But there was just something about the smelly guy that told her he wasn't a threat to her. If there was one thing she learned over the years since she started running it was reading people. That was half the reason Derrick didn't really bother her. She had known what he was the minute she took the job. So, obviously it was her own fault she had to put up with him. Aislinn picked up the phone. "Give me a number."

Cullen rattled off a number and she dialed. It rang twice and then a gruff, sleepy voice picked up. "Hello?"

"Yeah hi, sorry to wake you," Aislinn said.

"Yeah, who is this?" the voice said.

"Um, I tend bar. Do you know some guy named Cullen?"

A shocked, "Huh?" came from the sleepy voice. Cullen was watching Aislinn with amusement. His eyes sparkled a bit and he had a grin that reminded her of a kid playing a great joke on someone. He was taking note of everything about her. For a human she was either quite impressive or very stupid. There wasn't another person in this bar who had been willing to be within two feet of him, but the girl didn't seem bothered at all by his appearance or mood. He got the feeling that there really wasn't anything he could have said or done to have made her afraid of him. More than any of that, she was able to make eye contact with him and stare him down. It had been a long time since anyone had enough balls for that.

Aislinn growled her annoyance at the situation. "Look, I'm sorry I woke you up, buddy. But there's this guy in my bar and we're closing. He's too drunk to leave on his own. He says his name is Cullen and he gave me this number when I asked him if he wanted me to call someone for him. Can you come get him or not?"

Keith rubbed his face. He thought he was having a crazy dream. He looked at the cell phone and then put it back to his ear. "Cullen?"

"Yes, Cullen." The female voice at the other end of the line was sounding more agitated by the minute. "Are you coming to get him," she insisted.

"Yeah fine. Where is he?"

"The bar's called the Blood Pit. It's on the corner of Elm and Oak. Do you know it?"

"No," he said. "But I'll find it." Then there was a click.

Aislinn stared at the phone. Cullen chuckled. "He hung up?"

"Yeah, but he said he was coming." Aislinn went back to cleaning up.

Cullen reveled in the feeling of the spinning room. As he waited he watched the girl move about. The drinking had done precisely what he wanted. It drowned out the look, smell, and feel of Jenna, that bitch he wasn't interested in being mated to. He was trying to figure out what that scent was on the girl when one of the other girls walked up to her. That annoyed him to no end. Now there were two obnoxious smelling perfumes in addition to the rest of the odors in this room covering up the girl's scent.

"Ais, I've gotta go." She lowered her voice and looked over at Cullen uncertainly then back at Aislinn. But Cullen's ears were better than most and he heard every word she said. "I want to wait for you but Jeremy's outside already and he's being impatient. I don't know who to be more concerned about. Derrick or this guy you're looking after. It's not real bright of you."

Aislinn looked back toward the offices then over at Cullen. "I know. Maybe I can talk Derrick into watching him 'til his friend gets here."

"Fat chance on that. How's he gonna stalk you if he's gotta stick around here for some guy. Nope, he'll say that you didn't just kick him out so this guy's your problem. Then when he's gone and you don't have me around to give you a ride home, Derrick offers you a ride and guess how he'll expect you pay for it. Not to mention, the jerk's been drinking tonight. He's checked his brain at the door."

"It's okay Renee. I'll be fine. I've taken care of myself for this long." Cullen noted the tired, lonely sound in her voice.

Renee looked at Cullen again, just as some big football type poked his head in the doorway. "Renee," he yelled. "Are you coming or what?"

"Yeah," she answered sheepishly. "I've really gotta go," she said in that abused, manipulated, will-answer-to-any-jerk-that-pretends-he-cares-about-her way. She hugged Aislinn. "Be safe," Cullen heard her whisper.

"You too," Aislinn said knowingly. Renee blushed and then hurried away. As she reached the door the guy grabbed her by the arm and led her out.

Cullen held himself back. She was just another human in an abusive relationship and it wasn't any of his business. He growled under his breath and tried to stand up anyway. Suddenly the room began spinning again and he sat back down on the stool with a grin and a chuckle.

"Aislinn!" The voice that called the girl's name was slurred and angry sounding. Cullen looked up to see the girl hurry to some greasy looking guy who was standing in a doorway on the back wall. He tried to get her back into the office but the girl was smart enough to not let him draw her in. "Haven't you gotten rid of that guy yet?" His tone was annoyed and drunk.

"He's got a friend coming to get him. If you want to go I'll lock up behind me."

"And leave you here in my place?" He grinned luridly at her. "The only guy you get to stay here alone with is me." He tried to grab her, but she stepped back and he missed. That earned her a glare.

"You know that I don't work that way, Derrick. You wanna fire me go ahead. I don't play touchy feely with random fuck-offs."

Cullen grinned again. She was amusing. Her tone was assertive and she seemed to be in control, so he let her protect herself. It was nice to see that some people could. Cullen missed the end of their conversation to his swimming brain and his own thoughts. The guy disappeared back into his office and Aislinn was walking toward him when he looked up.

"So where is this friend of yours anyway?" She said. He could hear an edge of concern in her voice when she said that. She stared at Cullen and then over at the door.

"You know what," Cullen said and eyed the office door. "If you need a ride home or something…" His voice trailed off as he looked at her.

Aislinn's eyes meet his again. She couldn't help see there was something in there. He was just one of those people she knew could be trusted in the same way she knew that Derrick couldn't be. At the same time logic dictated that she not accept rides from drunken strangers.

"No thanks." She walked over to the main doors and looked out. There wasn't anyone there and the parking lot was abandoned except for a large black SUV and Derrick's dilapidated red Honda. Presumably he SUV belonged to this Cullen guy. She was considering calling a taxi. It would cost her but at least that was safer than any of her other options at the moment. Aislinn turned around to find Cullen standing directly behind her with a confused, appraising look on his face.

He just couldn't put his finger on it. He wasn't sure what she smelled like. But he was starting to think that he liked it, whatever it was. He figured that if it weren't for the alcohol he probably wouldn't be being so introspective or even care. The worst part was that he wanted a closer inspection. Not that she'd submit to that. She wouldn't even let him give her a ride. She was standing there looking at him cautiously. He closed his eyes and smiled, shaking his head. He could just imagine her reaction if he said something like, *I'll give you a ride home. You can take a shower. Then you can let me smell you.* He chuckled again. Alcohol hadn't felt this good in ages. *It's pretty sad with a little bit of amusement caused by a random female and alcohol beats out everything else in your life.*

Aislinn could see the thoughts spinning through his head. He was amusing himself with whatever it was he was thinking. She couldn't help wondering what it was. He certainly had a pleasant smile. As he was standing there she finally saw what was making him smell so foul. He was wearing a t-shirt and jeans under his duster. Everything he was wearing was black, so in the gloomy bar with all the smoke and him sitting behind the bar she hadn't noticed. But now that he was standing, with the coat open in the light from the main entrance she could see what appeared to be blood all over the front of him. She wasn't an expert but she was pretty positive from the smell that it wasn't human blood. That had a more coppery smell to it. She had caught that smell coming from people a number of times. People were always getting hurt. The smell of human blood wasn't pleasant, but it wasn't this foul either.

Cullen saw confusion on her face and followed her gaze to the front of his clothes. When he realized what she was staring at he pulled the duster closed and looked up at her again. That sobered him up a bit. He'd nearly forgotten the fight with the vamp he'd gotten himself into after he left Jenna's. He intended to go home after that, but spied this dive and decided to stop instead. *Maybe that was a mistake.* When their eyes met again they seemed to be staring into each other, trying to read the other's mind. That was when another large black SUV pulled into the lot.

Aislinn turned to look at who was pulling in. "This your friend?"

"Yeah, I think so," he said, still looking at her. He didn't want to be done with this yet. She had obviously seen the blood. Didn't she even care?

Aislinn looked over his shoulder toward the office, and then sidled past Cullen and headed for the bar. "Excuse me." She half jogged, half walked toward the bar and jumped over it in one motion. Cullen noted the athletic ability that her non-athletic build masked. She grabbed some stuff from behind the bar and then came around the side, all the while watching the office door. As she came back toward the main entrance she called back to the office. "Derrick, that guy's ride's here. I'm leaving."

Before Derrick could get out of the office to stop her she had moved passed Cullen again and out into the parking lot. "Have a good night," she waved and walked hurriedly toward the street.

The guy from the office came trotting across the floor and stared out the door after her but she had managed to get out to the road and was on her way toward town. "Shit," he said and glared at Cullen.

Cullen could see the look in the man's eyes and knew that whether it was tonight or some other night Aislinn was in danger. Something in Cullen was outraged at the thought. But the alcohol was making it difficult for him to think beyond doing something unfortunate to the man right then and there.

Keith walked up to Cullen as Derrick ushered him the rest of the way out the entrance and closed the door, locking it without a word. Derrick would never know how close he came to being ripped to shreds that night.

Keith followed Cullen's gaze as he watched Aislinn walking quickly down the road. "Hey, you all right?"

"Yeah," Cullen answered and looked over at his friend as he was led toward the SUV. "Congratulate me. I'm engaged to be mated."

Keith understood. He shook his head. He couldn't believe that Cullen was going along with this. It wasn't the way the Arnauk operated. As they neared the SUV Ranaild stepped out. Cullen threw Ranaild the keys to the SUV he'd driven here and Ranaild walked to the other vehicle. Keith headed for his side of the car. As they were getting in, Cullen saw Derrick appear out the side of the bar and head for the beat up car at the other side of the lot.

"Do me a favor," Cullen said. "Consider it a condemned man's last request. Follow that guy."

Keith stared at Cullen a minute and then shrugged. Putting the truck in gear he headed after the guy. It didn't make any sense but who was he to argue with Lord General Cullen Arnauk. "You gonna tell me why we're following him?"

Cullen smiled sardonically. "Cuz he's an ass and I want a reason to rip his throat out." "All right." Keith wasn't used to Cullen being like this. Firstly, he didn't get drunk. Secondly, he didn't disappear and then need rides summoned by strange girls in the middle of the night. Thirdly, he didn't show interest in human females. And if that wasn't enough, he didn't chase human males around for any reason. Keith glanced sidelong at Cullen. He knew that being forced into mating with Jenna Tairneach was the last thing in existence that he wanted, but this was just strange.

"Faigh muin," Cullen swore vehemently and brought Keith's attention back to the situation. Keith slammed on the brakes and Cullen dove out of the car before Keith could see what the problem was.

* * * *

Aislinn had been walking as fast as she could. She was just praying that she could reach her crappy apartment before Derrick could get his act together. It was only a ten minute walk from the bar but if he got in his car relatively quickly he'd be able to catch up.

When Derrick pulled in front of her, cutting her off, she knew that she was in trouble. Aislinn headed for the other side of the road as Derrick got out and followed her. "Hey Ais, are you sure you don't want a ride," he slurred.

God, I wonder how much he drank tonight? Aislinn's mind raced. He was between her and her apartment. *Just one more block.* Momentarily she thought she might be able to get around him. She was rather quick. Then there was the other option. He had tried this once before. She had cold cocked him and he had left her alone for a week. "Do you want me to hit you again?"

"You bitch," he said with a wicked glare. "You really do think you're too good for me. I'll teach you this time."

Aislinn set herself up in a defensive stance. As Derrick got closer she balled her hands into fists and punched him square in the face. Derrick grunted, but managed to catch himself just before he fell over. "Damn bitch!" he said, spitting out blood. "You on steroids or something?"

Aislinn took the opportunity to try and run around him but he yanked a black boxlike thing out of his pocket and caught her in the side with it as she tried to run. Aislinn felt the excruciating electric shock blaze through her body. Suddenly everything spun and she lost control of her legs. She found herself lying on the ground in confusion, unable to move and staring up at Derrick. He held up the black box and pushed a button so that she could see what he had done. Electricity jumped across the electrodes on the end of the taser. Derrick smiled an evil smile. "I bet you feel just as good unconscious as not."

A low growl caught Derrick's attention and he turned around but all he could see were shadows down the street. He figured he needed to work quickly before the stun wore off. Derrick shocked Aislinn again for good measure and shoved the taser back in his pocket. He had something more permanent in the car to deal with her. But he had to carry her over there. Another growl caught his attention and he looked behind him to see that guy Aislinn had been waiting on standing there out of nowhere. The guy didn't say anything and his face was shadowed where he stood with a street lamp behind him.

"Mind your own business," Derrick spit at him and headed for his car with Aislinn slung over his shoulder.

Cullen lost it. He couldn't believe that the piece of caoch would still be trying to get away with this even after being caught. He stepped up and knocked Derrick's feet out from under him. As Derrick fell Cullen grabbed Aislinn and pulled her to himself. The stun was starting to wear off and she looked up into his face. His eyes were like molten pools of amber. It was almost hypnotic. They seemed to swim between dark brown almost black and glowing gold.

Derrick stood up swearing and pulled the taser out again. He headed toward Cullen and Aislinn and jabbed the device at them. Cullen took the shock in his arm and then shook his head at the guy. Derrick finally figured out that this was not going to go his way. He turned and made a dash for his car but somehow Cullen was there first. Derrick tried the taser again but Cullen only grunted as the shock went through him and grabbed Derrick by the wrist that was holding the gun. There was a disgusting crunching sound and Derrick's screaming as Cullen's hand squeezed around Derrick's wrist and the bones gave under the pressure.

Aislinn was still a bit dazed as she watched Cullen beat Derrick to the ground and then toss the guy in the backseat of his car. Then, as if nothing had happened, Cullen came walking over to her. "Are you sure you don't want that ride home," he asked.

Aislinn swallowed deliberately. She just didn't get it. "Why did you do that?"

Cullen watched her. She still wasn't afraid of him. This little human girl had just been attacked and watched him throttle her boss. He knew that she had seen his eyes turn. He nearly killed the guy without thinking. The alcohol was warping his sense of control. "I don't really know," he said honestly.

Cullen knew that Keith was watching from the truck. He could see the black SUV down the road a ways. "That ride," he asked again.

"I just live a block down from here."

"Then I'll walk you." It wasn't an offer.

Aislinn could tell from the tone in his voice that he wasn't going to take 'no' for an answer. She took a deep breath. "Fine, it's this way."

Cullen walked with her toward her apartment building. "I think you need a new job." Aislinn harrumphed at him. "Yeah, well you gonna give me one? Here's my resume. College dropout with minimal bartending experience seeks nice stable job not working for an ass." She refused to look at him and he knew there were tears in her eyes from the shaky way she finished the statement.

"All right, you're hired," he said.

She stopped and looked at him incredulously. "Are you for real?"

Now he could see the glassy eyes. He wasn't sure if it had been his question or everything that had just happened that had caused her to be suddenly upset. But he didn't like the idea that it might be his fault.

"What do you mean," she persisted when he didn't explain himself.

"I have some influence with a number of different businesses in town. I can give you a job. Secretary," he shrugged, "waitress if you really want. If that's what you do."

Aislinn wasn't sure if she should take him seriously or not. "Who are you? Superman?"

Cullen chuckled and one corner of his mouth turned up in that amused smile he'd been wearing off and on all night when he looked at her. "I prefer Batman. I don't think I could pull off red and blue tights and Batman had better toys."

Aislinn shook her head. "I think you've done enough for me at this point," she said cautiously.

Cullen rolled his eyes and sighed in annoyance. "Why is it that people never do the smart thing when it's right in front of them? Look, I'm just offering you a legitimate job. You shouldn't have to put up with a creep like that."

Aislinn glared at him. What right did he have to be angry with her? It's not like she asked for his help. "And what about the other girls there? You gonna give all the people working for Derrick jobs elsewhere? Why are you so concerned with me?"

"Honestly?" Cullen ran his hand through his hair and looked back toward where the black SUV was parked. He knew that Keith was sitting behind the tinted windows watching the scene. "I don't really know. No, I'm not going help out everyone working in that dive. But I thought I might be able to help you out. If you want to keep working for that guy, be my guest. But my guess is that when he gets a grip after what I did to him he's going to be looking to take it out on someone. Who do you think is going to end up the target?" He was suddenly feeling very sober again and didn't like it.

Aislinn stood in silence for a minute staring at nothing on the ground. "You're right. I'm gonna have to quit. I can't stay there now. It would have been one thing if I'd just beaten him off like last time, but you really screwed this up."

Cullen growled at her. "Would you have rather--"

"Let me finish." Aislinn interrupted him. Cullen was shocked into silence. No one interrupted him. "No I wouldn't rather the alternative. But you didn't have to put him in the hospital."

"He's not in the hospital. At least I don't see you running to call an ambulance." Cullen shook his head. "You know what? Just forget it. I'm sorry I interfered." He turned and started to head for the SUV.

Aislinn watched him leaving for a moment. "Shit, wait!" She was standing there nervously. "God, why does the smart thing have to feel so shitty? Look, I just don't like owing people anything. I seem to be accumulating quite the bill with you. First you come out of nowhere and… Well, you know what you did. Now you want to give me a real job. How the hell am I supposed to pay you back for this stuff?"

Cullen could understand how she was feeling. He didn't like owing people either. "You can call us even for the first thing, considering you spent half your shift keeping an eye on me and then making sure I got home all right." She looked like she was about to argue but an authoritative look from Cullen kept her silent. Even if the glare she threw at him was screaming that she didn't think it was an even trade off. "As far as the job goes, I'm just offering you a job. Intelligent, reliable people are hard to come by. It's not as big a favor as you might think."

"I'm really not in a position to turn you down." Aislinn was feeling trapped. But she knew better than to think that it would be at all feasible to go back to her job at the Blood Pit.

Cullen nodded. He started searching his pockets. Empty handed, he looked up at her. "Got a piece of paper and a pen?"

Aislinn opened her purse and started rooting around inside. "Now you're asking a lot." After a moment she shook her head. "Not with me. But I know I have one inside." She pulled her keys out and without another thought about letting a complete stranger into her apartment she headed up the cement steps from the sidewalk and opened the main door. Cullen followed along behind.

Keith watched out the window as Cullen headed into the building with the girl he had just rescued. None of it made any sense. He was torn between getting out and following them and just asking Cullen what the hell he was doing. It was late and he wanted to go back to his bed. Jaylyn was already pissed that he'd left. If he didn't get back soon, he'd be sleeping on the couch.

Cullen was still just drunk enough to completely forget that Keith was waiting outside. The elevator was out of order so they headed up three flights of stairs. The place was entirely unpleasant. It smelled of mould and piss and there was garbage in the halls. It didn't look as though it had been cleaned in about a century and graffiti covered the walls and railings of the stairwell. He couldn't help the look on his face when Aislinn opened the door to her apartment and let him in.

"I know the place is pretty awful. But the rent is cheap." She was more than a little embarrassed by letting him see the place. She lived in efficiency in the bad part of town. There's only one look for places like that. Aislinn liked to refer to it as post-apocalyptic chic. The only thing worse would be being homeless. The one room she was in sported tattered wallpaper in an old 70's pattern. She slept on a mattress on the floor in one corner and the kitchen was only functional because of the microwave she got at the local Goodwill. She tossed her purse down on the table. She was kicking herself for letting him in here. She could just imagine where he probably lived if he was able to say that he 'had influence over a number of businesses in town.' She rummaged through some things on a small table in the kitchen/dining/living area of the room and managed to produce a pen and paper.

Cullen could see the embarrassment on her face when she handed him the stuff without looking him in the eyes for the first time that night. He put the paper on the table so he could write and it wobbled. He ignored it and wrote a name, number, and address on the paper. Then he wrote something else underneath that. "Here," Cullen handed her the paper and she looked over the information. "Go to the address there. The guy you want to talk to is Liam Arnauk. Tell him that Cullen sent you. I wrote him a note there. He'll give you a job."

Aislinn looked over the paper. The note he had written on the bottom of it wasn't written in English, but she could read it. "The girl's name is Aislinn. I'd appreciate if you found her a job. I'll call us even if you manage something good. Cullen."

Cullen was stunned. It took a lot to surprise him. But this girl had managed one thing after another tonight. "You read Gaelic?"

Aislinn was pleased by the shocked look on his face. She smiled at him smugly. "Actually I read and speak several languages. Gaelic is one of them."

"How? No one bothers with Gaelic." He couldn't help the curiosity. Who was she?

"I wasn't always living in crapholes like this and waiting tables in bars to make ends barely meet. Before I came here I was a college student. I was studying folklore and dead languages. Gaelic may not be completely dead, but it's pretty close. I find it interesting. Actually I was wondering why you were using it. Studying something like that in college is one thing. But it looks like you're using it on a casual basis. And 'no one bothers with Gaelic.'" Aislinn mocked with a grin and raised eyebrows. She could tell by the incredulous look on his face that she had managed to get a little past his guard and that didn't happen often.

"My entire family speaks Gaelic. We just always have." He was giving her that appraising look again. Cullen couldn't hold back his curiosity any longer. He stepped in close to her and moving very slowly so as not to scare her he leaned down and smelled her hair.

Aislinn felt an almost electric surge shoot through her as he stood so close to her. Her heart began pounding. At this proximity she could still smell the awful odor of whatever the blood on his clothes belonged to, but she also got a much stronger scent of him.

They both just stood there breathing, neither of them wanting to move. Cullen had never felt this compelled to touch a woman before in his life. Aislinn didn't know if she wanted him to go or stay. When they finally moved they just stood staring into each other's eyes as if they were trying to understand what was happening. But neither of them could wrap their brains around the situation.

Finally Cullen gently reached out and cupped his hand along the side of her face. Warmth spread from the touch through Aislinn's body. Cullen ran his thumb slowly over her parted lips. She took in a sharp breath as shock waves seemed to travel through her from the place where he touched. All the sensations were amazingly strong and resulted in a heat forming between her legs.

The minute the scent of her arousal hit him Cullen felt his wolf surge like nothing he'd ever experienced. No battle or woman before now had ever summoned his spirit like this. He wanted her. There was nothing else in the world right at that moment; just this enigmatic female standing proudly in front of him, challenging him, and drawing him in. He still couldn't place her scent. It wasn't lycan, was it? But it wasn't completely human either. Could he even be drawn like this to something that was neither human nor lycan? Was she fey? But he thought he knew those scents as well. Maybe the alcohol and all the competing smells from the evening were messing with his senses. He wanted to know.

Aislinn stared at him. She wanted him to do more. She couldn't believe how badly she wanted him to do more. She cursed herself for not being able to keep control. He was a complete stranger. An incredible, sexy, kind, complete stranger. As she stared into his eyes they changed again. It was like staring into molten gold. There were dark flecks swimming in this iridescent amber around his black pupils. Aislinn felt herself being pulled in, as though she could be happily lost in those eyes.

Cullen felt his wolf taking too much control. He forced himself to pull his hand away from her and step back. It wasn't until he wrenched himself back into the moment that he realized his eyes had shifted. She was just standing there staring. He could smell her arousal, hear her breathing, he could almost feel her heart beat thudding in time with his own. When he felt the stirring in his pants he knew that things had gone way too far. His brain was screaming, *You don't even know what she is!* But his heart, soul, and wolf were insisting, *Take her.*

Cullen closed his eyes, breathing heavily, willing himself to get control. Aislinn watched as he seemed to be trying to gain a measure of composure. She couldn't help herself. She really didn't want him to stop. She stepped toward him and placed her hand on his chest. "Are you all right," she said breathlessly. *This is insane*, Aislinn thought, *Derrick tries to rape me and now I'm encouraging my would-be protector to do who knows what.* This just didn't make sense. It was as though her body had taken over and it wanted this man, badly.

When her hand touched his chest Cullen thought he might lose it. He needed to leave or rip her clothes off. He settled for something in the middle. Leaning into her he pressed his lips to hers. The entire room seemed to spin and it wasn't from the alcohol. The kiss was long and lingering. Neither of them wanted to stop.

Aislinn felt her heart in her throat, goose bumps ran down her body, and she could feel the heat between her legs intensify.

The kiss became more and more inflamed. Cullen gently bit at her upper lip and she parted her lips to allow him to taste her. He snaked his tongue into her mouth and brushed against her tongue. Their breathing became increasingly ragged and Cullen's hands managed to find their way along her waist, move under her shirt, and then drift deftly upward as he began to explore her body. When he reached her breasts Aislinn let out a soft encouraging moan that soaked into Cullen's mind and called his wolf up full force. He wasn't going to be able to stop it if this continued. His mind was trying desperately to regain control of the situation while knowing that the fight had already been lost.

When the tentative knock came on the door Cullen turned suddenly toward it as if he had been startled and growled menacingly at the unknown intruder. For a brief moment he was in guardian mode and would have attacked anyone who came through that door. At the second knock reality grabbed hold of him and Cullen was able to reassert his mind over his wolf.

Aislinn watched Cullen's reaction and heard the growl issue from his chest. It was like some kind of weird guard dog sound. She remembered the sound in the street when Derrick had attacked her and knew it must have been Cullen as well. Oddly she wasn't bothered by it. She didn't really know why it didn't bother her. A third knock on her door, and she moved to see who could possibly be knocking. The only thing that kept her from locking the door instead of opening it was the fact that Cullen had proven himself more than able of handling the situation should something terrible be on the other side of the door.

Aislinn took a deep breath and willed her heart to stop racing in her chest. She looked back at Cullen before she opened the door. He was staring at it readily, as though he expected something bad on the other side. His eyes had returned to normal brown, and he stopped growling. So she opened the door.

Aislinn recognized the guy at the door as Cullen's friend who came to get him. She realized that he must have been waiting for Cullen all this time. She really wasn't sure how long they had been standing there kissing. But if Keith hadn't come knocking she was fairly certain that it would have gone much farther.

Cullen eyed Keith standing there, then let his head roll over his shoulders and sighed heavily. He knew logically that it was a good thing Keith had shown up. The last thing Cullen should have been doing was having sex with some girl he'd met tending bar. No matter how intriguing she was. No matter how much he wanted to take her. For a brief instant Cullen's wolf reared its head again and Cullen considered telling Keith to get lost. But instead he headed toward the door.

"Like I said," Cullen looked at Aislinn with a long suffering stare telling her he wished things were different, "take that note to Liam. He'll take care of the rest. It was," he paused and stared into her eyes with intense regret, "good to have met you."

Aislinn felt as though she wanted to cry. None of this made sense. Why should it hurt so bad that this complete stranger was leaving instead of staying to have sex with her? If she didn't know better she would have thought that her heart was mistaking Cullen for someone she had been in love with all her life. "Yeah, thanks," was all she could muster.

Cullen almost changed his mind about leaving when he saw the glassy look in her eyes. It just wasn't something he could do. He was supposed to be mated to Jenna. The arrangements were made. He shouldn't be having sex with some random girl. This was probably just his subconscious trying to get him in trouble and out of the arrangement. He nodded at Aislinn, pushed past Keith and headed down the stairs at nearly a run. When he reached the street he let out a yell and punched a nearby signpost hard enough to bend it in half.

Keith was completely baffled by the situation. He followed Cullen in silence to the SUV. They both got in and Keith started driving before he finally got up the nerve to ask, "What was that?"

"I've found myself saying 'I don't know' to similar questions repeatedly tonight. Just drop it."

The tone in Cullen's voice was dangerous and Keith didn't really know what, if anything, he could or should say. So they drove back to the den in silence.

Chapter 2

A man's as miserable as he thinks he is.
-Lucius Annaeus Seneca

Aislinn put on what she considered to be her best interview clothes. The outfit consisted of a pair of black dress pants, a white button up shirt, and a shear black scarf she tied at her neck. She put on a pair of black heels and combed her brown hair into a twist at the back of her head. She didn't really know what kind of business was at the other end of the address, but she figured that the look was conservative enough for just about anything and not overly dressy. She had bought the clothes to attend a funeral and hadn't been given another opportunity to wear them since. She sighed and remembered that she didn't even get to go to the funeral.

She took one last look at herself in the mirror before pocketing the piece of paper she'd been given and heading downstairs. She put this off for more than a week. When she had gone into work at the bar the day after she met Cullen she found out that Derrick ended up in the hospital after all. Luke said that he'd been told Derrick would be out for a couple of weeks or more.

When Derrick had initially gotten to the hospital he'd been unconscious. Some nice passerby doing a good deed had called the ambulance. Aislinn had decided to wait and see. She hoped that he would keep his mouth shut and leave her alone because he wouldn't want to have to deal with her accusing him of attempted rape. But when he woke up he fired her.

Then he decided to press charges against her for battery. She was arrested and spent the night in jail before Renee and Luke managed to put together bail money.

The story she ended up getting was that Derrick claimed she tried to steal some money from the register that night. Supposedly he caught her and she took off with the money. He chased her down and she and some big guy that Derrick didn't know beat him up and left him for dead. When Aislinn told the cops what really happened they suggested she bring up charges of attempted assault.

Everything was going to hell. Aislinn hadn't wanted to accept this job after Cullen had taken off that night. He'd given her that kiss, and then disappeared like there had been something wrong with it. She didn't understand why she felt betrayed by that. It was all too strange. On top of that, there was the court case, and now she owed Renee and Luke a lot of money. She tried to find another job at a different bar, but Derrick apparently had a few friends. No one was hiring Aislinn. She finally decided that she needed the money too badly to let her pride get in the way of taking the job she had been offered.

Aislinn had been so caught up in her misery that she didn't pay attention to where the taxi was going. When the taxi pulled up in front of Taigh-Olsda, the restaurant/bar/hotel attached to the most popular casino in town, the Madadh-alluidh Saobhaidh, she was positive that he had to have taken her to the wrong address. "Are you sure this is it?"

"Yeah lady. That'll be 13 even."

Aislinn handed the guy her last twenty and accepted her change. She took a deep breath, turned around, and walked toward the main entrance. When she got to the front door of the popular steak house a woman in expensive looking heels, a knee-length brown skirt, and a white silky shirt opened and held the door for her. "Welcome to Taigh-O\sda," the woman said warmly. Aislinn immediately felt as if she were in over her head.

Aislinn walked in with as much confidence as she could manage toward the front desk. An incredibly attractive dark haired woman with a clip board approached her. The woman's eyes were the same kind of dark brown as Cullen's and from the look of the woman she could have been his sister. Aislinn wondered if she had ever met a more attractive woman in her life.

"Do you have a reservation?"

"Um, no," Aislinn said. She pulled the paper out of her purse, noticing that her purse didn't match her shoes and wondered if the woman she was talking to noticed. "I'm here to see Liam about a job. Cullen sent me." She held out the paper to the woman.

The woman's dark eyes showed obvious shock. Aislinn was fairly certain that this woman wouldn't have believed her if it weren't for the note.

"Okay," the woman said haltingly. "Uh, wait here a minute. I'll go get Liam." She handed Aislinn back the paper and she headed through a door just off to the right of the desk.   Aislinn had to step out of the way as a couple came up to the desk and a different woman, also very attractive and with a similar look to the other approached the couple and spoke with them quietly. Then the couple was led off toward the restaurant entrance.

As Aislinn waited she couldn't help take in the delicious smell of steak that was wafting from the restaurant. Once the initial nervousness of the situation wore off some she decided to look around a bit while she waited. She took a few steps through the hotel lobby so that she could get a view of the inside of the restaurant through the entrance.

The lighting was low and the booths were high backed and mostly private so she couldn't tell how many customers were there. But it was relatively early. *The place probably picks up with the casino in the evenings,* she thought as she glanced across the elegant lobby to the casino entrance that was opposite the restaurant. The Taigh-O\sda had only opened for lunch about an hour before she showed up. So it was still pretty early. The casino was pretty empty yet as well. Both venues were definitely more of a night life kinda thing. She knew of this place by reputation and it appeared well deserved.

The lobby was decorated with an old Celtic feel. The floors and walls were cut, carved stone and large wooden beams arched up to the ceiling. The beams were decorated with elaborately carved Gaelic sayings that were most likely wasted on the average patron. But Aislinn was entranced by the intricacy and the beauty of it all. There were stained glass murals high on the walls that threw beautifully colored shadows across the floor from the sunlight streaming in. Tapestries lined the stone walls and sconces holding lighting that looked remarkably like flames. It was as though she had stepped into some different city. *No wonder this place gets so much attention*, she thought.

As she waited she contemplated the names of the two businesses. The name of the restaurant, Taigh-

Olsda, was actually "the pub" or "hotel" in Gaelic. The name of the casino, Madadh-Allaidh Saobhaidh, was "wolf den". She thought about Cullen's eyes and the growling. She didn't really know how to take it all. She was smart enough to make the movie world guess and jump to really insane conclusions. But she just couldn't force that thought into her head. *At the same time*, she thought, *I wouldn't have ever believed that there were druids until I'd had to run away from their creepy culty "circle."*

It wasn't too long before the woman returned and then asked Aislinn to come with her. She led the way back through the door next to the desk, passed a set of doors on the wall that shared a corridor with the restaurant. Waiters and waitresses were going in and out of the doors with trays and food, presumably room service for the hotel. The woman led Aislinn to a similar set of doors farther down the hall. "This way," she said with a smile, then hesitated and turned to look at Aislinn. Her eyes flashed with curiosity. "I'm sorry I just have to ask, how do you know, uh, Cullen?" Aislinn noted the strange emphasis the woman placed on his name. It was almost as if Aislinn shouldn't have been allowed to use it. The tone reminded Aislinn of a parent pointing out to a child that she should be more formal when speaking of adults.

Aislinn had really hoped that question wouldn't come up. She cleared her throat. "He helped me out last week. Uh, he thought the guy I worked for wasn't very nice and suggested I get a job elsewhere."

The woman looked at her as if she didn't believe what Aislinn said, but didn't press the issue farther. She just turned around and led the way through a door at the end of the hall into an office. There was a man in a gray suit shuffling paperwork at a desk. He looked up and motioned for Aislinn to come in. The woman immediately headed back out the door and closed it behind her.

He looked up at Aislinn with a piercing dark stare. Aislinn stared right back. He looked older than Cullen, but again there were those strange dark brown eyes and dark hair. Liam was much paler in skin tone than the woman who had brought her here or Cullen, as if he spent all his time in doors behind a desk. He seemed to be trying to see through Aislinn, but she put up her standard wall and waited for him to be done appraising her and say something.

"Meghan said that Cullen sent you here with a note for me." Aislinn stepped toward the desk and handed Liam the note that Cullen had written. He looked it over and then looked up at Aislinn with more of an interested gaze than before. "Okay, so do you have any experience with waitressing?"

"My last job was tending bar. But I'm a quick study," Aislinn offered.

The man nodded and looked back at the note. It was pretty obvious that this kind of thing didn't happen often. Somehow it made Aislinn feel good to know that Cullen didn't go around getting every woman he met a job. "Well Aislinn, I do have an opening for a new waitress. When can you start?"

There wasn't even an interview really. Aislinn filled out the paperwork, was given a tour of the place by Meghan, and was told what to buy as a uniform. That evening she went to the store and spent the last of the rent money on appropriate clothes for her new job. As she did it she wondered what her landlord was going to do when she didn't have rent on time. She shook her head. There wasn't anything she could do about it at the moment. *One step at a time*, she thought.

* * * *

Cullen had been into Taigh-Olsda several times throughout the week. It was his favorite place to eat so no one thought anything about it. But really he had been looking to see if Aislinn had shown up to get that job. He had been more than a little annoyed when she didn't show. *Muin*, he swore to himself. *If she wants to work for some jerk who tries to rape her then let her. She's just some random human female. Why the hell do I care?*

Jenna showed up at the den late that week. She was excited and waited all afternoon for Cullen to manage enough time to meet with her. For his part he had been finding as many extra things to do as he could come up with. The woman was driving him crazy. Ever since he had agreed to the mating she had been calling non-stop and making a fuss. As far as he was concerned, this was supposed to be an arrangement of convenience and nothing more.

Cullen was only mating with the girl as a favor to Brennus Tairneach. He was ancient. Jenna was his only child and he wanted his bloodline to retain some power in his clan. Cullen owed the man a great deal. Brennus had been an alpha when Cullen was still a child. If it weren't for Brennus Cullen would have been killed centuries ago. But as time wore on Cullen came into his own power. He had never been interested in being an alpha, but he was more than strong enough mentally and physically to do the job. He had created clan Arnauk a long time ago and it was now one of the most powerful clans on the continent.

At the same time Brennus was growing older and becoming less influential among the stronger members of the Tairneach clan. It was more than apparent that Jenna would not be able to succeed him and the vultures were clamoring for his throat.

Brennus' plan was simple. He called in an old favor. Here was his beautiful daughter Jenna. Cullen couldn't debate that point. The girl was attractive. Cullen owed him a favor and was more than strong enough to merge the Tairneach with the Arnauk. Brennus wanted the Tairneach name to be carried with one of Jenna and Cullen's children and when the child was old enough to rule Cullen was to give the Tairneach land to Brennus' grandchild. Brennus' only hope was that he would be around long enough to see it happen. But he had no delusions about his ability to hold his position as alpha for much longer.

When Cullen had received word that Brennus wanted to speak with him Cullen had been surprised, but happily went to visit the man. Initially Cullen had refused Brennus' request, but had noted the political turmoil in Tairneach territory. There were a number of lycans that were capable of overthrowing Brennus. The only thing keeping the situation from becoming volatile was a small group of loyalists who were backing Brennus. The main problem being that their backing was contingent on Brennus finding a suitable mate for Jenna so that they knew, if a challenge for his position were to happen, there would be someone able to take his place who wouldn't punish them for their loyalty to Brennus. Cullen had left that initial meeting feeling bad for Brennus and guilty for not wanting the man's daughter.

Cullen had done everything he could to help Brennus in some other way, but as the months wore on Brennus became weaker. Jenna was no closer to finding an alpha mate than she had been when Brennus had first summoned Cullen with his proposition. Finally Brennus asked again and this time Cullen had been unable to refuse. He couldn't handle the idea of the once strong alpha begging for anything. Cullen owed the man too much and had too much respect for him to refuse again.

Besides, he reasoned that if he hadn't found a true mate by now it was entirely likely he would never find one. Cullen didn't put much stock in the idea of a 'true mate' anyway. He had always assumed that when he wanted a family he'd pick a woman and mate with her and have a family. He had recently been thinking about it anyway. All of his close friends had gone that path long ago. Ranaild had two sons, Keith had a daughter and Jaylyn was pregnant again, Shona had grandchildren already. Jenna was attractive enough. And if he mated with her then he could take control of the Tairneach problem and not have to worry about his border.

He sat at his desk, rubbed his face in his hands and tried to not feel like his life was ending. Technically he should have been thrilled by this, a beautiful wife and an unchallenged addition to his clan holdings.

The truth was that a large part of the final decision involved the problem of who was most likely to become Tairneach alpha if he didn't. Gregorius was the best candidate. He was also the most likely man amongst the Tairneach to decide that he needed more territory and go after it. With the constant trouble to the south the last thing the Arnauk needed was to lose their strongest ally. Not to mention that Brennus may have been dying but the pack itself was still as strong as ever. The wrong man in charge of that pack could mean a great deal of trouble. So between the fact that there was no reason for Cullen to not want to mate with Jenna and the fact that he would be protecting the Arnauk in the process, he felt obligated to do it.

There was another knock on his office door. Cullen looked up to see a blonde head poking through the cracked door. "Any chance you're going to be able to talk soon?"

Cullen stared at the pretty blonde. She was smiling admiringly at him. "Yeah, come in Jenna." He watched her walk in. She was wearing a short black skirt and a tight pink designer shirt. He had to appreciate the sight. If nothing else she was an exceptionally beautiful girl. So why didn't that thought help?

She walked around behind his desk and sat against it, giving him an impressive view of her legs. "So when will I get upgraded to being able to see you without an appointment," she cooed. When she noted his gaze on her legs she smiled and parted them. Cullen couldn't help his eyes traveling up her thighs and noted that she wasn't wearing anything under her skirt. And she was a natural blonde.

"Sorry," he said with a heavy breath and pulled his gaze away from the sight. But his cock responded instinctively to the scent of the woman's sex. "I've got a lot of work to get done if I'm going to be able to take a vacation for the mating." He was pissed at himself for not being able to control his reaction.

Jenna was a more politically minded woman than anyone gave her credit for. It was the blonde hair that did it and the way she carried herself. He found long ago that men were more easily manipulated when they thought she was incapable of thinking past her next new pair of shoes. She was also more than intelligent enough to know that Cullen didn't want to be mated to her. She saw it every time he looked at her. There didn't seem to be anything she could do to change the situation. To some extent she didn't care. He was attractive, powerful, and would help her accomplish what her father wanted. If he didn't keep her satisfied she'd find someone who could. She was more than a little pleased to see that she had already managed to cause a reaction in him. She knew that in lieu of physical strength she had a great deal of power that men often overlooked, especially powerful men who thought too much of themselves and their abilities.

She smiled and batted her eyes at him. Then she lifted one foot out of her spiked heal and ran a stockinged toe up his calf, along his thigh, and stroked the bulge in his pants, before letting it come to rest on the edge of his seat between his legs. She smiled through her disappointment when he didn't reach out and touch her, considering the obvious invitation. "I've good news. I'm going into heat. I know that you and father decided that we should be mated next month. But then we'll have to wait another year before we can try to get pregnant."

Cullen felt as though he had just been punched in the chest. He studiously ignored staring at her spread legs. Not that he didn't notice the scent or completely miss the wet look of her sex. In the end he was still a man and it was a tempting site, but he managed to control his expression. Jenna frowned at the unimpressed look and the long pause before his answer. "Fine. Next week. I'll have the arrangements changed.

Good, she thought, *he may not like it but at least he had the right answer and maybe he's not as immune to my charms as I thought. There's got to be a man in the General somewhere.* "At that point," she cooed and bent closer to him, giving him a delicious view of her cleavage. The pink blouse was low cut enough that Cullen could just see the tops of her delicate, pink areola. She reached out and ran her fingers along the side of his face and down to his chest, "maybe you could offer to let me stay here with you until the ceremony." She leaned down as her hand continued to travel along his chest, over his stomach, and toward his lap.

Cullen suddenly had a flash in his mind of blue eyes, brown hair, and an electrical touch that set his wolf screaming for release and pushed Jenna's hand away. "If you want the mating plans taken care of and the time you made me promise to give you afterward then you'll get yourself home and deal with your end. I can't afford distractions. Especially if we're moving things forward." His tone was curt and he was rewarded with a pouty, annoyed look on Jenna's face. He reached down and moved her foot out of his lap.

"Fine," she answered. The soothing vixen tone dropped from her voice. "If you insist." She started to walk out, but turned and looked back at him. "So is this how it's going to be then?" She tilted her head haughtily and raised her eyebrows in a look that was cooling and Cullen though entirely unattractive on her pretty face. The girl reminded him far too much of her mother.

He sighed heavily and sat back in his chair, meeting her gaze with an equally cold stare. "How what's going to be?"

"Us. Are you going to hate me forever for getting stuck with me?"

Cullen stared at her, measuring her words. Her tone said that she wasn't hurt by the idea just curious. "Hate is too strong a word. Last I checked you didn't want to be doing this either."

"Maybe not but I'm at least doing my best to make do. You on the other hand are being a complete bastard. If you think that I'm going to spend my young, energetic life attached to a guy who won't give me the time of day and not look elsewhere for company then you're sorely mistaken." Jenna's eyes held a strong warning as she spoke.

Cullen tapped his pen on his desk with annoyance. "Jenna, I'm not going to deal with this right now. But I want you to think about what you just said to me and how exactly it would affect the legitimacy of your heirs. Or more accurately, your father's heirs. He's the reason we're both in this. If you can't handle the situation then you need to find a different patsy for your needs. Whatever they may be. I'm just the poor schlep who owed your dad too much to say no. This is how it is. You either cope or don't go through with it. Now, go home. Decide. I'll talk with you later this week." His glare held all the vehemence that was missing from his voice.

Jenna realized all too suddenly that she was about to get stuck in a forcibly monogamous relationship with a lycan who really wasn't the least bit interested in anything other than repaying her father and just intelligent enough to make her plans difficult. Her father underestimated her. He believed that she was weak because she wasn't a fighter. But she wasn't as dense as he thought. What she needed was an alpha without a brain and who she could manipulate. A lycan strong enough to hold the wolves at bay, but weak minded enough to let her lead. She was becoming increasingly more concerned that Cullen wasn't going to be appropriate for her needs. He was too clever. At the same time if she let him unite the packs and then got rid of him the Tairneach line would run twice the territory her father had. Maybe then her father would see what she was worth.

Cullen watched her eyes and could see the flashes of emotion. Whatever her thought process was, he didn't like the look of it. He waited for her to refocus on him. He didn't trust her. Brennus's only daughter and she was becoming more and more like her mother. As Cullen watched Jenna he remembered what Brennus had said about her. She needed a strong hand. Brennus had implied that he would prefer that any power over the Tairneach pack be passed directly from Cullen to Cullen's choice of an heir and bypass his daughter completely, as long as the child was born from Jenna.

Cullen had been there when Jenna's mother had been tried for attempting to kill Brennus. The man had put her to death and then coddled his infant daughter. He had loved Jenna's mother so deeply that he had put up with her attempts to kill him until it threatened to disrupt the pack. Brennus was so broken by what had happened that he had not touched another woman since her sentencing. Cullen could look back at it all and see Brennus' choices with his mate as being the beginning of his downfall. To compensate for what had happened with her mother Brennus doted on Jenna. Cullen was torn between feeling sorry for the man and being pissed as hell that his supposed friend had just sentenced him to a similar fate. *How the hell am I going to get out of this?*

Cullen cleared his throat in exasperation and jogged Jenna out of her thought process. Just as quickly as her sweet demeanor had vanished it reappeared again. "The least you could do is take me to dinner before I leave," she purred and batted her eyes at him.

His jaw tightened and he contemplated the displeasure of having dinner with anyone other than Aislinn. Then he kicked himself for not being able to get the girl out of his head. "Fine, I need to finish this," he said and shuffled some paperwork on his desk. "Go to the great room. I'll come for you in about an hour. We'll have dinner downstairs and then you'll return to the Tairneach manor."

Jenna sweetly smiled her grateful acceptance. "Then I'll be waiting in the great room." Jenna walked out of the office pissed. The weight of the situation was getting heavier and heavier. She hated her father for having dragged Cullen into this. She hated Cullen for having gone along with it. She even hated herself a little for not being physically strong enough to carry the Tairneach line without help. But she wasn't giving up just yet. She would either get Cullen to give in and let her have some influence or she'd get rid of him. At the moment she was leaning toward the later.

Cullen shifted his attention back to his primary concern for the moment. He sorted the reports in front of him into several piles; reports on the raids in his territory, the reports on the packs believed to be behind the raids, the reports on the political situations within the neighboring packs, and the pile he hated most, the reports on who within his own pack may be helping the raiders. He growled his frustration. He had read the reports over and over looking for a pattern or connection and was yet to find one. It only served to remind him of why his mating to Jenna was necessary. It would reinforce his numbers and keep his northern border friendly.

* * * *

Aislinn was shadowing Rissa and learning her new job. Aislinn was to the point where she was being trusted to take an order down, and bring out food with some supervision. Rissa was very nice and Aislinn decided that she liked her. She didn't look as much like Cullen as Meghan did, but she still had those black brown eyes and brown hair. The difference was in her facial structure. Rissa looked a little Asian. She was sweet and patient with Aislinn and had covered for her once in the beginning when Aislinn had forgotten a side dish at one table. Overall the past couple days were great. She felt welcome and was being treated fairly. It had been a long time since she had been around so many genuinely nice people.

Aislinn had just refilled the water at one table and was headed over to the next couple that had been seated. The large man wasn't dressed for dinner at the Taigh-O\sda and the woman with him certainly looked as though she was being paid for his company. But with the casino across the lobby it was a fairly regular sight. All it took was one jackpot for Joe Schmoe to be able to afford the steak.

Suddenly Rissa grabbed her arm and yanked her off toward a corner booth. "Lord Arnauk came in for dinner. When he comes in, if you have his table, everything else gets dumped and you deal with him. Without making it look that way though. It's important 'cause he's too nice to cut in line with other customers, but he's Lord Arnauk."

Aislinn nodded and filed the information away in her brain with everything else she had been learning and got ready to take a mental picture of 'Lord Arnauk'. When she came around the booth and saw Cullen sitting there with Jenna she stopped as though she had hit a wall. Aislinn felt as though someone had just slugged her in the stomach. She didn't really understand all the emotions that were overwhelming her at that point, but she was tempted to turn and run and hide.

Rissa looked at her with concern, but ultimately moved up to the table. "Lord Arnauk. You haven't been in for the past week. We've missed you," Rissa said in a good natured, friendly manner. Aislinn watched the blonde looked at Rissa with distaste and then went back to the menu.

"I've been around, just haven't had time to stop," he smiled back. His expression was strained and Aislinn thought maybe a bit uncomfortable. Then it was as though a blanket of calm acceptance overtook him and he smiled up at Aislinn hopefully. "I see you have a shadow."

"Yes," Rissa said with far too much energy. "This is Aislinn. She just started a couple days ago. So you'll want to be patient with her. But she's been doing a great job and learning quickly…"

Rissa kept talking but Cullen missed most of it when the air circulation shifted and Aislinn's scent wafted over the table. He took a deep breath, his eyes focused on her, and it was all he could do to keep his wolf contained. Jenna looked up at Cullen as Rissa asked for the second time if he needed a minute to decide on what he wanted. It only took a second for Jenna to register what had distracted Cullen so absolutely. She felt a distinct surge of jealousy run through her. Not that she really cared about who he was actually interested in. She knew that it wasn't her. But the fact that he was being so obvious about it in front of her and that it was just a little nothing of a waitress was annoying.

Jenna smiled a withering smile at Rissa and answered the question. "Why don't you give us a minute sweetie and then send- uh what did you say her name was? Aislinn back to get the order. We'll be happy to break in the new girl."

Aislinn met Jenna's stare and recognized the hatred immediately. *Ah this is more like what I'm used to*, she thought as she returned Jenna's smile. Rissa started to respond when Cullen interrupted her. "That won't be necessary. Just bring my usual. Jenna do you know what you want?"

Jenna shifted her gaze back to Cullen and adjusted it to be overly loving and attentive. Just to make sure she had his attention she slipped her shoe off and began trailing her toe along the inside of his thigh again. He glared at her but didn't do anything to draw attention to the situation. She found him hard as a rock when her foot reached its goal and she began rubbing her foot against him as she placed her order. Rissa took everything down and started to leave. But Jenna wasn't finished yet. She stopped Aislinn from leaving as Rissa disappeared to put the order in. Before Cullen could dismiss Aislinn Jenna began asking questions about when Aislinn was hired, how she liked the job, and how she got the job. All the while she continued to rub and manipulate Cullen's erection beneath the table.

Cullen's jaw was set. Jenna knew that the minute Aislinn left she was going to be in serious trouble, but Jenna was intent on making it clear that she was more than aware of his interest in Aislinn and that it didn't matter because he belonged to her now. Cullen was almost ready to break Jenna's foot off. Aislinn did a very good job of answering all of Jenna's questions without sharing the information that involved Cullen. He also noticed that Aislinn refused to look at him and he figured that if his taking off with Keith that night hadn't ruined his chances, this situation would. He had to do something about straightening it out the first chance he got. But for now he needed to end the foot job from hell.

"Jenna," Cullen sharply interrupted her. Aislinn wouldn't have believed that a tone like that could possibly come out of him. "I think that Aislinn has duties to perform."

Aislinn knew a dismissal when she heard one. She immediately took the cue and left the couple to themselves. She could hear the tones exchanged as she left and knew they were arguing, even if she couldn't hear what they were arguing about. She was trying desperately not to care that Cullen was here with that blonde, that he hadn't told her that he was 'Lord' whatever, or that she had nearly slept with him only to watch him take off from her apartment as though it had been on fire. *I don't care*, she kept thinking to herself. *I've got no reason to care. He was just some drunk that I met one night who did me a favor or three. I'm happy that he has a blonde bimbo bitch and I'm not at all jealous. I've got no reason to care.*

Chapter 3

Burning embers are easily kindled.
-Irish Proverb

Aislinn went through the motions of serving dinner and completing the rest of her chores for that evening. Cullen and his date who, Aislinn managed to find out from another member of the kitchen staff, was actually his fiancé ate, their dinner in relatively short order and then left. Jenna had been conspicuously silent on all the subsequent visits that Aislinn had to make to the table and Cullen had managed to catch her eyes with an apologetic stare at one point.

Aislinn sat in the back of the taxi on her way home. She felt rich in her ability to afford the small luxury each night. Walking would have taken at least an hour. But she would have done it if it had been necessary. She figured that if tips continued the way they were that she would be able to afford to move out of her shitty apartment and closer to the restaurant in relatively short order. She was calculating how much time it would take for her to pay for her missed rent, pay back her friends for her jail break, afford an attorney to deal with Derrick's lawsuit, and then move into town. Anything to keep her mind off of Cullen.

The taxi finally pulled up in front of her place and she slid out of the car, paid with some of her tips from that night, and headed toward the steps. When a figure moved out of the shadows near the main entrance and reached for her she turned, leaned back, and delivered a forceful kick to the figure's chest. It was a reflex she had developed over the years and had saved her life more than once.

Cullen staggered back into the wall holding his chest and trying to catch his breath. He had to admit it had been a long time since anyone caught him off guard like that and he was shocked that she had been strong enough to knock him backward even with that consideration. He was still trying to catch his breath when she glared at him and headed inside without a word.

Aislinn fumed as she virtually ran up the stairs to her apartment. *What the hell is he doing here?* She barely managed to get her key out and go inside before he appeared at the top of the stairs. She slammed the door and walked across the room, threw her purse and coat on the table, and kicked her shoes off. After a few minutes without a knock on the door she figured he must have gotten the message and left. She paced a bit before she decided that she wouldn't be able to calm down unless she looked to see.

Aislinn walked over to the door and stared at it a minute. When she started to feel like a complete fool she took the locks off and pulled the door open only to find she was face to face with Cullen. He took a deliberate step into her apartment forcing her back until he was able to close the door. They just stood there staring at each other without talking. Neither of them knew what to say.

Cullen finally started, "I need to apologize to you for Jenna-"

Annoyed, Aislinn cut him off. "No you don't. Why should you have to apologize?"

Cullen just wasn't used to people behaving with him the way she did. He smiled, chuckled and shook his head. "Do you have any idea how unique you are?"

Aislinn glared at him. She didn't get what he was trying to say. All she knew was that she could smell him and he was so close. She couldn't stop herself from wanting him and that was making her angrier and a little scared. "Do you have any idea how much of a jerk you are?"

Cullen had to laugh. When he saw the confused look cross her face he explained. "Sorry it's just been a long time since anyone seriously called me a name to my face. I'm sure plenty is said behind my back, but they generally make sure I don't find out."

"Are you really this full of yourself?"

He continued to smile. She growled under her breath. The smile finally dropped. Why was she growling? There were too many odd things about her. He was tempted to just ask if she was some weird kind of lycan that he had never scented before. "Look, I just thought that I owed you a bit of an explanation. I know that we haven't exactly gotten off on the right foot."

"So what? Why exactly do you want to be friends so badly? I mean this is virtually stalking. In fact I'd say that you waiting outside my place is definitely stalking. I'll admit that I do owe you for saving my ass the other night and for getting me that job, *Lord* Arnauk. When I figure out how to pay you back I will. But for now I think it'd be a good idea for us to keep our distance from each other."

Cullen flinched a bit at the use of his title. He had never hated his position before, but between Jenna and Aislinn he almost wanted to disappear and let the rest fight it out, deal with the raids, and the politics on their own. He nodded and headed back toward her door. As he got to the doorway he stopped and turned to look at her one last time before he left. "I guess I just thought maybe I wasn't the only one involved in that kiss the other night. I was hoping we could at least be on talking terms."

"At least on talking terms," she was glaring at him and her tone hit him harder than her kick had. "What are you trying to do? Start a harem? From what I hear you're engaged to that blonde bitch."

"That's a long story," he said, no longer finding her amusing.

"Okay, so explain why you would be back here after the other night and then dinner tonight? Why you could come back here and imply that you think we should be *friendly*." She crossed her arms and stared at him, waiting.

Cullen shook his head. "You know what? Never mind. You're right. I shouldn't have come here. Sorry." With that Cullen left and closed the door behind him.

Aislinn just stood there watching after him. As the argument she'd just had sunk in she threw herself down on her mattress sobbing. It was a long time before she fell asleep.

* * * *

Aislinn was standing in the middle of the street in front of her apartment. It was eerily dark and quiet. There were no stars or moon and the light from the street lamps seemed to be absorbed into the air as though it was being eaten by the darkness. The only sound she could hear was her own breathing and heartbeat.

Aislinn looked up and down the street and felt as though she was being watched. She looked up at her apartment. It may have been a hole but it allowed for some protection. She briefly considered going up there, but something in her told her that it just wasn't safe any longer. She looked down at herself and realized that she was completely naked. She didn't understand it but somehow it felt normal and safer to be naked than to be wearing clothes at that moment.

Suddenly out of the darkness she heard quiet whispering, unintelligible and frightening. She knew that she was in incredible danger. Something was coming for her.

Aislinn turned and started running down the street. She didn't know where she was running to, but she felt drawn through the darkness away from the whispering. Every time she stopped she could hear the whispering getting louder. She turned down one street and then another until the whispering was so close she couldn't stop to look around any longer. She needed to move faster. She could feel sweat running down her face and chest and back. The night air was cold on her bare skin. Her feet burned, slapping on the pavement. She needed to move faster. Slowly she felt herself changing. When she looked down she had fur and was on four feet. She was some kind of animal. She was moving much more quickly now.

As she kept running she could hear the whispering retreating a little into the darkness, so she stopped again and looked around. Everything seemed brighter now somehow and she reasoned out that it was because she was looking through new eyes. She found that she was outside of the Taigh-O\sda. She walked into the lobby and as the doors shut behind her the whispering became angry and frustrated. She walked through the empty lobby and found herself looking at a reflection of herself in one of the large windows.

It was a fuzzy image. The darkness outside caused the soft light inside to turn the window into an imperfect mirror. She didn't recognize what she was looking at. She was on all fours and shadowy. She was staring intently into her reflection when a figure came up to the window. Terror froze her solid as Rafe stared at her a lurid smile on his face. She started to backup to get away from him, but he was calling to her. Suddenly the voices came into sharp focus and she understood what the whispering was. They had found her again.

Aislinn sat bolt upright in bed. She was covered in sweat and the darkness in her small apartment was overwhelming. She jumped up and turned on the lights. She stared around the room into shadows that couldn't possibly hide anyone looking for Rafe. *I had another premonition*, she thought. Sometimes she wondered if it would be better to never dream. She took a deep breath and closed her eyes and concentrated on the last thing she remembered of the dream. She needed to get an impression of how close they were. How much time she had. She wanted to know what the other parts had meant as well. Why she had turned into an animal and why she had felt safe at the Taigh-O\sda.

* * * *

Cullen parked his SUV in the private garage attached to the Madadh-Allaidh Saobhaidh. He slammed the door shut and headed for the elevator. Once inside he inserted his key card into the elevator panel and pressed the button for the 13th floor. The floor directly below that was mostly storage and empty. From the 11th floor down to the lobby was the public hotel and the main face of the casino. The basement, which also needed key access, held the private training and workout facilities and swimming pool, and holding cells for the rare times that they were needed, as well as the security suites that monitored the entire building.

The 13th floor was the great room and the floor that contained guest quarters when people came to visit his pack. There were always people in the great room watching TV. I never mattered the time of day. It was the main gathering place for people with nothing better to do. There was the movie room which was virtually a theatre, the game room, and a small kitchen/dining area. Cullen's rooms were on the penthouse floor and had access to the roof. His key and a couple select others were the only keys that allowed access there.

He needed to take his frustration out somewhere. He had briefly considered hitting a punching bag downstairs, but that wouldn't assuage the problem in his pants that had been developing all day. Between Jenna's teasing, which only disgusted him, and Aislinn's scent he felt as though he was going to explode. Upon entering the great room he spied one of his usual targets for this kind of outlet. Normally he didn't go looking for company except during hunts out at the reservation, but desperate times as they say, and Celia was always willing.

He approached her with a heated expression and she looked up at him with her hazel eyes and a welcoming smile. He didn't have to say anything to her. When she saw him coming she ended her conversation with the other women she had been watching TV with and stood up to meet the Alpha coming toward her. His determined look told her what he was after.

Cullen looked Celia over. She was wearing a pair of jeans and a white t-shirt. She had on no socks and no bra from the looks of things. Cullen growled low in his throat at the thought, *That'll make it easier.* He looked over at the couch and briefly considered taking all of them, alpha advantages after all, but then thought better of it. Celia, to date, hadn't gotten attached to him and he didn't want any additional female troubles right now.

Celia pushed a strand of brown hair out of her eyes and smiled at him in that innocent way of hers that belied what she really was capable of. "I thought with Jenna around you wouldn't come looking for me any time soon," she said with a pleased sound to her tone.

"I'm not going to be very nice this evening Celia," he growled in warning.

Celia briefly considered that. It wasn't as though she disliked rough sex. It was that he'd never felt the need to warn her about it before. In the end though, she knew that she wouldn't turn down a chance to lie with him. She did a great job of giving him the impression that she could take or leave his company. But that was only because she had learned a long time ago that she would get more attention from him that way. There were about six females that Cullen had come to trade off in his bed over the years. Celia had become the unspoken leader of that small group of women and due mostly to her ability to appear off-hand and unconcerned with Cullen's preference for her she had quickly become the favorite for ending up in his bed on the rare occasions that he was in the mood for company.

Celia shrugged. "Whatever you want, General," she replied. She had never been upgraded as far as first name status. But she never stopped hoping.

Cullen turned and headed down one of the halls to a guest room. He never took any of the girls up to his actual rooms. Again, this was mostly to keep any of them from becoming too attached. He walked into the room and immediately took off his coat and shoes discarding them on the armchair near the door. When his shirt and pants followed in short order Celia knew that his comment had been even more serious than she had taken it. He was never this quick about undressing.

When he turned to her and she saw his angry face and his ready hard-on she knew that he was on a mission to get off and that was it. She felt a little scared. He had never inspired fear in her before. Without missing a beat he approached her and ripped her white t-shirt up and off. He only took a moment to run his hands down her breasts, waist, and stomach before unbuttoning her jeans and forcing them down over her hips. The fact that she wasn't wearing underwear only served to reinforce in his mind that he had picked right for this.

Without a second thought to foreplay Cullen whirled Celia around and pushed her onto her knees on the bed. His eyes shifted and his wolf growled angrily at the fact that this wasn't the woman it wanted as Cullen climbed up behind her on the bed. He grabbed hold of Celia's hips and pulled her back onto his cock as he thrust it forward, not even checking to see if she was ready for him.

Celia winced at his intrusion. She braced herself for the worst and spared herself a glance back at the angry lycan pounding into her from behind. One look at Cullen's face and Celia wished she had just taken it and not looked. He was staring at the wall above the head of the bed. His eyes were on fire and she imagined that this was the face his enemies saw just before he ripped their throats out.

Celia turned away from the scene and closed her eyes, tears squeezing out from beneath her lids and focused on the number of times he had fucked her and the passion had more than made up for the lack of love in his touch. She just held onto the bed and took the punishment of his cock ripping into her over and over again. She wondered what had brought him to this kind of mood and then decided that she didn't really want to know that.

Cullen growled anger and frustration and he plunged into Celia. All he could think about was that shortly the body beneath him would be Jenna and that the one he wanted would eventually go to someone else. He forced himself into Celia knowing that he was probably hurting her. But he also knew that she was strong and could take it. He had seen her accept worse from others in the name of rough play. He never considered that she might see it as different coming from him. He felt his balls slap against her mound, driving himself into her faster and harder. He closed his eyes and imagined Aislinn lying beneath him begging him to go harder and pleading for more. With the image solid in his mind he felt his sack tighten and pulled out of Celia just in time to spray her ass and back with his cum.

Falling back from her into a sitting position Cullen watched Celia slump down on the bed, burying her face in a pillow from the head of the bed. He knew that she didn't get anything out of what he had just done to her. Feeling guilty for using her like that he growled at himself and got up off the bed. Cullen rubbed his face with both hands and tried to block out everything that had happened that evening.

Cullen started getting dressed, leaving Celia lying naked on the bed. "Sorry," he said in frustration as he grabbed his coat and shoes then headed out of the room without looking back.

Chapter 4

Is math an sgàthan sùil caraide.
A friend's eye is a good looking-glass.
-Gaelic Proverb

Cullen sat in his office staring out the window. He was still trying to wrap his brain around the latest information he had received. Originally he had believed that the raids his southern border was suffering were perpetrated by the LaRayne. Stephen LaRayne, alpha asshole, of that pack had always been trouble. When he wanted to torment the human population he had a tendency to do it on other people's land so that the branch of the government that periodically monitored and helped to hide the lycan population would blame someone else.

Cullen had been in the process of explaining to the feds that he knew about the raids, they weren't originating from his pack, and he was in the process of getting the situation under control. "Muin," he swore as he looked over the reports that showed the raids moving closer and closer to the city. That wasn't like LaRayne. He didn't go any farther than he had to and he didn't chance his men getting caught, which was a distinct possibility of going too deep into someone else's territory.

At the moment the reports were scattered. The raids involved "animal-like men breaking into and searching buildings" in various locations. There was no information about what they were looking for or why. He also was confused by the "animal-like" description. When it was lycans the description involved terms like wolf or large dog. The implication was that the raiders were lycan. It could be one of the other weres. The descriptions appeared to put the raiders on four legs. Katta could do the kind of damage he was looking at, if they bothered to get organized. But the lions were the only ones that ever operated in a group.

The knock on the door had Cullen turning to see who wanted to talk to him. Most everyone had been avoiding him like the plague considering his mood lately. "Come," he called angrily.

Keith and Ranaild stepped into the room. They walked over to chairs in front of Cullen's desk and sat down without being asked. There were very few lycans who didn't care about Cullen's mood. Keith and Ranaild had been friends with the man too long to fear the mighty General Cullen Arnauk. "I've got word," Keith said, as he propped his feet up on Cullen's desk.

In an odd way Keith's disrespect and nonchalance made Cullen feel better. Ranaild just sat quietly. That's all he ever did, until he started drinking. "So?"

Liam and Serra just got back from their little espionage mission. "From what they heard the raids are originating from a group that has pretty strong affiliation with the Circle." Cullen was speechless. Keith smiled. He knew that would come as a shock. "I knew you'd like that," he chuckled. "When was the last time the druids came out of hiding?"

"I don't even remember. The real druids disappeared after Rome. Caoch," he swore under his breath. "I can only assume you mean the real druids and the real Circle."

Keith nodded. "Yup, the real Circle. So the real question is what do they want?"

Cullen's gaze drifted off into space as he considered the improbability of the situation. "Whatever they're after must be pretty significant for them to come out of hiding after all these centuries. Hell, even if they want something, raiding isn't the way they used to deal with things. Live and let live and all. The Circle my father talked about allowed themselves to be killed off and assimilated because they believed that was the way of things."

"Yeah, well look at it this way," Keith said, "if all the druids believed that was the way of things then there wouldn't be any left. Whoever is calling themselves the Circle at this point survived somehow and chances are that means that some of them didn't necessarily believe in that way of things."

Cullen agreed with is friend. "Okay so the Circle is behind the raids. But who or what is doing the raiding?"

"That we haven't found out yet. No one has really seen anything other than the aftermath and 'animal-like' shadows. From the sounds of it and from some research that Granad did we think it might be big cats of some kind. The Circle originally made lycans as guardians. If they're looking for something they're probably using hunters who are less likely to care about rules or trade loyalty for each other over loyalty for their creators the way we did. The raiders have been strong, have claws like you wouldn't believe, are quick, quiet, and managing to blend in and disappear. I'm guessing panthers, leopards, tigers, lions or some such. Hell maybe a combo. That would eliminate the possibility of a unified pride. You know how much katta hate interbreeding. Wouldn't want to chance a mutt."

"Sounds like you've thought this out pretty thoroughly," Cullen said, feeling like he hadn't contributed at all. "I had been considering katta, but it wasn't much of a guess at the time."

"Well, Serra, Granad, Liam and the rest of us have noticed you're distracted and we kinda get it. We're doing our best to get this monkey taken care of so that maybe the mating business won't be so overwhelming." Keith shifted uncomfortably and cleared his throat. "Actually we've been talking about that too." Keith looked to Ranaild for support, but he just sat further down in his chair and swallowed hard.

"What," Cullen asked, his eyes narrowing dangerously on his friends.

"The mating. We just wanted you to know that the pack at large, at least those of us high enough in rank to have a countable opinion," Keith looked at Cullen sympathetically, "don't think it's necessary."

"You don't." Cullen leaned back in his chair. It was obvious that no amount of glaring was going to have any effect on Keith.

"No. The way we figure it, if Gregorius gets his hands on the alpha spot in the Tairneach then we get into a fight. So what? We've been at peace so long some of our guys are forgetting to watch their own backs. Maybe it's time again."

Cullen sighed. Keith thought he looked a lot older all of a sudden. "Thanks, but I put a lot of effort into what little peace we have. Besides, the last thing we need is another clan war. The feds would be all over us. I for one don't want to go through that again."

"But Jenna Tairneach?" Keith said with some disgust.

"Yeah, Jenna Tairneach. It's not like there are any other women higher up on my list," Cullen lied.

When Cullen's eyes dropped to his desk at that last comment Keith growled his frustration at his friend's behavior. "Whatever," he said in annoyance. "I would have thought even Celia a better match for you than that galla Jenna, but what do I know."

"Enough, the mating ceremony is tomorrow. Everything is set. I expect you and all the others to be at the manor on the reservation same as the Tairneachs will be. I just want to get it over with."

Keith nodded and stood up from the chair. "Any other orders General," he asked with a salute.

Cullen turned back to the window in dismissal. Another move that was totally unlike him when interacting with his friends. Keith stormed out angry that Cullen was being such an ass and not even willing to look into other options. Ranaild stood solemnly and trailed after.

* * * *

Aislinn stood in the courtroom. Derrick was looking at her luridly from behind the prosecution's desk with his attorney. In the end Aislinn hadn't been able to afford much. She had at one point considered asking Lord Arnauk for help, but decided that no matter how good his lawyers probably were there was no way he would help her out after what she'd said to him that night.

Aislinn had asked Luke and Renee to testify on her behalf, but no one had been willing to lose their job. So with her cut rate lawyer and no witnesses the only thing she had to go on was the fact that she was half Derrick's size and didn't have enough money to hire a hitman. Her defense had been based on that and Derrick's previous history of sexual harassment.

Aislinn stood in there waiting for the verdict, hoping that if she lost she'd have a fine and wouldn't have to go to jail, possibly losing her job. At the same time her premonitions were telling her that she wasn't safe in her apartment and there wouldn't be a place much safer than behind bars, being watched in jail. *It's great when jail becomes a good alternative to life*, she thought with tears in her eyes.

Finally the judge came back into the courtroom. Everyone stood and then was told to be seated. The defendant was asked to stand. Derrick was grinning as the judge found Aislinn guilty of battery as a misdemeanor. She was fined $500.00, which to her sounded like a fortune, but at least it wasn't jail time.

On her way out of the courtroom Derrick caught her and cornered her in the hall. She felt completely defenseless. What could she do? Hit him again? "Get out of my way Derrick," she said with a tired but angry voice.

He grinned. "You should have just played along with me. If you want your job back, I'll pay off your fine and we can find a way for you to work it off somehow." He chuckled at that.

Aislinn looked around the hall and happened to catch the eyes of a courtroom guard who was standing near the doors. The man in uniform came over to her. "Do you need some help miss?"

"Yes," she said in such a grateful relieved voice that the guard almost arrested Derrick on the spot. "I just want to leave and he's, well, he's..."

The guard got the point and gave Derrick a look that caused the man to back off and allow Aislinn to move hurriedly down the hall. Derrick smiled at the guard, knowing there really wasn't anything he had done that the guard could do anything about at this point. He hobbled out of the courtroom on his crutches.

* * * *

Rafe watched from the back of the courtroom. *This is better than I thought it'd be. I don't think she could be pushed much lower*, he thought.

The last time Rafe had seen Aislinn she was full of fire. She had fought him like a hell cat to get away. He knew he'd track her down again. For now he was content to let her stew. It was obvious that the atmosphere of her life here was wearing on her. He wanted her so low that when he offered her help, she would accept because she lacked any other alternative. This court case had totally blown her cover. If there was one type of record you couldn't keep secret, it was a police record.

Rafe's contacts regularly kept track of police records. The minute Aislinn's name came across his desk, in the same area he was already headed, he knew he'd get his chance with her again. But, he was patient and had more important things to attend to for now. If she had ended up in jail he would have done something about that. But she could handle a fine. Besides, from what he had been told she was working for the Arnauk, and that might come in handy in the end.

* * * *

Cullen's stomach started to growl. He had been staring at the latest reports and avoiding leaving for the reservation. It was a three hour drive. He still had an hour or two before he had to leave in order to be there before sunset. He had been managing to find excuses to not leave all day. Everyone was waiting patiently. As far as most of the others were concerned this was Cullen's day. If he wanted to be late and piss off Jenna, that was his call.

The report he was looking at seemed to be calling his name. It was as though he knew there was something in it that he was just missing. His stomach growled again. Finally he decided to just take the damn reports with him. He pulled them together and headed down to the restaurant.

Cullen sat down in his normal seat more than a little nervous about possibly seeing Aislinn which pissed him off right from the start. He began spreading the records out to look at them while he waited. Just then a small commotion got his attention. He looked up to see Aislinn rushing through the restaurant and Meghan following her. He didn't even think about it. He just knew that something was wrong.

Cullen came up to the employee's break room. He could smell Aislinn and Meghan and he knew that they had gone in there. The door was open a crack. He could hear crying. He almost stormed in to find out why Meghan was making Aislinn cry when he heard someone start talking.

"Meghan I'm sorry," I didn't mean to be late Aislinn sobbed. Cullen stopped and listened, hoping he'd hear what was going on. He figured that Aislinn wouldn't tell him.

Meghan tried to be mad, but it was really hard to be the boss and yell at someone when they were already upset. "All right, just tell me why you're so upset. I can't very well send you out to wait on customers like this." Meghan tried to be comforting, but Aislinn pulled away in a manner that reminded Meghan of someone who had been abused.

Aislinn shook her head. "I can't. Please I just need to go to the restroom. I'll be fine." She sounded so defeated. Cullen knew how she felt.

"Aislinn," Meghan said in a sympathetic tone, "I need to tell Liam something. I know you told Rissa that you had to go to court today. Is this about that? What happened?"

"Rissa told you?" Aislinn was scared to death she was going to lose her job. God she had just been to court and found guilty of battery. Never mind that it wasn't her. She would have done it herself if she had been capable. As it was it didn't matter who had done it. She was the one who was found guilty and the Taigh-O\sda wasn't the kind of place that employed people with a record.

"Hey, don't be like that," Meghan said softly. She reached out to Aislinn again. "She was just trying to help. We're on your side here."

She shook her head. Well what was she going to say? It was public record. If she lied they could look it up. "Fine," she said with that defeated tone and more tears. "Remember when I first got here and I said that Cul- Lord Arnauk had helped me out with something?" Cullen felt his stomach turn.

"Yeah," Meghan smiled. "You're entrance here was kinda hard to forget." She was trying to be lighthearted about it but it obviously wasn't helping.

"Well my last boss had attacked me and Lord Arnauk stopped him. He ended up in the hospital and decided to sue me for battery and he just won. I got fined and he came after me again on my way out of the damn court." Aislinn's voice broke at that point. "I can't lose this job Meghan. If I do I'll never pay off the bills I had before, and now there's this fine. I don't have anywhere else to go."

Cullen almost went into the room. He stood there growling under his breath. *That piece of caoch. He had one hell of a nerve.* Cullen thought. *Wait 'til he sees what I do to him when I get my claws on him again.* Cullen was nearly of a mind to go back to the Blood Pit and burn it to the ground when Aislinn and Meghan came out of the break room and saw him standing there.

Aislinn's eyes went as wide as saucers and the tears started again. Meghan saw the standard Cullen Arnauk dismissal stare and gave Aislinn a reassuring glance before she hurried off down the hall. Aislinn looked like a scared animal about to bolt. Cullen took hold of her before she could run and led her down to the office further down the hall. When they walked in Liam looked up from his desk and upon seeking Cullen stood up.

"Lord Arnauk?" Liam looked between the two. "Is something wrong?"

"No," Cullen said shortly. "Can I use your office a moment?"

"Of course," Liam said in confusion and quickly let himself out.

Aislinn was still staring at him as though he was about to do something awful, and that cut through him worse than anything else that had recently happened. He could handle any one being afraid of him, but not her. "It's all right," he said gently. "You're not losing your job or getting yelled at or anything else."

It was the look in his eyes that calmed her down more than anything else. This past week had been worse than any in her life. Perhaps worse than her time with the Circle. She couldn't understand her need for his approval or touch, but being so close was more than she could handle right now. Aislinn stepped toward him, tears of frustration and embarrassment burning their way down her cheeks, and buried her face in his chest as she wrapped her arms around him. She didn't really know why she did it. She had refused any comfort from Meghan. She just needed to be close to him.

Cullen wrapped his arms around her automatically and leaned into the hug so that his check rested on the top of her head. They stood there feeling the warmth pass between them and feeling the need for more growing relentlessly. When she had finally calmed down he managed to pull back a little. He placed his hand under her chin and brought her face up to his. Slowly he kissed away the tears. Then he placed a small gentle kiss on her lips. At least it meant to be small and gentle, but as she kissed him back the intensity grew. They melted into the kiss and hands began to roam.

As Cullen felt his wolf beginning to stir he knew he needed to slow this and find out what he could do to actually help. Seducing her in this kind of state was just not a possibility. He gently pushed her down. Aislinn tried to lean in for another kiss, but he managed to catch her and stop it. Any more like that first one and his wolf would be unstoppable.

"Aislinn," he said softly. "We need to talk. I need you to tell me why you left me out of this court business."

She looked away from him. Her arms dropped and she stepped away. Suddenly he wished he hadn't asked. "I didn't think you should get involved."

"I was the one who beat the guy up. You shouldn't have taken the fall for that," he said with concern.

"I was certainly part of it, the cause of it, and I did hit him before that," Aislinn was sounding indignant and Cullen could see the argumentative side of her emerging. He knew if that happened there was no way that he'd be able to resurrect this conversation.

"You're right. You were part of it. But so was I. I could have helped you. I would have helped you." He thought about it a moment. "Maybe we can get it overturned."

"No, I just want to pay it and have it all go away," she said sadly and the tears started again.

He couldn't handle that. "What if I managed to make it go away without you having to be involved anymore?"

She looked at him uncertainly.

"Money can do a great deal," he said trying to sound as off-hand as he could. "Let me help you."

"I still don't understand why you want to," she said shaking her head. "I mean that night, this job, now you want to make this court case disappear."

"Can't you just let me? Do I have to explain it? Besides, I really didn't need to beat him up as badly as I did. I was pissed and drunk."

She nodded and walked over to him again. He pulled her the last couple steps to himself and held her again. Nothing had ever felt so right to him. He nuzzled into her hair and took in her scent, still wondering at the amazing way she smelled to him. "What are you," he whispered into her hair, entranced.

- 73 -

"I could ask the same of you," she responded just as softly. "What does it matter? Who and what are completely separate from intention. Whenever I look into your eyes I feel safe."

Cullen held her tighter, stroking her hair and breathing in her scent. "I'll take care of it. Just don't do anything until I tell you. Okay?" He finally pushed her away far enough that he could look into her face. She nodded. He let the air in his chest out, not even realizing that he had been holding his breath. "Now, Liam needs his office back, I want dinner, and you're going to eat with me."

"I can't. I have to get to work. I was already late," she said, sounding upset again.

"You can't wait on tables in this kind of mood. You won't make any tips," he smiled. "You'll eat with me and then you can get to work. You'll feel better by then. Besides, I'm in charge around here. If I want my waitress to sit and eat with me," he shrugged and smiled wider trying to get her to smile back, "then I get to have her sit and eat with me."

Aislinn was about to argue some more, but she didn't have the energy to. He took her by the hand and led her out to his table, only realizing that he'd left the records sitting there when he saw them spread about the table. *This woman is going to be the death of me,* he thought. He had never been so easily distracted by anything before. He pushed the records aside and motioned for her to sit.

Rissa was immediately over to the table and taking their order. "And while you're at it you can tell Meghan that Liam can have his office back and I ordered Aislinn to have dinner with me. She'll be back to work as soon as I'm done with her," he smiled over at Aislinn as he said it and was rewarded with an amused grin as she shook her head at him.

"You realize," Aislinn said as Rissa headed off to get their order in, "that the entire kitchen is going to be gossiping about this for a week?"

Kitchen, nothing, the entire pack it going to have a fit with this one, he thought. Cullen smiled deviously. "Just think of how much fun the rumors would be if they caught us in the office a few minutes ago?"

Aislinn blushed a bit. "You're a dangerous man I think," she said a bit breathlessly. "But not in any of the ways that everyone else believes."

Cullen grinned and winked at her. Aislinn reached for her glass of water and noticed that Cullen was staring down her blouse. When he finally met her gaze again she gave him a knowing, amused look.

"I'm only a man," he said with a wicked grin.

"I have a hard time believing that," she answered. As she set the water back down it spilled and ran across the table toward the papers he had moved out of the way when they sat down. "Shit," she said and grabbed the papers up, barely missing the torrent of water. As she held them up she felt the dark and light take her. Everything in the restaurant seemed to freeze in time, like a dream while she was awake.

* * * *

Aislinn saw a series of scenes flash before her eyes. First she saw a small, sleepy town. It was night and the streets were empty. She was standing naked, like in her other dreams, she moved and changed into her animal shape as she walked through the streets. She could hear the voices whispering but they weren't looking for her. They were looking for something. She walked through the streets. She couldn't see any people, but she saw buildings burning, and heard the whispering. She followed the voices to the buildings. It was as though the fire was frozen in its blaze, solid and blinding in the darkness. She walked into the building and found she was instantly in an office. The room was torn apart and books and papers were strewn about the floor. The bookshelves were thrown away from the walls and the desk was carved in half as though someone had taken out his anger on the innocent furniture.

The scene shifted, and again she was standing naked on a street. Again she heard the whispering, and again she found a burning building. Walking through the door she found herself in a library, just as destroyed as the office had been. The scene shifted again and again. Always she was taken to a burning building and always she found herself in a room of books.

Finally she was surrounded by people. There was no street. She was walking through trees. This felt much different. This time the danger was coming. In the other places the danger had already gone. There were people and wolves. They were celebrating something. She walked slowly through the crowds of people and wolves. They didn't seem to see her. She knew that she wouldn't be here. This premonition was not for her.

She had never had a premonition for someone other than herself. It was a strange sensation. She knew that the danger was fearsome and real and coming. She knew she was meant to warn these people. She walked through the woods. Everywhere she looked there was sex. Half of the people she looked at were as naked as she was. They didn't seem to see her. But she got the impression that if they could see her it wouldn't have mattered.

She found herself looking at a woman on her hands and knees. She was beautiful. Her eyes glowed amber in the night. Her dark hair flowed over her shoulders. On top of her was a large black wolf. He had mounted her and the woman was writhing in ecstasy as the wolf wildly humped against her. Aislinn walked around the pair. She was fascinated. And she was aroused. She watched as the woman moaned and the wolf growled. Beads of sweat formed on the woman's brow. She begged the wolf to fuck her harder. The wolf's eyes glowed that same amber, brilliant and needy as he thrust into her. His claws scratched her sides and she begged for more from him. Finally the woman began to cry out her pleasure and the wolf howled hungrily at the sky.

Aislinn reached down and touched herself as the couple cried out their climax. She could feel the wetness pooling in her own heated center as she stared in amazement at the pair. Then they both rolled off onto their sides. As she watched the wolf slowly turned into a man. All the while the creature's cock remained lodged in the woman's body. Aislinn stared in shock as she watched the wolf turn into a man.

She was snapped out of her realization as she heard the whispers getting closer. No one seemed to know what was coming. She tried to say something to the man and woman she had been watching but no sound came from her mouth, no matter how hard she tried. The voices were getting louder and more insistent. Aislinn felt compelled to move on. She knew there was more she was meant to see.

As she came out of the woods she passed a large standing stone and found herself in a kind of clearing. All around her there were men and women, wolves and women, wolves and men, and pairs of wolves rutting. The sounds of intense, unrestrained pleasure echoed through the clearing. She looked around at where she was. There was something here she was meant to understand. But she was missing it.

She turned and looked back the way she came. The voices were getting closer and she was getting scared. She could feel a hot breath on the back of her neck and eyes on her body. She knew that whatever was coming knew that she was here. She found herself staring at the stone she had passed. There was an elaborate carving on the large stone, but she didn't know what it meant. When she turned around she realized that she was standing in a circle of large stones. They were all covered in symbols. She looked from one to the other. They were Gaelic. Why were there Gaelic symbols here? Aislinn counted nine stones in all.

As she started to wonder where she was and why all the other scenes were books and this one was a circle of standing stones, she noticed the couple rutting in the center of the circle. Actually they were fucking in the middle of the entire wolven orgy. The apparently female wolf on the bottom was snow white. She was panting and heaving with the effort of the large black wolf on top of her. He was coal black. As she looked into the animal's eyes her heart shattered. She knew that it was Cullen. This was his wedding that everyone had been talking about. The snow white wolf was Jenna. Aislinn was watching him fuck her. The voices were getting closer but Aislinn didn't care anymore.

Suddenly an icy hand was on her shoulder. Aislinn turned around to see Rafe staring into her eyes. The voices stopped. "You see," he said. "Your destiny is with me. You're better than this. Do you want to be some beast, rutting in the mud, birthing puppies," he asked with disgust. "He doesn't want you anyway."

* * * *

Cullen grabbed up some napkins and had sopped up most of the water before he noticed the glazed over blank stare on Aislinn's face. She had gone deathly pale and there were beads of sweat on her forehead. "Aislinn," he said and waited.

When she didn't respond, he took hold of the papers and pulled them out of her hand. Cullen reached out and touched her face. Suddenly she gasped and looked wildly around the room as if she didn't recognize where she was. "Rafe," she hissed in a terrified whisper, pulling away from Cullen as if he had just bit her.

At that point Cullen didn't care what anyone thought. He virtually jumped the booth to sit next to Aislinn and take hold of her. She was trembling and fighting him. It took a moment for her to come back to reality. By then there were a number of people staring in concern. A glare from Cullen sent most of the back to their own business.

"Shh, Aislinn. I've got you," he whispered softly. "I won't let anyone hurt you," he promised.

Aislinn felt him wrapped around her. He was the safety that she never seemed to have no matter where she went. At first she was afraid she would start to cry again. When the tears didn't come she figured that she must have used up her allotment for the day. She pushed him back from her. "You won't be able to stop it. He's coming and he's going to get what he wants and then me as well."

Cullen let her push him away. The deadly tone in her voice seemed to reach into him and make it hard for him to breath. "What are you talking about?"

She looked over at the papers that were on the table. "You're looking for someone who is looking for something. It's in those papers and I saw it." Rafe was the only other person she had ever told about her premonitions, and she had regretted it ever since. She was trembling now. She knew that she had to tell Cullen. He was the one that the vision was for. He was meant to save all those people somehow.

Cullen started to say something but she stopped him so that she could just get it all out and done. "I sometimes see things. Visions, premonitions. Sometimes the past, sometimes the present, and sometimes the future." Cullen could barely hear her speaking. Her eyes were glassed over and she looked so weak she might fall over if the air touched her wrong. "I've always seen them for myself, but I think that one was meant for you. Rafe, that's his name, the one who you've been trying to find. He's coming to you. Tonight at your wedding." When she said that the tears that she had thought were dried up started to well in her eyes and her voice cracked. "The places he destroyed. They all had books and papers. He was looking for a book of some kind. Whatever it was he found it and now he is trying to find a place. He knows where it is and he'll be there tonight. During the celebration, while everyone is…" She stopped and her eyes met his. Cullen had completely forgotten that he was to be mated that night. He would have stayed there with Aislinn for the entire evening if this hadn't happened. "He's looking for a clearing with nine standing stones." *Then he'll be free to come after me again*, she thought.

With more strength then Cullen would have believed she had left she pushed him out of the booth so that she could get up. "I appreciate everything you've done for me. But now you need to go to them. He'll kill everyone." Then Aislinn ran out of the restaurant.

If it hadn't been for what she said he would have chased after her. But if the pack was in immediate danger he'd have to deal with Aislinn after that. Rissa arrived with their food as Cullen was picking up the papers and turning to leave. She stared at him with confusion.

Cullen took a minute to gather his thoughts. "Aislinn had to go home sick. When someone is able, please check on her." Rissa nodded. "I'm sorry I won't be eating. I need to leave." Rissa nodded again and then watched as Cullen swept out of the restaurant.

Chapter 5

Be wary of the man who urges an action in which he himself incurs no risk.
-Lucius Annaeus Seneca

Aislinn found herself back at her apartment. She had originally intended to pack up and run. She had about $200 in cash from tips hidden beneath her mattress and she figured that she could catch a bus and get out of town before Rafe finished with the wolves. But as she walked inside she only barely managed to lock the door behind herself. She had never had a premonition that strong before or during the day, not to mention the court case and then Cullen. Just thinking his name hurt. It briefly occurred to her that her premonitions had always given her information about the future in a fuzzy way. She knew that usually what she saw was a warning and not guaranteed to happen that way. But the one she had tonight was awfully close to happening for there to be much that could change it.

She walked over to her bed and collapsed onto. She didn't even manage to get her shoes off. Falling into a fitful sleep, she just prayed she didn't have any more visions for now. *I know I'm in trouble. I know he's coming. I know that Cullen Arnauk is someone else's. I don't need to know anymore right now,* she thought at whatever forces brought the premonitions on as she felt herself fall into oblivion.

* * * *

Cullen paced in the elevator. When the doors finally opened into the great room his friends cheered his entrance, until they saw the look on his face. "Every able fighter, even the ones who didn't plan on attending, need to gather in the garage and get out to the reservation. There's going to be a raid tonight."

They all stood in shock a moment, not wanting to believe what he was saying. It made no sense. Why would there be a raid on a lycan reservation. Was the source of their troubles recently really that stupid?

"NOW!" Cullen shouted when no one moved. Suddenly the room burst into action. An alarm that hadn't been used in decades was sounded and the pack snapped into action with a confused chaos that gave Cullen a sick concerned feeling. There was a reason that the Arnauk enjoyed the peace they had. For a very long time this pack was at constant war and always ready and able to fight. As Cullen looked around he wondered if Keith was right. Maybe it was time for the peace to end. This was not how the Arnauk went into a battle. He would have to deal with this as soon as possible.

A caravan of black vans and SUVs with tinted windows filed out of the parking garage at the Madadh-Allaidh Saobhaidh and roared down the road toward the reservation. The reservation was a 50 mile square of land that Cullen had acquired when he had first founded the pack. It was mostly wooded, with a small mountain range that bordered one side. A manor-like cabin was nestled into the forest at the foot of the mountain, and a number of older pack members had retired there. There were also a number of cabins that Cullen had allowed to be built in various locations around the forest. Most of those were the homes of lycans who preferred a solitary life for one reason or another, but still wanted the safety of belonging to a pack. The manor itself was just as elaborate at the den in the city, but it was also built to be self sustaining. There were not electrical lines that led out there and there were no cell towers that reached far enough into the territory for a signal. The manor ran on generators and solar power. The only outside contact was through a satellite phone in his office. The sat-phone only worked if it was taken outside and into the clearing, when the satellite it used wasn't being blocked by the mountain. There was no way to call ahead and tell people to watch for an attack.

The trip was only three hours long. But it felt as though it took all night. When they arrived in a rush of concern and warning, the people who were there were all stunned with disbelief. It just didn't make sense. Who would be stupid enough to attack such a large group of Arnauk on their home territory?

Cullen found the atmosphere of the entire place strange when he first arrived. There had been a number of bonfires lit and the celebration had started without him. Both things were completely out of the ordinary for a mating. Bonfires in general were out of the ordinary for the pack. These bonfires had an odd look and smell to them. They burned exceptionally high, had a greenish tint to the flame, and gave off a scent like burning flowers. That would be more than enough to scare all the local wildlife off. The pack preferred to not scare away any game that might be in the area. Especially considering that a hunt might occur as part of the celebration. Additionally, the fact that there were dozens of couples already undressed and rutting was also strange. That kind of thing should definitely have not started until Cullen and Jenna began their part. Cullen noted the oddities, but then dismissed them. His mind fought the idea of ignoring it briefly. But he decided that there were more important things to think about than the small problems with the ceremony setup.

Then there was Jenna. The minute the announcement was made that the ceremony might be canceled she started screeching and didn't stop. She followed along behind Cullen blaming the situation on him and accusing him of making excuses to cancel the mating. Cullen couldn't help but wonder what had her in such a panic. There was more going on with her right now than he knew, but he didn't have time to figure it out. The current plan was to make things look like everything was normal, in a way that resulted in everyone being ready when the attack came.

Convincing Brennus of the trouble was the hardest part. He was inclined to agree with his daughter about Cullen's motivations, even if he was making the accusations in a more diplomatic way. In the end Cullen agreed to set things up to defend from an attack while still going through the motions of the ceremony. If the attack never came then the mating would be completed and it wouldn't matter. If, however, the attack did come, then everyone would be ready and they might not lose as many lives.

* * * *

Aislinn felt herself being pulled into her dream. She fought against it as hard as she could. *I don't want another vision*, she cried into the blackness. As the scene flashed into view she was standing in the woods beside one of the large stones she had seen before. Rafe was standing next to her.

"I'm glad you could join us," he said in that sweet tone of voice that she had believed was sincere for so long. He had this ability to get into her head and change her perceptions. She doubted herself for so long, because he could make anything seem reasonable. She shivered as she thought about things she had done for him. That was, until she realized that he was doing something to her mind. At first, she had thought he cared about her, then she thought he was drugging her, but after she escaped she realized that he could get into her head and make her think things. It wasn't until she had been gone for over a year that everything started to clear and she started to make sense of things that had happened.

Aislinn didn't know if what she was seeing was one of her own premonitions or something Rafe was making her see. Aislinn tried to leave the circle of stones, but when she turned to go there was nothing behind her. There was nowhere to go. When she turned to face the scene again she could see the people milling about and Cullen and Jenna. She had her hands all over him, and although he didn't look very happy about it, he was allowing it. When Jenna reached down to stroke Cullen's cock Aislinn turned away. She found herself looking at Rafe, who was watching with great interest.

"You know. I had originally thought to bring you here when I first took you. This place holds power for people like us. You'll see. You'll come to appreciate me once I show you." His eyes never left the couple. He seemed to be waiting for something. "We're the same you know."

"I'm nothing like you," Aislinn hissed at him.

He just smiled. "I don't mean morally or ethically. I'm referencing our abilities. That's why I had to have you. You know how few of us there are left. The bloodlines have thinned over the years and most of us don't know what we are. But there are some. Once I have all of what was stolen from us I'll find the others as well. I'll make us strong again. If you really want the pet wolf so badly and he survives this, perhaps you can keep him once I've relieved him of his throne."

Aislinn's mind was racing. She was trying desperately to think of something she could do. But it wasn't as if she was really there. When she looked back to the scene playing out in the stone circle, she saw that Jenna had dropped to her knees in front of Cullen. He was breathing slowly and looking about as she sucked eagerly on his erect cock. Her hands toyed with his balls and inner thighs. He had his hands clenched into fists at his sides and was staring up at the sky with a frustrated expression. Aislinn was torn. *If he truly didn't want this then why is he letting it happen,* she thought.

"Because he has no choice," Rafe answered her thoughts.

"Get out of my head," she spit at him.

For a brief moment Rafe seemed pained. Aislinn realized that she had done something. She needed to think. But she couldn't if he was listening. She did her best to clear her mind and try to understand without thinking anything specific.

Rafe wasn't surprised at all. He knew she would learn quickly. But he was annoyed when he felt the wall go up and was thrown from her thoughts. He would have to get to her quickly when this was over. He needed to shake her up more. Her spirit wasn't completely broken yet. "You see, Arnauk doesn't realize that the real danger is sitting between his legs," Rafe chuckled. "Jenna was easy to manipulate. She truly believes that when she gets rid of Cullen that I'll take her as mine and together we'll run the two territories. The woman is blinded by ambition. She has no idea what's important."

"Fine, so what is important?" Aislinn said, deciding to play along. Carefully, she kept her guard up and watching as Jenna ran her tongue along Cullen's shaft. She felt chills run through her body. She wanted to rip the woman's throat out.

Rafe smiled and looked at Aislinn. His eyes were shining silver in the darkness, giving his face an otherworldly glow. "Power. Not political, or physical. But power like we had when we created them." Rafe walked forward and stared at the closest set of wolves rutting in response to their leader's example. "Look at them. Not even God himself was clever enough to create these creatures. These were made by our ancestors. Yours and mine. The power of life and change. They're magnificent. And I've improved on them. If you hadn't left so quickly you would have come to see what I mean. When I have you back, I promise that I'll finish." He smiled at her in a way that she was certain was meant to be sincere.

"What did you do to me?" she whispered in fear.

"I gave you the gift of the change. Oh it's not complete yet. But as I said, it will be." He walked over to Cullen and Jenna. She had reached between her legs to play with herself. Her fingers danced deftly over her clit, down into her wet slit, and then back to her clit. She was trying to convince Cullen that she needed him to mount her, but he wasn't going for it just yet.

As she reached down between her legs again Rafe became more excited. At first Aislinn figured it was because he was getting off on watching the woman toy with herself. But then she noticed that the movements of Jenna's hand weren't real consistent with any kind of masturbation that Aislinn could think of.

Rafe smiled at her pleasantly. "You are a bright one. Our children will be amazing."

"So what's going to happen when she does whatever it is she's going to do?" Aislinn asked hoping he was one of those moronic bad guys who liked to monologue before his big plan could come to fruition.

"His death is the signal for the others to attack. First, his own men that I've gotten to, then my men will come out of hiding. It's exceedingly simple."

Aislinn closed her eyes. There had to be something she could do. *Fuck it, if he can get into my mind because he wants to, I should be able to get into someone else's.*

"In time, pet," Rafe said with that awful smile. "I'll teach you in time."

Aislinn thought back to the earlier vision. The one that showed her Cullen's friend and she realized that there had to be a couple of lycans who had finished rutting and were sleeping off their exhausted energy lying around here somewhere.

Rafe glared at her and she glared right back. She turned away from watching Cullen and Jenna only to hear Rafe call after her that it was too late.

She plunged into the darkness outside of the Circle of stones and willed it to be as she had seen it before. Suddenly the forest in her mind lightened and shifted. She looked around and managed to find a couple of sleeping wolves. She knelt down next to them. She didn't really know what she was doing. She tried touching them, hoping that something would just happen like it had before. There seemed to be nothing until the woman stirred. Aislinn touched the woman's face and closed her eyes. She brought into her mind pictures of what she had seen Jenna doing and tied a fearful emotion to it. The woman suddenly sat upright as though she had awoken from a bad dream. Aislinn didn't know if it had worked, but she leaned down and did the same thing to the man. When he sat up and looked at the woman they spoke to each other. Aislinn couldn't hear what they were saying, and she was feeling drained. She looked around the clearing for more sleeping lycans. Everyone she found, she woke in the same fashion. Aislinn was unsure how many she had touched when she dropped out of the vision into darkness again.

"NO," she screamed into the black. "I need to know what happened!"

* * * *

The only thing keeping Cullen hard throughout the blow job was the image of Aislinn in his mind. He was praying the attack would come soon. He wanted it to interrupt the mating, buy him time to figure a way out of this. After having held Aislinn in his arms earlier that night there was no way he could go through with this. But with the prospect of an unknown enemy surrounding them he couldn't take the chance of starting a war with the Tairneach right here and now. If he stopped this mating ceremony at this point he would need a better than damn good reason.

Jenna was bringing him dangerously close to coming. He didn't want to give her the satisfaction. The relentless assault of her tongue on his cock was getting to him whether he wanted it to or not. He looked down and watched her pretty face bobbing up and down on his shaft. Her eyes half lidded staring up at him with a terrible devious glare. She seemed pleased by what she was doing, but not because she wanted to be sucking him off. Something she was thinking was pleasing her and he was afraid of what that was, especially since he was in such a vulnerable position. *Muin galla,* he thought angrily and wanted desperately to say it out loud and throw her off of him.

He watched a number of his own gathering at the perimeter of the standing stones. They looked concerned and they were watching the mating. Jenna finally pulled her mouth off of him. She had been going at him for so long her jaw and neck were sore and he was showing no signs of stopping her any time soon. She glared up at him and turned onto her hands and knees, presenting herself to him. The group that had taken up position between the stones started to advance. Cullen looked at Ranaild. His eyes were stone and Ranaild shifted his look from Cullen to Jenna in warning. He looked frightened.

Jenna started to panic. This wasn't how Rafe said it would go. He made it sound so simple. She almost thought the plan had been hers. She had a short stiletto blade, tipped with poison held nicely in her cunt. Since it was a stiletto the sides were dull and wouldn't pierce her flesh. But the tip would jab Cullen the minute he penetrated her. The poison was virtually instantaneous and Cullen would die, the fight would start and the Tairneach would take over.

As she watched the advancing Arnauk she knew that something had gone wrong. As she began to think about it, she wondered why she had agreed to this anyway. It was far too obvious for her. She looked around for Rafe. He said he would be here. Every time she thought his name she seemed to become more confident in the situation. She knew that he would come and save her.

"What is this Arnauk?" Brennus growled at the interruption in the ceremony.

Rafe continued to watch from the shadows. He was getting tired and was cursing himself for bringing Aislinn here. That was a miscalculation. He would see that she paid for what she had done. But at the moment it was all he could do, even with using the power from the stone circle, to keep the lycans' minds from noticing the enemy hidden among them. He was trying to come up with a way out of this. He needed more numbers and the only way to do that would be to take on a pack. He didn't like direct confrontation. Staring at Jenna at Cullen's feet calling out his name, he realized that he needed the bitch. As Cullen began to argue with Brennus, Rafe extended his influence over the lycans' minds to hide Jenna from them and to bring Jenna to himself.

"You tell me Brennus. Your daughter seems to be following in her mother's footsteps," Cullen growled back.

"She's done nothing save try to please you," Brennus replied coming toe to toe with Cullen.

"She has a knife," someone yelled. Cullen turned to see what was going on but Jenna seemed to vanish.

enna braced herself for the attack that never came. "Come here girl," Rafe said to her in annoyance. "I can't have you killing him now. This plan will have to be changed. Complications have arisen. If we want your father to believe that Arnauk was the cause of the bad ending here then you have to leave him to be the target of Brennus' anger. That will make it easier for me to convince him that you should be mine and that we need to go to war."

Jenna smiled at him dully. He hated the simpering look they got when he had to use his influence on them. He couldn't wait until he was done with this one.

* * * *

With Jenna's disappearance the mating ceremony was over and when the attack never came the pack was generally confused. Everyone seemed to have a headache or felt sick. No one even considered looking for Jenna. They all took turns being angry about her disappearance for different reasons, but a search party was never even suggested. The Tairneach left with promises of retribution for the embarrassment caused this night and threats should Jenna not reappear in short order. If Brennus hadn't been standing there when she vanished, arguing with Cullen, he would have blamed it on Cullen and possibly started the war right then. As it was, Brennus figured it would be best to remain on tentative terms at least until Jenna was home safe.

Cullen had his hands full explaining away the events of the evening. There were at least a dozen people who claimed to have dreamt that Jenna was going to knife Cullen with a stiletto that she had hidden on her person. No one said exactly where, but the implication had most everyone chuckling.

By the time everything was sorted out and calmed down dawn, was on the manor. Cullen took one look at the rising sun, felt his body begging for sleep, and looked around at the tired faces of his men. The best he could do was pray that Aislinn was safe.

It took a great deal of convincing and then finally an order to get a set of keys handed over so that he could drive back into town without sleep. He just had a bad feeling and knew that he wouldn't rest until Aislinn was safe inside the den. Keith insisted on going with him, but fell asleep halfway there. Cullen let his friend rest. It had been a long night for everyone.

Chapter 6

Nothing is so wretched or foolish as to anticipate misfortunes. What madness is it to be expecting evil before it comes.
-Lucius Annaeus Seneca

Aislinn could feel herself falling through darkness. The black was throbbing around her. Somewhere in the void there was a pounding. The echo became more and more insistent, louder. Then she felt herself being moved. She was aware of the black shifting around her. Someone was trying to reach her. Aislinn could feel an urgent voice pulling at her. Suddenly the black turned into the street outside of her apartment. She felt drunk as she watched the street lights pass above her. The lights passed over her one at a time. *Where am I going?* She thought. *Madadh-Allaidh Saobhaidh. I need to get to Madadh-Allaidh Saobhaidh.* But she couldn't make her body obey her mind. She was so tired. She closed her eyes and drifted into the black again.

* * * *

Rafe sat in the back of the long black limo. Jenna lay naked and prone across the seat opposite and a large lion lay purring at his feet. She would periodically look up, agitated, at the naked lycan that had her master's attention. As he stroked her head she went back to her patient waiting.

Rafe growled angrily. "These lycans are becoming more troublesome than I had originally thought they would be." The lioness sat up with interest and attention. Her large yellow eyes focusing intently on

Rafe. "Look at her," he said in disgust. "So easily manipulated. She actually believes she'll be leading the Tairneach to glory. She has no concept of how inconsequential she truly is. Now Aislinn and Arnauk, they will pay for putting me in a position to have to soil myself with this bitch. I don't like interruptions or delays. What's worse, I had my hands on the stones themselves tonight and now I'm driving away from the power. I could feel it. I used it. It would take so little to learn how to truly manipulate the forces that sleep there. The lycans have no concept of it. How could anything like that," he indicated the unconscious Jenna, "be capable of using the power there to its full potential?"

The lioness sniffed at Jenna with distaste. When a buzzer sounded the large cat growled and Rafe pushed a button on the panel. "Yes."

"We've arrived at the address you requested," the limo driver said.

"Finally," Rafe growled, opened the door and got out of the car. He looked around at the rundown buildings and the bums lying about the steps in garbage. He thought it fitting that she ended up here. *Serves her right for leaving me,* he thought. The lioness stepped lightly from the limo onto the street. She paced a bit. As she walked she lifted her paws from the ground as though she was stepping in something that was burning her feet. She looked up to Rafe for orders.

"I'll not go in that place. Go get her and bring her here. She shouldn't be any trouble," he said, knowing that after the evening they had she was probably completely unconscious. She was only a half-blood. She'd never be as strong as he was. None of the ones he'd found would ever be as strong as he was. Besides she had pushed herself much too far last night. If she truly wanted to get away from him she never should have shown him her potential. He had tried to get into her mind on his way here. But she was too far gone for him to even touch her dreams. That would make things exceptionally easy.

Rafe took one last look around and got back into the limo as the lioness headed up the stairs. One of the bums that sat near the steps got up and walked toward Rafe waggling a cup. This wasn't the type of area he wanted to be seen in, so Rafe got back in the limo to wait. He slammed the door of the car just as the old bum approached. The man proceeded to start wiping the windows of the limo, hoping for a handout, and Rafe sent the limo driver to deal with it.

* * * *

When Cullen pulled up in front of Aislinn's place everything looked normal. He elbowed Keith awake. "Hey, watch the door," he said as he jumped out of the driver's seat and headed up the stairs to the main doors of the apartment building.

Keith sat up. Looking around, it took him a minute to realize where they were. This was the apartment building where that girl Cullen had helped out lived. He watched the door the way Cullen asked. He couldn't help notice the bum lying face down in the garbage next to the steps. Keith got out of the SUV and looked up and down the street nervously. It just didn't feel right.

He walked over to the poor old man lying in the garbage and turned him over. "Hey buddy, you okay?"

The old man groaned. Keith winced when he saw the bloody gash on the man's chest. Something had cut him straight through his big, dirty overcoat. The old guy had a huge bump on his head as well. "Who did this to you, buddy?" Keith picked the old man up and put him in a sitting position on the ground near the steps. The old man couldn't answer. Keith pulled his cell out of his pocket and dialed 911.

* * * *

Cullen took the steps up to Aislinn's door two at a time. He could smell something on the stairs that had the hair on the back of his neck standing on end. A cat of some kind was here. When he got to her door it was slightly open. Fear and anger boiled in the pit of his stomach as Cullen threw the door open and rushed in.

There was no sign of anything being wrong. The apartment wasn't any more disheveled than it had been when he was here before. It almost looked as though the door had just been left open. The scent of the cat wasn't any stronger here than it had been in the hall. He figured that if there had been a struggle of some kind that the scent should be stronger. Maybe she went with someone willingly. Cullen couldn't tell anything from the look of the place except that Aislinn wasn't there.

On the table he noticed her purse and headed over to it. Inside were her keys, her wallet, and her cell phone. He picked it up and looked around again as if Aislinn might come walking out of the bathroom and yell at him for not knocking. She wouldn't have left here without taking her purse if she had gone somewhere willingly with someone. At the same time he didn't have any proof that anything had happened either. He was too tired to think.

Cullen sat her purse back down on the table and headed out the door. He took a deep breath in the hall.

He could smell her there. But that could just be because she lived here. He walked down the steps, considering that he could wait around and see if she came back for her purse. When he walked out the main doors he discovered Keith bent over a bum and talking on his cell phone.

One look at the bum had the feeling of fear returning to Cullen's stomach. When Keith hung up he looked at Cullen. "I called an ambulance. We should get out of here before it shows up. I don't have the answers to the questions they'll be asking."

Cullen looked back at the building and then got into the SUV without a word. Keith hopped in the other side, and Cullen pulled away from the curb. *What the hell am I going to do?* Cullen was pissed and tired and feeling helpless. Okay, so he went to check on her and she wasn't there. There seems to be evidence of something, but he didn't know what. "I am getting so muin tired of not having the information I need to make decisions anymore!" Cullen yelled and slammed his hands against the steering wheel.

"Okay, so you want to tell me why we went to that chick's place? And why it pissed you off," Keith asked cautiously.

Cullen kept driving. "We went to her place because I was worried about her and wanted to talk to her. I'm pissed because she wasn't there and it looks like either there's nothing wrong or something relating to last night happened here. But I don't know which. I should either be looking for her or moving on. Your guess is as good as mine."

Cullen's voice was deadly and Keith felt shivers go down his spine as he listened to the alpha's explanation. "Okay, so we go back to the den, we look up this Rafe guy. If something happened here and it had to do with what happened at the reservation then if we track him down we'll find out what happened to the girl."

Cullen growled. He didn't want to look things up any more. He just wanted to fix all the shit that was happening lately. "When exactly did everything go to hell around here?"

Keith didn't answer. He could hear the rhetorical tone in the question. "I'll take care of it. You get some sleep and by the time you wake up I'll have some kind of answer."

Cullen looked over at his friend. Keith was glad to see that what he said seemed to have helped some. The growl that came from Cullen next was low and resigned. They drove the rest of the way home in silence. Cullen pulled into the garage and parked.

As they walked into the elevator and pushed their respective buttons Cullen finally felt the tired hit him hard enough that he knew he'd sleep whether he wanted to or not. Keith got out on floor 13. Cullen hit the button for the penthouse as he watched the doors close behind Keith.

Keith figured that he'd gather up a couple people and get to work on figuring out who Rafe was. He wanted to see if he'd be able to get through to the reservation as well. Or maybe he'd try some cell numbers and see if anyone had left the reservation for home yet. But he guessed probably not.

Keith walked into the great room to find an unusually large group of people standing around. He was taking note of who was present and trying to decide who he should send to do what. He wanted to get this over and done with so that he could go to bed.

As he walked around the room, though, he finally figured out what everyone was so worked up about.

* * * *

Cullen walked out of the elevator and through his office/living room. His rooms included a main room right off the elevator that took up most of the penthouse area. On one side there was a large television with a comfortable couch positioned directly in front of it. He didn't spend much time in the great room with the others. When he felt the need for television he was much more likely to watch by himself. On the other side of the large room there was a desk and a number of file cabinets along with his computer. His favorite part of the room was a carpeted area against the far wall with one large arm chair and the wall itself was lined with bookshelves. He had a large collection of antique history books and a few modern fiction books.

He stared at his favorite chair and his books and sighed. He hadn't had any recreational time in quite a while. Cullen promised himself that as soon as all this was taken care of he'd get a new book or two, lock himself in, and read for a few days.

He headed for a door at the back of the room. He was already pulling his shirt off over his head as he entered his bedroom. Then his cell rang. Cullen dropped his shirt to the floor and dug in his pocket for the hated source of the noise. He heard the plastic crack as his hand closed around the phone. He pulled it from his pocket with the serious intent of throwing it against the wall. When he saw that the caller was Keith, he flipped it open and growled in a low warning tone into the receiver. "I thought you told me to get some sleep."

"Yeah yeah. Changed my mind. You need to come down to the great room. I can't decide whether we have a problem or a fortuitous circumstance."

"No. Figure it out then let me know tomorrow," Cullen answered.

"You'll be sorry if you don't get down here. And I'm not going to take the heat for it." Then Keith heard a click. He wasn't sure if Cullen was coming down or not. He was just contemplating calling him again when the elevator doors opened, and Cullen came walking into the great room, barefoot, shirtless and looking as though he was going to kill someone.

Cullen's glare was enough to make everyone step back. Rissa tentatively stepped toward Cullen and Keith followed her. "I hope it's all right," she said nervously. "I mean you told me to check on her, and when I got there she was unconscious and didn't look at all well. So I called Jake, and he helped me bring her back here. The doc in the infirmary said to put her in a bed, and he'd check on her in the morning. So I brought her up here and we weren't sure where to put her."

Cullen tuned out Rissa's voice as she tried to finish explaining the events of the evening. He couldn't believe it. Aislinn was lying on the couch, asleep. She didn't look well. She was pale and drawn. Her eyelids fluttered periodically as if she was dreaming, and her face looked strained and tense. There was sweat on her forehead, and she whimpered periodically. There was a small packed bag on the floor next to the couch. He just stared at her for a moment wondering if he had fallen asleep in his room and this was some cruel dream.

Everyone was waiting to find out if they were in trouble or if Cullen was okay with the fact that Rissa had brought an outsider into the den. Finally Cullen walked passed Rissa and Keith and knelt next to the couch. With as much control as he could muster he reached out and stroked her cheek gently. "Aislinn," he said softly trying to wake her up.

"That's why we spoke to the doctor," Rissa said. "She won't wake up. We tried."

Cullen looked back at Rissa. "You did good," he said with a soft smile. Rissa beamed at that and looked over at Meghan as though to say I told you so. When Cullen looked back down at Aislinn she appeared to have calmed some. Her facial features seemed to smooth over and her breathing evened out.

"Where do you want us to put her," Rissa asked enthusiastically.

Cullen thought a moment. He knew where he wanted to put her. But beyond the fact that it would send the entire pack into a tizzy because he never took any women to his room, he didn't know how Aislinn would react if she woke up in his bed. When he pulled his hand back her features tensed again and the whimpering started again. That was enough for him. "I'll take care of it," he said. Then to everyone's shock he picked her up off the couch and headed for the elevator. "Keith, would you hit the button," he called back over his shoulder.

Keith jogged up behind his friend and Cullen could hear him chuckling as he hit the floor button and the doors slid open. He stepped inside briefly to get the button for Cullen's floor. For a brief instant Cullen thought that he was going to escape without a smart ass comment. But he had no such luck. "So," Keith said with a wicked grin. "Do I have breakfast sent up tomorrow?"

"Actually," Cullen said with a growl. "I intend to sleep until lunch." Then he kicked at Keith so that he'd back out of the elevator and let the doors close.

* * * *

Cullen had never felt his mood shift from one extreme to another so quickly. He walked through his living area and into his bedroom. He carried Aislinn to his large platform bed in the middle of the room. As he looked down at Aislinn's sleeping form, she was leaning into him and her features had softened again. He laid her down on his bed and watched her there a minute. The sight of her lying on his bed asleep pleased him far more than he thought it should. He made a mental note to find some way to reward Rissa for taking such good care of Aislinn.

He wasn't sure if he should undress her or not. She was still in her work clothes. Finally he decided that he couldn't let her sleep in those clothes. He didn't want her thinking he did anything to her while she was sleeping, so he went over to his drawers and fished out one of his t-shirts. Cullen tried his best to be an objective adult, telling himself that he was undressing her so that she'd be comfortable. *I'm putting her in my t-shirt so that she won't be upset when she wakes up.* But he couldn't stop his reaction to the sight of her naked body.

He moved as quickly as he could so that he could honestly say that he wasn't ogling her while she was unconscious. It took all his effort to keep his hands to himself as he pulled her bra off. He'd never known a woman who slept in a bra. Cullen held the white lacy material to his nose momentarily before setting it aside with the rest of her clothes. He left her underwear on, pulled his t-shirt over her head, and then pushed her arms through the sleeves.

The back of his hand brushed against her breast, and he had to hold his wolf down. Every instinct in him was screaming for him to take her and make her his own. His wolf told him that she would understand when it was done. Cullen forced his wolf down. Breathing deeply repeatedly he told himself that he was too tired and there was no way he should even be considering any of the things his wolf wanted while she was unconscious. He growled deep in his throat as he pushed his jeans off over his hips. He left his boxers on and crawled into the bed. He had to pull the blankets back in stages to maneuver her under them.

Once he had both of them under the blankets, he slipped his arm around her waist and pulled her into himself. Her back was pressed against his chest, and his erection was pressed against butt. He groaned happily and nuzzled his face into her hair. Breathing deeply he started to drift off to sleep. He figured that if she didn't wake up on her own come morning, then he'd make sure the doctor came up and checked on her. He couldn't explain why he wasn't worried about this, but something in him said that now she was with him that she'd be all right. He'd take care of her.

* * * *

Aislinn awoke to sunlight streaming in on her face from a thin crack between the drapes on a large window and warmth radiating through her from behind her back. She blinked in confusion as she took in the strange wall, then the strange bed, then the arm that was wrapped around her. She lay still a moment. The last time she was in a room this posh was when she was first dating Rafe, before she knew what he was. The blankets were soft and satiny. She had spent so long sleeping on that mattress on the floor that she had forgotten what it felt like to be in a real bed. There wasn't any one thing she could see that stood out as extravagant. It was all normal bedroom furniture. But between the size of everything and the new/clean look of it all she might have thought she was in the best room at the Hilton.

Aislinn started to get nervous. All she could think about was the fact that Rafe loved places like this. The only reason she didn't jump screaming from the bed was because there was something about the feel of this that wasn't at all like it was before and it certainly didn't smell right. She took a deep breath and then started to blush. Aislinn rolled back. The arm loosened so that she could move and she found herself staring up into Cullen's face. He was wearing a hopeful, concerned look as he smiled at her.

"Good afternoon, mo mhúirnín bán " he said softly. "I won't ask if you slept well. I know you didn't."

Slowly the memory of last night solidified in Aislinn's mind: the court hearing, the premonitions, Rafe, and the mating ceremony. She took a deep breath then smiled as she realized what he called her. If he had intended to make her feel better about everything, she had to admit it was working. She cocked an eyebrow at him questioningly. "Mo mhúirnín bán?"

He smiled back smugly. "I thought you knew Gaelic."

She shook her head and decided to not give him the satisfaction of knowing whether she understood or not. "I guess I can assume then that she didn't manage to kill you," Aislinn said, changing the topic to something she thought was relatively important considering the position she was currently in on what should have been his wedding night or morning or afternoon or whatever this was.

"I'm afraid to ask how you know about that," he replied. Then he just couldn't help himself. She was awake. She didn't seem angry with him, and he didn't care about anything other than tasting her right then. He leaned down to her and nuzzled her nose with his own, testing her reaction. When she didn't pull away or push him off of her he pressed his lips to hers and kissed her softly at first and then deeper as she kissed back. It took a little coaxing, and she parted her lips allowing his tongue to dip into her mouth and slip along her teeth and tongue. As the kiss continued she felt waves of electricity surging through her body. Heat pooled in her stomach, and she twined her leg around his. She moaned softly into his mouth when he pushed his hips against her.

They parted briefly, staring into each other's eyes and trying to read the emotions there. Aislinn smiled at him. "I guess this means you're not married then."

"No, that didn't work out," he said with half a chuckle.

"Mmhmm," Aislinn continued. She could feel his need for her pressing against her thigh. She rubbed against him, teasing him a little. "And how did I get here?"

"Rissa brought you here last night. I asked her to check on you after you ran out of the restaurant. She found you unconscious. So she brought you here to keep you safe."

"And she put me your bed to keep me safe," she grinned.

Cullen smiled back at her and pressed his hips against her in response to her teasing. He growled softly. "Not exactly. I suppose I'm to blame for where you ended up sleeping," he admitted.

"And who dressed me?" Her eyes were on fire. He wanted to sink into those eyes. "Again I guess that would be me," he said. Then quickly added, "but I behaved myself." Aislinn leaned into him and nuzzled her nose along his jaw line then kissed and nibbled at his neck. When he started growling again she giggled. Aislinn began running her hands along his chest and the growling grew more intense. Suddenly he grabbed her wrists and pushed her back onto the bed. When her eyes met his again she could see that they had shifted, and she was staring at his wolf. She wasn't prepared for the intensity that she saw there. Her breath caught in her throat. *Does he really want me that badly,* she wondered.

"Aislinn," he said. His voice was guttural and deep with passion. "You need to be sure here. Too much farther and I won't be able to stop this."

She swallowed. She wanted him, but the look on his face and the sound of his voice was frightening. They were both breathing hard and fast. Cullen waited. He didn't want to take this somewhere she wasn't ready or willing to go. Aislinn was scared. She wanted this to be real so badly. Cullen started to pull away from her when she didn't answer. As he began to move back she realized that he was ending it and she couldn't handle that. She grabbed his shoulder to stop him from leaving her and kissed him heatedly.

When Aislinn kissed him Cullen felt his wolf overwhelm his senses. He pushed her back down onto the bed and immediately his hands found their way beneath her t-shirt, along her waist, and cupped beneath her breast. His thumb made small circles around her nipple, playing with the hard bud. He growled softly against her mouth. He could smell her arousal wafting from beneath the blanket and he needed a taste. She whimpered when he broke the kiss, but he growled insistently at her and she lay still to see what he was doing. The blankets were tossed off to the side and Cullen pulled the t-shirt up as he moved his head down to lick at one of her nipples.

Aislinn's breath caught in her throat. She watched as his tongue stroked her flesh. Soft, wet, warmth flooded from her breast, through her body, and pooled between her legs. Finally she let the air out in a moan that seeped into his mind and sent chills along his spine. He moved down her stomach, trailing his tongue across her skin and leaving a warm wet path that cooled in the air and sent a chilling sensation through her. Aislinn watched as he tore the waist band of her panties and pulled them from her body, dropping the ragged material to the floor next to the bed. Then he leaned down and pressed his face to the triangle of space at the top of her thighs. He stayed there breathing and growling for a moment. The warm air of his breath tickled her skin.

Finally, he couldn't take it any longer and he pressed her legs apart so that he could look at her. She watched his face, how his eyes swirled with passion and his heated expression. *This is how it should always be,* she thought. *Everyone should be wanted like this.* Cullen's control was stretched farther than he had ever had to take it. It was all he could to convince his wolf that while he could have her, he had to go slow and he had to remain in this form. He could feel the annoyance in his alternate half. Cullen could only hope that Aislinn would eventually understand and placate that part of him.

Cullen leaned down between her legs and began alternately kissing, licking, and nibbling her inner thigh. Her scent was overpowering. It seeped into his soul and called to his wolf like no one ever had. He worked his way closer and closer to his ultimate goal. If he gave the wolf any more control he knew that he wouldn't have bothered with the little pleasantries that were making her moan so deliciously. Normally with women it went differently. The wolf was set loose, and once he'd been sated the man would be allowed to play. But Cullen still wasn't sure what he was dealing with here. He didn't even really know how much she knew about him. She appeared to have figured him out, but that didn't mean she understood what it meant to be a lycan's lover, that her body was capable of handling what the wolf would do, or that she would be willing to let him be like that with her.

Aislinn thought she might explode if he didn't stop teasing her. He was being sweet and gentle and coming so close to touching her and then not. Finally she couldn't handle it any longer and she reached down, grabbed his head by the hair, and pulled his mouth to her center. Cullen growled with pleasure at her little show of force and took her hips to hold her still while he let his wolf have that taste he had been fighting for. Aislinn arched her back and moaned her appreciation as his tongue delved into her cunt and lapped at her copious juices. His tongue ran from her core to her clit and then he sucked her clit into his mouth. Her fingers twisted into his hair almost painfully, pulling him to her harder.

Cullen was losing his ability to think. He wanted to plunge into her and bring his own release. But he forced himself to make sure she was ready for that first. He alternated driving his tongue into her sopping cunt and suckling on her clit, listening to her moan sweetly for him. He released one hand from her hip and pressed one finger into her, stroking her walls and feeling her ripple around him. He listened to her breathing quicken and reveled in the thought that he had done this to her. He slipped a second finger insider her and she moaned louder. He continued to suckle at her clit, lashing it with his tongue and nibbling on the hard bud. With his fingers pushing insider her, he had lost control of her hips and she was writhing against him. Her moans were increasing in urgency, and her hands were pulling painfully at his hair as her hips thrust against his face and hand out of control.

The sound that came from her as her body convulsed in orgasmic pleasure was somewhere between a moan, a growl, and a screech that might be heard from a jungle cat. Aislinn didn't seem to notice, but the sound was enough to stop Cullen dead. He stood on his knees looking down at her, in wonder. When she stopped writhing from the pleasure coursing through her and looked up at him, her eyes were swirling blue and silver pools. If there had been any doubt left in his mind that she wasn't human it was melting into those eyes as he stared at her.

She wasn't sure what the change in his tempo was from. Aislinn blushed at the way he was staring at her. From the amused grin on his face, she assumed that he had been enjoying what he was watching. From the look of his tented boxers, she figured that he was due for his share of the fun. Aislinn sat up and turned around. Her premonitions from the before had given her a pretty good guess at how Cullen liked his women. With her back to him, standing on her knees she took the t-shirt off and tossed it aside.

When Aislinn moved onto her hands and knees Cullen didn't care any longer about the strange moan. He watched as she moved her legs apart and looked back at him expectantly. He didn't need any further invitation. He virtually ripped the boxers he was wearing off. He stayed himself as he grabbed her hips. He was losing control of the change and he felt his wolf asserting his need. His hands tightened and his muscles strained to force himself to enter her slowly. Her warmth wrapped around his cock as he pressed into her slick, wet sex inch by inch. Aislinn felt herself stretching around him, felt him pushing into her. His hands were impossibly strong on her hips. She knew there would be bruises where his fingers pressed into her flesh. His pace was agonizingly slow. She whimpered her need for more, but Cullen heard her cry and thought he was hurting her. With a growl, he released her hips and began to pull away. When he let go of her, Aislinn couldn't take it any longer and she pushed herself back onto him. The momentum of Cullen pulling away and Aislinn pushing back resulted in him sitting on his heels with Aislinn on his lap.

She was growling again and grinding herself against him. Cullen wrapped his arms around her and pressed his face into her hair, breathing her in. He growled in return and squeezed her breasts roughly as she continued to force herself down onto him, trying to take more of him in. Watching her amazed him. He pushed her onto her hands again, forgetting his previous concern and grabbed her hips. Both of them let out a needy groan as he finally started truly fucking her. His thrusts were long and hard. He was still holding back but not nearly as much as he had intended. His fingers dug into her hips and their bodies slapped together. The sounds of their growling and moaning mingled deliciously with the sounds of his cock slamming into her cunt.

It didn't take long. There had been so much build up and tension coming to this point that Cullen was ready to come from the very beginning. As soon as he felt Aislinn begin to tense beneath him, he lost it. He thrust into her hard a few more times as he released. Aislinn was so overwhelmed by her own pleasure that she nearly missed the molten heat spreading through her from Cullen's release inside of her. Aislinn's arms and legs were shaking as her cunt convulsed around his cock.

Cullen collapsed off to the side dragging her with him and into his arms as they tried to recover from the intensity of what they had just done.

* * * *

Rafe had arranged for a watch on Aislinn's apartment. He was pissed as hell and determined to have her. Nothing annoyed him more than someone denying him something that was rightly his. When Cullen and Keith pulled up and then left empty handed Rafe figured that at least the Arnauk didn't have her either. He left the watch on her apartment. She would have to return there some time and when she did he'd have her. Until then he had other business to attend to.

Rafe stroked Jenna's face. He hated having to waste his time with her. But she had access to something he needed. "Time to wake up," he said.

Jenna groaned. She was dizzy and sick to her stomach. She realized that she was naked and cold and lying on a floor. She sat up looking around and found herself in a large dimly lit room full of lush furniture. Plush, royal purple couches formed a seating area. There were matching curtains covering large windows. Jenna could see from the light trying to penetrate the curtains that it must be well into daylight hours.

"Come here I have something for you to eat."

Her brain felt numb, and she could feel his voice more than hear it. She thought it was the sexiest voice she had ever heard. Jenna looked around the room more and saw where the voice was coming from. "Rafe," she said in confusion. When she tried to get up her head spun. She tried but couldn't remember what had happened the night before. "How did I get here? Did we win?"

"I brought you and no," he replied flatly. She could hear the annoyance in his voice. Something about the feel of his tone warned her to be careful. "Come here and eat. It will help with your stomach and the headache."

Jenna got up and walked over to the bar he was standing behind. From there, she got a better view of the room. It looked to be a living room. In addition to the extravagant couches there were shelves upon shelves of books and expensive looking antiques of all kinds. *Just my style,* she thought as she mentally priced out all of the stuff in the room.

Rafe was pouring a drink for himself and her. He pushed it toward her as she sat on the leather covered stool in front of the wet bar. "This will help," he said contemplatively.

"You seem like you've done this before," she said as she accepted the drink, smelled it and then took a sip. Orange juice and vodka. There was also a plate with steak and potatoes on it. It was prepared the way someone might be served in a decent restaurant, but her stomach wasn't willing to chance it just yet.

"A couple times," he said with a wicked amused grin that told her it was more than a couple times. "Just eat."

At the obvious order she immediately picked up the fork and knife and cut into the steak. She wasn't real sure why she felt so compelled to do as she was told, but she didn't like it.

"You'll get used to it," he said. When she looked up at him he had that amused grin on his face, and now she was scared. "Good," Rafe smiled. "You're starting to get the idea. You and I need to talk. I think you'll find that we can arrange a mutually beneficial relationship."

Jenna wasn't about to be cowed that easily. At the same time she didn't know what her position was. The last time she talked to Rafe, he had convinced her to attack Cullen Arnauk during their mating ceremony, and now she didn't even remember what had happened. It couldn't have gone well from the tone of things. "All right, I'm listening, but do you think you could arrange for me to get some clothes."

Rafe heard the demand in her voice, but at least she knew how to phrase it right, even if she didn't have the tone correct yet. *She's trainable. Just like any dog*, he thought. He walked across the room to a door on the far wall and went through it. Jenna watched him enter the room and see could see a bed beyond the door after the light was switched on. When he returned he was carrying a silky black robe. He handed it to her and then went over to what appeared to be the main door. Jenna had just put the robe on when he opened the door, and a large golden, tan lioness came trotting into the room. Jenna growled instinctively as the cat entered.

"Play nice ladies," Rafe said even though the lioness gave Jenna an unimpressed look before alighting on the couch and making herself comfortable. "Jenna, this is Kara and your new escort. I suggest that if you leave these rooms, you not go without her. I can't guarantee your safety. They do tend to have minds of their own when I'm not around."

Katta, Jenna thought with disgust. She wondered how many of the beasts he had here. "Where are you going and why am I staying here," Jenna said before taking another bite of steak.

"I have business that you needn't worry about. You are staying here so that Brennus will be good and mad before I heroically return his one and only daughter to his possession," Rafe said dramatically, but with a tone of someone being put out.

"I'm not that dense. There's more to it than that." She took another bite.

He smiled at her. "Don't you remember what we discussed before?" Jenna felt herself starting to get sleepy. His voice was hypnotic. "It's not too late for you to mate with me. We simply won't have Arnauk's pack as well this way. At least not yet. You, my dear will be the alpha's female and I will be the Tairneach alpha. It's what you wanted isn't it?"

"Yeah, I guess," she said softly.

"Good. Now finish eating, get a shower," he said wrinkling his nose and stepping farther away from her, "and get some rest. You've got no need to leave these rooms, but if you do Kara goes with you. You're no prisoner here Jenna," he said with an amused look. "But our plan will work much better if you remain out of sight. I certainly think these rooms are nice enough to keep you happy for a while."

Jenna nodded, finished her steak, and then headed for the bathroom believing that Rafe was right and her best bet would be to cooperate with him. When she disappeared into the bathroom and the shower started Kara turned from lioness into her human form.

Rafe looked the woman over. She had always been one of his favorites. He had done well when he changed Kara. Golden cat eyes stared back at him. "Orders," she asked simply.

Perfect, he thought. "Like I said to her. She doesn't go anywhere without you. And behave. I need her unscarred for a while. But if she balks the suggestions I gave her. Put her back in her room and lock the door. Just let her have the impression she's in control for now. And don't let the others mess with her either."

The woman nodded her compliance and turned back into the cat. Rafe preferred them like that.

Chapter 7

*A gem cannot be polished without friction, nor a man
perfected without trials.
-Lucius Annaeus Seneca*

Cullen and Aislinn had fallen back to sleep. When
the hesitant knock came on the door Cullen groaned.
He looked toward the clock on the table next to the bed
and saw that it was nearly 9pm. He thought about that
for a minute. *Yeah, I guess it could be that late. The
ceremony, the drive into town, got back here, spent the
morning asleep then afternoon with Aislinn.* The
knock came again, a little more insistent. Cullen
hugged Aislinn to himself as he pressed his face into
her hair and took a deep breath. By the time the third
knock came he was crawling unhappily out of the bed.
Aislinn grinned at him before she pulled the blankets
back around her and cuddled down into the bed again.

Cullen headed for the door and opened it, knowing
that there were only a handful of people who had the
key that would get them all the way up to the
penthouse. Keith was on the other side of the door. He
raised his eyebrows at Cullen when he saw the man
standing there completely naked and the woman in the
bed beyond the door. Keith shook his head. "Please
tell me she's conscious," he laughed.

Cullen pushed Keith out of the doorway and back
into the main living area, closing the door as they went.
"Yes she's conscious," Cullen growled but couldn't
keep the smile from belying the tone in his voice.

Keith laughed openly at that. "Okay, I don't feel quite so used as I did before. I do believe this is the first time I've seen you smile in months. I think that whatever she did to put you in that mood should be bottled and put in an emergency box that the rest of us can get to and throw at you when you start getting pissy. Or we could keep here around on emergency stand by and the next time you get that glare on your face and come after one of us we can hide behind her."

"All right," Cullen said seriously. "You've had your fun. Now what's up?"

"Well, we can start with the fact that most everyone is back from the reservation and they all want a more thorough explanation than I have to give them. Not to mention I've been running interference with Celia and the rest. Everyone downstairs knows you brought her up here last night. Between Meghan asking if she'll be back to work at all and Celia's group trying to find out who she is and how she got this privileged so quickly, I'm going crazy. Mostly because I don't have the answers to give them. You kinda took us all off guard on this one, my friend."

Cullen nodded. "Sorry. I didn't plan it. As far as explanations for everyone go, I'll need to talk to Aislinn before I'll have the answers to any of the questions that are going to be asked. Give me an hour and I'll be down. Besides, I'm starving."

Keith grinned again. "Now if I leave you two alone, you will get dressed and make it downstairs right?"

"You know," Cullen said smugly and crossed his arms over his chest, "do I need to remind you of that little party back in Boston, new years, 1907. I don't recall complaining about all the trouble I went through dealing with the Merick clan while you were off with the alpha's favorite daughter."

"Ooo, low blow," Keith laughed. "All right all right I'm going, before you start digging up any more dirt on me."

"I wouldn't have to dig long," Cullen smiled.

"Ouch, I said I was going." Keith headed for the elevator and hit the button. "One hour," he reiterated as the doors slid open and he stepped inside.

Cullen ran his hand through his hair. He knew that this wasn't going to be an easy conversation. When he opened the bedroom door and walked into the room he was seriously tempted to jump back into his bed. He couldn't believe how much of a hold she had on him or how pleased he was by it. The word mate kept running through his mind. He didn't want to let her be around anyone else until he made their relationship permanent. Again he found himself forcing his wolf to concede to the human logic that it just wasn't going to work that way.

There were a number of things he needed to know from her. First, he had to find out what else she knew about what happened during the mating ceremony and how she knew about it. He wanted to know more about her, and that included her past as well as what she was. He stood there staring at her realizing how little he knew. At the same time he didn't really care. If he didn't need the information for protecting the pack he would have been perfectly happy just being with her.

Aislinn stared back at him. She could see him thinking. She sat up, drew her knees up to her chest, and wrapped her arms around them. She watched him and waited for him to decide what he was going to say.

When he didn't seem forthcoming with what he was thinking, she decided to break the contemplative silence. Aislinn smiled widely at Cullen. "I guess you don't worry much about modesty around here."

Her statement jarred Cullen out of his thought process. "Huh?"

"Do you always answer the door naked?" Aislinn almost started laughing, between his confused reaction and the look on his face.

"I knew it was probably Keith. There aren't many people able to get all the way to my bedroom door without making a lot of noise. And for the most part, no, I don't think much about modesty the same way you might." Cullen's voice was heavy and serious. Aislinn could feel the next question coming before it actually came out of his mouth. "That is if you're human."

Aislinn shifted awkwardly . "Well, I guess that you might have a right to ask that after the way we spent the afternoon. But I can honestly tell you that I don't really know. Not that I see why it should matter," she added with a knowing look. "In any case, I prefer to answer my door with clothes no matter who is there. I've never known any guys who were quite that free. Even with good friends. Maybe you could arrange for me to get something to wear for when I'm on my way out of here?"

"Aislinn," Cullen came over and sat down on the bed facing her. He knew from the tone, the run-on attempt at changing the subject, and the look on her face that he was in dangerous territory. He was speaking slowly and Aislinn figured that he was choosing his words very carefully. "As far as you and I are concerned, I don't care what you are. I want you here regardless. You can be an alien for all that matters," he smiled at her and she smiled back at the attempt to be light hearted. "But I'm in a difficult position when it comes to balancing my personal life with protecting the pack."

Aislinn's face dropped and became more tired and sad. "So if I were a danger to you would you get rid of me?"

Cullen quickly moved closer to her and reached out to touch her cheek. He forced her to look into his eyes. "No. I don't think I'd be capable of giving you up at this point. But, I need all the information I can get if I'm going to make sure everyone is safe."

Aislinn smiled at him weakly. She put her hand on the back of his, turned her face to kiss his palm and pulled his hand away. "I'm sorry but I told you the truth. I was born human. At least I thought I was. I don't know. Rafe," he felt her shudder at the mention of that name, "has confused me about a lot of things."

"All right, so start from the beginning. Who is Rafe? How do you know him? How did you know about the things you said to me at the restaurant the other night?"

"That's all a long story," she said and it was apparent that she didn't want to talk about it.

Cullen nodded. He got up and headed over to a table where he had left his phone the night before. He hit a button and waited, all the while smiling at her reassuringly. "Hey, Sarah?" Cullen paused and then growled into the phone. "I told Keith an hour. You'll get your explanations then. For now I need you to bring some clothes up here for Aislinn. I think Rissa had a bag for her downstairs last night." There was another pause. "I don't know," he answered, then looked over at Aislinn. "What size do you wear?" She raised her eyebrows as if to say the question wasn't polite. "Oh come on," he said exasperated. "I can't get you clothes if I don't know what to ask for."

"Six," she responded.

Cullen echoed the number into the phone. "And give me some time." Then he hung up and walked over to Aislinn with a frustrated air.

"You know I could have just worn my work clothes." She indicated the pile he had made the night before. "I was just giving you a hard time," she said apologetically.

Cullen mirrored the concerned look she was giving him and shook his head. "My frustration isn't for you. Please don't take it like that. And the clothes aren't an issue. There are plenty lying around here somewhere. We tend to go through them regularly," he smiled.

Aislinn smiled back but it was only half-hearted, and when he continued it dropped from her face completely again. "I'm sorry I have to push this. But I get the impression that you know a great deal that could help with some things we've been having trouble coping with."

"Can't we just go back to having sex," she grinned wickedly, but Cullen's eyes told her that she needed to be serious and answer her. She shifted uncomfortably, then shot a heavy glare at Cullen. "I'm not used to being able to trust people the way you're asking me to trust you right now."

Cullen was trying to be understanding, but he didn't have a lot of time. He was a bit hurt that she'd fuck him but wouldn't trust him. "I can't make you talk to me," he said and the hurt came through in his tone. "But you did say that you feel safe with me."

Aislinn nodded. She did feel safe with him. She wanted to trust him.

Cullen could see the conflict in her eyes as she stared at her hands and considered what to do. "Aislinn, I don't even know your whole name. I can tell you that the amount of trust I had to have in you to bring you up here was pretty high. I got used to trusting my instincts some time ago. I wonder why you're fighting yourself so hard right now. I give you my word that I won't hurt you. You may not know it, because you're not part of the pack, but my word is worth a great deal to me. I don't make promises lightly."

"All right," she said slowly. *I guess I have to start trusting someone sometime. God I hope he is what he seems to be,* she thought and tears almost came to her eyes. Aislinn hadn't wanted anything this badly in a long time. She hadn't dared to think she could have a family again, let alone a lover. She wanted this to be so much more than just a onetime thing. "The burning buildings," Aislinn started, remembering the vision she'd had in the restaurant.

Cullen nodded encouragingly. "I need to know how you knew about that and what else you might know."

Aislinn sighed. She figured that she might as well get it over with. *I suppose if he's going to decide I'm not worth the effort because of my past that it would be better for it to happen sooner rather than later.* Aislinn resigned herself to the possibility of a miserable outcome and decided to just give him the whole story from the beginning. "Okay, I guess I should say that I've had premonitions, visions for as long as I can remember. When I was little, I was told that it was just coincidence when I dreamed about things that happened. The visions didn't get detailed or strange until after Rafe." Cullen's eyes narrowed, but he sat silently, waiting for her to continue.

"In the beginning it was just vague impressions about things. My mother used to tell me that I was psychic, just like her. It always bothered my grandmother. She would tell my mother not to encourage me. They fought a lot about that." Aislinn's eyes glazed over and sadness over took her features. Cullen was tempted to comfort her, but he didn't want to take the chance that she'd stop talking. "I believed that for a while, that it was a weird coincidence. Like when you're thinking of a song and turn on the radio and it's playing. The visions didn't actually get strong or bad until I met Rafe. That was in college. About seven years ago. I was earning my masters in folklore." She smiled at him wanly. "Maybe I was always headed in this direction. My thesis was on gothic lit. You know Frankenstein, Dracula, and the reality that resulted in the fiction. My mother always argued with me about my college career. She didn't think I'd ever get a job with that kind of degree. I told her that I'd get my doctorate and teach it. I couldn't help it. I was just drawn to that stuff."

Cullen chuckled and grinned at her, thinking how gorgeous her eyes were. "I can only imagine what you're thinking about me." Aislinn blushed and he chuckled some more. "That's not what I meant," he said.

Aislinn cleared her throat and ignored the interruption. "I studied several dead languages as well. I can read or speak quite a few actually. Gaelic is only one of them. I figured that if I didn't end up teaching folklore then having experience with multiple languages would get me somewhere." She smiled at Cullen and he smiled back reassuringly, but remained silent and waited for her to continue. "Rafe was teaching one of my folklore classes. When I started taking his class was when the visions started getting scary. I didn't connect them to him at first. They were all disjointed and vague. It was as though something was trying to warn me that I was in danger."

She took another deep breath. "But Rafe, himself, was always very nice. Exceedingly so. He always smelled good. I don't know what it was, but he wore some kind of cologne that made me want to breathe him in. He ran a club after class that examined and discussed antique texts. I ended up joining the club and that was when we started dating."

Cullen shifted and his jaw tightened. "I guess I should have figured that," he scowled without thinking.

Aislinn smiled widely and her eyes brightened. "Are you jealous," she laughed.

Cullen nearly blushed. *Gods, how did I get so attached so quickly?* He growled. "Just concerned," he lied and she laughed some more.

Aislinn leaned over to him and tried to kiss him.

"If you start that," he said, "then I'll never get to hear the end of your story." When Aislinn's lip shot out in a pout, Cullen couldn't help but kiss it. "Please," he said as he made her sit down.

Aislinn sucked on her bottom lip where he'd kissed it as she remembered where she left off. "That was a bad phase in my life. After I started dating him I found myself pulling away from family and friends that I had known all my life. My world revolved around the guy.

I had no idea what I was getting into or what he was doing to me.

"After I told him about my visions, which I never should have done, he seemed to be even more interested in me. Since I was a doting girlfriend at the time, I was willing to do anything to please him or make him happy with me. He started taking me with him on weekends to a compound that he lived on. It was weird. After I got away from it I started thinking it was probably a cult.

"He referred to the compound as the Circle. When we were there the people treated him like he was God. They would do anything he told them to do. It was creepy. He told me that there used to be a council that ran the place, but he had convinced them that he would be a better leader than the council. I would nod stupidly and agree with him when he told me things like that, or when I was informed of how wonderful and brilliant he was. Each time I went there with him things got stranger. But since it happened in little pieces I just accepted it day by day. I stopped talking to my family and my friends completely. Looking back on all of it, I'm almost grateful that my separation from them happened the way it did. It's probably what stopped him from using them against me later.

"Anyway, the first couple times I went out there with him I noticed the exotic animals around the place. Lots of them. All kinds, and weird ones too. Animals that looked like a bear had bred with a gorilla. On any given occasion when I looked at them, especially the females, their eyes would glow and swirl. None of them were in cages. They were all just wandering around. Then there was the time I was there that I walked into an orgy. Animals and humans. At the time, I was exceedingly bothered by that." She smiled at Cullen as she put the emphasis on 'at the time.' "Even though it was so strange, Rafe was always able to explain it all away, and I would just accept it. Even now, there always seems to be this part of my brain that looks at things that should bother me and tells me that I haven't seen anything yet, and if I stare at anything long enough I'll see something unusual in it and that's okay."

Cullen reached out and took her hand, squeezing it as her story seemed to make her more and more uncomfortable. "I suppose I should be grateful for that. Remind me to thank him before I kill him."

Aislinn took a deep breath. She could see it in his eyes. He was completely serious. Cullen would kill Rafe. She wasn't sure if she should be grateful or frightened. She decided to ignore it for now. She just hoped that she hadn't traded one looney for another. "As time wore on I started having black outs. When I would go with Rafe to the Circle, I wouldn't remember what had happened to me. I started getting scared. I didn't like the things I saw there. I both wanted to know and still don't want to know what was happening to me that I can't remember. When I wasn't around Rafe for a long period of time, I'd start to wonder why I was going along with him. But it was like every time I saw him I just accepted it all and was happy to do whatever he wanted from me. When I questioned him about what happened during some of the blackout time, he would tell me not to worry about it. He was taking care of me. I was his favorite." She had chills at the thought.

"Finally, he decided that I should quit college and go live at the Circle. The suggestions he started making then got more and more demanding. I don't really know when I got control of my mind again. It might have been the day that I watched him order a man put to death. He fed the man to some of the lions that he had walking around." Cullen growled in distaste. This was the kind of thing that would keep weres and humans from ever being able to interact with each other.

Aislinn continued. "I was starting to think that I needed to get away from them, but I would lose the motivation every time I saw Rafe. I suppose I should thank Kara for giving me the incentive to get out. She was one of his favorites. She was always walking around naked and flaunting herself in front of Rafe. She hated me. She was the one who told me that he intended to get me pregnant." Cullen growled again.

Aislinn smiled at him. She was finding his apparently jealousy amusing. "It never happened. I left. It took more than I ever imagined it would. He sends people after me, and I have to move. Any time I started to get settled somewhere the visions would come back. More and more detailed. It got to the point where I could feel him coming for me and could move on before it became too urgent. I got better at controlling the premonitions over the years. But he never stopped. It was always just a matter of how long. The longer I was away from him the more I realized about what had been happening and what he did. So I tried all the harder to keep out of his reach. Random cash jobs in shit hole places until the visions came back and then I'd run. There were pieces of it all that I learned from visions, and things that I just remembered."

I can tell you that Rafe can influence anyone with his mind. He seems to be able to control people, large groups of people. Mostly you have to be kinda willing to let him. So he always comes off nice at first and slowly manipulates you into trusting him. He starts by giving you things you want or treating you the way you want, whatever will get you to trust him enough to let him plant suggestions in your head. He doesn't seem to be able to make people do things that they are drastically inclined not to do. Like if he had ever told me to kill someone, that wouldn't have worked. I don't think." Aislinn seemed to look into herself at that before returning to the story. "He can get into dreams, and he's been able to pull me out of my dreams. That's the worst because it doesn't matter where I am or how far, he can grab my mind and pull me to him. Sometimes I think that's worse than him having me physically. But he doesn't seem to be able to get into my head while I'm awake. So I try to sleep as little as I can, and usually at odd times of the day. Hence the bar jobs being my favorites. It gives him fewer opportunities to bother me. During your ceremony, while I was sleeping, he grabbed me out of my dreams and brought me to the ceremony. He was there. Watching you all and waiting to attack you."

"How could he have been there? There's no way a stranger like that would have gone unnoticed." Cullen wasn't sure if he should believe her or not. It just didn't sound reasonable.

"I told you. He can do things to people's minds. He could be standing right in front of you and if you're secure enough in the fact that he should have been able to be there he'd just whisper to you that he isn't and you'd believe it and move on."

"All right," he growled under his breath. This man was sounding more and more dangerous. "You were there as well," he prompted.

Aislinn could see him thinking about what she had said. She understood his unease. To some extent she had gotten used to the situation and was numb to the idea of Rafe. "The best way to describe it is an out of body experience. It's like my consciousness is somewhere. No one can see me or hear me, but I can see and hear them. I can walk around and touch things but no one can feel my touch. Or at least I used to think they couldn't." She briefly considered that she had managed to touch the lycans' dreams that night before continuing. "But I really don't know much about it. It all just sort of happens to me. The impression Rafe has given me is that he's able to do more to me because I'm like him." Just saying it left a bad taste in her mouth. "He keeps saying that' I'm like him."

Cullen could read the upset on her face and he moved closer to her, ignoring the fact that he didn't want her to stop her explanation. He squeezed the hand he was holding and put his other hand under her chin, making her look at him. "You are nothing like him," Cullen said.

Aislinn pulled away from him. She didn't want to discuss that topic. Cullen let her go. He didn't want to upset her more.

Aislinn continued with a topic that she was certain would get his attention. "Rafe had set it up that Jenna was supposed to kill you. When she did then the people he's gotten to inside your pack were going to attack the rest of you. His people would come out of hiding, and then he was supposed to take over.

Obviously it didn't work." At the mention of people in his pack, Cullen tensed and had to remind himself to let her finish.

"Rafe also mentioned that he had given me the 'gift of the change.' Whatever that means. And that he would finish it when he got me back. I guess I did notice some things about myself that had changed after I left him. I was stronger and faster. I could smell things better, and my vision and hearing got better. I never understood it, but I didn't have time to think about it, what with all the running. I don't really know what it means or what the change is for certain. But I think I can guess that at this point. I don't think anything would surprise me after everything I've seen and been through.

"My visions got stronger as well. Sometimes when I saw myself in them I would be something on all fours. I never really thought that it was anything more than a dream form of some kind. I mean, I've dreamt that I'm other people I know, or that I'm a shadow, or that I could fly. So why not dream that I was an animal? I never considered that the animal thing might be part of the premonition until I started to figure you out. Even then, I never really took that idea seriously. In my visions I'm on four legs, but I've never seen what I am. And Rafe's statement didn't include a description of what he's changing me into. I never actually saw all those animals at his compound change into people or vice versa, but I don't think that it would be a big jump to guess that they could."

Cullen nodded. He couldn't help his amazement. How the hell could anyone be making weres? It just wasn't possible was it? "I take it you've never changed into anything outside of your dreams then?"

Aislinn shook her head. "No." She stopped and looked contemplative. She was trying to think if there was anything else she knew that Cullen might find helpful to know. Besides, if she told him everything right now then she'd be able to say honestly that she didn't have any more information. "Um, I've heard him use the word druid. Between that, him calling the compound the Circle, as well as the research I did when I had that luxury, I was able to draw conclusions and make connections about that. It's not like the original druids in Europe from 500BC kept records or books so that I could figure out what a druid really is. But I could pretty much guess he wasn't the Winston Churchill kind of druid. I also know that Rafe has some weird vision of cultivating a 'perfect Circle.' I don't know what exactly that means, but I heard the phrase more than once. He has a crazy vision of something, and he's been planning to get it for years.

"I know from the vision in the restaurant and from the ceremony that he wants the standing stones for some reason, but you should have figured that out by now. I'm guessing from the whole druid connection and the Stonehenge associations that he either wants them for sentimental reasons or he thinks there's power there. I don't know for sure on that one either. Really I don't *know* anything. I only have a lot of partial information. Just enough to make Rafe keep coming, and not enough to do me any good."

She took a deep breath and moved to stretch. Cullen watched her quietly, realizing that he had almost forgotten she was naked during all of the seriousness. It was all he could do to keep from going after her breasts as he watched her change positions and get comfortable again. The number of things that she said that had him convinced she was a great deal more intelligent than she gave herself credit for only made her more attractive to him.

"Anyway, that's how I met him, why I don't know if I'm human, and how I knew about the stuff with you and the ceremony. Did I leave anything out? Oh yeah," she added sarcastically. "My full name is Aislinn Brianne Stevens."

Cullen noted the sarcasm in that last and knew that her self defense mechanism had kicked in again. He figured that he better be careful, or he'd be sleeping alone after the meeting. He definitely didn't want that. So he ignored the tone, and focused on the information he still needed that she hadn't already answered. "Do you know where this compound is? Can you find it again?"

"Yeah, I think I could if I had to," she said uncomfortably. "But I don't really recommend it. I mean, not that I don't think you guys aren't pretty tough or anything, but as far as the animal kingdom hierarchy goes I think lions, tigers, and bears would probably beat a wolf on the brute force and damage scales."

Cullen smiled at her. She certainly was a thinker. And he had to admit that she was right, as far as most of the pack was concerned. Being an alpha, by nature, put him above the rest, and he had more than a decent chance of being capable of dealing with the kinds of things she was talking about. However, the average lycan probably would have a tough time dealing with the average katta. If that's even what these things were. "I may be a bit tougher than you think," he said with his ego showing through. "But you're right in general. Especially if Rafe has the numbers you seem to be implying. Cullen was becoming increasingly more concerned. It felt good to know what he was up against, but at the same time there was a sinking feeling coming from it all. Aislinn's answers were creating more questions.

Then there was the one question that he needed an answer to, but didn't really want to know. "Do you know who in my pack is aiding this asshole?" Aislinn shook her head no.

Cullen looked over at the clock. He wondered where Sarah was with those clothes. He had promised an hour, and he intended to make good on that. He smiled trying to stop his brain for what brief time he had left before dealing with the council. He could tell that as far as Aislinn knew, she had told him everything. It came across in her tone and the expectant way she kept looking at him. It was as if she was waiting for him to kick her out and be done with her now.

Cullen decided that at the very least, he needed to make sure she was okay before they headed downstairs. He pushed all the frustrating information she had just given him out of his mind. He reached out and ran a hand over her shoulder and down her back smiling wickedly as he did. "We could both use a shower."

Aislinn smiled back. The relief she was feeling at the fact that he was still interested was almost overwhelming. "Trying to wash my scent off," she teased.

"Nope," he said as he stood up offering her his hand. "I fully intend to re-mark my territory the first chance I get." She raised her eyebrows at him as she took his hand. He pulled her up into his arms. He held her tightly to himself and breathed her scent in. "But I haven't had a shower in a day or so and, while you might not care, there are a few people who might. I just thought it would be fun to bring you with me. Though, I would be just as happy if you wanted to walk around with my scent all over you, advertising that you were in my bed. Less competition that way." He grinned at her devilishly.

Aislinn's face fell a bit. "Something occurs to me," she said. "I mean it's not like I didn't know you were in charge around here. But I guess I just didn't really think about it in terms of where things have ended up. I mean. What exactly am I dealing with here?"

Cullen looked at her carefully. She had the right to know. He was impressed that she knew the right questions to ask and worried that the answers might scare her off at the same time. *Well, I guess it's my turn to be worried about being dumped.* He had never been in that position before. "How likely are you to run away from me if you don't like what you hear," he asked only half kidding.

It was Aislinn's turn for the reassuring smile. "Pretty unlikely, as long as you tell me that you want me around and prepare me for whatever is going to happen when we leave this room. Or we could just stay here forever," she suggested hopefully.

He grinned at the joke. *We may be too close of a match,* he thought and wondered what the fates were getting him into with her. "If only. I wish we could hide up here. But seeing as we can't," he considered his answer carefully. "All right, you were honest with me, and it's not like I'll be able to hide the kind of thing you're asking about. Let's jump in the shower, and I'll explain while we get cleaned up. I don't have much more time left before I need to get downstairs."

Cullen nodded toward a door on the far wall and Aislinn headed for the bathroom. Cullen groaned as Aislinn walked in front of him toward the bathroom. He loved the swing of her hips, and the fact that she was naked certainly added to it.

She glanced back at him and chuckled when she saw his huge erection. "That didn't take much."

"With you it doesn't seem to," he smiled.

As they walked into the bathroom, Aislinn looked around at the enormous room. She had never seen a bathroom so big. There was an entry area with a small couch and a plush navy carpet on the floor. The tiles were gray marble looking, and they led up to a large tub in a raised platform. There were steps leading up to the edge of the tub. The tub looked like there were Jacuzzi jets in it, and it was impossibly deep.

Cullen noted the impressed look on her face as she examined the tub. "Maybe later," he said as he read her mind. "We don't have time for what would happen if we got in there." He grabbed her around the waist and dragged her to the shower stall in a back corner of the bathroom. "I actually don't tend to use the tub much. But with you around I might be inclined to spend some leisure time in there." As he was talked he turned the knobs on a walk in shower, and put his hand in the stream to see if the water was warm enough.

Aislinn let him pull her into the streaming water. "I just haven't had a real bath in a while and that is some tub. But don't let that change the subject. You were going to tell me what's downstairs."

Cullen thought about making joke about the casino and restaurant being downstairs, but decided that he didn't have time to mess around at this point. He grabbed up the soap and lathered his hands, then much to Aislinn's delight started to run them over her body instead of his own. She giggled as his hands slid over her and he started talking. "How often do you watch the discovery channel," he asked more seriously than she liked.

"Not often in the past seven years. I haven't had cable. You don't really mean-"

Cullen cut her off. "No it's not quite that barbaric, but the principle is the same. And you, mo mhúirnín bán," he added, making her smile and working his way over her breasts with his soapy hands, "are in the pack alpha's bed. Unfortunately, I've been around for a long time. After a certain point I stopped thinking I was going to find one woman I wanted to commit to," he paused trying to think of how to put the rest of what he was going to say.

Aislinn was a little amused by the way he was staring at her breasts and running soapy fingers around her nipples. He looked like he was concentrating on something vastly important. She couldn't believe he was that nervous talking to her about it. Cullen reminded her of a high school kid trying to ask a girl if she wanted to go steady or wear his ring. She leaned into him and reached down to his erection. As the soap from her body ran over it, she began gliding her hand up and down along its length. "So I get two things out of what you've just said. Firstly, there are several women, who might want to beat me up, given that this is a pack of wolves. The strongest of them is the one who should be in the alpha's bed."She grinned as she mimicked the way he had phrased it. "And secondly, that maybe you think that you might be interested in making some kind of commitment to me," she said tentatively, afraid to hope.

Cullen finally looked her in the eyes. "You are certainly clever. I'll give you that. You can turn me down," he said. His stare was intense. It was like he was trying to get inside her head. "But really that's a conversation for when we have more time than we do now, and for when you really understand what you'll be getting into if you agree to it. Just think about it," he said hopefully. "But as far as the first one goes, yeah there're a number of women who'll try to put you in what they think your place should be. I personally don't care if you end up an omega. But they'll think that if they make you look bad enough in that respect then I'll lose interest. So they'll try. The rest of the pack will probably be curious and inquisitive, but not dangerous. I suggest you stay away from any women who seem to be trying to pick a fight. It's worse than an actual wolf pack in the regards that it's not just physical prowess. There's an element of mental prowess that goes along with it. Brute strength can really only get you so far. And I have had a tendency of preferring the higher ranking females who've offered, over the lower ranks. So you can count on the ones trying to cause you trouble as being good fighters and thinkers as well. As far as the men go, you shouldn't have any real trouble with them. Except that since I've shown interest in you they might try to find out why." Cullen seemed to growl the last part.

Aislinn just stood there feeling his hands running along her body, stroking his erection, and listening. "Okay," she said curtly. Aislinn was starting to think he was just trying to add her to a pack harem or something. She didn't know what to think. She certainly didn't want to share him, regardless of what the hell he was or wasn't. But she couldn't stand the idea of leaving and never feeling him come inside her again. Her stomach was in knots and her brain was spinning. "Don't worry too much. A person doesn't survive on the streets for seven years without learning a couple things. I can take care of myself, better than you might think."

He moved his hips into her stroking, and his eyes rolled back into his head momentarily before returning to the conversation. She pulled her hand off of him finally, noting his disappointed reaction to the loss of attention. She grabbed up the shampoo and poured some into her hands, sniffed at the nonexistent smell and started washing her hair.

Cullen watched her soap her hair and couldn't help but reach out and toy with her breasts some more. This was taking longer than he should allow it to. "I'm not doubting that you can take care of yourself in most circumstances. But you aren't lycan, and they're going to have trouble with that. Although you may be able to hold your own against a human in fight, Aislinn, these women aren't going to be nice enough to stay in human form. That's not how pack rank works. They're going to try to test you, and there won't be anything I can really do about it. I probably won't even be around when they decide to mess with you, if they're smart about it."

Aislinn heard the concern in his tone. "Really, Cullen, I'll be okay." She turned away from him and leaned into the water to wash the soap out of her hair. She breathed out heavily. "Just one last thing," she added unhappily. "Not that I won't consider it if it's what you're looking for, but I just want to know up front, so there's not any confusion. Are you expecting me to join the ranks of all these women you have sex with and just wait around here for my turn in your bed? I mean, I was kinda getting the impression that you wanted more than that, and I don't want to misinterpret what's going on here."

Cullen realized the mistake he'd made in what he'd said and wished he could go back and reword the whole thing. The hurt in her voice was almost palpable. He stepped up behind her, the water streaming over them as he pressed against her. His erection found its way between her legs and pressed into the slippery wet that was still there. "I've never wanted any of them the way I want you," he said softly into her ear. "I'm not very good at this. But I give you my word that I'm not trying to add you to any ranks the way you think." He pressed his erection as deeply into her slit as he could get it from their angle and listened to her moan. "You are one great big long list of things I've never felt or done before. Every instinct I have is telling me to take you and claim you, and it's been all I could do to stop myself from acting on that."

Aislinn wasn't positive what he meant by 'claim,' but from the way he was talking she could tell that it was incredibly serious. Aislinn felt his cock pressing into her, and after what he'd just said, she needed more of it. She stepped so that her legs were spread farther apart and leaded forward until she had her hands braced on the wall of the shower under the shower head. She looked back over her should to see him eyeing her dangerously. Molten amber flooded his eyes, and he was breathing heavily. "What are your instincts telling you to do now?"

Cullen's emotions were too close to the surface. Aislinn just seemed able to push his buttons exactly the right way without even trying. Before he could push the wolf back down, he grabbed her hips and plunged into her. A low growl issued from his throat. One arm wrapped around her waist to hold her still, and the other arm reached under her to grab and torture one of her breasts while he pounded into her roughly. Aislinn let out an appreciative moan that pulled Cullen's wolf further to the surface, and his hands began to shift.

Aislinn felt claws rake her beast. The pain mingled deliciously with the pleasure, and she gasped. The water hit them as they moved together. Aislinn tried to adjust her hips to get more of him inside her, but she couldn't manage the right angle. She let out a needy moan. "Harder, Cullen," she begged.

When Aislinn's words registered in his mind, Cullen felt his wolf slip just a little more and his body shifted farther. He felt fangs grow in his mouth, and his face shift barely into his lycan form. He was holding it all back by a thread. Aislinn's moaning and begging was more than he could handle. His wolf wanted her too badly.

Aislinn felt her body yanked upright. Water hit her in the face, and she closed her eyes. His arm around her waist was like steel. She felt the claws on her breast leave, and then felt her head being pulled to one side. She let him move her how he wanted. She could still feel his massive cock thrusting into her. Her hands reached for something to hold onto, but only found the slippery walls of the shower. Then she felt the piercing pain. Cullen bit down on her neck just where it met with her shoulder. She drew in a sharp breath. It was a strange sensation. Something about it brought her over the edge. She felt heat pool in her lower belly. The pleasure rolled over her. Aislinn's body trembled with the sensations, and she cried out as he forced himself into her repeatedly through her orgasm.

Cullen tasted her blood as it rushed into his mouth. She was sweet, and her cries were needy. The combination mingled in his lycan mind as pure pleasure. When Aislinn climaxed he held on and forced himself up into her over and over again. Her pulsing walls brought him over the edge. Cullen started to fall forward as he lost control of his muscles through the convulsing pleasure of their orgasm. He released the hand holding her head to the side and caught himself on the wall of the shower.

Aislinn was finally able to open her eyes as they moved toward the wall. She only barely registered how close they both came to falling over. She reached out and helped Cullen to catch their fall as he came back to reality. She could feel his hot breath on her shoulder as the pain and pressure from his bite began to sink in. Cullen heard her whimper and pulled his mouth from her. He had left a very definite bite on her shoulder. A strange combination of pleasure and guilt swept through him at the sight of the bloody bite mark.

Sarah's voice jarred him out of the moment as she called into the bathroom. "If you both are finished," she said angrily, "I have those clothes you asked for."

"Caoch," Cullen swore and carefully put Aislinn down. His wolf completely retreated into the recesses of his mind. *At least he's pleased with himself,* Cullen thought in annoyance. "We gotta get moving," he said and flipped the water off.

Aislinn gave him a dreamy look over her shoulder as she joined him back in reality. "Yeah, sure," she said with a smile.

He stared at her and considered the fact that she seemed pleased with what had happened. Cullen briefly wondered if she understood the significance of what he had done. It didn't matter right then. He'd have to have a serious conversation with her about it later. For now they needed to get dressed and head downstairs.

He handed her a towel as she stepped out of the shower, and she wrapped it around herself. Aislinn stopped for a moment to look in the mirror before joining him in the bedroom. She winced at the painful looking bite mark on her shoulder. She could tell from where it was that she'd have trouble hiding it. She had a brief flashback to the first time she had a hickey in high school and wearing a turtle necks and scarves for a week so that no one would notice.

When she got into the bedroom, Cullen was already pulling his pants on. Sarah had left the clothes for Aislinn on his bed and disappeared. Cullen looked over at the clock and swore again. He was already 10 minutes late. He knew that Sarah would tell Keith what she walked in on, and Cullen would have to go through another round of tormenting as a result. Then he looked over at Aislinn and saw her smiling at him. Her eyes were on fire. He wished that the two of them could run off for a month or so, alone. He wanted time to really know her, talk to her, and spend time understanding her. He wanted to be with her forever. There was too much happening to afford that kind of luxury right now. It had been decades since he'd had the kind of motivation he was feeling right now to resolve an issue facing the pack.

Cullen growled under his breath as he finished dressing and watched her put her clothes on. It was just underclothes, a pair of jeans, and a t-shirt. Sarah apparently didn't bother to track down the bag that Rissa appeared to have packed. "I don't have any shoes," Aislinn said as she looked around the room.

"You don't really need them," Cullen said with a shrug. "We're not leaving the building. You'll find any number of people downstairs missing more than just shoes. I'll get you some when we have a little more time."

Aislinn heard the rush in his voice and nodded. She figured that shoes were the least of her worries right now.

Chapter 8

A kind word never broke anyone's mouth.
-Irish Proverb

The elevator doors opened onto the 13th floor, and Lord General Cullen Arnauk stepped out into a room full of people. As he looked around, he guessed that the whole of the pack, including those who weren't residing in the Madadh-Allaidh Saobhaidh were gathered. Most everyone was staring at him expectantly. Those who weren't staring at him were staring directly behind him at Aislinn.

Aislinn watched Cullen's face turn from passionate heat to emotionless stone as the elevator descended from the penthouse. He had been completely silent from the moment they stepped into the elevator. Now as they walked into the room she could see the reason why. *I've never heard of a pack of wolves this large,* she thought, looking around at the room full of people.

Cullen didn't say a word to her. He simply passed through the crowd, and she followed along behind. Aislinn hoped that he would give her some direction when it was needed. The people in his way stepped aside to let him pass. Aislinn noted that every person Cullen looked directly at lowered his eyes and slightly bowed his head, some more obviously than others. The differences were subtle, but it didn't take much to see that the larger the person the smaller the head nod. Aislinn quickly started taking mental pictures of who seemed to be higher in rank than others. She also watched the ones who seemed to dislike the show of submission, and the ones who appeared to do it with due respect. She felt like she had just joined an intricate chess game in the middle, and no one had told her who was playing which pieces.

Everyone in the room, with few exceptions, had a similar look to them. A person who had never met them before may have thought that any two of them were related. They all had the same dark hair and eyes that Cullen did. There were a few women and men who were lighter in shade or darker, but for the most part they all matched. Aislinn felt as though she stood out like a sore thumb, and not just because she was following along behind Cullen like a stray pup.

As Cullen walked into the great room there were slightly fewer people in there, and they were all arguing. One graying man was talking exceptionally loud. "How the hell could the woman vanish in full view of the entire pack and no one would say a word about it? No search party? No-" The man cut himself off in mid sentence when Cullen entered the room. Everyone turned and looked at him, Keith with a grateful, relieved look. The man who had been yelling gave the smallest nod of everyone that Aislinn had seen so far. He was as tall as Cullen but slighter built, and his eyes were an angry, resentful brown. He looked considerably older than Cullen, but he was certainly still in good enough shape to be trouble. "So our Lord finally makes his appearance," the man said, in a voice dripping with sarcasm. "And this little one behind him must be the curious cause of his late arrival."

Aislinn met the man's glare straight on, without blinking or flinching as he stared at her. He grinned back at her with a seemingly impressed and amused gaze when she didn't lower her eyes or cow to his stare.

Cullen didn't falter a single step. "Terrick, this is Aislinn," he replied. And that was all he said about it. "Now do you mind if we move this conversation into private quarters?" Cullen called out a list of names, and each of those people moved out of the room and down a hall. Then he turned to Aislinn with concern. "The mood in here is harder than I thought it might be." He pulled his elevator key card out of his pocket. "Don't lose this," he said, as if he was talking to a child. That earned him a glare from Aislinn which more than one person watching started whispering about. "If you need out of here go up to my room. I don't have any idea how long this is going to take. But don't leave the building."

Aislinn nodded to him. "Don't worry. I'll be fine," she smiled at him. "I'm not so sure about you though, from the looks on the faces of those people you sent wherever."

He let a smile toy with the corner of his mouth in return to her quiet comment. "I've seen worse." Then the fleeting bit of emotion was gone, and he headed down the hall that the others had gone down, leaving Aislinn to figure out what to do with herself in the mean time.

She let out a heavy breath. This was going to be interesting. Everyone was here for an explanation, and they were all going to wait around until they got one. That much was certain. While they waited, Aislinn was a tempting target. They didn't know how much she knew or didn't know about the mating ceremony. But in and of herself she was certainly a curiosity that they wanted to know about. It was just a matter of time before the questions started. She briefly considered going up to the penthouse to hide, but decided that if she was going to figure out what she was in for, the only way to do it would be to stick around and see what happened.

Aislinn looked around the room at all the people staring at her. It wasn't tough to pick out the ones who were merely curious about her and the ones who were pissed off. She counted three women who looked angry and six who looked amused. Those were probably the friends of the angry ones, who had to be some of the women that Cullen had mentioned. Aislinn was in the process of trying to come up with something to say to anyone when Rissa seemed to appear out of nowhere. Her eyes were sparkling with interest, and she was being followed by several other women who had the same amused inquisitive look as well.

Aislinn knew that she was about to be bombarded with questions, but she figured that anything Rissa wanted to ask had to be better than standing in the middle of the room like some kind of circus freak show. "Come on," Rissa said, "Let's go sit down. They'll probably be forever back there. When Lord Arnauk gets that tone we all know we're in for it." Then her smile got impossibly wide as she added, "Although he certainly seemed to change his demeanor when he was talking to you." The lilt in her voice said with no uncertainty that she was fishing for some kind of confirmation to the statement. Much to her disappointment Aislinn merely smiled back and shrugged. Aislinn was just relieved that she had found someone she knew and was relatively certain friendly.

Aislinn gratefully followed Rissa out of the room and down a different hall. The room they ended up in looked like a library. Sitting areas with couches and armchairs were arranged together in confidential little nooks and surrounded by bookshelves. Several people were already in the room. They looked up and watched as the small group of women entered and headed for chairs. Aislinn wondered if there was a single room on this floor that wasn't full of people.

"How many are in this pack anyway," Aislinn asked with a bit more emphasis than she intended.

Rissa ushered Aislinn to one of the big couches, and they all sat down. "I don't know exact numbers. It started out a lot smaller. Most packs are a lot smaller. But Lord Arnauk is, well, good at leading. There aren't many other packs this large, mostly because there aren't many alphas that can control this many people. Lord Arnauk seems to come by it naturally. Not to mention most of us just want somewhere safe to live, and he's got one of the best set ups." With that she introduced Aislinn to the other women who were with her. Then the questions started coming.

By the time Aislinn had finished avoiding directly answering any and all questions pertaining to what went on upstairs all afternoon, she was exhausted. Rissa was scowling. "And here I thought we were friends," she said with a pout.

"Oh don't you dare do that," Aislinn scolded. "We are friends. But you're getting awfully personal."

"Personal is all relative. Humans have way too strict a sense of what's personal. Besides, if any woman from this pack had ever managed to get up to Lord Arnauk's rooms, the first thing she'd do when she came back down is tell everyone. Then she'd rub his scent in their faces. You're acting like it's something to be ashamed of, for goodness sake. You have in your lap access to the best bragging rights in the whole of the pack, and you're keeping it to yourself!"

Rissa's exasperation was baffling to Aislinn. *Just one more thing I'll have to figure out,* she thought. Then something occurred to her, *wolves, rub scent in faces?* "Uh, you don't mean that literally do you," she asked.

Rissa's amused smile grew impossibly wide. "*What* literally?"

Aislinn cleared her throat. "The scent rubbing in faces part."

The other women present smiled and chuckled a bit, but for the most part the question was taken far too seriously for Aislinn's comfort. "Why? Where did he put his scent?" Rissa responded with a sparkle in her eyes that told Aislinn she had just said something far more interesting than she should have.

"Okay, Rissa, speaking as friends," Aislinn said, and Rissa nodded confidentially then moved in closer. "I don't have any idea what's normal around here. Think in human standards, which you seem to be familiar with, and then put me in your context. I don't really understand most of this. The mating ceremony, okay I kinda caught it in the middle. All the innuendo about what I should and shouldn't have managed to do around here is a little lost on me. Why don't you give me a couple hints about what you *really* are looking for me to tell you and maybe we can get on the same page."

Rissa took that as an invitation to get the dirt she was looking for one way or another. At least if she gave enough details that humans shouldn't know, and which might shock Aislinn, then she might find something out. "Well if you missed the beginning of the mating ceremony, then you missed the part where everyone would have presented themselves to Lord Arnauk. If you caught the middle then you know how that goes. The end would involve," she grinned as though this was the important part, "well, it's kinda like dogs. They'd shift to either their hybrid forms or their wolf forms. You ever watch the discovery channel?"

"Again with the discovery channel," Aislinn said in exasperation. She was more than a little shocked by the frank way Rissa was putting it, and from the look on Aislinn's face Rissa figured that whatever happened upstairs probably wasn't as good as she had originally thought if this info was new to Aislinn. Rissa figured that Lord Arnauk must have remained in his human form for whatever happened at least. "You can't be serious. You're just trying to mess with me now," Aislinn said angrily.

But the raised eyebrows on everyone's faces at her reaction had Aislinn feeling as though she had just said something relatively racist. "Nope, I'm not kidding," Rissa said with disappointment. She wasn't offended. She was just upset that she wasn't going to find out anything good. "A lycan in a form other than human will behave more animal than you're probably used to. And his," Rissa thought for a moment before coming up with an appropriate word, "genitalia will behave more like his wolf than human. They would have shifted, if all the assassination stuff hadn't interrupted things. He would have mounted her, swelled inside her while they had sex, they'd have gotten stuck together. He'd come inside her, and bite her hard enough to scar her. When they were finished the rest of us would have acknowledged what had happened while they were joined together. They'd be stuck like that for most of the rest of the night. If things were planned right, it would happen while she was in heat so that she'd end up pregnant as a result. Mating accomplished. Then usually the new couple disappears for a week or so to get it out of their system. The wolf does tend to get riled up when it claims a mate. And really that's the watered down version. Lord Arnauk never got past the human form part though. Really, they didn't come anywhere near finishing things. To some extent they never really even got started." Rissa grinned. "Then he came back here and took you to bed."

Aislinn was speechless. Her brain was trying to grasp what Rissa had just told her. Rissa continued in the silence. "But the men around here, especially Lord Arnauk refrain from any number of things if they aren't serious about a woman. Take Lord Arnauk for example." Rissa thought she'd approach things a little differently. She figured that there really wasn't any way all of the mating stuff had happened, but everyone knew Lord Arnauk's normal habits. If he had taken her up to his room, there had to be more to it than the two of them just having a nap in his bed. There was so much of his scent on her that she could almost be mistaken for him. And from the smell of things she had a shower before she came down. "Lord Arnauk never takes women to his room. He almost never takes all his clothes off. He tends to like women who are strong, intelligent, and show as few signs of remaining interested in him as possible. He never sleeps with the same woman twice in a row. He tends to make it short and sweet, with as little affection in it as he can manage. He's always on top, usually with the woman on her hands and knees regardless of the form he's in. And probably the most important thing is that he never marks women. He'll come on the floor before on a woman if he can help it. He never comes inside a woman. And if he does accidentally get some on someone he sends her to the showers immediately."

Aislinn couldn't believe how much Rissa seemed to know about Cullen's bedroom habits. She held herself in check. *Different cultures*, she reassured herself. "So do you know details about the sex life of everyone around here? Or have you experienced him first hand?"

Rissa saw the hurt look on Aislinn's face and realized she might have gone too far. Besides, her tactics didn't seem to be working. "No, Ais, I've never been with Lord Arnauk. He'd never lie with a theta," she said with a guilty tone. "But we do tend to be relatively open about this stuff. I could take you down the hall and show you a room where people who've gotten bored with waiting have started to entertain themselves in the mean time. We don't hide sex the way humans do. I mean we've all seen him with the women he beds. Like I said, he doesn't tend to take it private. That's why we're all so curious about you. It looks a lot more serious than he tends to get."

Aislinn nodded and bit her lip. On the list of things that Cullen supposedly didn't do, she'd managed to break the standard on more than half of them. Something about that brought a secretive smile to her face that had Rissa's curiosity back in full swing. Given what he'd said to her in the shower, she really didn't think she had the right to hold his past against him. *I guess maybe I shouldn't be too bothered by what she's saying. If this is the way they are at least I'm finding out before he wants to bend me over in the middle of the great room. God, he might want to bend me over in the middle of the great room. I guess we'll see if he wants me again. I mean it's not like I'm in love with him right? I mean right now we're just having a little fun. Right? No need to get panicky or jealous or bothered by the way things are around here.* At the same time, something about the idea of being 'mounted' made Aislinn a little heated.

In the brief silence, a woman who had been standing off against a wall and just listening stepped in. "Perhaps she has nothing to tell." The woman was one of the stand outs from before. She had three other women with her. She was the angry one while the others looked amused. She would have been easy to spot one way or another. She was blonde with green eyes in a room full of dark hair and brown eyes.

Rissa shifted uncomfortably. "Aislinn, this is Meredith." Aislinn smiled at the woman, but didn't respond.

"Perhaps," Meredith reiterated. "Lord Arnauk took her up to his room for some reason other than what everyone is assuming, and the girl has nothing to tell."

"He gave her the key to the penthouse Meredith," Rissa defended.

"So he's protecting her for some reason. That doesn't mean he's fucking her." Meredith walked over to the seating area. She looked down her nose at one of the women in a chair across from Aislinn, and the woman did the head nod thing, jumped up from the chair, and allowed Meredith to have it.

Aislinn couldn't help the amused scoff and eye roll that followed. She had no intention of falling into a who-fucked-Cullen-better argument with this woman. Besides, from what Rissa had said, Aislinn was fairly confident that she'd win hands down. Just knowing that gave her a little more confidence in dealing with this bitch. *Bitch,* Aislinn smiled, *oddly appropriate.*

Meredith tilted her head in a superior fashion so that she could look down on everyone even from her sitting position. "I'll ignore that seeing as you're probably ignorant of the way things work around here, this time. But for future reference little one, I'm a beta. That means that everyone less than that gets out of my way when I want. You don't have any rank at all."

Aislinn caught the implication, but was not about to bow to this woman. She'd lost just about everything over the last seven years, except her pride, and she wasn't going to give that up now. Aislinn met the woman's gaze dead on as she talked. "I don't think that I'll be giving up my seat to you. But thanks for the warning just the same." Rissa gave Aislinn a warning look. Her eyes were like saucers and a little scared.

Aislinn's comment dropped the smile from Meredith's face. "I don't think you realize what you're dealing with here, little one."

Aislinn ignored Meredith and looked over at Rissa questioningly. "Okay that's several times I've been called 'little one.' Is that supposed to be an insult?"

Rissa swallowed and looked over at Meredith who was now fuming. "Yeah, uh, you are a little petite to be much of a threat to anyone Ais. Meredith is a beta."

Aislinn heard the warning in Rissa's voice. But she just didn't feel threatened here. For seven years she had been warned ahead of time if she was in danger.

She had yet to get any warnings about this place or these people. Not to mention, they had no idea what she was capable of. "Big things come in small packages," she answered Rissa, and then looked back over at Meredith. "Did you want something? Or are you just in the habit of interrupting conversations you're not invited to?"

Meredith sat forward in her chair. "You must be pretty confident in your abilities to think you can speak to me like this and not have to worry about retribution."

"I guess you could say that," Aislinn answered. "Or you could say that it's hard for me to not be amused by the fact that someone so grand and mighty as you seems to be threatened by little old me. If you were confident in your position, you wouldn't be bothering to try and find out who or what I am. You'd have moved on with your life, believing that no one like me could get in the way of whatever you had going on with Cullen. I'm guessing that you must not be that important around here or you'd be in that meeting that Cullen called. So no, I'm not all that worried about you. It doesn't add up in a way that would make me."

Rissa couldn't believe what she was listening to. She had to admit that she didn't really know much about Aislinn. She knew that Aislinn had been nice and had learned her job quickly at the Taigh-Olsda. She knew that Lord Arnauk had shown some favoritism toward Aislinn from the beginning, and there were rumors that he had gotten her the job in the first place. Rissa knew that Aislinn had a weird scent, and she didn't think that Aislinn was human, even though that was the way she talked. But if she wasn't human Rissa didn't know what she might be. She had never actually had a personal conversation with Aislinn beyond the random chat in the break room or while waiting tables. This was definitely not something she had expected. She just hoped that Aislinn could back up what she was saying. Rissa certainly didn't think that Aislinn looked capable of it.

Meredith's eyes virtually bulged out of her head. "Have you no respect for Lord Arnauk? You've no right to use his name."

Aislinn looked over at Rissa, who was wincing a bit and looking at her as though Meredith was right. But Rissa was keeping her mouth shut on this one. "Well," Aislinn said, "he told me to use his name. What? You slept with him and you never earned the privilege?"

Rissa leaned in conspiratorially. "You didn't tell me you could use his name."

Aislinn shrugged. "What's the big deal?"

"No one but a few of the elders get to call Lord Arnauk anything other than Lord Arnauk or General. He's the alpha Aislinn," she said as if Aislinn had missed something very important about the word alpha.

"Okay, but I'm new at this. I don't get all the rules here. I just do what he told me to do. He's never once told me to not call him Cullen. Frankly if I slept with someone," she added looking at Meredith incredulously, "and he didn't let me use his first name, I wouldn't be continuing to sleep with him, whatever he was."

Meredith couldn't take the condescending tone any longer. "That's enough. If you don't adjust your attitude, then his scent that still clings to you won't be enough to keep me from teaching you a lesson about pack etiquette."

Aislinn shook her head. "You don't intimidate me. Either do what you think you want to do or go away."

At that Meredith began growling. Aislinn just continued to glare at her sharply. With no warning Meredith shifted into her hybrid form, and then leaped at Aislinn where she sat. Aislinn only had a second to contemplate the change she saw with fascination before the woman was on top of her. Rissa barely managed to get out of the way as Meredith grabbed hold of Aislinn on the couch. The force of the attack caused the couch to vault backward and both women went rolling to the floor. A circle cleared around them in the room. *Great,* Aislinn thought, *Cullen tells me to avoid fighting, and the first thing I do is get into a fight.*

With that thought in mind Aislinn used the momentum from the roll off the couch to continue the roll until she was on top of Meredith. The shocked lycan pushed Aislinn off, and then got to her feet turning to continue the attack. Aislinn was on her feet as well. Faster than any of the people in the room expected, Aislinn launched her own attack. Meredith was thrown completely off guard as the smaller woman began a volley of punches and kicks that quickly had her backed against the wall.

Before Meredith could get her mind back in the situation Aislinn managed a punch to her face that had blood pouring from the lycan's nose. If Meredith hadn't changed into her hybrid form, the blow probably would have broken her nose. Meredith was blinded by the pain and let out a growl that caused the onlookers to step back. She started flailing at any shape she could identify. Aislinn dodged each swipe as though she was bored with it. She had figured that a lycan would be faster than this. She led Meredith around the room ducking out of the way of each clawing attack and taunting the woman as they went. The room of people had fallen into deadly silence. They couldn't believe that this little, human outsider was making such a fool of one of their betas.

Finally, Aislinn grew tired of playing with Meredith. She grabbed Meredith's arm as the woman tried to claw at her again and flipped her so that she landed face first on the floor. In a blur of movements Aislinn had the woman pinned. Meredith growled furiously. Aislinn was impossibly strong, and the angle at which she was holding Meredith's arm left the woman incapable of getting any leverage to change the situation. It sent shooting pain up the woman's back and felt as though Aislinn was about to rip it off. "You shoulllldn't be abllle to do thiiis," Meredith hissed through clenched teeth in a guttural voice that shouldn't have come from her throat as she struggled to get control of the situation.

Aislinn's voice had a deadly quality to it. "Don't make assumptions about things you know nothing about. I suggest that you submit to the superior fighter here."

* * * *

Cullen took his place at the head of the table. Nearly all of the pack elders were present. The few who weren't there were still at the reservation cleaning up after the failed mating ceremony. "All right Terrick, you were saying?"

"I was merely voicing a concern about why no one bothered to look into Jenna's supposed disappearance. It just seems strange to me that she would vanish into thin air. All of you seem to think that there was nothing wrong with that." When Terrick said that, there were concerned looks exchanged around the table. It was as though something in their minds clicked all at once, and they realized that they should have arranged a search party or something. As Terrick continued an uneasy silence enveloped everyone. "And what about the insane way you came up with the idea that you were going to be attacked, and then there was no attack."

Cullen glared at him for the way he phrased that part, but he didn't interrupt the man's tirade. Terrick was making valid points. One of the things that kept Cullen in charge was his willingness to listen when other alphas might not.

"I heard that Jenna was stopped from killing you because several people had *dreams* that warned them it was going to happen? Are we going to get a real explanation?" The people in the room were looking at each other with concern. They all agreed with Terrick. What was worse was that most of them had been there. They had seen Jenna vanish and none of them had been bothered by it. Why didn't they go looking for her?

"Why don't I start from the beginning, and maybe by the end some of the questions you're asking will be answered," Cullen replied calmly. Then he launched into a rendition of the story. He started with the night that Keith had brought him the information about the Circle being behind the raids, included some of the information about Aislinn, and ended with the ceremony. "I can only guess that this Rafe person had something to do with why none of us cared that Jenna disappeared. According to Aislinn, he was standing there watching us all, and no one questioned his presence or the presence of his men."

Cullen looked around the room to be sure that he had everyone's attention, then continued. "Aislinn said that distance from Rafe has a lessening affect on his abilities. I, for one, am feeling it necessary to question not only my own actions that night, but things that I observed on the way in that were unusual as well. I don't know about anyone else, but I seem to remember strange greenish bonfires. I'm guessing that the bonfires had something to do with it as well. Right now, I have quite a few questions that still need answers. So I can't do more than tell you all what I have and attempt to arrange for additional solutions. Aislinn was only able to shed *some* light. She is, for the most part, ignorant of the finer details. Rafe seems to want something. She thinks it has to do with our standing stones. We've owned that property since I came to leadership, and our possession of it was never questioned. I always believed them to be an attractive landmark and a reminder of our past, but it seems there may be more to it than that. We're going to have to look into quite a few things to get the rest of the answers we seek.

"However, I believe the worst threat is the possibility of traitors amongst our own number, and the now imminent threat posed by the Tairneach. While Rafe is a problem, we don't really know what he's after. Regardless of his intentions anyone in our pack helping him needs to be routed out."

Terrick growled his annoyance. "Don't you think it would have been better to deal with the Tairneach when Brennus first started all this caoch as opposed to waiting until the girl was beneath you to deal with the fact that you preferred this random human you picked up at some bar?" Cullen had to use every ounce of control he had to keep from launching across the table at Terrick. He had known that the subject would be broached, but Terrick was taking too many liberties with his position in the pack and ignoring half of what Cullen said. Terrick was just trying to cause additional descent and Cullen didn't need that.

"How do you know that you can even trust her," Celia asked with more jealousy than Cullen would have expected from her. "If she's having these visions is she even human? How much do you really know?" Celia didn't like the way Cullen was referring to Aislinn at all. From what she had heard about where Aislinn spent the day, Celia was feeling a strong desire to rip the girl's throat out.

Cullen growled a warning that wasn't wasted on the others who looked as though they may voice an opinion. "I have Aislinn under control. If I feel she's a threat in any way, I will deal with it myself. Right now, we need to find out what this guy, Rafe, is trying to accomplish and keep an eye on the Tairneach. There's no guarantee that there isn't a connection, seeing as Jenna appears to be involved with him now. I want a sizable guard placed at the reservation, specifically watching the standing stones. I want someone looking into the buildings that were burned down and finding out what books have to do with it. I want someone looking for Jenna. I want any information on strange behavior on the part of anyone in this pack previously, presently, or suspected. Someone let those assholes in and lit the bonfires. I want to know who. And I want someone taking what background information Aislinn has and looking into Rafe. Am I missing anything?" All the while Cullen was talking Keith was diligently taking notes. He knew without it being said that he would be in charge of picking the 'someones' for each task.

Sarah looked at him. "What about Aislinn?"

Cullen glared at her. "What about Aislinn?"

"Should someone look into her," Sarah said with an incredulous tone. "I mean if she's capable of the things you say she is…"

Cullen eyed Sarah, but decided that until someone other than him said she was okay he wasn't going to hear the end of it. "You're in charge of the women. I'm not worried about Aislinn. But if you'll feel better doing an investigation, then be my guest. Let me know if you find anything."

Sarah felt better when he didn't tell her 'no.' Not good enough to stop her from doing a background check, but better than when Cullen had been talking about everything Aislinn could apparently do. As for the others in the room they all appeared to be happy with the way things were being left. The only exception being Terrick, but he was never happy.

* * * *

Cullen and Keith were headed to the kitchen. They were often headed for the kitchen. Cullen hadn't eaten all day, and his stomach was growling. The meeting had ended with everyone being relatively satisfied with the explanations they were given, but also everyone was uneasy with the situation in general. How do you prepare to deal with a person who appears to be able to make your mind only see what he wants you to see and to make you think what he wants you to think?

When the men entered the kitchen, there were a couple girls giggling and speaking conspiratorially in one corner. Cullen smiled at them. It was nice to see something normal around here. The girls blushed and giggled some more. Cullen chuckled and shook his head as he opened the refrigerator door and started fishing for something interesting.

Keith, on the other hand, went over to the girls to see what secret they were sharing and to cop a feel. He had no shame. The girls smiled at him as they saw him coming. They knew he was harmless. He had a mate. That never stopped him from flirting though. Keith had been getting increasingly worse since Jaylyn got pregnant and decided that she didn't want to play anymore.

Cullen pulled a container of something that resembled chili out of the fridge. He was sniffing at it and trying to decide how old it might be when Keith started roaring with laugher. "She didn't!" The girls started giggling again.

Cullen was trying to ignore the conspiracy. He didn't like gossip. He fully accepted that Keith would find out anything important, and then let him know if it was necessary. Everyone in the pack loved and trusted Keith like he was a best friend or brother. Cullen threw the container in the microwave and was fishing a fork out of a drawer when the girls took off out of the room. Keith came over to where Cullen was standing at the counter. Cullen could tell from the look on his face that he was dying to share whatever he had just found out. Keith was beaming with amusement, but Cullen was hungry and had a rough evening. He wasn't interested in playing games, unless it involved Aislinn and his bedroom. He smiled. The microwave dinged, Cullen grabbed the container, and moved over to kitchen table. He sat there eyeing the food and considering calling down to the Taigh-O\sda for some steak.

Keith sat down across from him and waited until Cullen had put the first spoonful of food in his mouth before blurting it out. "So while we were in the meeting, Aislinn got into a brawl with Meredith and forced Meredith's submission." Cullen virtually choked on the mouthful of food and Keith beamed at his accomplishment. "Oh that's not the end of it. I guess she made a complete fool of Meredith in the process. It wasn't even a close fight."

Cullen wiped the food from his mouth and looked at Keith as though he had grown a second head. Keith grinned from ear to ear. "I take it you didn't know she was capable?"

Cullen cleared his throat. "The closest I ever came to finding out if she could fight was when she told me she had previously beaten up her asshole boss from the bar. But there was that time I snuck up on her, and she managed to kick me hard enough to knock me backward several feet." Cullen thought about that as he said it.

Keith nodded. "Well from the sounds of things, she may very well be alpha bitch material after all." He shrugged and stood up from the table to get something to drink out of the fridge.

* * * *

Rissa and Aislinn were seated on the couch in the games room facing the large screen TV. Shortly after the fight with Meredith, Rissa had given Aislinn a tour of the floor, just to get her out of the room with all the whispering and uncertain stares. It didn't take long for Rissa to realize that Aislinn just wasn't like the other women. She didn't see rank as an issue. She was too human in that respect and operated from the 'all men are created equal' point of view. Rissa didn't quite agree, but she thought it was nice that Aislinn was so inclined to treat everyone nicely as long as they returned the favor.

They had spent some time in the kitchen since Aislinn hadn't eaten all day. Then they made some popcorn, picked out a movie, and camped out on the large couch to wait for the meeting to be over. Aislinn seemed disinclined to go upstairs to bed without Cullen. She didn't say why, but Rissa got the impression that she was almost afraid to go to sleep.

They ended up watching some sappy romance story. It was just getting to the part where the guy finally realized he was in love with the girl and was going after her, when Celia came into the room with her eyes on fire. She was accompanied by two of the women who had been with Meredith earlier that evening. Aislinn shook her head and went back to watching her movie. She couldn't believe she was going to have to go through that again.

Rissa leaned over to Aislinn and put her and on her shoulder. "That's Celia. She's ten times worse than Meredith." Aislinn met Rissa's gaze and read the warning in it. Aislinn sighed heavily and tried to continue watching the movie.

Celia studied Aislinn for a moment. Celia was much more contemplative than Meredith. She was a planner. She didn't necessarily intend to get into a fight with the girl. If Aislinn could be put into line with the others, then there wouldn't be a problem here. From what Celia could tell she didn't look like much. Under the General's scent, Celia could pick up Aislinn's . Her scent was confusing, but from what General Arnauk had said, that wasn't surprising. Celia was trying to size Aislinn up physically when she noticed the mark on Aislinn's shoulder just at her neck, half hidden by the collar of her shirt.

Celia stormed over to the couch where Aislinn and Rissa were sitting. She grabbed the sleeve of Aislinn's shirt, rage flaring in her amber eyes, and yanked on it to get a better look at the mark. Rissa jumped out of the way instinctively. Aislinn pulled away from the woman and readjusted her shirt. "What the hell do you think you're doing," Aislinn said, standing up and backing away from Celia.

Celia looked like she was about to explode. She took a deep breath and let it out. *He took her to his room, gave her the key, and marked her*, she thought. As she added it all together in her mind, it came down to one thing. The General had chosen a mate. If that was what was going on here, then Celia was about to be ousted from her position whether she liked it or not. "Did he mark you," she fumed.

The suggestion started the entire room buzzing with excitement. Cullen had been around a long time and had never seemed inclined to mate with anyone. Jenna had been a political convenience and wasn't expected to disturb the order of the pack. If he chose a mate like Aislinn, then things were about to turn upside down, in the female ranks anyway. The pack was already dividing into the group that was happy for him and the group who was disgusted that he'd pick a non-lycan outsider.

"It's none of your business. If you don't want to end up like Meredith I suggest you leave me alone." The deadly calm in Aislinn's voice was almost enough to make Celia back down. Almost.

* * * *

The last thing Sarah wanted to deal with was contention over pack rank right that instant. She was standing in the great room surrounded by the six women who were going to be directly affected if Sarah decided that Aislinn's fight with Meredith constituted a rank change. She growled with annoyance. "There are more important things to be dealing with right now. As far as I know, I have not been told that the girl will be here permanently. I'll need more information before making that kind of decision. But if she's capable and wants to take up the challenge, then you know full well how this decision will fall."

Sarah pushed her way past the frustrated women and headed down the hall to find out where Keith and Cullen had gone. She could pretty well guess. It was always the kitchen or Cullen's office. It depended on his mood. Since he had appeared to be in a decent mood, outside of the meeting, she figured the kitchen. She was growling to herself and almost missed the commotion that began emanating from the opposite direction. Sarah stopped and listened. She already knew what it was. Celia had gone looking for Aislinn. Sarah quickened her pace toward the kitchen.

She stormed into the kitchen in a rage that instantaneously started Keith laughing again. Cullen pushed the chili aside and got up, apologizing to his stomach as he did. He was already guessing what Sarah was going to say before she said it. When Cullen heard Celia's name in the same sentence as Aislinn's, he stormed through the door of the kitchen and down the hall. If this was what was going to happen on the first night she spent with them, he couldn't help but wonder what the future held. It's not like he could take her with him everywhere he went.

As Cullen, Keith, and Sarah entered the doorway of the games room they heard Aislinn's deadly warning. Cullen started to head toward the women, but Sarah stopped him. This was a matter of female rank and none of his business technically.

Neither Aislinn nor Celia noticed the addition to their audience. They were too busy staring each other down. Celia growled low in her throat. Aislinn was good enough at sizing people up to know when to hold her ground and when to run and hide. This seemed to be a tossup. Celia was neither rash nor mouthy as Meredith had been. She was just angry. Aislinn watched the woman pace around her, thinking.

Celia's eyes were concentrating on the mark that Cullen had left on Aislinn's shoulder. It wasn't quite deep enough to scar. It would heal. But, that didn't change the fact that he had done it in the first place. "How did it happen," she asked in a dangerous low voice.

"Why are all of you so stuck on how exactly we had sex? I don't get it," Aislinn glared at her. "It's none of your business." Cullen stiffened and Sarah gave him a harsh glare at that.

"On the contrary. They're stuck on it because what the alpha does with his women is everyone's business." Celia grinned. Sarah had to hold Cullen back as the face off continued. Celia leaned in closer to Aislinn. Neither woman was willing to drop her gaze from the other for an instant. "Did you bite him back? Taste him?" Aislinn didn't answer. "No? Shame. I would have. Did he do it on purpose? Did he tell you what it means? Do you have any idea what it takes to be the alpha bitch?"

Suddenly Celia stopped. She tilted her head, and her eyes looked over Aislinn's shoulder to the three elders who had been watching. She smiled broadly. "Have you come to make sure I didn't hurt her?"

Aislinn wasn't sure if Celia was trying to distract her so that she could attack, or if there was something that was actually drawing her attention. Celia stood upright and dropped the threatening demeanor as though it had never been. She looked at Aislinn with more hatred than Aislinn had ever seen, and at the same time there was a tear in the corner of her eye. She stepped in closer to Aislinn. Speaking in a whisper so low that Aislinn could barely hear what she was saying. "Do you love him," she asked.

Aislinn swallowed hard. She didn't have an answer.

"Then you and I will have to finish this later," Celia said.

Aislinn looked at her in confusion, then followed her gaze to the group in the doorway. Cullen was eyeing them both cautiously. The woman with him looked pissed, and Keith had a disappointed air about him. He obviously wanted to watch a fight. Celia nodded in submission toward Cullen, and headed out the door. A man who had been standing against the wall immediately followed her. He had an annoyed air about him, and Aislinn shortly heard arguing from down the hall.

She was waiting to see what Cullen was going to say. She was pretty certain that he wouldn't be happy with her. To her surprise he came over to her and started looking her over for injury. "Are you all right?" The rest of the room stared on in shock and amusement.

Aislinn tried to stop his fussing but wasn't very successful. "Yeah, I'm fine. I told you I would be."

Cullen stopped as she growled at him and he grinned at her. "Picking up bad habits," he said.

"Huh?" Aislinn was frustrated. It had been a difficult evening.

"The growling. Not generally a human habit." He smiled at her. He was greatly amused by the fire in her eyes. The idea that she had held her own against Meredith made him feel better about her fitting in. Then there was watching her with Celia. No matter how concerned he had been for her safety he had to admit that she had looked and sounded impressive. He leaned in and kissed her. It took her and all the others totally off guard.

Aislinn could feel his fingers on her chin gently guiding her mouth to his. His lips burned against her and she felt passion rolling in her stomach. She reached up and took hold of his shirt, partially to keep herself from falling over. When he ended the kiss, she stood with her eyes closed for just a second longer and took a deep breath, feeling his scent seep into her and wash the frustration she had been boiling with out of her system.

He ran his fingers over her face and smiled at her. "Have you had enough for one evening?"

"What?" It took Aislinn a moment to catch what he was saying.

"Would you like to go to bed," he added. His eyes swirled with the suggestion.

Aislinn couldn't help but join him in the smile at that point. "Sounds nice."

Keith and Sarah approached the two. "We hate to interrupt. But," Sarah said. She looked considerably less pissed off than she had a minute ago. The anger had been replaced by a bemused resignation. She reached out and pulled the neck of Aislinn's shirt aside to see what Celia had been ranting about earlier. Then she gave a motherly look to Cullen. "I take it that Aislinn will be staying with the pack on a permanent basis?"

Cullen cleared his throat and, upon seeing Aislinn's uncomfortable stance with Sarah examining the mark on her shoulder, he pulled Sarah's hand away. "Aislinn has been told that she can stay as long as she wants. Anything more has yet to be discussed in detail."

Sarah crossed her arms and her tone adjusted to match the motherly look in her eyes. "You were behind her when you did that."

Cullen looked around to see how many people were witnessing the conversation, and he watched Aislinn carefully. He had started to explain it to her earlier, but she just didn't seem to understand the significance. He was certain she wouldn't completely get it until she was dealing with it firsthand. "This isn't the place to talk about that," he said and eyed the onlookers suggestively.

Sarah shook her head and then looked over at Aislinn. "Are you okay with being in his rooms or do you think you might want rooms of your own at some point? I mean, he's only likely to get more aggressive, and if he takes the play too much farther then you may end up stuck with him whether you like it or not." She looked at Cullen. "But if he's smart he'll do it by the book instead of taking things into his own hands." She looked back at Aislinn. "I know you probably don't get this right now. But if he gets out of control there won't be a way to stop him, and the entire pack should be involved if it really does go that far."

Aislinn looked at Cullen and then at Sarah again. She was sounding more and more like his mother. Aislinn's brain was wheeling. Everyone seemed to be awfully concerned about this and she was starting to join them. The real problem was that the entire explanation was more than anyone seemed willing to say in detail and all the veiled information wasn't going to help. She looked over at Cullen. He looked concerned. She smiled at him. *Hell, I haven't felt this good about someone ever.* "No, I'm okay in his bed. As long as I'm wanted."

Sarah looked at Cullen then back to Aislinn. "Girl, if you actually doubt whether or not he wants you there, then I can think of a few elementary classes we give to the children that you need to sit in on. My concern is more that he doesn't seem to have a grip on where to draw the line." Cullen growled at her. "I am happy for you," she responded to the growl with a sincere tone. "Just be careful. And get around to making sure she knows what she's in for. I'm only half kidding about sticking her in one of the classrooms." Then she walked off shaking her head.

Cullen watched after her like a child who had just been scolded for doing something he knew he shouldn't have. "Well that went well."

"I did catch the sarcasm," Aislinn responded. Keith just stood there watching and waiting with a goofy grin on his face as if something great were about to happen.

"Aislinn, that was Sarah. She's one of my best friends, and for all intents and purposes, she's in charge of the women. There are too many in this pack for me to deal with all of it myself. At some point you'll have to spend some time with her and get your position around here straightened out. But with the rest of the complications at this point I think it best if that waited."

Aislinn nodded. "Alpha female," she said earning an impressed look from Cullen. She looked at Keith quizzically as he just stood there amused. "Is there something growing out of my forehead," she asked Cullen.

He shook his head and glared at Keith, who only returned an unimpressed look. "Have you actually met Keith?"

"That first night we met. At the bar."

"Yeah," Cullen breathed out. It was all like a bad dream now. "Well, this is Keith. He's a pain in my ass and my right arm. He's mostly harmless, though his mate is not. Where is Jaylyn anyway? I'm surprised you're still wandering the halls."

"You know, one of these days you're going to hurt my feelings," Keith replied good-naturedly. Then he looked at Aislinn again. "In case you don't know it yet, he's none too subtle when he wants to get rid of someone. Jay doesn't care where I am as long as I end up in bed with her eventually. He's just afraid that I'm going to say something to embarrass him and so he wants me to disappear. That is an impressive bite mark Cul," he said rather loudly, not wanting anyone to miss the fact that Cullen had finally chosen a woman to mate with. "You were behind her when you did it. I can tell from the angle. Nice! When's the actual ceremony?"

Aislinn blushed furiously. "Well it seems as though Cullen was right about the embarrassment factor," she said, in an authoritative voice that raised Keith's eyebrows.

"Oh yeah, this one is much better than Jenna," he chuckled. "She even has your annoyed tone. This is going to be fun. Things were getting rather dull with all the attacking and raiding and mystery. Give me a nice simple way to pick on the boss and my day brightens immensely."

Cullen reached out and took hold of Keith's shoulder. He pushed the man out of the way, and with a hand at Aislinn's back he guided her past his friend, heading toward the elevator. By morning everyone in the pack would know that he had bitten Aislinn. He couldn't decide whether he should try to talk to her about it again or not.

When they got into the elevator Cullen reached for his key only to realize that Aislinn had it. She was holding it up to him with a smile on her face. He nodded to the panel, and she put the key in and hit the button for the top floor. Cullen was torn between being tired and being playful. "By all the Gods you're beautiful," he said in a soft serious way that sent chills up Aislinn's back. His arm went around her, and he started kissing her.

He couldn't help it. All he wanted was to be inside her. When the elevator doors opened they virtually fell into the room, almost forgetting to grab the key. By the time they were in the bedroom, they were naked, and by the time they were in the bed, Aislinn's legs were wrapped around his waist. They never did get a chance to have a conversation that night.

* * * *

Rafe backhanded the man who had come to report in. The large lycan only barely moved from the force of the blow. He was as unimpressed with Rafe's physical abilities as Rafe was with lycans. Rafe didn't understand why his ancestors had been so enamored with them. *Of all the weres they could have created they chose wolves*, Rafe thought with disgust. *Wait until they see what I do.* "How did Arnauk get his mongrel hands on her?"

"I don't have that information. Just that she's there. He's keeping her in his rooms."

Rafe paced, allowing anger to bleed out and mar his generally placid appearance. If she was in his rooms that implied more than Rafe was willing to concede. "I need her out of there. You'll arrange it."

"The way he's treating her, there are fairly solid rumors that he intends to mate with her."

Rafe roared and threw a nearby chair across the room. "I want her back untouched!"

"It's too late for that."

"Then I want her back as unmarred as possible. Before he mates with her. She's mine. I don't care how you do it. Just bring her here." Rafe moved in so close to the lycan that the lycan snarled at the proximity. An odor that made him sick permeated the air around them. He wanted to rip Rafe's throat out but couldn't bring himself to do it. Rafe smiled at the lycan as if he knew what was going through the man's mind, and it amused him. "You'll do as you're told. You know what will happen to her if you don't."

Rafe swept out of the room, leaving the lycan standing there. A tear formed in the large man's eye. Somewhere in the back of his mind he could feel fear and pain. He let his head fall back, on his shoulders and a howl bleeding with misery echoed through the building. Rafe smiled when he heard the sound. He looked over at the tiger that was walking beside him. "Bring me some more of their women."

* * * *

Jenna was pacing back and forth in her room. She was getting increasingly antsy. The large lioness just stared at her with distaste. Kara mostly slept, but always seemed to be awake when Jenna wanted to try and get out. Jenna wasn't stupid enough to think that she wasn't a prisoner. It had only been a day and she wanted out already. Her brain was warring between knowing that Rafe wasn't going to share his power with her and not caring.

Her logic told her that it wasn't like her to not care, but every time she thought about it in detail, Rafe would float into her mind and she would give in and go take a nap.

Kara was watching her uncertainly. Usually they didn't fight it this much. She was starting to think that Jenna had more of brain than Rafe was giving her credit for. The girl was playing him at least a little bit, and Rafe was far too full of himself to notice. She was going to be trouble. Kara watched Jenna pace and hoped that Rafe would be back soon to reassert himself. She didn't want to have him summoned. He hated that. But she also didn't want to get into a fight with the girl. She hated the smell of lycans.

Chapter 9

Cullen had to give Keith credit. He was nothing if not efficient. Cullen was looking over the pile of reports on his desk. It had only taken Keith 24 hours to produce a background report on Rafe Senach. Cullen was reading over the man's information. He looked relatively innocuous, if the reports were to be taken at face value. There really wasn't much more to it than what Aislinn had told him the other day, except some previous addresses that Keith already sent people to check out, along with the address of the compound that Aislinn had been held at. The idea of what the man had done to her had Cullen contemplating the things he intended to do to Rafe.

Cullen also had a list of names. On the list were three bookshop owners, a couple collectors, and a librarian. All of whom shared the last name Senach with Rafe or, Keith had found out, were related to a Senach. Keith had done some digging and had pulled up some information on the family name. Apparently a lot of Senachs had been dying recently. They were a fairly normal family from public appearances. They didn't participate in politics. Most of them were teachers or writers. Cullen picked up a history book that Keith had provided with the report. It was written by a woman who called herself Alissa Morgan and covered information on ancient Scotland, Ireland, and Wales. That hit a cord with Cullen. Keith had found out that 'Morgan' was her pen name, and she was one of these Senach. Keith was currently in the process of trying to find a couple of them. All of the unexplained deaths recently had Cullen wondering if the entire Circle was the problem or just this one member.

Cullen sat back in his chair and tried to remember what his father had told him about the Circle. Cullen hadn't thought about his father in a long time. Dyfan Arnauk had died long before Cullen had become strong enough to be an alpha. Cullen always wished he'd been around to see the pack. The only thing Cullen knew was that the Circle had spent the last thousand years keeping their heads down and practicing pacifism to a fault. That was why the Pack Council, the leaders of the various were groups, and the Circle Council, the leaders of all the various druid groups, had parted company in the first place.

The various pack leaders weren't willing to go quietly into the night, so to speak, and the Circle Council hadn't been willing to stand and fight, when Rome. They wanted the Pack to play guard dog, but avoid direct confrontation. It just went against Pack instinct and after a few hundred years the Pack left the Circle on its own. It wasn't a bad separation. Both sides of the issue agreed that they weren't compatible any longer. Like an amiable divorce. That was what the Circle had been like: live and let live.

After a dozen decades or so, the Circle had been hidden for so long most of the people who had been a threat to them were either involved in different wars or dead. Another couple hundred years and even the lycans started to forget about them. By the time Cullen's father had told him stories about the Circle, they were legend. Most lycans didn't believe the stories any longer. The main legend that had survived was a story about how the were races were created by druids. But that couldn't have been true could it? Lycans were born, not created. All the ridiculous werewolf movies the humans liked to make up and the biting caoch drove him nuts.

Most lycans thought of the creation legend as similar to the Greek legends the humans had. No one really believed it. If you wanted to make a lycan, or any other were for that matter, two of them got together and had a good rut. Biting could be fun, and with the human obsession to be more than a boring old human, he could understand why they made that crap up. Everyone just assumed the druid stories were similar. Or the druids were trying to look like Gods in the eyes of the lycans. He didn't even know if the stories were told to kids any more. Could there be something more to it?

Cullen was debating over what he should say to Aislinn about it. She seemed to have accepted that Rafe had done something to her. The way that it sounded, from her description of the compound he was calling the Circle, he was either recruiting weres or he might be creating them. If he was creating them, who knows what he had done to Aislinn. If he had been trying to turn her into something Cullen didn't understand why she couldn't change. Rafe couldn't make someone half into a were could he? It didn't make a lot of sense. Cullen pushed the thoughts out of his head and went back to the reports. There really was no guarantee that's what was happening anyway. It was incredibly unlikely, wasn't it?

Keith hadn't been able to produce any concrete information on anyone in their pack causing trouble, but there was a list of tentative names of men who had been acting more agitated than usual and people who had been out of contact. That list included reasons for the inability to get a hold of them.

As far as the bonfires and Jenna went, there wasn't anything new or helpful on that front either. Jenna was still missing, and the Tairneach were threatening war. Cullen had even had a phone call from one of the feds who kept an eye on the pack interactions. He'd spent part of his afternoon reassuring the man that he had it all under control. He just wished he believed what he had told the fool on the phone.

The questions about the bonfires led to omegas. The omegas said that Jenna had told them to build the fires, and she gave them bags of plants to throw on the flames. Cullen had been given a small pouch containing an assortment of plants that the omegas had put on the fire to turn it green. Apparently Jenna had said that it was for decorative purposes. Now half the omegas who had been at the reservation that night were panicking and thinking it was all their fault.

There was a knock on his door and Cullen groaned. He had too much information floating around his brain at the moment. He didn't want any more. When Aislinn popped her head in the door and smiled at him, he couldn't help but smile back with relief. He waved her in, and she closed the door behind herself.

"I was thinking about dinner. You interested," she asked, as she walked around his desk and stepped up to him.

Cullen grabbed her hips and pulled her down onto his lap so that she was straddling him, her hands on his shoulders. She was nose to nose with him. He nuzzled her playfully. *Gods I got it bad,* he thought. "You have no idea how glad I am that you're not Keith."

Aislinn smiled wickedly. She settled down onto the growing erection beneath her and chuckled. "I think I can guess how glad you are that I'm not Keith." She put her arms around his neck and kissed him passionately. This whole experience was scaring her, but not in any of the ways that Cullen thought it might. All she could think about each time he touched her was that every time she had found something good in recent history, Rafe had shown up and destroyed it.

"How has your afternoon been?" Cullen pushed her hair away from her face. He was contemplating shoving the reports off of his desk and taking her on it.

Aislinn giggled at the look in his eyes. She knew exactly what he was thinking. "Didn't you get enough last night and then this morning," she teased, knowing that if he wanted more she'd willingly give it, and she hoped the smile on her face told him as much. "All the women are avoiding me," she responded to his question. "So it's been a pretty uneventful day. I guess Meredith told them all that I broke her arm. If I did," Aislinn looked skeptical, "I really didn't mean to. But she has it all wrapped up and keeps whining about it. There appear to be two groups of people."

While she was talking Cullen was running his hands under her shirt and heading for her breasts, causing her to smile through the annoying topic. She breathed out with an odd soft growling purr that had him listening more to her breathing than her talking as he cupped her breasts and pushed his hard-on against her. Aislinn tried to continue but was finding it more and more difficult. "Half the people I run into seem curious about me, amused for some reason, and inclined to sniff and move on. The other half, mostly women, are acting as if I insulted their mothers." If Cullen kept up his play, then she'd never get to talk to him about what was going on.

"They'll get over it," Cullen said in dismissal and pinched her nipple, causing a delicious moan. He smiled and moved her off of his lap onto the desk. He sat her on the edge of the desk and nuzzled her nose with his angling her face up. He was pleased that she seemed to be taking this all with such acceptance. "As long as you think putting up with them is worth it."

Aislinn put her hands on either side of his face and stared into his eyes. "Tell me that you want me," she responded softly, with a seriousness that nearly drove Cullen back into the wall. Normally a woman speaking and acting like Aislinn would find herself assigned to some job as far from the den as possible. But Aislinn inspired him to want to do any number of things to her, most of which involved his bed and her on her hands and knees.

Cullen stared into her eyes. Emotions crashed over him like a tidal wave. "Aislinn, I-" A knock on the door interrupted him, and Keith walked in without waiting for a response. When there was no smart ass comment about walking in on Cullen standing between Aislinn's legs with such obvious intent, Cullen knew that something serious was happening.

Keith didn't wait for Cullen to ask what was wrong and only briefly considered suggesting that they send Aislinn out of the room. There were some things he wanted to know about Aislinn that Cullen didn't seem willing to broach with her, and he figured that this would be as good a time as any. He had never seen his friend so obsessed with a woman. There wasn't a lycan in the pack that couldn't see where this was going. Hell, half the women who had been chasing him for decades had already given in and moved on to lesser targets. The only problem was that most of the elders were uncomfortable with Aislinn. She was too much of a mystery. What was worse, Cullen didn't seem to be in any hurry to figure it out. With all the time they spent together, if Cullen had been talking to her, then he'd know her family life history by now. Keith stared at her contemplatively, and Aislinn stared right back. That was another reason to be nervous about her.

Keith didn't bother to wait for an invitation. He just started his latest report. "Jenna has turned up. Apparently, there's a mating about to take place. Brennus and Gregor are both dead and Rafe is to be the alpha of the Tairneach." Keith sat down in the chair across from Cullen's desk. He propped his feet up and waited for a response.

Cullen took a deep breath and stepped away from Aislinn. "When did this happen?"

"This morning I guess. Our contact in the Tairneach says that Rafe showed up with Jenna on his arm and a group of weres of all shapes and sizes backing him up. Odd weres too. A bunch of them were mix-breeds. Made some pretty speech that had everyone growling with approval, and then Brennus promptly handed the pack over. Shortly thereafter, Brennus's body was found along with Gregor's. The story is that the two men killed each other fighting over Brennus's decision. No one is contesting it. I wonder why. Who knows what Rafe's doing to their brains as we speak." Keith shifted uncomfortably and looked over at Aislinn. "You can't do that kind of caoch, can you?"

Aislinn looked confused. "What? Mind control? No. But Rafe seems to think I have the potential. He talked about teaching me. I think that it's part of the reason he won't back off and let me go. He keeps saying that I'm like him." Then she turned to Cullen. "But I'm not."

Cullen heard the tremor in her voice. He had been concerned that this might come up. He pulled her to himself and hugged her. "I know. Don't worry. I think Keith was more interested in the possibility that you might be able to do something to help the situation." He gave Keith a meaningful glare over Aislinn's head so that she wouldn't see it.

Keith wasn't sure he liked the way Cullen was coddling her. There were times that Aislinn appeared strong and intelligent. But all it took was mention of Rafe and she seemed to crumble. The guy had gotten to her badly, and Cullen was dangerously protective of her. Keith only hoped that the situation would improve once they were mated. "Yeah, that's what I meant," he said unconvincingly. "Look, what we know is that we're about to be at war with a pack that was already our equal and has now added lions, tigers, bears, and the Gods know what else to their numbers. To make matters worse, the new alpha has no trouble randomly killing anyone who might see reason and can play games with people's heads. I don't know about you, but I'm scared shitless. You'll have to forgive me if I start grasping at straws and being suspicious." Keith's joking demeanor was completely gone. Cullen knew that the only thing keeping him from joining Keith in serious terror was Aislinn. It was impossible to think about anything unpleasant when she smiled at him.

Aislinn got down off of Cullen's desk. Keith was right. She knew how he felt or worse. Rafe terrified her. She thought back to the night at the mating ceremony, as much as she didn't like that. With a great deal of effort she pulled herself into the moment and tried to be as helpful as she could. She knew that if she was going to fit in around here, then someone other than Cullen needed to trust her. Otherwise, they were all going to start thinking that the only reason Cullen liked her was because she was doing something to him when no one was looking. Well, beyond having sex with him. She smiled to herself. "I don't know what I'm capable of. I seem to be able to manage things when I put my mind to it. I'd never tried getting into other people's minds before that night at the ceremony, but I managed a little. I don't know. Maybe if I put some effort into it I could do some of the things Rafe does. But it's more than just some mental ability he has. He uses something else too. He's always got a smell about him. That's part of his ability to mess with people. Maybe you could all wear gas masks or something."

Cullen considered that. "Maybe not gas masks, but I think that figuring out what was in those bonfires just became top priority." Keith nodded, impressed at Aislinn's thought process. Cullen figured that there were only two ways to figure out the herbs Rafe had used. Involve the feds, which he desperately didn't want to do, or find the druids. He looked at Keith. "Do you have any more word on the Senachs?"

Keith shook his head. "They've all disappeared. Every address we've found is abandoned."

Aislinn looked at them uncertainly. "Senach?"

"Yeah, that's the name of all the people who were involved with the book shops and such from your vision," Cullen said and pulled the report out of the pile on his desk. He looked at her with interest. "Mean something to you?" He half wondered about suggesting she touch the files again, but she pulled back from it when he showed it to her, so he set it back down.

"That was my grandmother's maiden name. Brinah Mong Senach," she said uneasily. "Do you think I could use your phone?"

Keith sat forward in his chair and cocked his head at Cullen with a look as if to say, 'see she's trouble'. Cullen ignored Keith and reached across his desk, picked up his phone and handed it to Aislinn. She stared at it a moment, the old familiar number from her childhood running through her head. She hadn't spoken to any of her family in so long. "When you say they've all disappeared, do you mean in a bad way," she asked with fear tinting her voice.

"We don't know," Keith said suddenly sympathetic. "Some are dead," he said slowly, and Aislinn winced at the phone. "But most are just gone. No trace. They could have left on their own."

Aislinn nodded and dialed the number. With each ring her heart sank a bit. As the fifth ring cut off and an elderly female voice said "Hello," Aislinn was so relieved she almost jumped for joy. "Grandma?"

"Who is this," Brinah asked not wanting to hope.

"Grandma this Aislinn," she said softly. "How are you?"

There was dead silence on the other end of the line for a moment, and Aislinn could hear a soft sob. "How am I? Child how…where are you?"

"Grandma, a lot has happened. Uh, I don't think that the whole story should be said over the phone. I have to ask you something strange," she paused and tried to think of what exactly to say. "Do you know anything about a Circle?"

There was dead silence. "Aislinn," she said seriously, with the authoritative tone that can only come from a person's grandparent. "If someone has approached you saying things about that, then you need to get away from them. Do you understand me?"

"Grandma I wish that I could. I'm not with them, but I guess a lot of people with the last name Senach have been disappearing. I was worried about you. Has anyone been bothering you?"

There was some more silence as Brinah tried to figure out what to say to her granddaughter. "All these years and now this. Sweetheart, are you in trouble? Have you been in trouble? Is someone making you call me?"

"Yes and no. I'm okay Grandma."

There was a heavy sigh. "I left all of that a long time ago. I don't use the name and I didn't think that I could be tracked down easily. When Fearguis called and warned me that we were being hunted I didn't take it seriously. You tell whoever is bothering you that if they let you go, I'll not fight them."

"Grandma I don't really know exactly what you mean. I'm okay. I'm safe. I'm not with them or the people hunting them."

Brinah sighed with relief. "Then where are you child, and how do you know about this?"

"I'm sorry about everything Grandma. I wish I could explain."

"Just tell me that you aren't involved with the Senach. Things are too dangerous right now. If you want to learn about that part of you then I'll help you. You don't need the Circle."

"I'm not involved with them, Grandma." She could see Cullen and Keith staring at her. She knew they needed information. From the way her grandmother was talking, Aislinn knew that her grandmother could give them the information that they needed. "But one of them is after me. I'm safe. Don't worry. I'm with some people now who are protecting me. But I can't come home. I just called to see if you were safe, and because maybe you could tell me something about what's going on."

Brinah was getting nervous. "I don't know what I can tell you child. I haven't associated with them a long time. I left when I married your grandfather."

"So tell me what you can. I mean anything might help. The man who's after me, he does strange things. I need to know if there's a way to stop him from doing them."

"That depends on what he's doing Aislinn. You're scaring me. It doesn't sound as though you're safe. Who is this man who's after you?"

"His name is Rafe."

Brinah nearly dropped the phone. She caught herself and tried to stay calm. She knew that she needed to get to Aislinn as quickly as possible now. "Okay, I can tell you that he is not someone to play games with. If he completed the training that he had been chosen for, then he's an alchemist."

"I don't understand what that is. Alchemy went out in the dark ages. Isn't that turning lead to gold and nonsense like that?"

Brinah smiled into the phone. She had always been very proud of her granddaughter. She was impressed that Aislinn knew even that much. "There's a great deal more to it than that. Wasn't your thesis on the fact behind myths child?"

Brinah thought about that a minute. "Okay, so what kind of alchemy makes someone able to control someone else's mind?" She said it before thinking. She was getting caught up in learning something new. Her brain had been hungry for learning for so long now. It was part of why the pack wasn't bothering her. She felt like she was back in school again and absorbing new information. The kind of thing her grandmother was now suggesting fascinated her even more than pack dynamic.

"A very dangerous kind. Aislinn you need to get very far away from this man."

Aislinn felt guilty that she was scaring her grandmother so much. That shocked her out of her desire to learn something new. Aislinn had been missing for seven years, and here she was on the phone leaving her grandmother with the certainty that she was in danger. She owed her grandmother more than that. "Grandma, I really am okay. I'm safer here than anywhere else. These people can protect me better than running away can."

There was more silence. "You have a great deal of faith in these people you're talking about. You seem to have acquired a lot of knowledge about things I worked very hard to make sure our family wouldn't have to be concerned about. Who are you with Aislinn?"

Cullen was watching her. His heart jumped a bit each time she professed how safe she was with him. Keith could read the pleasure his friend was getting out of this on his face. He shook his head. Keith had never thought he'd ever see Cullen this gone over a woman. Aislinn was searching for the right words to explain the situation without making matters worse. Hell, if her grandmother knew about druids, and was maybe possibly a druid herself, then who knows what she might know about the lycans.

Brinah could almost feel the pause in the line. "Okay, child, you don't have to tell me. I'll just have to trust you. If you insist on staying where you are, and you have Rafe after you, then you'll need to do something about his abilities. I can't help you from here. You don't know anything about mixing compounds." It had been a long time since Brinah had done anything remotely druidic other than hide and keep secrets, but she knew she needed to get to her granddaughter somehow.

"Grandma, if you think for one second that I'm going to bring you here then you're crazy." Aislinn sounded like the original defiant child.

"Don't you dare use that tone with me, Aislinn Brianne. I'm still your grandmother, and you'll do as you're told. Whether you think it or not this is partially my fault. If I had remained with the Circle you would have known how to do these things yourself. Or if I had done a better job with leaving they never would have found you."

"Grandma," she tried to interrupt.

"No, you're my granddaughter. You need help. Whoever is protecting you won't be able to do it alone, not if Rafe is doing what it sounds like. I would have thought that with your curious nature you would want to know more about all this anyway. I guarantee you that you won't find any of the things I can tell you in a book." Brinah paused and her voice softened. "Besides, it wasn't all bad. Over the years I've regretted not passing it on. Maybe it's time."

"Hold on a minute Grandma." Aislinn covered the phone with her hand. She looked at Cullen and Keith with raised eyebrows. "Well, Grandma seems to know something about what Rafe is able to do. She wants to help. But that would mean bringing her here. I don't know if I like that."

Keith looked at Cullen. "You said to find the Senach and get what information we could. But, I personally don't want to lead Rafe to the woman. Especially if he doesn't know about her. He seems to be taking them out one at a time. She'll be in danger if we go there. She'll be in danger if we bring her here. And that will be one more non-lycan in the den. You're call."

"I don't see much choice in this." He looked at Aislinn. "What can she do here that she can't do over the phone?"

"She said something about mixing compounds, alchemy, and that I couldn't do it with phone instruction. She'd have to be here. But it seems that she can do something about Rafe's mind stuff." Aislinn's brow was furrowed, and she was shaking her head. "I didn't even know that she was a druid. How could she have kept this secret all this time?"

Brinah was getting tired of the silence on the other end of the line. "Aislinn," she called into the phone.

Cullen nodded to Aislinn. "Tell her we'll come get her, but she's not to involve anyone else."

"I'm sorry grandma," Aislinn said into the phone. "I was making sure it would be all right. I guess they're going to come get you. But you can't tell anyone what is going on. Not mom or dad or anyone."

"Child I've been keeping this secret since long before you were born. I'm not about to start sharing now. But I would point out that your family loves and misses you. Some day you should do something about that."

Aislinn couldn't bear to answer that comment. She nearly started to cry. *I miss them too,* she thought. Cullen cut in again. "Tell her that a woman named Sarah Arnauk will come to get her. If your grandmother is close enough I'll send her tomorrow." Cullen gave Keith one of his looks that sent his friend into action without the direct order. Keith got up and pulled out his phone to call Sarah.

"Grandma, um, a woman named Sarah Arnauk is going to come and get you. She'll be there tomorrow. So get everything ready. Okay?"

There was a long pause before Brinah answered. "Druids *and* lycans then. Well at least it's the Arnauk. No wonder you think you're safe where you are," Brinah said to her granddaughter with a knowing tone. "I guess I didn't do a very good job at protecting you," Brinah said apologetically.

Aislinn almost dropped the phone. "You know about that too?"

"The story is too long for the telephone dear. I'll be ready when she gets here."

"All right Grandma," Aislinn said softly. "I guess I'll see you soon. I love you."

"I love you too," Brinah replied, and they hung up.

Aislinn stared at the phone for a short time before she put it down. Cullen came up behind her and put his arms around her. "Grandma knows about your pack."

"We've been around for a long time Aislinn. There are a lot of people who know about it. We just do a very good job of making sure that the only people who know are people who won't say anything," Cullen said, trying to be reassuring, but feeling a bit uneasy by it. Apparently the Circle kept tabs on the Pack. "Aren't you the one who pointed out that you seem to have been headed in this direction your entire life?"

"Yeah, I guess so," Aislinn turned in his arms and rubbed her face into his chest. She always felt better when he was holding her. "Can we get dinner now? Before the next disaster strikes. I need to figure out what to tell my grandmother about you."

At that Keith started laughing. The first real good laugh he'd had in days it seemed. It felt good. "That's the funniest thing I've heard all day."

* * * *

Rafe stood in the middle of the room surrounded by the sounds of people in misery. The lycans he was holding captive were Arnauk and Tairneach alike. He walked over to one of the women who was chained naked, on her knees, with her arms behind her. She immediately began growling at him, and he smiled at her unimpressed. He pulled a dagger from his belt and slowly ran the blade across the woman's naked breast, cutting deep. She refused to give him the pleasure of hearing her cry out. He looked at her with amusement. "Maybe if you continue to behave yourself you'll get lucky, and I'll keep you for myself." She spit at him. "It's either that or I give you to the troops. Trust me, no matter how unpleasant you think I might be, it could be worse. Have you ever considered what it would be like to be bent over by a were-elephant-bear? Just think, an elephant's size, strength of both, and the claws of a bear. It's an amazing sight." He grinned again and held up the bloody dagger. "A present for your mate. To keep him docile."

Rafe sheathed the blade and took it with him as he left the room and mounted the stairs. He had several things to attend to. Jenna would be mated to him that evening, then the rest of the Tairneach should fall in line. He figured that he could keep her around until he had complete control of the dogs, and then he could give her to one the men who had been eyeing her. She was attractive. She just wasn't his type. But she'd make a decent prize for someone.

Rafe intended to put the army together and head for the Arnauk reservation within the week. He'd been cheated out of his birth right for long enough. The stones were going to be his. He couldn't believe that the Circle had left it under the control of lycans all this time. The Circle Council would have to acknowledge him once he had possession of the stones. Then he'd force them to finish his training. One way or another. All that left was Aislinn, and he was about to resolve that as well. He opened the door to a room where a large lycan was sitting. "You haven't brought me what I asked for," he said sharply.

"Cullen hasn't let the woman out of his sight since she arrived. I need more time."

"You have 24 hours." With that he threw the blood coated dagger on the table. "It's still warm. If you return without the girl again it won't be." Then Rafe slammed out of the room.

* * * *

Jenna was pacing her room. She couldn't believe how uneasy she felt in her own house. Tears streaked down her cheeks continuously. She couldn't stop them. Since Rafe had killed her father everything in her died as well. Her ambition to rule had stemmed out of the fact that her father had never believed she was capable. She had just wanted to show him. Now he'd never see, and Rafe wouldn't have been here to kill her father if she hadn't brought him here. Jenna couldn't understand what the hold Rafe had on her was, but it seemed to wearing off because she could definitely see more clearly since she'd watched Rafe kill her father. More tears streamed down her cheeks.

The lioness was watching her warily. The girl was good. Kara saw the wheels turning in her head. When Rafe was present, the girl simpered and pleased. Then Rafe would leave and she would turn into a plotting galla. Kara had told Rafe about the quick change behavior, but he had his mind elsewhere. He was far too confident in his own abilities to see it as a threat. Kara resolved to keep a closer eye on Jenna.

Chapter 10

Bàthaidh toll beag long mhòr.
A little hole will sink a big ship.
-Gaelic Proverb

Rafe stood in the great room of the Tairneach manor. One thing he did like about Brennus Tairneach was his taste in decorating. The manor was huge and richly furnished. Everything was brocade, silk, antique, or plush. A grandfather clock on the wall began to chime. The moon was high and could be seen through the skylights in the ceiling of the great room. Every room in the manor seemed to have a fireplace. That was Rafe's favorite part about the manor. It was as though the fates had planned for him to be here. He was seriously considering having the cabin on the Arnauk reservation remodeled in this fashion. Large green tinted fires blazed in every fireplace, and no one questioned the oddity, even though the nights had been far too warm to justify lighting them.

Jenna stood in the middle of the room. She was naked except for a large ruby signet ring hanging from a thick gold chain around her neck. It had been her father's ring. Rafe had been gracious enough to let her keep it. Rafe walked up behind Jenna. He was in a relatively good mood, so he allowed her to wear the ring during the ceremony. He found it morbidly amusing in some way that he was about to mate with the girl while she was wearing the ring that had been on her father's hand when he died.

Rafe smiled as he thought about the look in Brennus's eyes when he died. Rafe pushed Jenna down to her hands and knees roughly. Then he dropped his pants and took up his position behind her. The movement brought some halting applause. Rafe was pleased by the turn out. He grabbed hold of Jenna's hair and yanked her head back as he thrust into her. She cried in pain as he forced himself into her dry cunt. She hadn't been ready for him. How could she be? He disgusted her, but this wasn't the time to fight him. Jenna knew that she'd have her chance soon enough. She stayed herself with the thought that she would be there to see him die.

Kara watched Jenna submit to the punishment that Rafe put her through. He appeared to be thoroughly enjoying himself. He seemed to be using this as practice for when he turned himself into what he was calling 'perfection'. Kara seethed with jealousy. The idea that Jenna wasn't appreciative of what Rafe was giving her was beyond Kara's ability to comprehend. Aislinn had baffled her the same way. Having Aislinn around had been worse though. Rafe actually wanted her.

Rafe continued to fuck Jenna until she finally responded. Jenna was doing her best to cooperate through her revulsion. She managed to imagine herself in a different enough situation that when she faked her orgasm he believed it. Rafe considered himself to have been infinitely generous, allowing Jenna to come first.

Rafe yanked her upright by her hair as he released into her. Positioning her the way he wanted, he bit down on the crease between her neck and her shoulder. Since he wasn't were yet, his teeth weren't exactly made for this part of the ceremony. He bit down hard on Jenna's shoulder, his teeth finally pierced her skin and drew blood. There was some additional applause at that point. He had at one time considered this ceremony to be barbaric, but now that he was in the middle of it he could see the appeal. He swallowed the blood readily, and then pulled away from Jenna to admire his handiwork.

Jenna had yet to fulfill her half of the mating. It wasn't as if this could work the way it was supposed to. He wasn't a lycan. She hadn't even bothered to take her wolf form. Rafe was only doing this because it would send a message to the pack. Jenna decided that the positive point about it was that at least she didn't have to force her brain believe this was an actual mating. She felt no bond with him. She was totally unsatisfied, and her wolf wasn't anywhere near interested in the situation. She took his arm in her hand and brought it to her mouth. She bit down just hard enough to draw blood, but she made sure that the wound would heal without scaring. She didn't plan on keeping him around for life.

The ceremony didn't last long at all. Rafe watched the weres he had created rut throughout the great room. There were a number of differences in the tendencies of each of the species. He vastly preferred the habits of the katta. The lycans tended to make each session of sex long, drawn out, and overly intimate. The cats liked theirs short, sweet, to the point and then they moved on.

Rafe and Jenna spent the rest of the evening mingling with their pack. Rafe was enjoying playing the part of the alpha male. Jenna was frustrated, angry, and ashamed. She tried several times to escape the ceremony, but Kara would appear and send her back into the mix. Rafe mostly ignored her after he finished fucking her. Various members of the pack approached her, and Jenna stood bored and indifferent as they knelt in front of her and showed their respect by pressing their faces against her sex and taking in her scent mingled with Rafe's.

Jenna couldn't help a grateful shiver when Maon approached her and spent a great deal of time licking her clit. He had been enraged by Rafe's treatment of Jenna that evening and pitied her. Besides, there were currently three women kneeling in front of the new alpha lapping at his latest erection. There was no way Jenna's scent was still clinging to Rafe after the little display they put on. The point of this half of the ceremony was for the pack to acknowledge the joining of the alpha pair. This certainly wasn't how it was normally done.

By the time dawn rolled around, Jenna was sent back to her room and Rafe retired to his. He had cleared his morning for sleep, but he had several appointments that afternoon. Then he would begin assembling the army.

* * * *

Sarah boarded the plane angrily. She sat in the seat fuming. She was still pissed when she took the taxi to the address that Aislinn had given her. She had more important things to be doing than collecting the grandmother of the alpha's bitch. Cullen had been insistent, however. He didn't know who to trust, and his solution to the problem was to only involve the people he thought needed to know. Sarah and Keith were the only two on that list right now. So Sarah was on her way to Brinah Senach's home, while Keith dealt with the information that Sarah had dug up on a couple of the elders.

Keith had been in the middle of a delicious dinner at Taigh-Olsda, talking about Aislinn's grandmother when Sarah had missed another meeting with Elise. She had managed pin down Ranaild's son Iain on the fact that his mother had been missing for quite some time. When Sarah tried to talk to Ranaild about it, he had also turned up missing.

Sarah though she should be the one looking into it since she had discovered it. Unfortunately, Cullen was adamant that Aislinn's grandmother be dealt with delicately. Keith was not the delicate type, and Sarah was the perfect candidate, in Cullen's eyes. *Well right now neither am I,* Sarah thought in annoyance. She had also suggested that Aislinn go after her own grandmother, but Cullen wasn't letting Aislinn out of the den for any reason. Aislinn had protested, loudly. That made Sarah less angry with Aislinn; however, it didn't change the situation. Cullen was the alpha and Cullen told Sarah to go.

Sarah told the taxi driver to wait while headed up a path that led to the front door of a pretty little white house. Before she had a chance to ring the bell on the door, it opened hastily. A small woman with gray-white hair, pulled nicely into a bun on the back of her head, and wearing jeans, a t-shirt that said 'don't underestimate me', and carrying a duffel bag appeared in the doorway. She eyed Sarah with the same striking blue eyes as Aislinn, nodded, and then locked the door.

Sarah was nearly bowled over by the woman as she headed for the taxi. "Are you coming," Brinah called back to the startled lycan.

Sarah got herself together and moved back down the path toward the taxi. Once they were both in the backseat, they exchanged introductions as the driver pulled out and drove to the airport. "I don't think I will," Sarah said, indicating the t-shirt. "You certainly weren't what I was expecting."

"And what were you expecting dear," Brinah said. Her tone and words belied the appearance that she was giving.

"I don't know. A grandmother," Sarah said. "I guess I can see where Aislinn gets it."

"I don't think I know what you mean by 'it,' but I'll take that as a compliment." Brinah looked out the window impatiently.

"We can't get there any faster. I got the earliest flight. We should be there by dinner." Sarah watched Brinah.

"I haven't seen my granddaughter in a very long time. You'll have to excuse my haste."

Sarah nodded. The rest of what she wanted to say to the woman would require privacy and that was something they wouldn't have until they were back at the den. Sarah and Brinah spent the rest of the trip in silence, save for a few pleasantries when it got too uncomfortable.

* * * *

Cullen wasn't willing to concede that any of the names on the list that Keith provided him could be in the process of betraying his loyalty. "I want more proof," he stormed, as he threw the list down on his desk. The names on the list were people who were too close to him. "I refuse to start ripping out throats until I know without doubt that these people have turned. Rafe has to have done something to them."

"You're the one who wants to believe Aislinn when she says that they won't do anything that they would be drastically disinclined to do in real life." Keith argued.

- 203 -

He thought that all of the men and women on the list should be caged for their own good until this was figured out. He didn't care who they were.

Cullen growled. "Is there anything else?"

"Not until Sarah gets back," Keith said.

"Good. I've had enough news for this afternoon. I'm going to find Aislinn."

Keith got up and walked with Cullen out into the hall. "You *find* Aislinn an awful lot you know," he said with a chuckle. "She in heat or something?"

Cullen rolled his eyes. "Do you have to make this into a joke?"

Keith shrugged. "No, I don't *have* to make it into a joke. It's just more fun that way." Keith's voice took on a mocking tone. "The mighty Lord General Cullen Arnauk chasing after a woman." He started chuckling again. "Actually, the best part is that she seems so clueless about the grip she has on you. I can't decide if it's denial, or if she's just that dense." Cullen growled a warning at Keith that caused him to start laughing again.

* * * *

Aislinn was getting seriously bored with the way things were turning out. Cullen refused to let her do anything that might put her in what he saw as danger. If she hadn't been sleeping with him, she probably would have put up more of a fight about it. But she just couldn't argue with him when he got that concerned, hurt tone in his voice and asked her to stay upstairs in the den for a little while longer. She was just too used to always having something to do. This sitting around was driving her nuts. All she did was think about the next time she would get to be with him. Those thoughts only made sitting around more miserable. She squirmed in her seat a little and looked around to see if anyone had noticed. She still couldn't decide why she was so infatuated with the guy. *Maybe I just don't know what's bad for me. First Rafe and now Cullen. He's a werewolf,* she told herself. *What am I doing?*

She growled to herself and turned the page of a decent book she had found in the library. At least there was plenty of entertainment on the main floor, even if no one except Rissa would talk to her. Aislinn fully planned on making Cullen let her have a job after this was all over. Alpha or not, she didn't see anything wrong with waiting tables at the Taigh-O\sda. That way she could feel useful. There was also the thought in the back of her mind that she'd like to have her own stash of cash somewhere, just in case. She couldn't help feeling like this couldn't possibly be real. She was waiting for Cullen to get tired of her and move on. With all the talk about the women who were after him, it was impossible for Aislinn to completely believe that he wanted her more than one of them.

She couldn't concentrate on the book she was reading and looked out the window instead. Every time a plane flew by, her stomach would jump. She couldn't wait to see her grandmother. It had been so long, and she missed her family so much. Aislinn tried to tell herself that they were safer this way, but that didn't make the hurt stop. Although, she had to admit, Cullen had been a fairly good bandage for that pain recently.

God, she thought, *and then there's Cullen again. Can't I stop thinking about him for just one minute?* Her heart nearly beat out of her chest. The way he touched her was more than she could handle. *I'm in love with him,* she finally admitted to herself as she stared out the window. *The question is if he feels the same and then what do I do about it.* According to Rissa an alpha male could choose any female he wanted. They generally tried to find a woman equal to their abilities who could compliment their position in the pack, but that wasn't a prerequisite. There was supposed to be someone out there that the fates intended for each of them. That didn't stop people from mating with whomever they liked. It just made matters more complex for the few lycans who put effort into trying to find the one who was meant for them. Rissa said that Cullen had been around a long time and had chosen not to mate on several occasions. At least one of those occasions had been badly handled. The girl had been wrongly given the impression that he was in love with her. Ever since that mismatch Cullen put a lot of effort into making sure that he spread himself thinly, so as not to accidentally make a girl think he was interested. Then there was the Jenna incident.

She was so lost in thought that she missed Celia's approach until it was too late. Celia took the book out of Aislinn's hands and tossed it aside. "We have some unfinished business little one. I'm surprised you're out and about all alone. Have you finally qualified for grown up status?"

Aislinn stared back at Celia. She had learned quite a bit about Celia. If the woman thought that Aislinn had just been sitting around doing nothing and waiting for Cullen to have time for her then Celia was mistaken. Aislinn had spent most of time quizzing Rissa about the supposed competition, and she was feeling pretty confident in her position with Celia at this point.

"I could say the same of you Celia. Doesn't Mack usually follow you around?" Aislinn's tone was haughty. She didn't bother to stand up. It wasn't necessary yet.

"I would be careful to not talk about things you don't understand little one," Celia growled in warning.

But Aislinn had been planning for this and wasn't about to pass up an opportunity to use the material she'd been preparing. "So I heard that you've turned him down three times now. That's either cruel or stupid. I mean I guess I kinda pity you. Do you actually prefer the idea of being alpha over mating with someone who you were meant to be with?"

Celia's eyes were wide and the anger that had been kindling in the back of them flared into a blazing fire. "You ignorant galla. You have no idea what you're talking about," she spat vehemently.

"I know that Mack believes you're his mate. If he's feeling it for you then you should most definitely be feeling it for him too. I think that the reason you're so pissy is because you want something you can't have, and at the same time you need something you won't accept." Aislinn flashed a superior smile at Celia. The people in the room who were listening to the conversation were starting to look frightened. Everyone thought exactly what Aislinn was saying, but no one had the courage to say it to Celia's face.

In a shadowy corner of the room Mack stood watching and listening. He decided that he very much liked Aislinn, and that she made an excellent match for Cullen. Now if only some of her common sense would rub off on Celia. Or at least shock her into reality. He readied himself to help Aislinn, just in case she couldn't back up her sharp tongue and smiled, hoping she'd torment Celia a little more.

Celia was struck dumb by Aislinn's gall. The only woman in this pack able, physically, to stand up to Celia was Sarah, and with good reason. No one was dense enough to talk to her this way. "You're not one of us. You have no rank. You have no right to speak to me this way," Celia growled menacingly.

"We haven't established that yet." Aislinn stood up at that point. "I should probably tell you that I had a dream last night. You will lose this fight." Aislinn had been doing a lot of dreaming lately. For the first time in years, she wasn't afraid to sleep, as long as Cullen was there. She didn't really know why, but Rafe didn't seem to be able to get into her head when she was with Cullen. There was something about being with him that made her feel stronger, more confident in herself. She didn't know if Rafe's inability to bother her was because of Cullen, or the way Cullen made her feel. Either way she was more rested than she had been in a long time.

Doubt flashed in Celia's eyes. Everyone in the pack had heard about what Aislinn was capable of. Celia considered that she may be bluffing to put her off guard. Then again if she wasn't and Celia started a fight and lost then she'd look like a fool. Celia hesitated. It was just long enough for Cullen and Keith to enter the room.

Cullen and Keith stopped when they saw the women standing toe to toe. Cullen growled a warning at Celia that Aislinn stopped with a pleading look. Keith started laughing again, and Celia stormed out of the room. Mack then appeared from a corner to go after her. He nodded at Aislinn as he left.

"I suppose it's good that you interrupted," Aislinn said, as she walked over to Cullen. "If Grandma came here and found me bruised there might be trouble."

"Then you two need to lay off the rough sex? That really is a shame," Keith chided.

Aislinn was getting used to his running commentary. Cullen ignored it so she didn't see why she should let it bother her. She slid her arms around Cullen's waist and nuzzled her face into his chest. Cullen responded by wrapping her in his arms and placing an affectionate kiss on top of her head. After everything Rissa had said about Cullen not touching women affectionately in public, every time he was like this with her she felt a little stronger in their relationship.

"Eww," Keith mocked. "Get a room."

"Don't tempt me," Cullen said. Then he looked at Aislinn with a wicked grin and raised his eyebrows.

"You serious," she asked incredulously. Things had been getting increasingly more intense between them. He didn't seem able to stop touching her. Not that Aislinn minded, but Rissa said behavior like that was how couples got just before mating. Aislinn didn't know what she thought about that, especially after learning how it was done. Besides, Cullen hadn't said a word about mating. Everyone else did. They joked and suggested and poked fun, when they knew Aislinn was in hearing distance. But Cullen never said anything about it. After everything Aislinn had been told about his habits with women, she still wasn't certain what he was doing with her. He was showing her a great deal more attention than anyone else he had been with in the past. However, he hadn't actually defined the situation, and she was scared to make him. As long as it was uncertain, she could still hope.

Cullen looked seriously hurt by her response. "If you're not interested then maybe an early dinner instead?" He was wondering if his wolf was making a mistake. She was always pulling back from him just enough to make him nervous. He wanted her so badly, but she seemed reluctant. He wasn't used to chasing women, as Keith had put it. He kept trying to come up with a magic thing to say that he knew she wouldn't be able to turn down. He didn't think he'd be able to handle it if he suggested mating, and she told him that she'd prefer to just be friendly. At the very same time, he knew that if friendly was all she wanted he'd take it for as long as she was willing to give it. *Life would be much easier if human over thinking didn't complicate wolf instinct,* he thought.

Keith dropped his eyes and looked embarrassed. It was a rare occasion that someone was capable of making the alpha obviously upset. It wasn't any fun to pick if it actually ended up hurting his friend. From the way Cullen sounded after Aislinn's reply there was no doubt that she'd stung him that time. Keith wasn't even sure what she had said that was so terrible. Cullen appeared to have lost his ability to read signals when it came to her. He was usually a savvy diplomat, and never showed when someone got to him. Keith often wondered if it was even possible to get under his skin. Keith had never seen Cullen lose his confidence so readily as when he was dealing with Aislinn.

Aislinn looked into Cullen's hurt expression. She hadn't meant anything by her response. "You just took me by surprise," she said apologetically. She smiled hopefully at him and softened her voice, hoping that Keith wouldn't hear her confession. "I don't actually think I'm capable of telling you 'no.'" Aislinn bit her lip. He didn't look like he believed her. Aislinn's brain raced to find a way to repair the misunderstanding and to get his smile back. She felt like her heart was being ripped in half by the upset look on his face.

"It's okay Aislinn," he said, trying to sound normal and reassuring. But the look in his eyes didn't match his voice. "You don't have to spread your legs for me every time I ask. Come on, we'll go to dinner." He started to pull her toward the door, trying to force a change in subject.

Aislinn was overwhelmed with frustration. *You stupid jerk,* she thought. *If I could arrange to never leave your bed I would.* Aislinn was so scared that she had just messed things up with Cullen that she did something she had been telling herself she'd never be able to do, no matter how long she might be here. People were always having sex out in public around here. She knew they wouldn't find anything she did embarrassing or unusual. That didn't change the fact that Aislinn had been raised with human ideals, and the idea of public sex sent butterflies fluttering through her stomach.

Aislinn stopped him and leaned into him. Her left hand on his shoulder urged him down so that her lips were right next to his ear. "If you don't believe what I said then maybe you'll believe what you feel," she said softly.

Cullen could hear a slight tremor in her voice. Her face had flushed, and he could feel her hand running down his arm. When her hand reached his she pulled it to herself. With what little confidence she could muster and praying that he didn't pull away from her and make her look like a complete fool, she guided his hand beneath the waistband of her jeans, inside her panties, and pressed his fingers into her slit. When she pulled her hand away to give him more room, his hand remained behind.

She started speaking into his ear again as his fingers slid into her wet folds. "I've been thinking about you all afternoon," she said. "I think that's pretty good proof."

Cullen knew that Aislinn was shy about sex in public. She had been easy to read on that. So it wasn't hard for him to see how far she had to push herself for this little display. The only problem was that his wolf wasn't concerned about her modesty factor, and he had been thinking about her as well. He growled with pleasure into her ear and buried his face against her neck as his fingers slid deeper into her wet heat and his thumb played with her clit. His other arm came around behind her and pulled her against himself so that she could feel the desire growing in his pants.

Their passion was palpable. More than one person in the room was watching the display, entranced.

Cullen growled again as her rapid breathing in his ear spurred him on. "I need you *now*."

"All right," Aislinn answered breathlessly without hesitation. His fingers were driving her mad. Somehow she just didn't care about where they were any longer.

In one sudden movement, Cullen pushed her against a nearby wall and his wolf pushed her jeans off over her hips. He pulled his cock out of the front of his pants and picked Aislinn up. His fast movements showed how much he wanted her. Her legs wrapped around his waist, her back on the wall gave leverage, and in one fluid movement he entered her warm, slick, needy body. Aislinn's growling, cat-like, moan of pleasure was the sweetest music he ever heard. She sang to his wolf. The beast was even starting to accept being caged while making love to her. He'd do anything to get a taste of her. Once he had her wrapped around him Cullen was able to gain some measure of control and his movements become slow and purposeful. He took his time, pumping into her in long strokes so that he rang more of the sweet sounds out of her.

Aislinn's strange growl had everyone's attention. The couple was far too caught up in the sudden passion overload to notice the looks that they were drawing. Cullen kissed and nuzzled her neck as he slowly made love to her. The onlookers' discussion of what kind of animal made the sounds she was making was getting quite involved. As the couple started to get more intense, the keening cat-growl got louder. Finally Cullen forced his name from her with a long hard thrust as she came, and he followed her into pleasure.

As the people in the room watched him come inside her there was a shift in conversation from confusion about what the hell the girl was to amusement over the fact that their alpha had just made such a blatant physical statement about how he felt for her. Keith smiled at the two of them. That was the moment that he decided, whatever Aislinn was or what trouble she may cause, he would be putting up with it. Cullen had waited too long and had almost lost his chance to find a mate he could care about. If he wanted Aislinn this badly, who was Keith to complain about it? Keith stood there, a bit misty eyes out of happiness for the big fool, and waiting for them to gather themselves so that they could all get something to eat.

Cullen braced himself against the wall and held her up. Aislinn's face was buried in his shoulder out of exhausted passion and uncertain embarrassment. When Cullen managed to get a grip on his legs he held her to himself and headed for a nearby armchair. He sat down with Aislinn straddling him. There was just enough room in the armchair for both of them. He smiled at her. His amber eyes met her silver and they started kissing again.

Cullen's tongue delved into her mouth. He couldn't believe that she had given in to him in the middle of the library. He smiled as she continued to kiss him and he stared at her with an amused considering look. He knew she had no idea how much what they had just done meant, not just to him, but what it said to the people who were watching as well.

"What," she asked breathlessly. Then she ground her hips down on his rapidly re-hardening member.

"You amaze me, mo mhúirnín bán," he said softly. "You didn't have to do that."

She was still kissing him, trying to coax him into round two. "Does it feel like I didn't want to," she asked in between kisses.

He chuckled and pulled her hips down hard on himself as he lifted up to meet her. A satisfied growl issued from his throat. He was staring into her eyes again. Aislinn stopped her insistent sexual onslaught and stared back at him. Their eyes were mirrors of each other's uncertainty and desire.

When Keith saw Cullen pulling Aislinn's shirt over her head, he let out an exasperated sigh. "Looks like dinner is on an undetermined hold," he said to no one in particular. There was a round of laughter in the room that the couple didn't notice. Keith started to check out the books on a nearby shelf. He figured he'd give them a little time before insisting that they get it together. The public show would go a long way with the rest of the pack. The people who loved and respected Cullen would be happy for him, the ones who thought Aislinn was doing something to his brain would see exactly what she was doing, and that it had nothing to do with mental manipulation, either way it would get her some more respect. *Ah politics,* Keith thought as he picked a book and sat down to wait.

* * * *

For once Sarah's plane was running on time. That never happened. Sarah and Brinah managed to even catch a taxi in short order and they were at the den well in time for dinner. The Madadh-Allaidh Saobhaidh was not wasted on Brinah. She was shocked into an impressed silence at the den's setup.

They got into the elevator. Sarah inserted her key and hit the button for 14. "I'll show you your room. Then we'll find Aislinn and Lord Arnauk. I'm sure he'll want to have dinner downstairs. He always does." She smiled at Brinah. Sarah was dying to start the conversation and get some answers, however it had been a long morning and then a long afternoon and they were both tired and hungry. But mostly Brinah was in a hurry to see Aislinn. Sarah sympathized. She didn't know what she would do if someone close to her vanished and then popped up again several years later in as much trouble as that girl had managed to get involved in.

"Does the entire pack live here," Brinah tried at polite, non substantial conversation.

"No, but most spend time here at some point. There's room for everyone if need be." Sarah had arranged for Brinah to have a room on floor 14. There were several guest rooms there, and it was a lot quieter than the main floor. They dropped her bags off in a room that Brinah thought might belong in the Hilton. There was a small sitting area with a television, chairs and an overstuffed couch, a walk in closet on the far wall, and a large private bathroom. Everything was conservatively, but beautifully decorated in navy and green. The huge bed had large comfortable, inviting pillows, and Brinah nearly said that maybe it'd be okay to find Aislinn in the morning.

"Are you sure this is my room," Brinah asked with a smile at Sarah.

"Definitely like Aislinn," Sarah said in amazement. Brinah had the same confident but friendly demeanor that made Aislinn so outgoing. She was just a bit more abrasive than Aislinn. Sarah could see Aislinn aging into Brinah quite easily. She shrugged as she looked around. "These are just guest quarters. The casino does very well."

Brinah nodded in amusement. "Lord Arnauk has managed quite well for all of you then."

Sarah knew that Brinah had no clue that Aislinn had gotten involved with Cullen. Sarah hadn't intended to set things up to be any easier for the two of them, but she couldn't help supporting her alpha when given the opportunity. "Lord Arnauk does well by all of us. He's a business man, diplomat, warrior, politician, and anything else the pack needs. There isn't a more prosperous or influential pack on this continent," she said with pride.

Brinah considered Sarah's tone during the little informative lecture as they got back in the elevator and wondered what she was missing. When they got out on the 13th floor the entire place was buzzing. Sarah explained to Brinah that the 13th floor was the main area of the den. She was telling Brinah about the different recreational rooms on the floor and was in the process of telling Brinah that Aislinn seemed to be spending a great deal of time in the library. Sarah felt like a tour guide. "I figure that Aislinn will be easier to find than Lord Arnauk. He's usually dealing with the latest conflict. Aislinn spends a lot of time reading." Brinah was smiling, eager to see her granddaughter.

When they walked into the library most of the crowd that had gathered for Aislinn and Cullen's scene had dispersed. There was one couple rutting in a back corner of the library. Keith was sitting in a large armchair near the door thumbing through a book with a devilish smile on his face. He noted the time when Cullen and Aislinn had fallen asleep in the chair, but he wasn't about to be the one to interrupt. Not after the little argument that had preceded the show. When he saw Sarah and the elderly woman come in, he jumped and ran to intercept.

Sarah looked at Keith with frustration as he tried to turn them both out of the library. Brinah stopped dead and turned on him. "Young man, I don't know who you are. But you can stop what you're doing and explain yourself," she snapped.

Sarah glared at Keith. "What she said. But I would like to add, do you know where Aislinn or Cullen is?"

She could tell from the look on Keith's face that something was up.

"Uh, yeah," Keith fumbled. "Why don't you let me get them for you. Just wait in the great room. It'll only take a minute."

But Brinah caught sight of the back of Aislinn's head and refused to be ushered out of the room.

* * * *

Cullen's head was lounged back against the chair and his eyes were closed. His hand was trailing gentle petting strokes up and down Aislinn's spine. He didn't think he had ever been this comfortable in the whole of his life. Aislinn was still straddling him. He was still inside her and he was entirely unwilling to let her move. She had tried twice, but he growled and pulled her back to himself. He was taking the afternoon off.

Aislinn finally gave up and had fell asleep on his chest as he petted her. She was curled against him with her head snuggled securely against his shoulder and her arms folded against him at his waist so that she was almost hugging him. He held her tightly and listened to her breathing. He could barely make out what sounded almost like a purr each time she breathed. It had started when he began stroking her bare back. He was trying different patterns of stroking, to find one to make the sound louder. He didn't really understand why the little sound pleased him so much. Then again, everything about her seemed to please him. He was listening intently to her and ignoring all else.

He had completely forgotten that they were expecting Aislinn's grandmother. At that moment, he didn't care what Jenna or Rafe was up to. He believed that he would be happy for the rest of his life if he could just stay there holding her and trying to make her purr.

The gruff throat clearing that caught his attention had him wanting to kill the owner of the voice. He ignored it, assuming that it was Keith. When someone tapped the hand he was using to stroke Aislinn's back, he got really mad. He opened his eyes to deliver one of his patented glares to the intruder, only to find himself staring at an elderly looking woman with Aislinn's startling blue eyes.

Cullen took in a deep breath. *This is probably not the best way to meet her family,* he thought. When he started to move Aislinn rumbled her dislike of his change in position, and he settled back down.

Brinah was obviously not happy. There were voices warring inside her head. One said that this was perfectly normal behavior for lycans. The next voice pointed out that Aislinn was not a lycan. Then there was the voice that said how much he appeared to adore her. That was countered with the fact that if he cared as much as he appeared to, by the look on his face and the way he held her, that he would not have put her in this kind of position. It had been a long time since Brinah had been exposed to this kind of behavior. She understood that this was the way lycans behaved, and if she had raised her daughter and granddaughter as druids then this type of thing would have been common place there as well. At the same time, Aislinn had been raised human, and this was not how humans behaved. She didn't know whether to admonish or accept. She settled on the one thing that would have been common to all three species. She softly asked Cullen a very simple question. She didn't want to wake Aislinn.

Yet. "What exactly are your intentions toward my granddaughter young man?"

Keith thought he was going to die. The glares that Brinah was doling out were incredible, but the 'young man' thing was priceless. He was trying his best to muffle his laughter when Cullen started squirming. In the silence, Brinah added, "You do that and you'll wake her up. Just answer my question."

Cullen felt trapped. He was pinned and being questioned by a girl's grandmother. *How the hell did I get into this?* He thought.

Aislinn lay perfectly still. She had no intention of facing her grandmother like this. There was no way she was opening her eyes until she figured a way out of this, even if she had to play dead. She had never been this embarrassed in her entire life. She hoped that Cullen wouldn't take offense, but she wouldn't be doing this again anytime soon and that was all there was to it. She felt like she was going to be sick.

Brinah stared at him expectantly. Finally Cullen decided that honesty would be best. All he had was the truth. "I don't know. We haven't gotten to that conversation yet."

Brinah's eyes flared with anger. "Don't you think that's something you should have talked about before turning her into the afternoon entertainment?"

"That's not what it was like," he whispered back just as angry. He couldn't believe how much of Aislinn's attitude was being handed to him through her grandmother. Brinah's eyes were flashing and she talked to him as though he was child. He felt like a teenager who had just been caught having sex with his girlfriend by the girl's shotgun toting parent. He had human television to thank for that image.

"Well. I'm going to tell you what it will be like." Brinah fumed. "I am going to step out that door and you are going to wake her up and get her dressed, so that when I come back in, I can say hello to my granddaughter with some semblance of decorum. And, at some point very soon, you and I are going to talk about what you think you are doing with her." Then Brinah turned on her heal and headed out the door. Sarah followed her out into the hall, but was smart enough not to say anything. Brinah was talking to herself angrily the entire time they waited.

Cullen could tell that Aislinn was awake. Her breathing had changed repeatedly throughout the short conversation. "You can open your eyes now possum," he said softly.

When Aislinn looked up at him, she had turned a brilliant beet red blush that made him smile. "I can't believe Grandma found us like this. I think I'm going to die," she said aloud. *And what do you mean, you don't know what you're doing with me,* she thought.

Cullen shook his head. "I won't let you do that. Just put your clothes back on. It'll be fine. I'll take the heat." Cullen saw the concern in her eyes and wondered if it was entirely her grandmother that caused it.

Aislinn jumped up and grabbed her clothes from the floor where they'd been thrown, blushing repeatedly as she accidentally made eye contact with various people about the library. When she and Cullen were fully dressed, Cullen went over to the door and pulled it open. Brinah glared at him heavily and walked into the room, headed straight for Aislinn. Before anything could be said, she grabbed Aislinn into a hug that nearly forced all the air out of Aislinn's chest. After some time, she pulled away and stared at Aislinn a moment.

"Well, child, you certainly do look to be in one piece. I have missed you so much," she said and hugged Aislinn again.

"I missed you too grandma." Aislinn said still blushing. "I don't even know where to begin."

"Well," Brinah smiled at her, "why don't you introduce me to your friend, and then we'll go find Lord Arnauk. It's been a long time, but I do remember some of my schooling. Pack etiquette says I should really have gone to talk to him first, seeing as I'm in his house. Then we can do all the story-telling that needs to be done." She was standing there staring at Aislinn unblinking, as though Aislinn might disappear. Cullen, Keith, and Sarah were impressed with Brinah's statement. They never would have expected her to know anything about pack life.

"Uh, okay, grandma this is Lord Arnauk," she said, indicating Cullen.

Brinah's eyes caught fire again. "Now I definitely want to know what you think your intentions are," she said angrily.

Aislinn blushed again. "Grandma, it doesn't matter what his intentions are. Can't we just go sit down and talk about what we need to talk about?" Cullen didn't like the way she said that it didn't matter. The terrible feeling that his wolf was wrong started to creep into his stomach again. *Way to ruin an afternoon,* he growled at himself.

Brinah interrupted Aislinn. "Child you can't possibly know what you're dealing with here. It's more important than you can possibly realize. As far as I'm concerned, I came here to protect you and it looks as though I'm a bit late. Rafe and now this?"

Keith was chuckling, and Sarah was looking pained. Cullen for his part was completely bowled over by the fact that now he had two women who didn't seem to understand that when he was in the room they were supposed be intimidated, let him talk, and behave with subdued respect. He had never fully appreciated that luxury of his position until now, as all the lycans in the room looked on. "Enough," he said with emphasis and managed to get the women's attention.

Brinah's glare got much worse, and she placed herself between Aislinn and Cullen. That was a big mistake. Cullen started to growl. His wolf was concerned that Brinah may try to take Aislinn away. As far as he knew, Aislinn might actually go with her. Brinah was her grandmother and so far Aislinn hadn't said whether she intended to stay or not. But the look on her face when she called her grandmother and talked about her family had been plain enough. Cullen considered that he would do anything for her. If she wanted to go back to her family, then he should help her to do that. A pain started in his chest then he thought about that.

"Alpha or not, you don't get to talk to me like that or growl at me. You need my help and you won't get it being threatening. I have every right to protect my own, and you should have some respect for that," Brinah said with an air of authority that made Cullen back off a little. "I asked you what your intentions are."

Aislinn started to say something again and tried to move passed her grandmother to get to Cullen, but she was cut off before she started to talk and then blocked before she could move. It was a talent that she figured must be born out of being a parent.

Sarah elbowed Keith to stop the laughter and then indicated that he should help her clear the room. It was obvious that the group would not be getting out of this argument without trouble, and it was one of those arguments that might not go quite as badly if the witnesses were limited.

"Regardless of my intentions," Cullen replied, trying to remain calm. "I don't think Aislinn would allow anything that she didn't intend."

That comment went a lot farther with Brinah than Cullen realized. The alpha's acknowledgement that Aislinn had a choice in the matter settled her anger quite a bit. But Brinah wasn't done. "You're behaving very possessive of my granddaughter. Do you intend to mate with her?" Cullen wasn't sure whether he should be pissed by Brinah's attitude or impressed by her apparent knowledge.

Aislinn felt her grandmother's words sting in her chest. "Grandma, please," she said softly. She couldn't believe this was happening.

Cullen looked at Aislinn. This wasn't how he intended to have this conversation. He had no idea what to say. He didn't want to scare her off. He wished he knew what she was thinking, but a bond had to be pretty strong for that and would only happen if he mated with her. He rubbed his face with his hands. Aislinn recognized the move as something he did when he didn't know what to say or was upset. She was getting pretty good at reading some of the things he did.

Brinah wasn't about to back down, and she reiterated the question. "Do you intend to mate with her? I think we both have a right to know."

Aislinn couldn't take it. If he really didn't want to say, then she didn't think he should have to. Before Cullen could respond Aislinn moved around to face her grandmother. "Grandma. I love you, and I've missed you. I don't want you to take this wrong, but I can handle myself. Cullen and I get along very well and he makes me happy. If he doesn't want to take things farther, then that I'm okay with that. I need you to leave this be. I'm not a child who needs to be protected in this way. We have a much more dangerous problem then my love life right now."

Brinah could see the pleading in Aislinn's eyes, and she didn't want this to come between them when she had only managed to get her granddaughter back just moments before. "All right, I'll let it be for now." Brinah hugged Aislinn close to her again, but continued to glare at Cullen over her shoulder.

Cullen was relieved and dismayed by Aislinn's interruption. There was a part of him that just wanted to say it and get it over with, but the part that was afraid of rejection still held him by the balls. He was thinking about the way she had phrased what she'd said. He decided that one way or another, he had to get up the courage to tell her that he loved her. And it needed to be soon. Or at least before her grandmother killed him.

Cullen led the group back to his office, ordered up dinner from the Taigh-O\sda, and the rest of the evening was spent filling Brinah in on the last seven years of Aislinn's life and the latest information about Rafe.

Chapter 11

Every guilty person is his own hangman.
-Lucius Annaeus Seneca

For the most part, Sarah and Keith had been supporting Aislinn being in the pack because Cullen so obviously wanted her there. He was the alpha, and if he wanted this non-lycan outsider then whether they thought it was a good idea or not, Keith and Sarah backed him. He rarely asked the pack to just do something because he said so. Besides, she seemed to make him happy, and they were his friends. They had never taken the time to talk to Aislinn because they talked to Cullen. Sarah and Keith had heard the edited version of Aislinn's story from Cullen during the elders' meeting, but hearing the detailed version from her own lips was much more compelling. They found themselves feeling for her and actually wanting to help.

Brinah's eyes were wide and she looked as though she may cry. Aislinn tried to gloss over some things, but Brinah seemed to have an innate sense of when she was skipping ahead and forced the extra information out. The only thing she was able to keep from her grandmother was the fact that Rafe had done something to 'change' her. She couldn't bring herself to let her grandmother know how different things really were. She knew that her grandmother was looking for a way to bring her home. Brinah was shaking her head and looking scared when the entire rendition, from Rafe creating his own Circle, to his obsession with Aislinn, and now finding the standing stones, was finished.

Brinah let all her air out as if she hadn't breathed for the past hour. "You are all in a great deal more danger than you have any idea. I suppose," she said in a defeated tone, "I would be talking to air if I suggested that you abandon this place and take shelter somewhere far away."

Cullen growled at that. "We're not druids. We don't run and hide."

Brinah looked at him with fear painted in every feature on her face. "Then you put all your lives in danger."

* * * *

Ranaild entered the lobby of Madadh-Allaidh Saobhaidh. He felt like his life was coming to an end. To some extent he figured that one way or another he would be dead. Either Rafe would kill him, or Cullen would kill him. Hell Aislinn was rumored to have closet fighting abilities. Maybe she would kill him. Any way it happened, he would probably be dead by the end of this. He may even have to kill himself if he couldn't find a way out. He had done his best to avoid harming anyone. But with the dagger coated in his mate's blood tucked into the back of his jeans to give him the strength to go through with his assignment he headed for the elevator, inserted his key, and hit the button for the 13th floor.

As the elevator proceeded up, it stopped at the 3rd floor. A human couple stared at the stormy faced lycan in the elevator. One look at the man had them deciding to wait for the next one.

When the elevator finished its agonizing ascent to the main floor of the den, Ranaild nearly vomited on the floor. He walked unsteadily into the great room. Everyone who saw him got out of his way. They didn't know why Ranaild was upset, but he wasn't a lycan to mess with when he was angry. He was one of Cullen's best men, and a pack elder. They assumed that whatever the problem was, it would be above their heads. No one even asked what was wrong.

Ranaild asked an omega where Cullen and Aislinn were. When he was told that they were in an office meeting, just down the hall, he decided to take a seat and wait. He just needed an opportunity.

* * * *

Cullen stared at Brinah with angry fire. "I don't accept that as an option."

Brinah glared right back. "Then you're a fool."

"The druids were never so powerful that what you're suggesting could be possible." Cullen was speaking with a deadly calm, and his features had taken on the stony look he got when dealing when someone he was trying to intimidate and control. Brinah was unimpressed by Cullen's appearance. That all by itself was impressive, but it reminded Cullen of Aislinn's fire and softened his demeanor toward Brinah slightly.

"We've told you why we brought you here. Now you need to tell us what you know about Rafe, and what we can do about his mind altering caoch. Then if you don't want to stick around and find out how it'll turn out that's your call."

Brinah's eyes narrowed. "I find it interesting that Aislinn did all the talking, and the story was for the most part hers, for years, before you all came into the picture, accidentally. It's interesting that you seem to count her as one of you. If anything she's a watered down druid. Not a lycan."

"That doesn't change the fact that Rafe is trying to take a piece of my territory. Stop trying to alter the subject. I'm getting the impression that you may not be able to be as helpful as you originally seemed to indicate. If the only reason you told us you could help was so you could come here and attempt to take her home with you, I'm afraid you'll find that Rafe is more intent on getting his hands on her than you understand. You'd be risking both your lives leaving. Your presence here now negates the possibility of leaving without the danger of him following you."

Aislinn found Cullen's calm strange to watch. He was always so passionate with her, it was as though he was another person. She didn't like the way her grandmother and Cullen were arguing. "That's enough, both of you! Grandma, you said you could help us make something."

Brinah looked at her granddaughter. Her eyes were searching Aislinn's. Cullen wasn't the only one referring to her as being with them. She was afraid she had permanently lost her granddaughter, and she had only just gotten her back. A tear formed in the corner of her eye. She leaned toward Aislinn and reached out to put her hand on her cheek. "If you choose this life here, you'll never be able to go home Aislinn. There are a great many people there who love and miss you."

Aislinn's breath caught in her throat. Cullen sat there waiting for her response. She didn't even look at him. If she managed to get away from all of this, and he dealt with Rafe, she could very easily go back to her life with her family. Rafe hadn't changed her enough to make a human existence impossible. Cullen watched her with her grandmother, and he saw the loss in her eyes. She didn't want to make the decision. He knew from the way she had spoken to him about her mother and her grandmother before that she missed them all terribly. He could easily understand that. He knew how he would feel if he was pulled out of the pack. Even so, he would willingly leave it all for her. He couldn't make her make that choice. Especially, since she didn't seem nearly as interested in being here as he was in having her here.

After a silent pause that seemed to last an eternity, Cullen shifted in his chair. His voice softened significantly, but his face went more stony, if that was even possible. There was no emotion to be seen in his eyes. The stranger Aislinn was looking at made her go numb. "All right. Brinah, you show us what we need to do to make something to stop Rafe's mind altering abilities. When we deal with him, and it is safe, you and Aislinn can go home."

The look on Aislinn's face when he said that ripped into him, even if no one could see it. How could he do that? Was he just going to shove her out the door? "Isn't that my decision to make," Aislinn said in a cracking voice.

Cullen's stomach turned. "I'm not going to ask you to leave your family for this," he responded.

"So you're done with me. Just like the others." Aislinn couldn't stop the tear that dropped from her eye. She stood up and walked away from his desk. She had expected it to happen, but not this soon. Aislinn thought about the afternoon they'd just had. *Not now,* she thought. *Not when I've finally let my guard down.*

"This is nothing like the others," he said.

"Right," she answered, then walked out of the office, slamming the door behind her as she left. The shock wave that rolled through the room made Cullen flinch. He almost went after her. Almost. He decided that she needed to cool off, and if he was going to go through with this then chasing her would give her the wrong impression. *I'll talk to her when we're done here,* he thought. With more effort than anyone would ever know he turned his attention back to Brinah, Sarah, and Keith.

* * * *

Aislinn stomped down the hall into the elevator and hit the lobby button. She needed to get out of here and get some air. She knew there wasn't anywhere inside this building that she could hide, and she just didn't want to deal with her thoughts right now.

Ranaild only barely made it into the elevator before the door closed. She shot him a teary eyed glare when he joined her. It nearly broke his heart. Whatever had happened in that office wasn't going to make his intentions any easier.

Neither of them spoke. He didn't really want to talk to her. If he started feeling too bad for her, he might change his mind. Ranaild wasn't sure how she managed to get out of Cullen's sight, but there was no way he could pass this up. When the doors opened again, he wondered why the fates seemed so damned determined to give Rafe what he wanted. Aislinn slipped through the lobby straight for the front doors. Ranaild followed her. He couldn't believe how easy she was making this.

She took off out the doors of the Madadh-Allaidh Saobhaidh, and then down the sidewalk. She wrapped her arms around herself. The cool air was helping. She was trying desperately not to cry. *I knew it,* she thought. *Nothing in my life ever stays good. I don't know why I let myself get so attached so quickly. I knew that something would ruin it.* Her brain was swimming, and she just wanted it to stop. She didn't even notice Ranaild following her down the sidewalk.

Ranaild decided to let her get as far from the den as possible before he took her. She was moving at a good clip. From what he could tell there wasn't anyone else following her. He kept looking behind them and watching. He sniffed at the air, but didn't catch wind of any pursuit. He seemed to be in the clear.

Finally, Aislinn stopped on a corner. There was a taxi sitting and waiting for a fare. Ranaild stepped up behind her and took her by the arm. She looked up at him with a shocked, angry glare. He returned an apologetic look, as he pulled the dagger from behind him and brought it covertly around to jab into her side. Her anger turned to fear as she realized what was happening.

Ranaild guided her toward the taxi. "Open the door," he said in a frightening flat tone, pressing the dagger further into her side. Aislinn silently did as she was told. They both got into the taxi and Ranaild gave the driver directions to where he wanted to go.

Aislinn looked down at the dagger, covered in dried blood, which was pressing into her side. Then she looked back up at Ranaild. She knew him. She often saw him talking to Cullen. She knew that Cullen had trusted him.

* * * *

Celia watched as Ranaild sat brooding in the chair he'd angled so that he could watch the hallway. He was acting strangely. Everyone who had been in the elder meeting knew the possibility of one of their own being on the wrong side of all the mess that was going on. The rumors had everyone in the pack on edge. Celia thought about that as she watched Ranaild.

There had been a reason that Cullen had taken her as a lover and companion. Ultimately she was one of the best in the pack. She had earned her position the hard way. She was intelligent, observant, and devious enough to see it in other people when sometimes it was overlooked. Ranaild was acting just strangely enough to get her attention.

When Aislinn came out of Cullen's office in tears and Ranaild rushed after her, Celia watched with an uneasy realization that he might be one of the traitors. She couldn't believe it. Ranaild? Celia went over to the elevator panel and watched only long enough to see where the elevator stopped. Then she hit the stairs. She flew down the flights of stairs as fast as she could. She knew she wouldn't catch up if she waited for the next elevator, but she might be able to track them if she got to the lobby before the scent was lost in the throng of people coming and going.

Mack watched Celia dart for the stairwell and immediately trailed after her. He didn't really know what she was up to. but it was a rare occasion that she ran anywhere. He was going to find out where she was going.

Celia almost raised the alarm, but she couldn't bring herself to it without proof of what she thought she was seeing. She had been friends with Ranaild and Elise, his mate, for too long to do that to him and his family if it wasn't true. At the same time, if it was true she'd rip his throat out herself. Elise? When was the last time she'd spoken with Elise? The thought was fleeting, gone the minute she came slamming out the lobby doors.

Celia headed for the elevator and immediately picked up Aislinn's scent. She'd know that galla anywhere. When she saw Mack come through the stairs' doors and into the lobby she swore to herself. *Doesn't he have anything better to do?*

"Whatcha up to Cel," Mack said nonchalantly as he approached her.

"Mind your own-," Celia started. Then she thought better of it. If what she was thinking about Ranaild was true, it might not be bright to chase after him alone. "Caoch," she swore. "Just come on. Follow me and try and keep out of sight."

Mack knew it must be serious when Celia stopped herself from trying to get rid of him. He nodded and followed her out. He picked up on Ranaild's scent as they went, and it only took him a minute to recognize Aislinn's as well. Everyone in the pack had caught the new girl's smell. She was weird, hard to place. The rumors about her being 'not quite human' had everyone looking to get a whiff.

Twice Ranaild almost saw them. Celia's heart was racing. She stood behind the newsstand and hid, waiting for him to keep going before continuing to follow him. "I can't believe it. He really is following her. That piece of caoch."

"What the hell is going on here Celia?" Mack asked with a growing fear of what she was going to say.

Celia looked around the corner. Seeing that Ranaild was moving again and watching Aislinn, she pulled Mack along behind her and headed after them. "I don't really know. Ranaild is following Aislinn. I don't know where Aislinn is going, but it's all too weird," she said hurriedly.

Mack grabbed her by the arm, hard, and stopped her. He pulled Celia to face him, and she lost sight of Ranaild. She fought Mack's grip, but couldn't manage to move him. Ranaild was one of his closest friends. Celia did a lot of stuff that pissed him off, but this was the limit. "Don't you even suggest what I think you're suggesting. Aislinn shouldn't be out here. If he's following her, he's probably just keeping an eye on her."

"Well we'll never know that now," Celia said angrily, as she wrenched her arm free and ran off in the direction in which they had disappeared.

Mack came walking up behind her. She was pacing the sidewalk where the scents mingled and then ended. "They got into a car," he said.

"Faigh muin! I caught that myself. I never should have brought you. You didn't see the way he looked."

"I know that Ranaild wouldn't do what you're suggesting."

"You didn't see the way he looked." Celia paced. It didn't feel right. "I agree with you. It doesn't make sense. Ranaild has never... He wouldn't... Would he?" The confusion in her voice concerned Mack.

"I don't think so. Look, if Aislinn is actually missing then the entire place will be in an uproar. Cullen is far too gone over her. I'm betting that Ranaild is just keeping an eye on her. We'll head back. If there aren't alarms going off, and warnings of Cullen bringing the apocalypse down on us all if we don't produce her from the shadows, then I think we can safely say that this isn't what you think it looks like."

Celia didn't want to, but she let him talk her into heading back and seeing. *What do I care anyway? If Aislinn ends up gone, then things can go back to normal.* She didn't even realize that she was leaning into Mack as they walked down the sidewalk, and she didn't think about how his words had been more reassuring than they should have been. She hated how much she liked him. She growled under her breath.

When they got out of the elevator on the 13th floor and walked into the great room, nothing seemed amiss. "I guess maybe," Celia said looking around. Cullen was still in the meeting with Keith, Sarah, and that human woman Sarah had brought up. More odd rumors. She was getting tired of all the secrets. It wasn't like Lord Arnauk. *Lord Arnauk*, she thought. Her mind took on a mocking tone, *Aislinn wouldn't continue sleeping with a man who wouldn't let her use his name.*

"You guess maybe what?" Mack asked smugly, smiling at her.

"You're probably right," Celia snapped. "There. You happy?" *Gods why can't I shut my brain off? How many times did he tell me that he'd never mate with me? Why did I think that I could change his mind if I just kept myself available. Is he an asshole, am I a complete fool, or both?*

"Both," Mack said out loud.

Celia didn't realize she had been projecting. But Mack had always picked up on her thoughts so easily it didn't really surprise her that he'd heard, but it did embarrass her sometimes. "I'd thank you to keep your opinions of what you know I don't intend to say to yourself."

"Cel, why do you fight me so hard? Is the fact that I'm not the alpha really that bad? You wanna break off and form our own pack? It's not like we couldn't manage. I just always thought that the family we had here was more important than rank. But you tell me what you want to do, I'll do it."

Mack's sincerity seeped into her. She knew he'd do anything she asked him to do. Ambition aside she did care about him. She hated to admit it, but she did. She growled and rolled her eyes. The worst part was that she was going into heat. She hadn't been with anyone in so long, and it was really getting to her. The little chase they went on didn't help much either. "Come back to my room. We'll discuss reality later," she offered begrudgingly.

Mack leaned into her and tilted his head cautiously to the side, as he slipped an arm around her waist and bent down to kiss her. She hadn't let him touch her since that time they had been out at the reservation on a hunt, and they nearly ended up mated. They had been so into each other that night. Cullen had thrown her over for one of the other girls, and Celia had gone with Mack for lack of another option. He thought he was going to catch fire when she moved into him for the kiss. Her hands slipped up his shoulders and grabbed the material of his shirt fiercely.

In seconds the kiss went from experimental and tentative to explosive passion. Celia's tongue delved into his mouth and danced with his. Without breaking the kiss, Mack picked her up by the waist, and her legs wrapped around him. He backed them into the elevator, and they fumbled for the key to the panel. Mack had to put her down as they exited the elevator and stumbled down the hall for her room. Both of their eyes swirled amber.

Celia's door slammed behind them, and she began tearing at Mack's clothes. He grinned, watching as she ripped them to pieces and pushed him back toward the bed. Celia knew that he was stronger than her. He was letting her run the show to prove a point, but at that moment she didn't care. Her clothes quickly followed his in shreds onto the floor.

Mack found himself pushed back onto her bed. The scent of her overwhelmed him. He'd never managed to get into her room before. He just hoped she'd be this enthusiastic about him when it was all said and done. Any way it turned out though, he knew he'd wait for her forever if he had to. Celia looked down at Mack's form on her bed. She couldn't decide what she wanted to do to him most, until she caught the look in his eyes. The first thing she wanted was to wipe that adoring gaze off his face.

Celia climbed onto the bed, and much to Mack's delight she turned away from him, then straddled his face. She pressed her sopping sex down onto his mouth while she leaned down and took his cock into her mouth. Mack grabbed hold of Celia's writhing hips and plunged his tongue into her. Dying for a better taste, he let his wolf slide out into his hybrid form. Celia moaned with delight as his cock grew in her mouth. She licked around its head, and then plunged back down onto it. Mack's tongue was much longer and more maneuverable than his human tongue. He drove it deep into her pussy, lapping teasingly at the walls and the more sensitive spots, until he could just reach her cervix. Breathing her scent in his wolf form was what told him that she was about to go into heat. He growled at the temptation. The scent wasn't strong enough for him to catch in his human form, but inside her sex and in his current state he couldn't miss it. She would probably get her heat that night or the next morning. But really it was close enough to make pregnancy a concern and for the scent to cause his wolf to fight for more control than he should allow.

He growled hungrily. He had already purposely let his control slip. Now the intelligent half of him was arguing with the beast. She belonged to him. The fates had dictated this from the day they were born. She brought him here. She was the one who started fucking him. He could feel her hot wet mouth sliding up and down his shaft, her hand playing with his knot. She had to know what she was doing. Mack pushed Celia off of him and grabbed her by the waist before she could get away.

"What do you think you're doing," she squealed, as he forced her onto her hands and knees.

What does it feel like, came the guttural response in her mind.

Celia couldn't restrain the moan of pure bliss that escaped her mouth as he drove his huge member into her wet heat. He filled her completely and then forced the knot inside as well. She was panting with the effort of trying to pull away from him. At the same time, her wolf was screaming at her to just hold still. She cried out breathlessly as he managed to completely take her onto himself. They both stood still on their knees, on her bed, minds blank and just feeling the ecstasy of being joined together.

Mack's voice was almost angry in her mind. *Tell me to stop now and I'll leave.* He didn't want to end up accused of raping her in the morning.

Celia whimpered. "Can't you just do it and we'll argue about it tomorrow?" She bent her elbows and buried her face in the bed, trying desperately to contain her own wolf. *Gods that feels good!*

Mack smiled as he picked up on her thought. Her bending down only gave him a better angle and he pushed himself deeper, the head of his cock buried against her cervix. She moaned and pushed back against him. *Tell me you want this,* he thought at her, fighting his wolf desperately to keep from fucking her brains out without the approval. His human half wanted something more. Celia had been stomping on his pride too long. He thrust against her once. *Say it,* he demanded.

Celia moaned into the pillow. *All right, Mack please fuck me. I want you to fuck me.* As she finished the thought, he felt her shift in his hands.

He watched fur grow along her back and sides. His claws dug into her hips, and he began fucking her with quick hard thrusts that made her growl with delight. He could hear her begging for more in his mind, and it was driving him crazy. When he began to swell inside her he stopped, and pulled out, suddenly realizing how dangerous a position they were actually in. *Elders won't be happy with this*, he thought at her in warning. Not that he wouldn't do it if she let him. He didn't care what the elders had to say on that account. He just figured that he'd give her a last chance to get out of it. Then she wouldn't be able to accuse him of trapping her.

It was the stopping that did it. Celia was too close to being in heat and too far gone with their rutting to allow for a lull at this point. She turned on him, forcing him onto his back. She sat down on him, growling her delight as his swelling member filled her again. She began humping him wildly, and he watched as her breasts bounced beautifully before him. He reached up and squeezed them savagely, causing her to moan some more. He pinched and twisted her nipples, then pulled her down to him so he could suck on one while she fucked him.

When she started to come he stared into her eyes. He thought it was the most beautiful thing he had ever seen. He was mesmerized by the exquisite look of tortured bliss on her face. Mack forced a couple quick thrusts up into her while she writhed above him, and he joined her over the edge.

Cullen, Celia's mind moaned sadly as she realized that this was truly the end of her ambitions to alpha bitch. Even if he didn't mate with Aislinn, Celia had just given herself to Mack.

When Cullen's name drifted into his mind from Celia's, Mack went into a rage and nearly threw Celia through the wall. He pushed her off of him so forcefully that both of them felt the pain of his swollen member being ripped from her body. Mack's wolf howled in misery and retreated back into him, leaving the human standing staring glassy eyed and pissed at Celia on the floor.

"Galla," he swore at her. "I can't wait to see the look on your face when he mates with Aislinn. He doesn't want you. He never did," Mack spat at her. "I don't know if I do now." Of all the things she had ever done to him, this was the worst.

She shook her head at him, *You don't understand.*

Mack didn't want to hear it. He turned and walked out of the room, slamming the door behind him.

Celia had never seen that look in his eyes before. She hadn't meant it. *Gods what did I just do?*

The pain they were feeling doubled as a partial bond took hold. They didn't complete the mating, but there was just enough done for them to know how much misery the other felt.

* * * *

Brinah had a new respect for Cullen. The pain on his face when Aislinn slammed the door was evident. "All right," she called, but Aislinn was gone. Brinah decided that if Cullen was willing to send Aislinn home, then she would give them what she could. Brinah also had to admit that to some extent he was correct. If what Brinah wanted was her family to be whole again, then she would have to have Rafe dealt with. There was no way she could explain to her daughter, after having hid it this long, what was going on, and that they would have to move and change their names and hide. Brinah really didn't have a choice. "The first thing you have to understand is that Rafe has two things going on. He's a druid and an alchemist. The druid half gives him some ability to move in dreams, influence thoughts. It's kind of like a hypnotist. The alchemist half gives him the knowledge to work with herbs and elements to make compounds that can aide his abilities, make people more pliable and willing to let him influence them."

Cullen picked up the bag of herbs he had on his desk that had been added to the bonfires at the mating ceremony. He couldn't believe that it had only been a few nights ago. He handed the bag to Brinah, and she poured the contents out on the table. She looked through the contents. "Okay, I'll give you a list of what I will need. This doesn't look too complex."

Cullen looked over at Keith. His friends had remained silent throughout the meeting. When he met his friend's eyes, he could see the sympathy there, and it made him angry. He didn't want to be pitied. He was doing what was best for Aislinn. "Get Brinah what she needs," he said flatly. Keith nodded and took down the list of things that she wanted and the quantities.

Brinah sat thinking. "That will allow me to make a compound that will counteract the one he's using. But that won't stop him. It will only make it harder for him." She thought some more. Cullen could see her mind working over what she had been told earlier. "If he's making weres, then he has to have recreated something ancient. When I was still with the Circle, that kind of alchemy wasn't practiced any longer. I know that in ancient times, when Rome threatened the Celts, the Circle created a compound that when mixed with animal blood and ingested over a period of time would give the person who drank it the characteristics of the animal that the blood came from. It was a lengthy and painful process. When it was completed, the person was able to change into that animal. Hence all of you. It was done by a small group within our number that thought we should fight back. Seeing as we weren't fighters, and Rome was so powerful, they theorized that the only way for us to protect ourselves was to have guardians that were stronger than the Roman legions."

Sarah shook her head. "I always thought that was a story told to us when we were children to make us more sympathetic to the druids. I thought that the druids started that story because they wanted to guilt us into protecting them. Make it seem like we should show them respect and loyalty."

Brinah smiled. "In the end, all creatures with a brain assert themselves. We watched the lycans grow and move on to create their own identity, and we were pleased to see it. Humans who didn't understand us or what we had done turned it all into stories about druids being shape shifters, able to speak to animals, and things like that. Everyone creates their own legends to make what they don't understand make sense. I'm sure that even *our* stories about that time have become tainted over the years. Believe what you like about your origins. The truth about history isn't what the current dilemma is about. Right now, if Rafe is using ancient alchemy to create weres, there is nothing I can give you to stop that. Once it's done then it's done. I can only tell you that it is possible."

Cullen nodded. "If it takes a long period of time to do, are there stages? Does it just stop if you stop drinking the compound?" He was trying to ask the questions without bringing up Aislinn. She had obviously not told her grandmother about what Rafe had done to her. So he didn't want to make things worse between himself and Aislinn by saying something she didn't want said. He had a hope that Aislinn would understand and not leave hating him. The thought of her leaving ripped through him and he lost track of the conversation momentarily. Brinah's answer snapped him back into the moment.

"I don't know for certain," she said. "It was taught as history when I was a child. The details of the compound and how it worked weren't included in the lesson. There were some, like Rafe, who tried to find the old compounds and spent a great deal of time researching our past. I was never one of them."

"You talk like you knew him," Cullen replied in a despondent tone.

"A long time ago. He wasn't a very friendly child. I was on my way out of the Circle at that time. He was still very young. He just had... cruel tendencies.

There wasn't a member of our group who didn't know about that child."

Cullen nodded. "So then what about the stones. Apparently he wants them for some reason."

Brinah didn't really want to explain that one, but she had come this far. "The stones aren't what he wants. The stones are just a marker. He could find what he wants in any number of places. The stones are just an indication that he definitely found the right spot. We used the stones to demark the location of an intersection of ley lines. It's a point of power. If you know how to use the power, it can be a very dangerous place." Brinah took a breath. "It's a place for holding rituals. The site could be used to make compounds stronger, if that's what he's doing. It's hard to say what kinds of things he might be up to if he's determined to take possession of that location. You'd be better off dealing with him in a different place."

"Is there anything else significant that you might be able to add to this?" Cullen wanted to be done with the meeting.

"I'll keep thinking. But from the sounds of things, he has you outnumbered, with stronger fighters, and he's using alchemy to undermine your ability to fight him. It doesn't sound very promising."

Cullen nodded. "No it doesn't," he said. At that moment he just didn't care. He got up from his chair and headed out of the office, leaving all of them sitting there.

Keith and Sarah looked at each other. This wasn't good. Sarah was the one who spoke. She was completely unable to hide the frustration in her voice. "Brinah. I totally sympathize with you wanting your granddaughter back. But it seems to me that someone who left her own family, or Circle, or whatever you had behind, to marry someone and cut yourself off from everything you knew, might understand what's going on between them."

Brinah stood up and met Sarah's anger head on. "I was in love with my husband. What happened between us is totally different from an alpha lycan adding an additional female to his numbers."

Sarah's eyes shifted and swirled with amber as her wolf tried to surface out of loyalty toward Cullen and this ignorant woman's words against him. "Eistigi liom. I have never seen Cullen Arnauk in love with a woman the way he is with your granddaughter. I had always been given the impression that druids were observant and intelligent. I don't understand how you can't see that."

Brinah stood her ground and waited. She refused to perpetuate this argument. Cullen had yet to prove to Brinah, in any way, that he was in love with Aislinn. Brinah couldn't believe he'd give her over so easily if he were really in love with her.

Keith was the one who broke the battle of silence. "Do you women think that we can deal with this in the morning? I don't know about both of you, but I've had a long day. Tomorrow promises to be longer. The women agreed without a word, and Brinah was escorted to her bedroom. She thought about looking for Aislinn, but decided to give her some space and find her first thing in the morning. When Aislinn had been a child she had always preferred to be upset by herself. She would come looking for comfort when it was wanted.

* * * *

Cullen went up to his room. He waited for a time, trying to think of what he would say. He lay on his bed feeling how empty it was. If he could fall asleep, he might wake up to find her in his arms and have this evening be just a bad dream. Well, aside from the afternoon in the library. He closed his eyes and smiled painfully as he remembered how it had felt sitting in that chair with her lying on his chest. He could almost hear the soft purr-like sounds she had been making. There was no way he could sleep.

When Aislinn didn't come up, he started to get nervous. It took some effort but he decided to go looking for her. Keith's comment about chasing after a woman echoed in his brain again. The longer he was away from Aislinn, the more Cullen's resolve to let her go was breaking. He was thinking that he should just apologize or tell her it was a misunderstanding. Maybe he should try the truth and say he had thought it would be what she wanted. Then he could ask her to stay with him instead. Depending on how angry she was, maybe he'd beg her to stay.

When Cullen had searched the entire building, including the casino and every other room she had never been in he began to panic. He virtually threw a couple customers out of the elevator and hit the button for the basement.

Cullen stormed into the security suite. There were computers and monitors along all of the walls. One of the monitors was even monitoring the security suite that monitored the casino. That was the room that the human cops saw if they ever needed into the Madadh-Allaidh Saobhaidh surveillance system. This room contained the system that monitored the rest of the building.

Cullen violently pulled the chair out from under the man who was watching the monitors with disinterest. The poor guy landed on his butt on the floor, and then scrambled to bow his head to the angry alpha standing over him.

"Find Aislinn," Cullen ordered. "I need to know if she's anywhere in this building. If she isn't, I need to know when she left." Then he stood there with his arms crossed, waiting.

It took a second for the lycan to realize that Cullen meant for him to do it instantly. He jumped and fidgeted as he played with buttons and moved cameras and checked monitors. After so much time passed that Cullen was pacing the man said, "I don't think she's here General. It'll take me a little bit to find out when she left." There was an intimidated tremor to the man's voice. He knew that was not what Cullen wanted to hear.

Cullen growled menacingly. Fear boiled up in him. He knew she was in danger. He just felt it, and his instincts were rarely wrong. "When you find her, call me immediately." With that, Cullen stormed out of the room and back to the elevator.

He paced in the elevator as it headed up. He didn't know what to do. He had no idea where to start looking. It was incredibly late, and everyone was already in bed. She may have just taken off and was fine. He kept trying to reassure himself, but he couldn't shake the feeling that there was something terribly wrong.

When elevator doors opened on the 13th floor, he stood there a moment looking down the hall. It was mostly empty. The carpet was well worn from all the people in his pack that came and went on this floor. He could hear a television down the hall where all the insomniacs were currently getting their fix of some bad horror flick. He walked down the hall like a zombie. He was the alpha. He was supposed to know what to do.

Chapter 12

The first and greatest punishment of the sinner is the conscience of sin.
-Lucius Annaeus Seneca

Every time Aislinn started to speak during the taxi ride, Ranaild jabbed her with the dagger. It didn't take long for her to realize that she needed to keep her mouth shut. The taxi driver kept looking in the rearview mirror, concerned. One look from Ranaild and the man would go back to minding his own business.

By the time the taxi pulled up in front of the Tairneach manor, it was nearing dawn. Ranaild had the man stop at the end of the drive just outside the gate. Ranaild got out first. He was tired, and his guard was down. He figured that he was home free at this point. He just couldn't make himself feel good about it. When Aislinn noticed that Ranaild wasn't paying attention, she turned and ran after the taxi that was pulling away from the gate.

Without even thinking, Ranaild let his hand fly. The dagger he had been holding all evening hit Aislinn in the back of the thigh. It lodged deep in the muscle and sent searing waves of pain running all the way up her body. Aislinn cried out in pain as she fell to the ground, and tears of anger began to pour down her face as the taxi drove away. She slammed her hands on the ground in frustration. That was it. She didn't have anything left. Her cries died out and she went limp, resigning herself to her fate. Maybe Rafe was right. Maybe she was destined to be his.

With an emotionless demeanor, Ranaild came over to her. "For what it's worth, I'm sorry," he said as he picked her up and threw her over his shoulder. He reached up and pulled the dagger out of her leg. Blood poured from the wound. There was a trace scent of Elise from the blood that had dried on the dagger that mingled with the coppery fresh smell of Aislinn's blood. The scent reached into Ranaild and reminded him of why he was betraying his pack, his alpha, his friend, and himself. He put the dagger back in the waist of his pants, not bothering to wipe it off. With the blood on his hands now, it didn't matter that it was on his clothes as well. Then he headed toward the manor. The gate at the end of the drive swung wide without Ranaild having to ask. He was expected.

Aislinn didn't bother to fight back. The last ounce of fight left in her was lost in the dash for the taxi. After what had happened with Cullen and now this, Aislinn felt drained. She lay over Ranaild's shoulder like a rag doll and watched the ground pass beneath his feet as he headed through the gate.

* * * *

Rafe sat up in bed and picked up the ringing phone on the night stand. "This better be good." As the voice answered back, a disgusting smile crept across his lips. "By all means let them in. I'll be down momentarily." Rafe jumped out of bed and threw on a black robe and slippers. He hadn't bothered to rise this early in a long time, but what kind of host would he be if he didn't greet his guest personally.

Ranaild stood in the front room of the manor. Blood dribbled down Aislinn's leg and was leaving drops on the white and gray marble floor. He stared at the blood and weighed the odds that Rafe might not release Elise or that Ranaild would get Elise back and not be allowed to leave unharmed. But, even if Elise was given back to him and they were allowed to go, was the price worth it? He felt cold and empty.

Rafe walked into the room. When he saw the blood on Aislinn, he was angered at first. But his features smoothed over as he reminded himself that a leg wound would heal. At least he had her now. "Put her down."

Ranaild did as he was told too well. Aislinn felt her ass hit the cold marble and winced as the pain in her leg shot up her body again. She was starting to feel strange. She figured that the loss of blood must be making her nauseous and dizzy. She just didn't think she had lost that much blood. And blood loss didn't explain the pain in her arms. All her muscles felt tight and her ears were ringing.

"Where's Elise," Ranaild said coolly. He had made the decision that if Rafe did anything other than what he had agreed to Ranaild was going to kill him where he stood one way or another.

Rafe smiled at the man. He knew exactly what the lycan was thinking. "Why wouldn't I hold up my end of the bargain my friend?" he said with that terrible smile playing along his lips. "After all, I wouldn't want to deprive you of the lifetime of self loathing for what you've done." He was amused. Lycans were so easily manipulated. He leaned over to a large tiger that had a lion's mane and said something softly to the animal. It trotted off down a hall.

"Now if you don't mind," Rafe said, "you can wait in the entry way." At that, another large cat appeared and ushered Ranaild back toward the front door. Ranaild vaguely noted the number of annoyed looking lycans around the room who were allowing the katta to run their manor. Rafe walked over and knelt down next to Aislinn. Her blue eyes flashed at him and silver mixed with amber swirled in their depths. "You certainly are beautiful when you're angry," he said staring into her eyes. He noticed the amber flooding into her eyes and stared with confusion.

Aislinn couldn't help but be frightened. She did her best to channel that fear into her anger so that Rafe wouldn't have the pleasure of knowing how much he scared her. But between the pain, the sick feeling, and his eyes boring into her, Aislinn didn't have the same kind of control over herself as usual. She decided that the best thing she could possibly do is channel all of her remaining energy into blocking Rafe out of her mind. If nothing else she didn't want him able to use what had happened that night to torment her. She'd rather be raped than that.

When the block came up Rafe's attention shifted. He didn't care nearly as much about how she ended up with an additional bloodline, as he cared about whether or not he could control her. Rafe tried to get into her head. He had been frustrated enough when he stopped being able to find her dreams. But having her right in front of him and not being able to get in was pissing him off. He stood up and without thinking, he pulled his hand back and slapped her across the face, sending her sprawling on the floor.

Aislinn was shocked. He was much worse than the last time she had been face to face with him. Something about him was more twisted than before. This was not the man she had originally met. This one wouldn't have been able to play at nice the way Rafe had been in the beginning. This one was leaning toward insane. She hadn't even seen the slap coming when he hit her. She lay on the floor. She could feel him trying to get into her head again. She refused to let him.

"You've gotten better at this since meeting the lycans. I wouldn't have thought you could learn so much so quickly and on your own," his voice shifted strangely from sincere to menacing and angry then back again as he talked. "I'm torn between being annoyed and being impressed. I don't think you want me to put you through what I'm going to do to you if you continue to hide your mind from me, Aislinn."

There was a sound in the hallway, and Aislinn looked up to see a disheveled, abused woman barely walking, being led by the arm down the hall. When Ranaild saw her, he had to be held back in the entry way. Rafe knelt down next to Aislinn and spoke softly to her. "Look how weak they are. They are so attached to one another that they'll sacrifice their lives to be together. They'll have nowhere to go now. Every time they look at each other, they will know that he betrayed his pack to save her. They'll spend their lives running away, feeling guilt rack them, and all because lycans have a terribly misplaced idea of loyalty and love." Rafe stood up and sneered at them. "Pitiful."

Elise was shoved into Ranaild's arms and they stood there holding each other. Elise's sobs could be heard all the way down the hall. The few lycans present could feel the pain that had been caused by what Rafe had done. They all stood uncertain why they were allowing this to happen.

Jenna appeared in the doorway. She was watching the couple and toying with a ring on a chain around her neck. She looked over at Rafe and could see the wheels in his head turning. Before he could change his mind about letting them go, Jenna waved her hand and the pair was ushered out the door.

Aislinn laid her head back down on the marble floor. The cold felt good against her feverish face. She took a couple long breaths and waited. She didn't know what Rafe intended to do next, but there wasn't anything she could do about it.

Jenna watched. She knew that Rafe intended to make Aislinn his alpha. Here she was again. She had even allowed herself to be subjected to a mating with the muin bastard, and he was going to throw her aside the minute he didn't need her any longer. For now his connection with her was keeping the Tairneach accepting of him as alpha. He still needed her a while longer. That would buy her time. She fondled her father's ring on the chain around her neck, and her eyes fell on one of the larger lycans in the room. He nodded to her submissively and she smiled back. *Not yet,* she thought at him, *but soon.*

* * * *

Cullen was standing in the security suite. The lycan on security duty had found Aislinn on the tape. His heart sank into his stomach. He watched Aislinn walk through the lobby and out the front doors. He saw the direction she had gone in, but who the hell knew where she went after she left the building.

He continued watching and saw several different members of the pack coming and going at the same time. A couple of them even watched her leave. But she had that air of someone doing exactly what she should be doing, so no one stopped her or said anything.

Cullen pulled his cell phone out of his pocket. He called Keith. When the tired voice came through the line Cullen growled at the phone. "Aislinn is missing," he said simply.

That woke Keith up. He looked at the clock on the night stand. It said 7am. The sun was just barely peeking through the windows. "How long?" He said getting out of bed. Jaylyn growled a complaint. She spent most of her time in bed recently, seeing as she was heavily pregnant and due to drop any time now.

"Since she left the meeting yesterday," came the deadpan over the line.

Keith was surprised that it had taken this long for Cullen to call. "Where are you?"

"The security suite." Cullen was still watching the tape. She looked like she was fine. She just left. "I'm watching the camera footage of her leaving the lobby. There are a few others who left at the same time. I'm going to start calling and see if anyone saw anything. I want you to get Brinah working on that stuff she said she could do. I get the feeling I'm going to need it sooner than I originally intended."

"I'm on it." Keith had already left the room and was headed into the elevator. He'd need Sarah, considering he didn't know what room Brinah was in. He put his cell phone back in his pocket and headed for Sarah's room.

Cullen watched the tape and paused it. He stared at the man who left shortly after Aislinn. Ranaild. He opened his cell and searched for the number then hit send. On the other end of the line Ranaild held his phone up and looked at the caller ID. Then he looked over at Elise. She stared at him with tears in her eyes. They were walking down a deserted street, headed away from the Tairneach manor. Ranaild couldn't face it yet. When he knew that Elise was safe, he would probably go to Cullen and confess what he had done. For now, he silenced his phone and placed it back in his pocket. Cullen left a message, telling Ranaild to call him back.

Cullen forwarded the tape to the next people out the front door. Celia and Mack. Cullen growled and shook his head. That's just what he needed. He found Celia's number in his phone and hit send. Again no answer. Celia was down the hall in the gym. She was running the track, trying desperately to get Mack and what had happened out of her head. He was asleep at the moment, so at least the only misery she was feeling was her own. Cullen growled a message to call him back into Celia's voice mail and moved on to the next number.

Cullen dialed Mack angrily and listened to the phone ring and ring. He was about ready to rip the computer panels out of the desk when Mack picked up the call. "Yeah," a tired voice said into the phone.

Cullen's dead pan voice was eerie and had Mack listening to the man on the other end of the line with even more attention than usual. "You and Celia were on your way out of the building last night about the same time as Aislinn. Did you see her?" Cullen was answered with an extended silence that had him wanting to crawl through the phone and shake the man on the other end of the line.

"Yeah, Ranaild was following her." Mack was suddenly sick to his stomach. Celia had been right. "Cel thought that he was up to something and was trying to follow him. I thought that you'd stuck Ranaild on her as a tail and talked Celia down and brought her back to the den." The apologetic tone on the other end of the line did nothing to stem Cullen's temper.

Cullen threw the cell phone across the room then proceeded to have a temper tantrum that included destroying quite a bit of computer equipment, scaring the shit out the poor man on duty, and drawing the attention of half the floor. The lycan on duty had to jump several times to get out of the way. Suddenly Cullen stopped and stared at the ceiling with his hands balled into fists at his sides. "The report," he said far too calmly. He looked over at the security guard. His eyes were wild swirling amber. His wolf was ready to go at anyone who breathed wrong. "I wanted more proof. I ignored the report. His name was in the report," Cullen said to the confused guard. Then he turned and left the room.

* * * *

Aislinn's head was swimming. She wasn't sure how long she had been unconscious, or when exactly she had passed out. She was naked and on her stomach, tied down to a bed. She tried to move her arms and legs, but pain shot through her body and she drew in a sharp breath before lying still again. When she tried to open her eyes, the light from the room stung and sent a new pain into her head. She closed her eyes again. Somewhere in the background, she could hear people talking, but couldn't quite make out the voices. She couldn't remember where she was or how she had gotten here, but she was scared and cold and in pain. "Cullen," she said softly not really thinking that he'd be there or hear her.

"Does Arnauk tie you down to beds as well?" Rafe's voice sank into her and suddenly she remembered what had happened to get her there. Aislinn pressed her face into the bed. She didn't bother to try and pull away. She knew that it wouldn't get her anywhere. When Rafe's hand touched the back of her leg she flinched. Pain sliced into her again and she went still, her breath hissing out of her. Rafe chuckled and continued touching her.

Aislinn could feel a bandage on the back of her leg. Rafe's fingers probed the sensitive wound and pain shot through her. "I do have to apologize for this one," he said and poked the bandaged wound again.

Aislinn's head spun with the pain. When she finally groaned and her breath choked out of her with the sound, Rafe removed his hand. "The incompetent lycan who brought you to me stabbed you with a dagger coated in lycan blood. You've been tainted. I don't think there's much to worry about. But we won't know how much of your change has been affected until I finish it."

Aislinn's brain was swimming with what he had said. "What did you do to me," she whispered, afraid to know the answer.

"You'll see," he replied, stroking her hair. "Trust me."

Aislinn shivered at the thought. She could feel his breath on the back of her neck. After being with Cullen, the of passion and pleasure she had felt with him contrasted sharply with the revulsion and terror she felt when Rafe's hands began to explore her body. Aislinn knew that if she protested, it would just get worse. She laid perfectly still and bit back her disgust as she felt his hand stroke up the inside of her thigh. When he reached her sex, he pushed his fingers into her. "Hmm, I wonder what you were dreaming about to be such a welcoming target for me," he said angrily, pissed because he knew that if she had been thinking about him she wouldn't be like this. Then Aislinn felt his attempt at a caress turn to agony as he dug his fingers sharply into her sensitive flesh. "How are you blocking me Aislinn? You're not that strong." After he finished the question his fingers let up and he waited. The pain he had caused ebbed slightly, but the sting was still there. A tear formed in her eye and trailed down her cheek.

When she didn't answer right away, he dug into her again. "I asked you a question." This time his brutal fingering lasted longer and Aislinn couldn't hold back a strangled cry.

Finally, he stopped and she answered him this time. "I don't know," she whimpered quickly. She pressed her face into the bed, crying.

"That's not a very good answer," he said soothingly. He was stroking her again. He gently rubbed her clit and the tender area he had been torturing. When she seemed to gain control of herself, he moved to stand in her line of sight so that he could look at her and asked again.

"I really don't know Rafe. I just did it. I wanted you to stop. I don't know what I did. I just thought about making you stop."

Rafe listened, his eyes narrow and angry. He was staring into her eyes contemplatively. "Lucky for you, I believe you." He put his fingers to his mouth and Aislinn saw blood on his finger tips. He breathed in her scent and then licked the blood and juices from his fingers while she watched. "Don't get too comfortable pet. We'll be leaving for the reservation soon. I've decided to move things up. I'm far too excited about bringing you back into the fold. My little lost lamb." Rafe moved around to where she couldn't see him again. She was terrified that he was going to touch her again.

She heard metal scraping and rattling. There was a pause, then she heard him behind her again. She felt his hand on her and she whimpered, numb with fear. Then she felt a sting that could only be described as a shot. Was he drugging her? Rafe chuckled again when she flinched. "Don't worry lamb. I'll protect you from the wolves." His voice started to echo in her head. Her mind started to fuzz over. "If you continue to block me, pet, then I'll find a way to make you less inclined to block me. I'll start with giving you the choice to cooperate and accept that you belong to me. If you fight me, you'll only make me hurt you more." His voice terrified her. Her body felt like it was on fire. Her muscles ached and the room began to spin.

"Lesson 1," Rafe's distorted voice blurred in her ears. "The quicker you come, the sooner I'll stop." Aislinn felt something, probably his fingers again, press inside her. At least it wasn't painful this time. She lay there crying, much to his delight, as he plunged into her over and over. Aislinn couldn't believe her body was responding to him. She was torn between holding out and giving in. She briefly considered imagining Cullen holding her and letting Rafe have what he wanted. The idea of Cullen only brought more tears. The room began spinning more. Rafe said something else. She could hear frustration in his voice. The distortion was getting to be too much. She wasn't sure how long he continued his assault before blissful blackness settled over her, and she lost awareness of what he was doing to her body.

Rafe was pissed when she passed out. "I didn't give her enough for her to black out already." He stomped across the room and grabbed the omega that was standing by to see to his needs. He got no pleasure from torturing someone who couldn't respond with the fear and submission he found so arousing. He forced the frightened omega to her knees and pulled his cock out of his pants. She hesitantly obeyed his obvious intentions and began sucking on his member. She wasn't very enthusiastic or good at it, but Rafe was worked up from tormenting Aislinn, and he came quickly. Pushing the omega away he pulled his pants back up and went to check on the other arrangements he had been making.

* * * *

Keith and Sarah pulled Brinah out of bed to start working on the compound she had told them she could make. Brinah argued at first. "I understand that you're all in a hurry. Is there truly no time for me to talk with Aislinn.? I had hoped she would be able to help me."

Keith looked at Sarah. He had been trying to find a gentle way of breaking the news, but Sarah was still angry at Brinah from the day before, and she was happy to explain. "She ran off out of the building after you and Cullen argued, and she got upset," she said shortly. "From what we can tell, she may have been picked up by one of Rafe's men. We're not completely positive. Right now the plan is to attack the Tairneach, risk all of our lives, and maybe manage to find her. I guess the assumption is that she's *not* bull headed enough to take off on her own and just not come back. Which means that someone must be stopping her from coming back. Which means Rafe probably got to her. But, like I said, we don't know for sure."

Brinah was wide eyed. "You're going after Rafe, and you don't even know if she's there?"

"Cullen is upset. When you upset an alpha you have problems."

Brinah was torn between telling her that it was ignorant to go charging off to attack a place over the possibility that they may have taken one person captive and asking why they hadn't left yet. She opted for not causing any additional trouble. "So do you have the things I asked for? I'll need a kitchen. And there are a few other things that occur to me might be helpful. I'll get you a list of ingredients for those as well." She was wringing her hands and shifting her weight form foot to foot.

Sarah rolled her eyes and took off out the door to handle other duties and left Keith to finish with Brinah.

The Arnauk were drastically out of practice. It had been a couple decades since they had been on war footing. When Cullen had spoken to the elders after the failed mating, everyone had left the meeting believing that Cullen would get it all under control. He always did. The call for fighters to mobilize took everyone off guard. Cullen was pissed and impatient. At one point in time a call to mobilize would have had the entire pack assembled at the den within hours.

As the day wore on, Cullen grew more and more agitated. Brinah wasn't finished with whatever she was making, and a large number of his pack were still missing. He didn't know whether it was because they had joined Rafe or because they hadn't gotten the call or because they were on their way. He promised himself that he wouldn't let the pack get this out of shape ever again. For now, though, there was nothing he could do about it. He paced and swore and scared people away from himself. He decided that regardless of who he had, how many he had, or whether Brinah was ready, by nightfall they would be leaving for the Tairneach manor.

* * * *

Ranaild and Elise had managed to get to town. Elise had been chained and beaten so often that she had only barely managed the walk. She wouldn't have made it if Ranaild hadn't carried her most of the way. He was debating taking her to a human hospital. But the need to be as far from the Tairneach as possible made him opt for the first public bathroom they came too.

Ranaild carried Elise into the nasty gas station bathroom and sat her on the dirty graffiti covered sink counter. They hadn't talked since they left the manor. Elise could see and feel the self loathing in him even though he refused to look directly at her. Ranaild wet a bunch of paper towels and made Elise let him look at her wounds. He was wiping dried blood away from a particularly nasty looking one on her side.

Elise's voice trembled a bit when she asked him, "What did you do to get me out of there Ranaild?"

He stopped cleaning the gash in her flesh and finally met her gaze. He stared into her eyes for a very long time. Tears formed in his own eyes. She reached for him, but he wouldn't accept the comfort she was offering. "Whatever I had to do," he finally said.

Elise didn't ask him anymore. She submitted to his poking and prodding. When he was satisfied that she was able to keep going, he helped her down and they headed out the door. He couldn't stop thinking about how much he hated himself right then. He wasn't strong enough to have protected her the way he should have. He wanted to kill Rafe for what he had done to Elise and for what Rafe had made him do. He wanted to kill himself for betraying his pack.

Elise was the one who saw the Tairneach convoy. Her hands dug into Ranaild's arm and she pulled him back around the corner of the gas station to hide as they drove past. Her heart was racing. They were headed for Arnauk territory. "They must be on their way to the reservation," she said as tears filled her eyes. "They're going to attack again. It's all they've been talking about for days. When they were going to take the stones."

Ranaild looked at Elise. "You know I love you," he said.

"I don't like the way you said that Ranaild. What are you going to do?"

"If I call Cullen and warn them they may be able to do something about it. But after what I've done..." He couldn't finish it.

"So we weren't going home, were we?"

"I'll take you back to the pack Elise. You'll be safe there. But if I were Cullen, I wouldn't let me live."

"Then we won't go back. Ranaild, I don't want to know what you did. I don't care. I just need to be with you. We don't need the pack. We can go somewhere else." The panic in Elise's voice almost made him think that it could work.

He shook his head. "I'd never be able to live with myself knowing. And there's the boys, Elise. I've got to tell Cullen. I can tell him other things too. I can't just disappear. I wish I could."

Elise wanted to stop him, but she knew that if he didn't follow his heart then he wouldn't be the man she mated with. She nodded agreement with tears in her eyes.

Ranaild fished his cell phone out of his pocket. The 1 message caption was running across the face of the phone. He knew that it was from Cullen. He wondered if the alpha had figured it out or if it was just a call. It didn't matter. He dialed Cullen's number and listened to the phone ring with the morbid feeling of a man going to his own funeral.

* * * *

Cullen was sitting in his office going over the report he had neglected earlier. He was trying to decide if Ranaild was the only traitor, or if he needed to jail all of the people on the list. His phone rang and he picked it up to see who was calling him. When he saw the caller ID his wolf went into overdrive. He flipped open the phone and growled into the receiver, "Tell me why I shouldn't rip your throat out."

"I can't. I'll lay down at your feet and offer you my throat when this is over. But for now you need to know some things. Rafe has loaded the Tairneach up. They're all headed for the reservation. I just watched the convoy pass us. I give them two hours to get there."

Cullen was confused. "Why should I listen to you?"

"I've done enough damage. I'm on my way back to the den. You can deal with me when you return. I'll accept the repercussions of my actions. I'm sorry."

Cullen's wolf retreated in confusion. Cullen felt as though his beast was pacing in his mind. He wasn't sure how to deal with Ranaild now, and that made him angrier. It would have been much easier breaking Ranaild's neck before this phone call. Ranaild proceeded to give him the names of the other men he knew were being manipulated by Rafe. He left the detailed explanations for a later date, when there was more time.

Cullen stormed out of the office with a new list. He had to further cut his numbers. He pulled several of his best men who weren't on the list to round up the men that Ranaild had named. The last thing he needed was inner pack conflict when they went into battle, even if he was neutering his numbers.

Finally, he decided that he couldn't wait any longer. The Tairneach had a two hour lead by the time he straightened everything out. If Ranaild was correct, that would place them on the reservation by now. Brinah had only just finished the alchemical formula she said would counteract the compound Rafe was using. It was a foul smelling liquid that she told people to spray themselves down with. Keith was complaining that it didn't mesh well with his aftershave. Brinah insisted on going with them. Cullen hadn't thought it was a good idea but he had enough other things going on that he just didn't have the energy left to try and stop her. Overall it was a hectic mess.

Chapter 13

Vae Victis!
Woe to the Defeated!
-Brennus of the Senones

Aislinn was sick of passing out. She never knew where she would be waking up. This time she was in a sitting position and her hands and feet were still tied. It occurred to her that Rafe must have thought she was fairly dangerous to think that tying her up unconscious and sick was necessary.

The pain was subsiding, but she still ached all over as if she had the flu. She opened her eyes to find that she was in a car, probably a limo. She was on a black leather seat which was facing Rafe and Jenna. Rafe was leaning back and looking out the window, oblivious to the fact that Aislinn's eyes had just opened. One hand was on Jenna's knee. She didn't appear to care or notice that Rafe was touching her. Jenna was staring at Aislinn with a vicious glare. Aislinn didn't know what this particular glare was for. Jenna would probably come up with a reason to glare at the pope. Aislinn could only figure that Jenna was still dwelling over Cullen. Rafe's other hand was stroking a golden tan lioness, who lay at his feet. The lioness appeared to be pleased by the petting, as she was purring her approval.

Jenna reached down and touched Rafe's hand on her knee. "Your new pet has awakened." *And how I hate her,* Jenna seethed.

Aislinn was becoming more and more cognizant. She realized, with a great deal of embarrassment, that she was the only one who was naked. Well, unless you count the lioness. She immediately burned a brilliant shade of red, then grew angry at herself when her obvious upset appeared to please both Rafe and Jenna.

Rafe was in a causal suit that looked to be tailored and Jenna was in a loose fitting, expensive looking red silk dress. Between the blond bimbo in the red dress, the greasy looking weasel in a suit, the black leather limo seats, and the lion at their feet, a person would have thought that they were in some bad rock video. Aislinn rolled her eyes at the thought. She leaned into the leather seat, felt her body aching and closed her eyes with the intention of going back to sleep.

"Aren't you even curious where we're going," Rafe asked in a way that might have been friendly if it weren't for the fact that she was tied up and naked.

"No," Aislinn answered, without opening her eyes.

"Usually there's more fight in you lamb. I'm curious what has you so defeated," Rafe cooed in irritatingly fake sympathy.

Aislinn didn't answer. She could feel Rafe squirreling around in her brain. She made her mind go blank. She refused to give him ammunition for abusing her. The way she saw it, she couldn't protect her body from him, but she sure as hell wasn't giving him her mind again.

Rafe pulled his hands from the two women, braced his elbows on his knees, pressed his hands together, and leaned toward Aislinn. His eyes narrowed dangerously and his voice seethed, filled with threat. "Do you remember what I told you about blocking me lamb? Or were you too out of it to remember out last conversation?"

Self preservation being her number one priority, a thought suddenly occurred to Aislinn. The more she fought him, the more she had found she could do. She didn't really know her limitations, but she seemed to manage to do things she wanted badly enough. She let a picture float into her mind of what she remembered of their last conversation.

Rafe smiled and sat back. "That's it lamb." He continued to work himself into her mind. He figured she was tiring of fighting.

Aislinn was glad it was working. She let him in just far enough to see what he expected to see. Beyond that she stayed safely inside herself and waited for his reaction.

"I've always been impressed with your talent Aislinn. I had thought it an unusual thing to find in a human outside of the Circle."

Rafe was fishing, and Aislinn knew it. She wasn't sure what he was after finding out, but she wished that he would get to the point. She wasn't feeling well enough to play this game right now, and she let him in far enough to catch that thought.

He chuckled. "Fine," he answered her unspoken comment on his behavior. "I was informed by one of my men in the Arnauk clan that your grandmother has paid the Arnauk a visit. Personally escorted to the building by the female alpha." The fear that Rafe picked up on after his statement wasn't purposely given to him. "So I did some looking. It seems that you and I are more alike than I had thought," he said with a jovial tone. Then his voice suddenly dropped and took on his usual deadly monotone. "Why exactly did you keep this from me?"

Aislinn didn't see a reason to not tell him the truth. As long as he remained focused on her, he might leave her grandmother alone. "I didn't know. She never told our family."

Rafe watched her as she spoke. She could feel him in her mind, and she let him reach a place that would let him know she was telling the truth. She figured it would get more difficult if she had to make him believe a lie.

"So then," he continued, "I suppose you're going to expect me to continue to believe you were never trained to use your abilities?"

Aislinn didn't answer him. She knew it wouldn't matter what she said to that one.

"Fine. I'll leave this for now. But don't think that the topic won't be revisited. Especially if you continue to develop skills miraculously out of nowhere. Let's just hope it won't be necessary for me to bring Brinah Senach in, after we've destroyed the Arnauk, and question her." He put an unusual emphasis on the name Senach.

He sounded so definite about destroying the Arnauk. It sent chills down her spine. She moved to find a more comfortable position. But that wasn't easy, considering the way she was tied.

Rafe watched her breasts bounce as she moved, and he was tempted to play with them. He moved across the space between the two seats and helped her into a sitting position.

Aislinn glared at him. "I would thank you for the help, if I weren't naked, tied up, and drugged."

"Naked," Rafe questioned. "I would have thought that all the time you've spent with the Arnauk, on your hands and knees, would have made you accustomed to being naked," he said, in an innocent sounding voice.

Aislinn was uneasy with the Jeckel and Hyde voice distortions. She was having a difficult time reading his mood, and that played havoc with figuring out how far she could push him. She wondered if he was doing it on purpose, or if he really was that crazy. "I don't know what you mean," she said angrily.

One of Rafe's hands reached up to cup her breast. He kneaded the flesh gently and ran his thumb over her nipple until it hardened in his grasp. Aislinn grimaced and pulled back as far as she could, sitting up in a car seat. His gentle touches tended to turn cruel fairly rapidly. She let him into that thought and pressed her legs together tightly at the agonizing memory.

Rafe smiled at her again. "How insightful you are, lamb," he said sweetly. Then he grabbed her by the hair and yanked her head back, exposing the bite mark on her neck. He did he dug his nails into her breast, and he leaned in close to her ear. "Did you think I wouldn't notice? So you let that mongrel lay claim to you? You're lucky I'm still willing to touch you." He threw her back against the seat, and then returned to his own. "Don't worry lamb. The big bad wolf will be dead soon, and if on all fours is the way you like it, very shortly I'll be more than able to oblige."

When he said that, Aislinn couldn't help wanting to know what he meant. She relaxed and reached out with her mind, with the intent of reading his thoughts. Part of her couldn't believe she was trying this. All she managed to get was an image of a thing that looked rather like a cross between a lion and a bear, with Rafe's insane eyes staring back at her.

Rafe felt her intrusion into his thoughts, and anger flashed red hot on his face. He leaped across the limo and backhanded her so hard that she fell off the seat onto the floor. Pain, from the sudden movement and from the impact, swirled in her brain, almost knocking her unconscious again.

"*Never* do that," Rafe said manically. "Apparently you still don't know who is in charge here or where you fit in." Rafe went back to his seat. He was furious. An image of his hands around her neck and her breath being slowly squeezed out of her drifted through his mind.

Aislinn stared up at him defiantly. She couldn't manage to get back up into the seat herself. On the floor, the lioness was uncomfortably close to her and leaned down to sniff at the blood running from Aislinn's lip, which had split with the impact of Rafe's attack. Kara's large cat tongue snaked out of her mouth and licked the blood off of Aislinn's face. Aislinn pulled back in revulsion.

Rafe smiled triumphantly as he watched Aislinn try to escape Kara's wet caress. He sank down into his seat once again relaxing into the comfort of the soft leather. "We have at least an hour before we reach the reservation." Rafe's eyes flashed with pleasure at Aislinn, and she knew that he was about to cause her more pain. "I'm bored with the trip. Jenna, entertain me."

Jenna felt the man's touch on her mind. She knew what he wanted her to do. She pushed her vehemence at being used like this down. If he knew how little control he actually had over her, then he would attempt to fix it. She didn't know if she could regain her senses in time to use the upcoming opportunity to her favor if

Rafe did that. So she moved to Aislinn and helped her back up onto the bench seat. *Besides,* Jenna thought, *it's not as if I won't enjoy tormenting the druis for what she's done to me.*

Aislinn was watching Jenna move. The woman had a blank stare on her pretty face, as she laid Aislinn on her back across the bench seat. Aislinn was at a strange angle with her hands tied behind her. Rafe watched with delight as Jenna untied the bonds on Aislinn's ankles, then forced her legs apart. Aislinn started to squirm to get away, but there was nowhere to go. Rafe's smile broadened, when she looked at him pleadingly, as if he might save her.

Jenna dropped the shoulders of her red dress off her arms and let it puddle on the floor around her knees, as she knelt between Aislinn's legs. The angle was bad; Jenna had to arch awkwardly, fighting to keep Aislinn's legs spread, so that she could accomplish Rafe's mental order. Jenna was just glad that the asshole thought she was too stupid to do anything about him. He tended to only send her orders, and never really messed with actually reading her thoughts, as long as she smiled mutely and did as she was told. The few times he had tried to read her, she was able to use her experience with sending thoughts in her other forms to protect herself. All lycans learned how to think selectively in order to communicate in their other forms. Jenna was counting on Rafe's overconfidence and tendency to underestimate lycans.

Jenna only sneered for a moment, when she caught the full intensity of Aislinn's scent emanating from her sex. Rafe's eyes glowed happily, as he watched Jenna bend down and draw her tongue along Aislinn's thigh. Her hands pressed against Aislinn's knees to force cooperation. Aislinn was in too much pain, from whatever Rafe had injected into her to be capable of fighting with much strength. Even Jenna was able to subdue her this way.

Aislinn flinched when she felt Jenna's tongue stroke her sex. While Aislinn had nothing against oral sex with other women, Jenna touching her was just as paramount to rape as Rafe's touch was. When Aislinn tried to get away, she hit her head against the car door. Rafe's smile broadened. Kara laid her head down on her paws with disinterest. Jenna repositioned herself and moved down on Aislinn with more enthusiasm than Rafe had expected. He was pleased that Jenna appeared to be thoroughly enjoying this. He reached down and started stroking himself through his pants. *I may have to make this a regular thing. Keep the bitch around to play with instead of giving her away as a prize.* He would have to think about it. He adjusted himself and moved for a better angle to watch the show.

Aislinn squeezed her eyes shut, trying not to think about the woman licking gently at her nether lips. Jenna slipped her tongue over Aislinn's pussy with infinite care. She made sure to stroke every inch of bare flesh with her tongue, before moving to suckle on Aislinn's clit. Rafe watched the agony on Aislinn's face, and the tears squeezing out of her eyes. He pulled his cock out of his pants and began to stroke himself in earnest as he watched the two women.

Jenna took turns between sucking on and licking Aislinn's clit. The more Aislinn wriggled to escape, the more delight Rafe took in watching. Aislinn fought to control herself and not let Rafe take any more from her. Her mind reeled with the tormenting sensations that Jenna was causing. Aislinn wondered if things like this were what she had blocked out of her mind and never managed to remember, from the last time she was with Rafe.

Aislinn shuddered and tried to relax. When Jenna felt the fight go completely out of Aislinn, she released her hold on Aislinn's leg and inserted a finger, then two into Aislinn's now dripping cunt. Jenna smiled with pleasure as Aislinn whimpered and pressed her face to the leather seat. Aislinn hated her body for reacting to the woman's mouth. There didn't seem to be anything she could do to stop the impending orgasm. At least it wasn't Rafe. Aislinn gasped as her body tightened, and her cunt rippled around Jenna's intruding digits. Jenna continued her tongue lashing and stroking until Aislinn lay limp again, panting for air. Then Jenna withdrew her fingers and, much to Rafe's delight, sucked the last of Aislinn's juices from them, while she stared into his eyes.

Rafe toyed with himself, trying to decide which of the three women in front of him deserved the pleasure of helping him find his release. He finally decided that Aislinn would be receiving that gift soon enough, and Jenna had hers not too long before, but he had been neglecting Kara since their move into the Tairneach manor. Kara. The one truly loyal follower he had. He had never been forced to manipulate her in any way. If he asked her to do something, she willingly did it. She worshiped him. Rafe had often wondered why he felt nothing for her. Perhaps she ruined her chances with him when she posed no challenge. He didn't know. Every so often he felt obligated to reward her for her loyalty.

Rafe nudged the lioness with his toe, and she eagerly stood and presented herself for his approval. Rafe made sure that the large cat was positioned so that he would be fucking her right in front of Aislinn's face. "Watch this," he said grabbing Aislinn by the hair and forcing her face to angle up. Jenna sat back on the seat to watch Aislinn's misery. All Aislinn could think was that at least it wasn't her.

* * * *

Cullen had left some men at the reservation to defend the territory. But the vast majority of the Arnauk had returned to the city in order to find out what happened after the mating ceremony. No one expected another attack on the reservation so soon. Cullen had word that a significant force would be coming. But the preparations for the battle had only just been started.

An alarm blasted through the manor-like cabin, as the Tairneach vans crashed through the front gate. The driveway to the cabin was long. That gave them some small amount of time. The Arnauk inside the grounds scrambled to assemble, in order to defend their territory. Men and women took up positions at windows holding guns and waited.

The Tairneach pulled up in front of the cabin. As the lycans and other weres got out of the vehicles, the Arnauk began a volley of gunshots that forced the Tairneach to jump for cover. Rafe completely ignored the battle. He got out of the limo and his driver open the trunk, as if nothing were happening. He pulled a duffle bag out of the trunk that clinked of glass, before he headed toward the wooded area that concealed the standing stones. Jenna spared a glance of concern for her men, who were taking fire, before trailing along behind Rafe obediently. Kara was left to drag Aislinn along.

Aislinn was shoved out of the limo. Pain shot through her body again, and she fell to her knees, then onto her chest. The gravel from the drive dug into her breasts as she hit the ground. She only barely managed to lift her head high enough to not scrape her face on the driveway. Kara growled impatiently and shifted into her hybrid form so that she could carry Aislinn.

She reached down with a golden clawed hand and took hold of Aislinn's limp form. "You make me ashamed to be a woman. When I took the change I didn't roll about on the ground whimpering. If I'm going to have to put up with you being around again, the least you could do is make an attempt at dignity," Kara snarled as she flung Aislinn over her shoulder like a rag doll.

Aislinn looked up toward the cabin. It was obvious that the Arnauk would lose this battle. The Tairneach had already reached the front door and were climbing in some of the windows. As Kara toted Aislinn easily into the woods, she saw someone crash out of a window on the top floor and scream before hitting the ground. Aislinn let her head fall back down, as Kara entered the woods and trailed after Rafe and Jenna toward the standing stones.

* * * *

Cullen drove like a maniac. The caravan of SUVs blasted down the highway, trying to close the distance between themselves and the Tairneach. Cullen had called in a favor that was owed to him by some friends on the highway patrol and was managing to make it across the state in record time.

As he gripped the steering wheel of the lead truck and gunned the gas even more, his cell rang. He reached into his pocket with the intent of taking note of the caller ID for a future pummeling. The name of his federal contact flashed across the display. Cullen closed his fist around the cell, and an audible crunching noise told everyone else in the truck that calling the man right now was not a good idea. Cullen tossed the cell into the backseat, nearly hitting Sarah in the head with it.

Keith tried desperately to find humor in the look on Sarah's face, when Cullen's cell went flying passed her head. Even he was having a hard time seeing the good in this situation. The truck reeked of the lovely perfume Brinah had whipped up, which caused Keith to wrinkle his nose and try to put his mind on something else to keep himself from being sick. Keith was trying to calculate the odds of getting disemboweled by a were-tiger or whatever else he might be about to fight. "Well," he said, trying to lighten the tension in the truck, "At the very least, if this stuff we're sprayed down with doesn't stop Rafe from his mind control caoch, we might be able to stink the lot of them off our territory."

Cullen's growl told him that his attempt at humor had not been appreciated. Keith grumbled a bit and settled back to watching the road speed past them. At this rate they would make the reservation in less than an hour. Hopefully that would be soon enough. Though what they were going to do when they got there, he wasn't sure.

Cullen knew that his pack was uneasy. His brain was working overtime for a solution to this one. He knew that if Rafe didn't have Aislinn, he would have waited and thought it out. It didn't make sense charging into this, and he was pissed at himself. *How many people are going to die*, he asked himself over and over again. But, that thought wasn't enough to stop himself in the head long charge. He didn't know how he was going to do it, but he would bring her out of this safely. Then he was going to hunt down Ranaild. He felt like his entire pack was falling apart, and it started with him.

"Brinah," Cullen demanded with a growl. "Are you able to do anything like what Rafe can do?"

Brinah shifted uncomfortably in her seat. She had been wondering when they would get around to that. "Most of the Senach were able to do things similar. All of our talents lay in slightly different places though. My talents tend toward premonitions, but I closed off that part of my mind a long time ago. There are consequences to seeing the future." Brinah hesitated, as though there was a bad memory attached to that statement. "I believe Aislinn is fairly gifted in premonitions as well. I was never very good at using my talents, and I never put the effort into developing them. They always used to control me. Then I fell in love with a human and left the Circle without looking back. I forced that part of me into silence. I can't claim that it could be of any help to you now. Aislinn's abilities always concerned me. I tried to stop her mother from encouraging her. She seemed to manifest the talent for dreams without even trying. I'm sorry, but I don't think there's anything I can do to Rafe or the Tairneach to help you, in that way."

A defeated silence fell over the truck. Brinah was so worried about Aislinn that she twisted the handle on the bag she was holding until it ripped off. "I did make some salves and things that might help anyone who becomes hurt," she said hopefully, as if that would fix everything. "What you truly need are some druids who can heal wounded or some who can manipulate nature. Those are the Senach who would be able to help here."

Cullen was pissed, and Brinah's voice was just pissing him off more. "Got anything to bring life back to the dead," he asked sardonically. The people in the SUV went back to riding in silence.

That talent takes more than my kind have had for centuries, Brinah thought sadly. For the first time since she had left the Circle, she was regretting her decision.

* * * *

Rafe walked up to the Circle of tall stones. He ran his hand over the surface of each stone with reverence. When Kara entered the Circle carrying Aislinn, he indicated for her to be dropped in the middle of the Circle. Kara tossed Aislinn off of her shoulder, onto a stone slab set into the ground, in the middle of the Circle.

Aislinn hit the stone slab hard, and all the air was knocked out of her lungs. Kara smirked. She didn't know what Rafe was turning Aislinn into, but she had a hard time believing that it would be anything Kara needed to worry about. So far Rafe had professed, on several occasions, that Kara was the best of his work. She had always been pleased with that.

Rafe was excited. His lifetime quest was finally going to be achieved. First he would complete his change, and then he would force the Circle Council to accept him as the head of the Senach. He read the rune carvings on each of the stones carefully and proceeded to place jars of herbs in front of each stone. When he had finished his circuit of the stones, he walked to the center. Aislinn had managed to come to a sitting position. Jenna watched expectantly, and Kara kept an eye on Aislinn.

A small spotted cat, rather like a leopard, came bursting through the trees and into the clearing beyond the stones. He slowed his charge and slunk up to Rafe at nearly a belly crawl. Then he changed into human form. He stood up on two feet, breathing hard and trying to catch his breath. "A caravan of Arnauk was spotted."

Rafe smiled widely, much to everyone's surprise. His eyes glimmered with power. He believed he had already won. "Fine. Let Arnauk and his pitiful little pack in. He seems so fond of my mate. Let him come see our union. Then," he looked down at Aislinn, "I'll kill him. A gift for you on our wedding day lamb."

* * * *

There was no sneaking up on this fight. Cullen pulled his truck up before the main entrance. The gate was down. There was no question that the Tairneach were already there. They had numbers and positioning, so the best thing the Arnauk could do would be to try and sneak in. They had the advantage that they knew these woods and hills better than the Tairneach could possibly know them.

The pack already had their orders. The men and women piled out of the trucks, stripped their clothes, and bodies began to shift. As each of the lycans completed the change to hybrid or wolf, they headed in different directions along the wall. Some of them vaulted the wall, while others slipped along the outside of the wall headed for different entrance points. Cullen, Keith, Sarah, and a select group of others formed up and headed, in human form, through the front gate on foot. Brinah was told to stay with the trucks, but she had ideas of her own. She trailed behind at a distance, scanning the scene for any evidence of Aislinn. She could feel the power here.

Cullen led his group toward the standing stones. They dropped clothes as they went, but remained in human form for the moment. They would wait for Cullen's lead. As the half naked group of men and women passed their second home, they could see the Tairneach and the strange weres watching them. It was an uneasy passage. There was no immediate attack. Cullen guessed that Rafe was so confident in his position he wanted to gloat before destroying the Arnauk.

Cullen could smell blood on the air, and his wolf howled at the loss of his friends even before he saw the bodies piled along the side of the cabin. He told himself that at least those deaths were over the territory and not because he was dragging his men into a fight over a woman. He could scent the various intruders throughout the woods. The strange green bonfires were lit, but the caoch that Brinah made overpowered the smell. Cullen could clearly see the enemy lycans and weres hiding amongst the trees as he neared the standing stones.

As Cullen and the others cleared the edge of the woods that surrounded the stones, his control was nearly defeated. A path between the weres who surrounded the stones opened in front of them. The were-cats grinned at them as they passed, knowing they had the advantage. There really wasn't anyone present who believed that the Arnauk could come out of this alive.

Rafe was standing bare-chested. He wore only a pair of expensive looking suit pants. He had drawn a number of runes on his chest in woad. It was a strange anachronistic vision. Aislinn was naked and on her knees. Her body had been abused. He could see dried blood trailing from a swollen lip. There were numerous scratches across her breasts and bruises covered her legs. There was a were-lion standing behind her. She had Aislinn by the hair, pulling her head back and holding a knife to her throat. Jenna stood by, and she smiled as though this was all exceedingly entertaining. Cullen's wolf reared. He felt his fangs extend in his mouth and his hands grew claws.

Rafe walked over to Aislinn. "If Arnauk moves from where he is," Rafe said nonchalantly to no one in particular, "attack him. And I should probably tell you." Rafe petted Aislinn's hair. She pulled back and the knife sliced her skin. A trickle of blood flowed from the cut, and Rafe used a finger to wipe it. He placed the finger in his mouth and smiled down at her affectionately. Then he looked at Cullen. "Several of your men are still alive. I'll let them live, and you and your fool followers all go unharmed, as long as I get the word of the mighty Lord General Cullen Arnauk that none of you will ever return to this place or pursue my mate." His hand reached out and stroked Aislinn's hair again.

Aislinn's eyes were on the ground. She hadn't looked up at Cullen since he walked into the clearing. He could see tears glistening on her cheeks. Throughout Rafe's talking Cullen could hear howling in his ears. *She's right there. Go to her,* his wolf cried. His human side kept the wolf check. Cullen had known that he would be outnumbered, but it looked as though Rafe had brought every Tairneach there was here to fight the Arnauk. That didn't take into account the were-cats and other beasts that Rafe had apparently created. Cullen's pack was significantly smaller to begin with. Subtract from that number all the men Cullen had lost to Rafe already, and the men he had guarding the men Rafe had turned against him. Could Cullen sacrifice Aislinn to get the rest of the pack out of this?

Keith was the one who spoke. His voice startled Cullen. "I don't think so Rafe," he said with a half smile. Cullen looked at Keith. "This is our land," Keith said. "We all fought and bled for this territory long before Aislinn was a consideration. She's not the only thing at stake here, even if she's the only reason you're here," he added, giving Cullen a wicked grin. Cullen looked to Sarah, who nodded in agreement with Keith.

Cullen's gaze fell back to Rafe and he shrugged. "You heard him," he said with a deadly growl that spoke of his wolf surfacing.

Rafe briefly looked annoyed, and then his features smoothed over again. "As you like it. My life will most likely be easier with you dead, even if I lose a few men in the process. But I wouldn't want you to miss the show you've come to see."

Rafe walked over to a number of jars that were on the ground in front of Aislinn. He opened the first jar, dipped his finger, and pulled it out covered in woad. He stepped over to Aislinn and began to draw runes on her chest. Cullen couldn't handle Rafe touching her. His wolf broke free. He shifted in to his hybrid form and moved to attack Rafe. But, before he could get to

Rafe, he was jumped by several of the weres that were surrounding them.

Cullen found himself tearing madly at the flesh of a creature which looked like a cross between a gorilla and a tiger. The man had wild, cat-like eyes and claws that sliced into Cullen's side. He had a huge barrel chest with long arms, but short legs. The creature was colored like a tiger, orange with black stripes across his back that blended into the muscular ape-like chest. His grip nearly broke Cullen's arms as he wrenched them behind the lycan's back, and with the help of several other cats, forced Cullen to his knees. When Cullen looked up he saw all his people in similar positions. They must have tried to join him in the attack. He growled and snapped wildly at the men holding him, but there was no breaking the ape-cat's grip.

Aislinn's scream blazed into his ears. Immediately Cullen's rage shifted its target, and he turned his head to see what had happened. Rafe was standing over Aislinn's writhing body. She shrieked in agony, and began to shift. Her arms and legs shortened and her head took on the look of one of the cats. Her body soon followed. She was covered in brown fur. Black stripes started at the nape of her neck and covered her back, bleeding into spots that vanished into the white fur covering her stomach and the insides of her legs. She was smaller than the other cats present. Rafe probably did that to keep her more controllable.

By the Gods she's beautiful. If Cullen hadn't already been on his knees he would have fallen to them. When the change was completed, Aislinn lay still. She was whimpering a little, but the worst of it was over. She tried to stand, but her legs wobbled. She ended up sitting back down. *Four legs is different than two,* Cullen thought gently. She looked around at herself in confusion, and then seemed to understand when she saw her tail. There was a pause in her movement as it folded out from under her.

Rafe looked down on his work. His face and eyes illuminated with hubris. He had done better than he imagined. He dropped the jar of woad to the ground and walked over to the last jar left. He started speaking in Gaelic, asking the fates to bless his transformation. Energy crackled around the stones. Rafe opened the jar he had picked up. This one was red. He held it up, and the weres surrounding the Circle started howling and screeching.

Rafe put the jar to his mouth. As he drank the liquid, the woad on his chest started to bleed. Sweat beaded and ran down his face. Dropping the empty jar, it and it shattered on the stone slab. With a roar of triumph, tinged in pain Rafe's body began to transform. His dark hair grew into a wild mane. His body grew larger than any lion since prehistory. Rafe's fur was white, and his roar sounded bear-like. Polar bear and lion. There may have been other things in there, but the main combination was obvious. The other jars sitting in front of the standing stones shattered, and various liquids poured out onto the ground, seeping into the earth.

Rafe paced back and forth in front of his audience. The weres raised a cheer that rang in the ears of the Arnauk. For the first time in centuries, Cullen Arnauk felt fear.

Chapter 14

A kingdom founded on injustice never lasts.
-Lucius Annaeus Seneca

Brinah watched the transformation from behind a large stone. The weres were ignoring her. She didn't have strength or speed. She was a weak old woman to them and they were waiting for orders from their leader. She understood why he needed the stone circle so badly now. He had shortened the process. This way he didn't have to go through weeks of pain and waiting. Instantaneous power. But there was always a price for things like that. Brinah wondered what the price for that kind of power would be. She watched her granddaughter lying weak and disoriented on the ground. She wanted to go to her, but she was fairly certain there would be no getting to her while everyone's attention was on Rafe. As she waited, she stared at the liquid seeping into the ground from the broken jars, trying to figure out what had been in them.

Jenna stared in terror as Rafe finished his transformation. With the victorious war cries of his men ringing in his ears, and Aislinn lying at his feet, Rafe didn't notice Jenna walk toward Cullen.

As Jenna knelt in front of him, Cullen growled and snapped at her. His fangs only barely missed her face. She smiled and leaned in toward him, ignoring the danger. When she got closer, Cullen caught Aislinn's scent. Jenna smiled at him. "She does taste good doesn't she," Jenna said and then kissed Cullen deeply.

Cullen was stunned for a moment before he began growling, and Jenna pulled away from the kiss. Her eyes sparkled an unfathomable depth of sadness. Cullen couldn't help but wonder what Rafe had done to her. Jenna spoke very softly, and amidst the din of roaring beasts, he almost missed what she said. "The enemy of my enemy Arnauk. On my signal, call your attack."

Cullen watched Jenna stand up and step to the ape-cat holding Cullen. The beast growled at her. But Jenna was used to men who growled, and she didn't pause for a single moment. She reached up to her shoulders and dropped her red dress to the ground. It pooled around her feet like a bloody puddle. The man holding Cullen stared appreciatively at the beautiful blonde. She stepped closer to him. Jenna placed a finger on her lips and her tongue snaked out to wet her finger. She slowly trailed the wet finger down her chest and over her breast, circling her nipple with it before reaching toward the ape-cat. The man's erection jumped up in front of him. There were few men alive who wouldn't have responded to Jenna's display. She touched the ape-cat on his chest, and he unconsciously released Cullen as the confusion of roaring cheers grew louder.

Cullen immediately jumped to his feet, rounded on the ape-cat and with a feral growl shoved Jenna aside, and lunged for the man's throat. The two beasts rolled to the ground amidst a blur of claws and teeth. When Cullen stood up, there was ragged flesh dangling from his jowls.

Rafe was menacing Aislinn with evil intent. He moved up behind her barely cognizant form. He was so intent on his target that he completely missed Jenna's actions. He pawed at Aislinn, and she turned to face him. She pulled her tail between her legs, backing away from him. She stumbled a bit as she moved, and Rafe was on top of her. His size dwarfed her in all ways. Aislinn cried out as he maneuvered her beneath him. She couldn't see how he could do this and not rip her apart. A gigantic paw held her down as he pressed against her. Aislinn wiggled away from him as best she could, but that mostly entailed lying flat on the ground and trying to use her tail to stop Rafe's intrusion. Her struggles only seemed to spur him on.

Brinah picked up the remainder of the jar at the foot of the nearest standing stone and stared at the substance Rafe had used to aid in his transformation. It had been so long since she learned these things. The residue in the jar was red and smelled of herbs. There must have been blood in it. She looked up at Rafe as he attacked her granddaughter. Using the glass from the jar, she slit her palm and dropped some of her own blood into the mixture, then poured what was left of it onto the ground. Nothing happened. She was panicking, but she was convinced that the only thing needed to disrupt Rafe's transmutation would be a change in the formula, before he left the Circle. As she looked around for something more drastic than her own blood, her eyes fell across the rest of the stones. *Eight more jars.*

Cullen saw Rafe trying to mount Aislinn, and his attention shifted. He howled in rage, calling out the attack, and there wasn't a wolf on the reservation who didn't know that Cullen Arnauk was pissed. Jenna joined her howl with his, and in unison all the Tairneach seemed to come to life. When the Tairneach jumped sides, there was some confusion at first. It was as though no one was sure who should be fighting with whom, but the Arnauk shortly got the idea and the true fight began.

The weres were outnumbered by lycans more than three to one. However, the battle was fought as though the sides were nearly even. The body count piled as fangs tore at throats and claws disemboweled stomachs.

Cullen tackled the were-bear-lion that was Rafe and the pair toppled over, leaving Aislinn cowering on the ground, watching the fight. Her head was spinning, and she couldn't quite make out what was happening yet. She felt as though she was trapped in one of Rafe's nightmares. Cullen was greatly outmatched in strength, but Rafe had never been in a hand to hand fight, was slower than the lycan, and was new to his form. The two men grappled and rolled. Cullen weaved, avoiding Rafe's gigantic paws and swiped at him in return, tearing chunk after chunk of flesh from Rafe's hide. Rafe tilted his head like a bear and roared a lion's rage at Cullen, drool dripping from his jowls.

Kara watched the insanity break out around her. When Jenna called the Tairneach, it was clear that the bitch had been planning this. Kara charged Jenna, intent on destroying the woman. Jenna watched unimpressed. Just before Kara reached Jenna a large lycan appeared out of nowhere, crashed into her side, and pinned her down. Kara grappled with the lycan, roaring her rage at the loss of her target and Jenna disappeared into the fray.

Brinah worked her way around the Circle of stones. As she managed to spill blood into the fourth reagent mixture on the ground, Rafe started to falter. At first, he wasn't sure what was happening. Something didn't feel right. Cullen charged him again, taking him to the ground. The were-bear-lion wrapped his arms around the lycan and tried to crush him. Cullen growled in pain as Rafe nearly broke his back. Brinah was feeling light headed when she reached the sixth stone. She pushed herself to complete her task. She sliced open her other hand and spilled blood in the mixture that was still seeping into the ground. Rafe suddenly dropped Cullen. He stood disoriented, looking around with a fog over his eyes. When he saw Brinah, he roared in anger and charged.

Brinah ducked behind the seventh stone as Rafe ran at her. In his rage, Rafe ran into the stone, which wobbled on its base and began to fall over. Brinah scrambled out of the way just as Cullen hit Rafe in the back and knocked him over the stone, rolling into the clearing beyond the stones. Brinah watched in dismay as the pair rolled out of the Circle and toward the woods. She was feeling the effects of the blood loss, and she wasn't sure that contaminating the rest of the stones would affect Rafe's transformation, if he wasn't inside the Circle.

Aislinn felt the battle rage around her, as if she wasn't really there. It was as though she was in one of her dreams, staring down at everything. Her body burned as though she was on fire, and her head swam. When she moved the world spun. Somewhere in her mind she registered that her grandmother was standing nearby. Aislinn watched Brinah pick up a broken piece of glass and slice into her wrist. Aislinn cried out, but it came out more like the screeching growl of a jungle cat. Forcing herself to her feet, Aislinn ran to her grandmother with a drunken step.

Brinah was near passing out. When Aislinn reached her, she thought she was being attacked at first.

Brinah fell back onto the ground as Aislinn butted her head against her grandmother in lieu of arms to hug her. Aislinn wasn't sure what to do. She tried to calm down and force herself to become human again. She never realized how much it would hurt. It felt as though she had been in pain forever. Her body twisted and contorted, shifting a little, and then fear and the pain seemed to cause her to shift back. Aislinn looked around at all the others. There had to be a way to do this. She concentrated on being herself again. She needed to help her grandmother. Her body began its awkward shift once more. It was nowhere near as smooth and graceful as the others all made it look. Aislinn didn't manage to get all the way back to human. She ended up in her hybrid form as she stabilized. The pain was more than she was able to deal with though, and she lay on the ground staring at her grandmother with pleading amber eyes.

When Brinah realized that the animal in front of her was Aislinn, she grabbed her granddaughter into her arms. It was all she could do to remain calm. Seeing all the cuts and bruises on Aislinn's body, Brinah pulled open the bag she carried. Her hands shook, but she managed to find the small bottle she was looking for. She pulled the cork out of the top of the bottle and poured the solution into Aislinn's mouth.

Rafe was still holding his own in the fight despite the fuzzing of his senses. He didn't think it could last much longer. He managed to get in a hard swipe, and knocked Cullen back several feet. Cullen was starting to tire and was fighting the pain of several broken bones from being repeatedly hit by the were-bear-lion. He rolled to a stop, dazed momentarily. Rafe headed back to the stone circle intent on killing Brinah before she could cause any further damage. Seeing him coming, Brinah crawled for the ninth stone.

Aislinn felt a cooling sensation through her body, and suddenly her senses cleared. Realizing that she hadn't quite managed to shift all the way to her human form, she sat on her knees staring down at herself. Most of the fur was gone from her stomach, but there was still quite a bit across the backs of her arms and over her legs. She had spots that bled into her hairline, down her neck and collarbone. They turned into stripes, flowing down her back and trailing off, becoming spots again across her hips and down her thighs. Her hands were still claws and she could feel fangs in her mouth. With a measure of gratitude she realized, she had no tail in this form. When she saw Rafe charging in her direction, Aislinn assumed that he was after her until she followed his gaze to where Brinah was sitting near the next stone.

Rafe singled in on Brinah as she added her blood to the base of the ninth stone. Lunging just in time Aislinn managed to throw Rafe off balance enough to miss Brinah, as she crawled away and lay down just beyond the Circle amidst the melee. Rafe grabbed hold of Aislinn, growling his rage as they rolled into the center of the Circle and came to a stop with Aislinn beneath him, pinned to the stone slab. He growled into her face as she struggled to push him off. "Rach-air-muin," Aislinn spat at him. Rafe grinned and leaned down. His tongue snaked out of his mouth, and he licked Aislinn's chin up to her lips, trying to force his way in between.

Brinah passed out watching her blood seep into the damp ground at the base of the ninth stone. The first of the pain shot through Rafe's arms and legs, as Cullen plowed into him for the last time. As the men grappled, Rafe roared in pain. For all his strength he wasn't able to combat the twisting of his body as well as Cullen Arnauk at the same time.

Cullen's jaws closed on Rafe's throat with a sickening crunch, and he yanked his head back, tearing Rafe's throat from his neck. Cullen fell away from Rafe's body, spitting the bloody mass of flesh onto the ground, relief surging through him. Cullen sat there breathing heavily for a moment before he came to his senses and looked around for Aislinn. He let his wolf slip back and took on his human form, feeling some of the tension ebb.

All around them, the sounds of battle were coming to an end. Slowly the Arnauk and Tairneach, who were left alive, gathered around the stone circle for orders. They stood uneasily together. Bodies riddled the ground. The smell of blood was so thick, the lycans couldn't scent the difference between each other. Mates sensing loss searched through the crowd for each other in fear, crying out mentally for their missing halves. There was a growing group of were-cats, being herded together to be dealt with when Jenna and Cullen were able to give their joint attentions to the problem.

Appearing from the shadows with the dying of the fight, Jenna stood over Rafe's mangled form, her body apparently untouched from the battle. She kicked at the dead were-bear-lion with one foot, as if to make sure he wasn't coming back. Then she looked over at Cullen with a relief that made him start to wonder if he had misjudged her. But that moment was fleeting. The small glimmer seemed to fade, and the relief was replaced with Jenna's standard dark smile, her fingers fiddling noticeably with a ring on a chain around her neck. Cullen recognized the large ruby signet that had been on Brennus Tairneach's hand for the whole of the time that Cullen had known him.

Jenna turned to the two large lycans trailing behind her protectively. "Have the others gather the bodies of our dead and make ready to leave."

The large man bowed his head in compliance. "What about the cats," he sneered, looking over at the group of creatures that were being gathered together. It was taking quite a few lycans to keep them all in line. There were a few excessively large mixed were-beasts that the lycan guards were having trouble with.

Jenna looked over her shoulder at Cullen, who was still sitting on his knees trying to gather his strength. "I think that Rafe and his followers have been a Tairneach problem for long enough. Let the Arnauk clean up the mess." She grinned weakly at Cullen. "I wouldn't want you to get the wrong idea about me," she said sweetly and walked away from the gory scene in the Circle of standing stones.

"Jenna," Cullen called after her. She stopped momentarily and turned to him. "Brennus would have been proud," he said, loud enough that most of the Tairneach present wouldn't miss it.

Jenna's eyes fell away from his with a teary thoughtful glaze across them, as if she didn't really believe it. She looked at Cullen again with a sad grateful stare, before turning and disappearing into the woods on her way back to the cabin.

Cullen shook his head and started to stand. He felt his body crunch. He had a lot of healing to do. Rafe may not have been very skilled at fighting, but his strength had been monstrous. Every time he managed to make contact with Cullen, Rafe broke a bone or ripped a gash in Cullen's flesh that would scar horribly before he had a chance to heal. Still, he would survive. *Barely,* he thought.

Cullen's eyes fell on Aislinn. She was so amazingly beautiful. His heart was near exploding with how much he needed to hold her. She hadn't managed to change out of her hybrid form yet, but she appeared relatively unharmed. A number of claw slashes along her waist and arms appeared to be healing quickly. *Unbelievably quickly,* Cullen noted, watching the scratches on her breasts fade away.

Suddenly he realized he was staring at her breasts. His breath caught in his chest, as his eyes traveled to the small scattered spots and white fur that began just under and along the sides of her breasts. The spots darkened to mottled black in color, where the white fur blended into the same brown color as her hair, and increased in number traveling around her sides. The spots seemed to dip and gather in just the right places to accentuate each curve of her body. The leopard like markings kissed the tops of her shoulders and faded along her collar bone. He was dying to press his lips to her skin and taste each gorgeous spot. They ran up the sides of her neck and along her hair line. Her face was more human than it should have been, even in hybrid form.

Cullen wondered how many women Rafe experimented with before he came up with this. Aislinn's features were most definitely cat-like. Her upper lip curved up just enough to appear like a muzzle, without losing the thick human lower lip. Her nose was somewhat flat against her muzzle, but was oddly wider than a cat's should have been. His tongue wet his own lips unconsciously. He felt his arousal growing even through the pain of his injuries. Her eyes were what captured him the most. There was no cat there. They were too round. The pupils took up too much area. He smiled. Somehow those eyes were lycan. Amber replaced the silver that they had been before and swirled around the black dilated pupils. Flecks of iridescent blue mingled in their depths, causing them to shift from gold to green and back again. It was hypnotic to watch.

She had gone to Brinah's collapsed body and was kneeling next to her grandmother. Aislinn pulled Brinah up onto her lap, stroking her grandmother's hair, tears streaming down her face. Her gaze shifted alternately from the strange spots that covered the back of her arms to her grandmother's face. She didn't think she could take one more thing. She just didn't have the strength left. She believed that Cullen didn't want her, Rafe had raped her and changed her into this thing, and now her grandmother was lying dead in her arms. She trembled with the excess of misery that flowed through her. *I knew I never should have let you come here,* she thought as she stroked her grandmother's hair gently. Aislinn wouldn't let herself think it in words, but she felt as though this was her fault.

Cullen forced himself to stand and walk to Aislinn. She was concentrating so hard on her own thoughts that she didn't notice him coming. As he walked around behind her, he watched the spots blend into stripes. The change was so subtle it was difficult to tell where the stripes ended and the spots began. He studied the elegant slant of the stripes across her back, trailing the line of her waist and leading his eyes to follow the curve of her hip. He winced and let out a sharp escape of air as he knelt behind her. Cullen's presence startled her and Aislinn flinched away, as if he was going to hurt her. She refused to look at him.

"Aislinn," he started and tried to reach for her. Cullen felt more pain from her reaction, than he did from his broken body.

She shied away from him. "Stop," she interrupted. Her voice was trembling, and she held herself protectively away from him. "Just stop. Whatever it is I can't do it right now. Just leave me alone."

Cullen felt tears well up. He held them down, but he moved back, falling to sit a few feet away, watching her back. He was tired of not knowing what to do. It seemed to be a perpetual state of mind since Aislinn appeared in his life. As much as he wanted to hold her, he didn't want her to associate him with the types of things that Rafe had done to her. So, forcing her to let him hold her was out of the question. He sat on the ground, those few feet from her seeming like miles, and feeling broken in so many ways.

Keith approached them tentatively. He could tell from their expressions and the way Aislinn was holding Brinah that he needed to be careful. He knelt next to Cullen. "You got hit hard. Are you able to make it to the cabin on your own feet?"

Cullen didn't answer. He just stared at Aislinn's back.

"All right," Keith said on a long tired breath. "I'll send someone over to get you back to the cabin. I know you haven't bothered to pay any real attention, but you don't look like you should be conscious." He cleared his throat and looked at Aislinn's stooped form over Brinah's body. Lowering his voice, hoping he wouldn't upset Aislinn more, he added, "Didn't Brinah say that she made something to help with healing people?"

Aislinn couldn't help but hear the conversation. Her ears seemed impossibly better than they had been before. She wished she could turn off all her senses. It was overwhelming. Without looking at them, she grabbed Brinah's bag and shoved it toward them. Then Aislinn went back to mourning over Brinah's body.

Keith took the bag with a sympathetic look at Aislinn's back. He opened the bag and looked at the assortment of small bottles and jars. Some of them held left over reagents, but most of them were full of foul smelling liquids. He wasn't sure what exactly he was looking at. "Well," he said with a shrug. "What's the worst that could happen?" He picked one of the corked bottles out of the bag, popped the cork out of the bottle, and took a small sip. A gentle cooling sensation seeped into his muscles, and he felt a great deal more awake all of a sudden. He tipped the bottle up and drank down the rest. His entire body tingled pleasantly and his scratches began to knit together before their eyes.

Keith pocketed one of the full bottles, hating the fact that he was being so practical as he looked at Aislinn and Brinah. He figured that the stuff would be useful, but with Brinah dead they were going to have to figure out how to make it again on their own. He uncorked another of the small bottles and handed it to Cullen. "I hope this is the same stuff I just drank. It looks and smells the same. It's foul, but it feels nice once it's down."

Cullen didn't respond at first. His eyes hadn't left Aislinn. Keith got the distinct impression that he was on his own for the rest of the evening. One look at Rafe's dead form, and he figured that Cullen had earned the evening off. He nudged the bottle into Cullen's hand and finally got his friend to drink the stuff before he left Cullen alone. Keith took the bag to deal with the worst of the injuries. His brain went over the list of things that would need to be accomplished before he could go find his bed. At the very least, he figured he'd have to figure out what to do with the large number of were-beasts they had taken prisoner. It wasn't as if they had facilities to keep these guys captive.

Aislinn sat there, crying over Brinah, for what seemed like an eternity to Cullen. But he wasn't going anywhere. He could wait. All around them, bodies were gathered, and the battle was cleaned away. There were even omegas cleaning the broken jars from around the stone circle. They moved quietly, not wanting to disturb the angry looking alpha or Aislinn. Eventually, Sarah approached Aislinn. The crying had stopped, and now she was just stroking Brinah's hair gently and staring off into the woods.

Sarah crouched down next to Aislinn. She looked over at Cullen, but was greeted with a blank expression. Sarah was tired and finding it difficult to be sympathetic, but forced her voice to be gentle when she spoke. "Aislinn, can you let us take Brinah with the others? You need some sleep. There will be a memorial to honor all the dead in a couple days and all the bodies will be burned."

Aislinn took one last look at her grandmother. "I want to be there when her body is prepared." Her voice was devoid of emotion.

"I'm sure that can be arranged. Can I get you to go up to the cabin now?" Sarah suggested and looked over at Cullen again.

"Where can I sleep?" Aislinn asked.

Sarah's features took on an unsure and concerned look as her eyes met Cullen's. He didn't respond. "There are plenty of rooms. I don't think anyone is worried about assigned beds tonight. If you won't be sleeping with Cullen, then I'm sure you could take any room on the main floor." Sarah watched Cullen's jaw tighten. Aislinn stood without looking at either of them and walked away toward the cabin.

Cullen rubbed his face with his hands and growled. His body wasn't nearly as pained as it had been, but he still felt as though he was being torn apart. He stood to follow Aislinn and a couple omegas instantly appeared to try and help him. He waved them off angrily. He wasn't about to let Aislinn see him weak right now. Not wanting to let her out of his sight, Cullen limped along after her with the concerned omegas cowering behind.

Sarah caught up and grabbed his arm, pulling him to a stop. The glare that he leveled on her would have had most lycans bowing and scraping. At the very least, another lycan would have released his arm, but Sarah had known him too long and wasn't giving way.

"What the hell," she asked.

Cullen wrenched his arm away. "What do you think?"

"I think you haven't bothered to say the two things that might magically fix the entire situation. I think men are morons, and you, Lord Arnauk, are no exception," Sarah growled at him in frustration.

"Difficult to say anything when she tells me to stop and not touch her or talk to her," he growled back.

"And of course you listened." Sarah said incredulously. "Because *you* always listen when someone tells *you* what to do. By all the Gods I need to figure out what she says and how she says it."

"So how do *you* think I should fix this," Cullen said sarcastically, still glaring and snarling. His mind was grasping for anything that might work and rid him of his uncertainty.

Sarah leveled her tone. She could hear how much he was hurting. "Tell her that you're sorry and that you love her," she said simply. Then she walked away.

Cullen sent the omegas off and hurried after Aislinn, following her scent through the cabin to find what room she went to. He was just grateful she hadn't decided to run off again. He stood outside the door to the room aching to go inside. He knocked, but there was no answer. A few lycans passing by were trying to ignore their alpha politely. He tried the door and found it locked. So he knocked again. "Aislinn I need to talk to you," he said through the door. There was no answer, and a few more people pretended not to stare. Cullen's pride was getting to him. He couldn't take doing this in front of the pack, not after the display he had made of himself over her already. He growled and headed down the hall, up the stairs, and went to his room.

Aislinn stood on the other side of the door listening to his footsteps retreat down the hall. She went over to the bed and laid down. She was trying desperately to not feel any more. All she wanted was to be in his arms, but she didn't think she could handle leaving if she gave in now and spoke with him. She assumed that he wanted to explain, tell her why he didn't think she should stay with him, how it would be better for her to leave. She didn't care what his reasons were. She kicked the blankets back and then pulled them over herself.

Aislinn didn't sleep very well. Every time her eyes closed she was plagued with nightmares. She dreamed about Rafe, about Jenna, about her grandmother, but the worst part was that in all the dreams she was alone. She wished she had never met Cullen. Maybe she wouldn't feel the loneliness so badly if he hadn't shown her what it would be like to be with people again.

Cullen lay awake as well. He was afraid that she'd run away, and he wouldn't get a chance to do anything about it. He was pissed. That was easier than being hurt. *She over reacted. It's her own fault for taking off like she did. She won't even let me explain. And how dense does the woman have to be that she can't see what I did to get her back?* Cullen's mind reeled all night long.

Chapter 15

Hawdd cymod lle bo cariad.
Reconciliation is easy where there is love.
-Gaelic proverb

Cullen threw his bedroom door open before most of the rest of the pack was awake. He couldn't believe that all his injuries seemed to have healed overnight. He figured he should get that stuff Brinah made on tap.

The only lycans awake that early after the night they had were either omegas, who were getting breakfast ready and finishing the clean up, or others who hadn't slept the night before. Most of them were people who had lost mates in the fight. Cullen felt a strange guilty, bitter jealousy. *At least they had mates to lose*, he thought angrily.

Cullen went down to his office. There were several handwritten notes on his desk. Cullen recognized Keith's scrawl. The first one said, "Don't wake me up on pain of death alpha boy!" Cullen couldn't help the grudging grin. He tossed that one in the garbage, and considered waking Keith up on principle. The second one said, "The feds showed up after you went to bed. I handed them the cats for safe keeping and made the report. You're welcome. Not to say you probably won't get a phone call. Did that make sense? Who cares I'm tired." The third said, "Word was sent to the den with a list of the deaths." The fourth said, "Arrangements being made for the memorial service, including pyres for burning the bodies. We're giving it three days to allow for everyone who lost someone to be contacted and get here." The fifth said, "Anything else you want, take care of it yourself. Although I would point out that your schedule looks pretty clear to me. Leaving you a few days to straighten out the mess you made with the lovely were-mystery-cat-girl who is currently sleeping in the omega's quarters. By the way, I assigned someone to keep an eye on her. Just in case."

Cullen sat the last note down. *Keith should be the alpha,* he thought and he was serious. Not that any of the things his friend had taken care of wouldn't have been handled personally under different circumstances, but Cullen wasn't entirely sure that he ever wanted to deal with any of this ever again if he couldn't get Aislinn back. He created this pack so that lycans could be safe and have families. *What the hell's the point if I can't have one of my own? It took so much for her to trust me. Now I'm starting all over again with a strike on the record, her grandmother dead, and who the hell knows what Rafe did to her.* He was staring out his window.

* * * *

Aislinn got out of bed. She laid there staring at the ceiling for some time before she decided to get up, find some clothes, and figure out what she wanted to do. He hoped it was early enough that she wouldn't have to face anyone who would make it difficult. She stood and turned on the light. She felt remarkably good considering, what she had been through. If it weren't for the bags under her eyes and the headache from all the nightmares, this would have been a relatively good morning.

She looked in the long mirror on the back of the closet door. She still didn't look human. She examined herself in the mirror. Tears filled her eyes.

Well, if he wanted me to leave before, now he'll really want me to go away. She couldn't believe, even a small bit, that he would want some kind of cat-thing when so many of the female lycans in his pack were interested. *Maybe Celia can have what she wants now.* She wiped the tears off her face and pulled herself together. She had spent seven years of fear and running not crying. She didn't need to make it a habit now.

She had no idea how to make herself look human, but she didn't want to leave the room looking like this, or at the very least without finding some clothes. She opened drawers and the closet looking for something to wrap around herself so that she could go find a bathroom. When she didn't find anything, she contemplated the sheet on the bed. *I don't even have a toothbrush.* Finally frustration got the best of her. She was feeling trapped. Aislinn threw the door open and looked out into the hall. She waited patiently, hoping that someone would come walking by and she could ask for help.

When a pretty dark haired girl came walking down the hall, Aislinn stepped out to talk to her. The girl yipped and backed up. Aislinn almost growled at her out of spite, then caught herself. Here she was, looking like one of those things that had just invaded and killed people. No wonder the girl was scared of her. "Don't," Aislinn said holding up her hands, "I just need some clothes and maybe a toothbrush. I'm on your side." The last words came out almost sarcastically.

Recognition flowed over the girl's face. She bowed her head submissively and blushed. There wasn't a lycan on the reservation who didn't know who Aislinn was, what had happened last night, and how their alpha felt about her. "I'm sorry, miss, I didn't recognize you. I can get you some clothes," she said sweetly, not raising her head.

"Um, just Aislinn, okay? Uh… what's your name?" she said, not sure how to handle the girl's suddenly overly respectful tone.

"Milis." The girl looked up and smiled broadly. Usually the higher members of the pack didn't ask the names of omegas for something as simple as getting some clothes. They'd just send the omega running. "What would you like?"

"It doesn't matter. Just clothes." Aislinn answered with relief and quickly added her size to the statement. Milis nodded and headed off down the hall.

Aislinn went back into her room. She sat on the edge of the bed. Her stomach growled, and she really needed the bathroom. She hoped that Milis wouldn't take too long. Aislinn's prayers were answered, when Milis returned almost as quickly as she had left. She brought jeans and a plain white t-shirt, a bra and underwear, and socks and shoes. "Thank you so much Milis."

The girl beamed at Aislinn as though nothing else in the world could have made her as happy as having brought Aislinn these clothes. The girl was being so sweet that Aislinn thought to take advantage of it. "Do you think you might be able to help me with one more thing?"

Milis nodded happily. "Of course."

"Well I was wondering where the bathroom is," Aislinn said hastily. "But when I get done with that." She paused and tried to think of how to put it. *Fuck it*, Aislinn thought angrily. *There is no delicate way of saying I'm ignorant and don't know how to control this curse that's been dumped on me.* "I don't know how to change this back to normal," she said uncomfortably.

Milis' happy look turned to uncertainty. She shifted and seemed to think about how Aislinn had said that. "Normal?"

"Human looking," Aislinn responded, but that didn't seem to help Milis return to the happy helpful girl she had been moments before.

She nodded and looked at Aislinn sympathetically. "I'm sorry. I think you're asking me to help you learn how to shift. That's really kind of a personal thing. Parents teach it to their children privately. It's rather a—"

Aislinn had the overwhelming fear that she would be like this forever. She interrupted Milis. "Well I don't have parents or anyone else to teach me anything," she said angrily and teary eyed.

Milis lowered her head again. "I am sorry, Miss. Perhaps one of the betas or Lord Arnauk—"

Aislinn interrupted her again, the anger in her voice increased, and a note of sarcasm filtered into it. "Lord Arnauk has more important things to do than deal with me."

Milis raised her eyes at that. Obvious confusion and disbelief marred her face. "Miss, Lord Arnauk brought the entire pack out here looking for you. He risked and lost a lot of lives to get to you, not the least of which was his own. It may not be my place to say, but the tone you used when speaking of him wasn't what I would have expected from that. He wouldn't have done this for anyone else that I know of." Milis looked personally offended.

Aislinn could see from the near fear in the girl's eyes, mingling with the rest of her emotions, that normally Milis would not have been quite this bold. *But she doesn't know about what happened in the office.* "Fine. Thank you for your help," Aislinn said shortly. "Just point me toward the bathroom."

Milis returned the snippy tone and sent Aislinn down the hall. After getting cleaned up, Aislinn headed outside. She wanted to clear her head. As she walked across the lawn, she started to rethink the day in Cullen's office. She thought about how little was actually said. She thought about how they continually seemed to be misunderstanding each other. *But there wasn't anything to misunderstand. He was getting rid of me,* she thought. When she looked up she found that she was standing in the clearing just outside the standing stones.

Horrible memories raced into her mind. She had to work hard to block the image of her grandmother's body lying on the ground. She wrapped her arms around herself, shivering.

* * * *

Cullen watched Aislinn head across the lawn toward the woods. He instantly got up and headed out of his office, down the hall, and through a side door. He'd be damned if he was going to let her take off without a word. He didn't trust her to stay put for an instant. When he got out the side door he saw a pretty little brunette following quietly from a distance. *Keith's idea of a guard. If Aislinn wants to leave that little thing isn't stopping her.* Cullen scared Milis as he came up behind her. "I've got her. Go on back to the cabin."

Milis nodded gratefully and disappeared back inside. She had looked frustrated. Cullen wondered what Aislinn had done to upset Milis. *Hard to say with*

Aislinn, he thought angrily. *She seems to have a gift for that.* By the time he caught up with her, she was standing in the clearing outside the stones and holding herself. Cullen felt his anger melting when he saw the obvious signs of her upset. She had lost her grandmother, and he knew that other things had happened. He was compelled to go to her, but he didn't think he could take it if she pushed him away again.

Aislinn heard the footsteps coming up behind her. As a breeze filtered past, she caught his scent and knew Cullen was watching her. Her heart raced in her chest. She was so tired of feeling like this, and now she wasn't even positive that she was thinking straight. *What I wouldn't give for a premonition now.* Her dreams lately had all been nightmares reflective of her day life. She waited to see if he would do something or if he intended to just stand there watching her. *Well, I suppose it's encouraging that he isn't just letting it go. I suppose I'm going to have to talk to him eventually.* When he didn't do or say anything, she walked toward the standing stones. The one that had been toppled in the fight the night before was still flat on the ground. "Is someone going to stand it back upright?" she called out to him.

Cullen let her voice sink into him. *At least she sounds willing to talk,* he thought as he stepped out of the edge of the woods and approached her. He noticed she was still in her hybrid form and wondered if she liked it that well or if she was having trouble controlling her change. When she tried to hide her face from him, he guessed the latter. The last of his anger ebbed away and was replaced with guilt for not having been able to keep her safe.

"Someone will probably stand it back up. There have been other concerns to this point." He managed to get up next to her without her trying to get away. Something about Aislinn's demeanor made him a bit braver, and he let an arm slide around her back. When she didn't pull away, he put his other hand beneath her chin and made her look at him. He smiled at her, reading the hurt and confusion in her eyes. "Besides, it's awfully heavy," he said softly, trying to sound light and make her smile. There was a long silent pause. He stared into her amber eyes and felt a terrible ache, as he took in all the cat-like features of her face. "Tá tú hálainn," he said breathlessly.

She dropped her eyes from his and moved to bury her face against his chest. She just couldn't keep looking at him.

"You don't believe me," he asked gently.

"How could a wolf find whatever the hell I am beautiful," she asked with annoyance.

"I thought we already had this discussion. I do remember telling you at one point that it wouldn't matter," Cullen said, in his most sincere tone. His stomach was turning, he was so nervous. If he didn't take this opportunity, he didn't know if he'd get another one. "Besides, I do find you incredibly beautiful. And it's not just because of what you look like or smell like. I like the way you make me think and feel. You're intelligent and capable. I never knew what I wanted until I met you."

Aislinn looked up at him. She wanted to believe him so badly.

Sarah's words echoed in Cullen's mind. *She better be right,* he thought, knowing that if Aislinn ripped his heart out they'd be finding a new alpha for the Arnauk.

He cleared his throat, and Aislinn could see a nervous schoolboy looking at her through his eyes. "Aislinn Brianne Stevens," he said, with a lopsided grin, using her full name. She finally smiled back and it gave him courage to continue. "Tá grá agam duit."

Aislinn felt her heart start beating again. She didn't even know that it had stopped. He leaned down and nuzzled her face up so that he could kiss her, afraid to wait for a response. Electricity shot through them both as their lips met. Her hands slid up his chest and gripped his shirt in her fists as though he may try to pull away. His arms wrapped around her more tightly. One hand slipped up into her hair. It took some coaxing, but she opened her mouth to his inquisitive tongue, allowing him to explore the new fangs. She sucked on his tongue gently and bit at it as he tested the sharpness of one fang.

He smiled against her mouth at her little game. He kissed her nose and then nuzzled his against it again before looking down into her eyes as if to ask for her answer. Her brilliant amber eyes swirled with blue flecks. Cullen hadn't thought they could be more beautiful than they had been before. He had to admit, he liked the amber better than the silver. *She'll need to learn to control that*, he thought, pleased that he might actually get the chance to teach her if she'd let him. He refused to let go of her, afraid that her mood might shift against him again. She still hadn't answered him, but she seemed happy with what he had said. In the silence, his next thought was out of his mouth before he realized what he was saying. "Mate with me."

Aislinn was shocked. She pulled back a little so that she could look into his face and try to read him. She actually considered invading his mind to see what he was thinking. "How do you go from wanting to get rid of me to wanting to mate with me over night," she asked suspiciously.

Cullen's brow furrowed and upset seeped into his eyes. "I never wanted to get rid of you. It killed me to suggest that you go back to your family. But it seemed like that was what you wanted, and you were afraid to say it. I know how I would feel if I was told to choose between the pack and…" Cullen stopped as he realized where that one was going.

"And me?" Aislinn asked. "What would you do?" Her voice softened and sounded more curious than angry. "I mean. I'd never ask you to do that. But…"

"I already made that choice," he said definitely. He stared into her eyes hard. "If I can't have you, I don't want any of it."

"I don't understand. I mean, I already left my family to protect them. And now," she looked at the spots on her hands, "there really is no going back to them. Not like this. I'll miss them until the day I die. But if it had come down to it, and I could have gone back or stayed with you." She shook her head and seemed to look inside herself. "I would have stayed. I just didn't know how to say it to my grandmother." She looked at Cullen again, understanding resolving her features.

Cullen leaned down and kissed her. The passion in that kiss exceeded everything he had ever felt. His hands roamed over her body, trying to pull her closer. Heat rolled low in Aislinn's belly, and the scent of her need rose between them as readily as his steel erection pressed against her hip. Cullen growled and pulled back to look down at her. "So is that a yes?" he prompted hopefully.

Aislinn smiled at him as she tried to catch her breath. Relief and need overwhelmed her. "Now?"

Cullen grinned excitedly, hoping that the emotional roller coaster ride was ending. "If you want now I could probably arrange it. But it generally takes a bit more than an announcement in the great room. And there are quite a few people who lost mates last night who might not be enthusiastic about attending a mating ceremony alone the morning after." He bent to kiss her again, licking her lips and then sucking and nibbling on her lower one.

Aislinn moaned into his mouth as he kissed her. Encouraged by the sweet sound, Cullen's hands found their way beneath her shirt. He growled with pleasure as his hands found soft fur covering her back. He let his fingers dance along her back wondering where each stripe was and wanting to see her naked again.

"Then when," she asked.

He laughed and hugged her tightly, burying his face in her hair and breathing in her scent, dying to possess her. "Mmm," he rumbled. "I'll have to see what the atmosphere of the pack is like before I answer that." He kissed her neck and then started to nibble and suck on her ear. "But I want to hear you say it."

Aislinn pulled back from him and looked into his swirling amber eyes. His wolf was close to the surface. Cullen stared back at the glassy look of her own amber eyes. "It's not really fair, you know," she teased him, blinking away the happy tears and delaying saying it. "I don't even know your full name," she said, remembering that morning not so long ago when he weaseled her full name out of her only to use it against her a few moments ago.

He grinned back with a tortured look on his face. "Cullen is ainm dom. That's it," he played along, letting a heavy Scottish accent that had long since dropped from his speech color the statement. "My parents were from a day and age that didn't use names the same way you do. Cullen of the clan Arnauk. Now say it."

She grinned and giggled. "Oh really," she continued to tease. "How old are you anyway?"

Cullen growled his frustration at her game, and his eyes narrowed. "Lost count. Say it."

Aislinn's eyes softened, and she leaned in for another kiss. He dipped his head down and kissed her gently, balled his hand in her hair, and then pressed his nose into her hair and breathed her in again. "Please say it," he asked against her ear.

Aislinn bit at his neck. As much fun as teasing him was, she didn't think she should make her alpha beg. She spoke so softly into his ear that he nearly missed it. "Tá grá agam duit, Cullen. Yes I'll mate with you. And anything else you may want of me."

Cullen's wolf howled with joy. He crushed her to himself just breathing her scent and reveling in the fact that she was his. She said she would be his. He felt himself begin to shift. Cullen growled as his control slipped and his wolf surfaced. He knew that he wasn't going to be able to stop this. He looked around for any witnesses to what he was about to do. His senses were a bit fuzzy, with his focus on Aislinn, but he didn't see or scent anyone in the woods. He didn't even manage to get out of his clothes before the shift started.

Aislinn felt is grip on her grow almost painful as a rumbling growl in his throat warned her what was coming. Aislinn found herself facing Cullen as he shifted into his hybrid form. She'd seen him like this last night during the fight, but she never really got a good look. She'd never seen anything but his eyes shift before. His muzzle began to protrude, and his skin color darkened. His ears moved back and up on his head, his hands grew claws, and his entire body grew larger. He groaned as his jeans became uncomfortably tight, especially with the raging hard-on in his pants. He hadn't lost control like this since he was a young man.

Aislinn's hand came up to his face, and she traced his features. Where Aislinn's face was more human than beast, Cullen's was just the opposite. His nose and mouth protruded from his face too far to make kissing as Aislinn knew it possible. She was considering how to go about it when he leaned in and licked her lips. His voice was a grumble monotone not meant for speaking, "Mmm, I coullldnn't lleet mmy betterr hallf haavve all the funn," he said.

Aislinn could see the pleasure in his eyes as he began pulling at her clothes. She couldn't help being amused at his impatience. In hybrid form Cullen may have been big and strong but he had no manual dexterity. He ended up ripping her bra off when he couldn't get the clasp. From the tone of his growl, she knew that he wasn't finding the clothing dilemma at all amusing. He ripped at his own shirt, and then his jeans getting them off. Considering how tightly he had grown into them, there really wasn't any other way.

His gaze on her was intense. Aislinn felt drawn to him in a way she couldn't express. She knew she was about to find out what he had been holding back from her before. Her body trembled with anticipation. He growled at her and she felt his voice in her mind. *On your hands and knees*, came the insistent, needy, order.

She looked at him in surprised confusion.

You didn't think we relied on voices in other forms did you? He growled again. *On your hands and knees.*

"I've still got a lot to learn," Aislinn grinned as she obediently turned away from him and knelt on the grass next to the fallen stone. She looked back over her shoulder at him as he watched her. He was growling nearly continually, a soft insistent rumble deep in his chest with each breath. His member stood out in front of him proudly. It was a good inch or more longer than it was in his human form, and it was as thick as her wrist. She wiggled her butt anxiously. She wanted to feel him insider her so badly. Then she noticed the thick knot growing at the base of his shaft. That concerned her a bit. She remembered what Rissa had said. She suddenly realized that the differences here might be more than she was necessarily prepared for.

Cullen saw some doubt filter across her face, but it had gone too far for him to stop now. The most he could do was try and temper the beast, but he was afraid his wolf was going to win this time. As she wiggled deliciously in front of him he fell to his knees behind her. Reaching out, he ran a clawed hand down her striped back before taking her by the spotted hip. His other hand held her hips still in front of him. The only thing keeping him from letting loose all his pent up need for her was the promise to his wolf that he would get what he wanted. He didn't need to rush. Cullen leaned down to take in the scent of her sex. His tongue dove into her glistening slit to lap at the juices spilling from her. She moaned and wiggled some more, trying to impale herself on his tongue.

Aislinn's growing need for him far outweighed any fear she may have felt about his massive erection or what he intended to do to her with it. She felt a beast inside her fighting against her human common sense, and she suddenly understood what he meant when he referred to his wolf. His tongue drove into her. He licked the walls inside her in a way that no human tongue possibly could. She writhed in ecstasy, as he managed to bury his tongue all the way back to her cervix and continue the onslaught on her senses. She moaned again, the sound increasing in intensity. "Cullen please," she begged, when he pulled his tongue out of her and began circling her clit deftly.

She whined and wiggled her sex against his face. She couldn't help it. He growled out loud again and sat back to regain some control. She looked over her shoulder with a wicked grin and watched him lick her juices off his muzzle.

Her eyes flashed feral as her cat growled at him. He couldn't help but give in to that sound. He straightened up behind her, and grabbed hold of her hips with a strength that would leave hand print bruises. Slipping the head of his cock up and down her slit, he felt her try to push onto it, coating the head in her slick wet heat. Aislinn fought his grip on her hips trying to push back, but he was too strong for her. He groaned his pleasure at her desire for him.

"Stop teasing," she demanded desperately.

As you wish, he said to her. His claws dug into her hips, and he drove himself into her. He wasn't capable of being slow or gentle at this point. Aislinn cried out as pain and pleasure seared through her, and she stretched around him. Once he was completely inside, he bent over her and wrapped one arm around her chest while the other arm braced him, so that he wouldn't put all his weight on her body. One clawed hand gripped and dug into the flesh of her breast. Her cunt rippled and gripped at his huge cock. She couldn't believe how intense it was. Suddenly, he began thrusting into her with long hard strokes. He withdrew so far he nearly pulled out then slammed back into her with furious need. Each thrust wrenched an exquisite moan from her mouth. Cullen found himself grateful to Rafe for having managed a hybrid form that allowed for such music.

Aislinn's claws dug into the ground to hold her in one place throughout the intense punishment her body was taking. She had never thought to find pain so exquisite. Between the claws, his size, and the strength of each thrust she was torturously coming to her climax. Cullen felt her pushing back against him as her cunt squeezed and rippled against his shaft. His cock began to swell inside her, locking them together for the rest of the duration of their coupling. He growled loudly, knowing that he was nearing his limit and trying desperately to hold out for her.

After what seemed like forever, he felt her body tense. Aislinn's cries of pleasure changed, growing louder and higher in pitch. The strange growling moans that had so intrigued him before were stronger, and strangely fitting coming from her now. Cullen grabbed her roughly by the shoulder. He pulled her up and back, so that she was on her knees with her back to his chest. He rammed up into her, grunting with each thrust. Aislinn let out a cry of pleasure that Cullen thought must be echoing through the woods, all the way to the cabin. Pushing her hair to the side, he bent to place his mouth on the join between her neck and shoulder. She let her head fall to the side, anticipating his bite. Cullen gave a few final quick thrusts and bit down on her shoulder hard as he released into her. He held her there, one arm wrapped around her waist and the other around her chest. Her hands gripped the arm across her chest, holding on as he pumped into her. Her claws pierced his flesh and caused blood to drip from her fingertips. His mouth sucked at the wound he had created as he emptied his seed into her.

Aislinn felt a strange energy filtering up through her from the ground. It was as though she could feel everything. She knew how many birds and squirrels had been witness to their coupling. She could feel sadness and concern for what had happened the night before coming from the cabin. When she closed her eyes, it was as though she could see everything all at once. She could feel the sunlight beating down on them. *I can feel Cullen,* she thought in awe. She could feel everything that had brought him to this point: what he had felt for her from the first day, his fight with himself ever since, how angry and hurt and worried he had been, how much he loved her. She could even feel the pleasure he was getting from making love to her. She let herself bask in his orgasm, amazed. It all soaked into her. She felt like she was swimming in his emotions. Then, just as suddenly as it had all come to her it retreated back to a corner of her mind. It was still there, only softer, like he was whispering to her how much he cared for her. Aislinn started breathing again. She hadn't realized that she was holding it all in.

Cullen felt the bond take hold. Somewhere in the back of his mind he could feel Aislinn's love for him. He had been told long ago about what it felt like to bond with someone. He knew that once the bond was formed, he should be able to sense her moods. That was the easy explanation. But there was more here than that. He could feel Aislinn's amazement at what was happening, and the pleasure she took from it, and he could feel why as well. It wasn't as detailed as reading her mind, but there was more than just the surface emotions she was feeling.

Cullen let his head fall back on his shoulders. He took a long deep breath as he came back to earth. His wolf retreated, sated. The wolf didn't care about the emotional side of things. He had gotten what he wanted and was pleased. Cullen wrapped his arms around Aislinn's waist and dragged her onto her side as he collapsed to the ground, her bottom tucked tightly against him and her head coming to rest on his shoulder.

Aislinn felt his body change, returning to his human state, with the exception of the swollen member lodged inside her. He kissed her back of her head, amused when she tried to pull away from him to turn around. "You'll have to wait a bit," he said. He grinned as he felt her arousal at the idea that he was stuck inside her like that.

Aislinn could hear the grin in his voice and felt his amusement. "So why didn't this ever happen before," she asked, cuddling back against him. There was something about the idea of his penis swollen inside her that pleased her a great deal.

Cullen felt her walls squeeze down on his shaft. He chuckled. "You keep that up, it'll take longer," he warned. "I never let my wolf get that involved before," he said, as if that was enough explanation.

Aislinn could feel that he had been trying to protect her. "It seems as though your wolf has retreated and you're still, well…" she wiggled against him in lieu of saying that he was stuck inside her.

He laughed and hugged her to hold her still. "Don't you like it," he asked but already knew that she liked it very much.

"I didn't say that," she said and blushed. "And you are finding this way too funny."

Cullen stopped and just lay there, feeling her and finding himself more content than he had ever been. He couldn't help the curiosity about why the bond seemed so strong. "Do druids bond when they marry or whatever?"

"Huh? I don't really know about druids. That would have been something to ask my grandmother."

Cullen instantly regretted asking. He could feel her sadness welling up. He wrapped himself around her and changed the subject. "I'm in a lot of trouble you know?"

Aislinn could feel that he was trying to change the subject. He didn't want to mar what had just happened between them. She decided that she agreed and let him move on. "Oh, then why are you so amused by the idea? I just realized that we're going to have an awfully hard time lying to each other," she joked.

He smiled. "Do you intend to lie to me?"

"No, but we've built such a wonderful relationship on misunderstandings at this point. I'd hate to completely change the dynamic now," Aislinn said sarcastically.

"Too late. It appears as though you will know each and every time I say something stupid, and what I actually meant. No more excuses." He squeezed her tight.

She nuzzled against his arm. "So what happened to needing to set up a ceremony and now not being a good time?"

"Well, it kinda got away from me," he said honestly. "Maybe I made my wolf wait too long. Or maybe I just wanted you so badly I couldn't help myself."

Aislinn could feel the truth in what he was saying and was near tears of happiness that he really wanted her that badly. He hugged her closer, and they lay there for a while just feeling how much they loved each other.

Cullen was still lodged firmly inside Aislinn when they heard the footsteps coming. He started growling a loud warning, praying that they wouldn't get caught quite this red handed.

"I don't think that's going to work," Aislinn said and felt Cullen's confusion and ego. She giggled. "Are you really that full of yourself? What am I saying? I can feel that you're that full of yourself."

The footsteps were getting closer, and Cullen increased his volume.

"It's Keith," Aislinn said. "Last I checked, he didn't care about your warnings. Why are you so concerned about it? Are we in that much trouble?"

Cullen grumbled. Now he was mostly annoyed at the interruption. "Trouble isn't the right word. But the elders won't be happy. Don't worry. I'll deal with it. How did you know it was Keith?"

"Yeah, how did you know it was me?" came a far too amused voice from directly behind them.

"Hard to explain. Go away," she said, voicing Cullen's feeling for the intrusion.

"I feel so unloved," Keith said. "You do know what this looks like don't you?" He walked around the two of them and then sat down on the toppled stone.

Aislinn growled at him and did her best to maneuver into a less exposed position.

"Hey," Keith said in mock offense. "You're just lucky I came looking for you myself instead of sending an omega. I at least have the common courtesy to ask if this is going to be announced, or if it's going to be hushed up until more appropriate arrangements can be made. Then again, if I'm not wanted I can just head right back up to the cabin and-"

"Don't bother to finish," Cullen interrupted. "You're such a pain."

Keith smiled down at his friend. "Congratulations," he said in the most earnest tone Aislinn had ever heard out of the man.

"You have to be the most impossible person I have ever met," Aislinn said in exasperation. "You shift from bad standup comic, to overbearing know-it-all to sentimental all in one breath. Is there a persona you don't make use of?"

Cullen started to laugh. "I was going to suggest that you get to know Sarah and Keith a bit better, but you certainly seem to have Keith pegged."

Keith raised his eyebrows. "And here I was trying to be nice. I guess I've learned my lesson. Be warned, kitten, you're fair game now."

Aislinn grumbled. "Is this really the time and place and situation for friendly banter?"

Cullen could sense her annoyance at the intrusion on their moment. A look at Keith and his friend stood up to make a polite exit. At least he knew when each different persona was appropriate. "I just needed to see if we would be headed back to the den before the funeral. I have to point out that there are quite a few people still missing. And I really should establish if this is to be public knowledge."

Cullen thought about it a moment. He didn't want to offend Aislinn by suggesting that they keep it a secret, but he thought that as far as the pack went, with everything that had happened the day before this wasn't the best way of handling his mating. Whatever his motivations had been, he was still the alpha and there was protocol to follow.

Aislinn nuzzled against him. "It'd probably be better to save the announcement for later," she said for him.

Cullen smiled and hugged her. She had caught his entire thought process. "Just make sure that people stay clear of the stones for a couple hours would ya?" he said to Keith.

Keith nodded. He started to walk off again, but stopped. "I suppose I should offer to make it official for you, if you want."

Aislinn's mind drifted to the 'acknowledgement' part of the ceremony Rissa had mentioned and then to Cullen's talk about lack of witnesses. He felt her unease at the suggestion. "No. Not yet. But thanks," he said. With that, Keith headed back up to the cabin.

Chapter 16

There are more things to alarm us than to harm us,
and we suffer more often in apprehension than
reality.
-Lucius Annaeus Seneca

Jenna walked down the stairs into what had been a basement wine cellar. Rafe had turned it into more of a dungeon torture chamber. She was considering having the place burned. It smelled of blood and terror. Along the wall where there had once been numerous wooden racks holding bottles of carefully chosen, rare vintage wines, there were now rows of naked, battered, whimpering women.

"Let them all go," Jenna said, without emotion.

Large lycans circulated through the room pulling chains off of the tired, beaten, women. Jenna may have been a bitch, but even she saw some things as going too far. She'd have her revenge, but not like this. She still owed Cullen Arnauk for embarrassing her at their mating, and the idea that two men had wanted Aislinn over her had Jenna seething with jealousy. She felt like she still had something to prove, but kidnap and torture wasn't her style.

The women were given clothes and ushered to the great room to wait for cars to take them back to the Madadh-Allaidh Saobhaidh.

"Mistress," one large lycan said as he approached Jenna and nodded his head respectfully. Maon was burly, even for a lycan. He had a head full of dirty blond hair that he pulled into a loose pony tail. His eyes were wild green, and he always wore a suit coat.

Jenna had considered mating with him, but her father had never approved. Still, that hadn't stopped her from spending more than one long night in his bed. If she was to remain head of this pack, he was one of the ones she would need. "What about the cats that were left behind? We've got them locked up for now. Do you want anything in particular done to them?"

Jenna heard the innuendo in his voice. She smiled at him sweetly and reached up to stroke his stubbled chin. "Keep them locked up for now. I may need them later." She walked back up the stairs, and he followed her. "Make sure that all of our people who Rafe mistreated are taken care of. I want everyone in this pack seeing me as a savior." Maon nodded and left her side to deal with his orders.

Jenna ascended the main stairwell of her home. She headed straight for the room that Rafe had taken as his own. It had been her father's room. On the one occasion that Rafe had brought her to his bed, she had noticed a mess of papers and things on her father's desk, and she was curious to see if it was all still there.

She pushed the door open. The room reeked of Rafe, but there was still a hint of her father's scent left. It brought a tear to her eye. She pushed the upset into anger and headed for the large mahogany desk. There were several scrolls laid out and a couple books. It was all written in Gaelic and would take some time for Jenna to wade through. She knew the language, but only barely. Her father had forced her to learn when she was a child.

Jenna flipped through the papers looking for something to tell her what they were. Rafe must have thought they were important, or he never would have kept them. The man had been very methodical.

* * * *

Cullen and Aislinn woke to the sound of a small animal shuffling in the bushes nearby. Aislinn stretched against him, and she felt his cock slide from her body. Cullen groaned in disappointment at the apparent end of their morning.

Aislinn lay there with her eyes closed for a moment. She felt as though the ground was pulsing beneath her. It was a pleasant sensation, kind of like a forgotten memory or something on the tip of her tongue. It felt familiar, but she couldn't quite remember what it was and she didn't know why. As she felt Cullen move next to her, she lay still and with her mind reached for the love and pleasure she had felt before. The strange sensation from the ground faded away, as Cullen seemed to fill her.

Aislinn turned in his arms and eagerly pushed him over onto his back. "If you're upset," she grinned wickedly, her eyes took on an amber sheen, and she straddled him where he was lying, "I' m sure I could find a way to cheer you up."

Cullen's growl took on a needy sound, and Aislinn felt him harden beneath her. She moaned uncontrollably. She didn't understand why she wanted him so badly when they had only just awakened from an incredibly intense round of love making no more than a couple hours earlier. His eyes were glowing already, but he curtailed his desire to take her again. "We don't have time," he growled with annoyance.

Aislinn pouted as he grabbed her hips and pushed her over onto her back. He leaned down and kissed her. "Come on. Before Keith comes looking for me again." He swatted her on the butt and got up.

Reaching out, Aislinn tugged at his hard-on as he tried to move away. Cullen growled, grabbed her again, and pulled her close. She could see and feel the amount of forced control that he had to use to stop from responding to her touch. Her own need mingled with his, and she started growling low in her throat, nuzzling against his neck.

Cullen took a deep breath and forced himself to release her. "I promise you, we will revisit this. But we need to take care of some loose ends first, piseagan." He kissed her forehead. Even that was almost more than he could handle. He growled again. Holding her hands away from him, he picked up her shirt from where he had thrown it earlier and put it in her hands. The amount of overwhelming disappointment that emanated from her nearly changed his mind.

Aislinn looked over the mauled t-shirt, then pulled it over her head, knowing that there was no point in looking for her bra first. He had totally destroyed that. Smiling at the thought, she reached for her torn jeans and noticed that her hands were human. "Hey," she said excitedly. "I look normal again."

Looked up, Cullen saw her examining her arms and legs. He smiled, but had to look away. It was far too tempting a site. *I'm going to have to arrange the ceremony soon.* He knew he wasn't going to be able to control his wolf's need for her to the extent that he should. *Everyone is going to know,* he thought with concern.

"I heard that," Aislinn said. "How much trouble are we really in?"

"You heard that?" Cullen's brow furrowed and he looked at her. He crossed his arms over his chest to remind himself to not touch her.

"Yeah," Aislinn said haltingly. "I thought that was normal."

"It is. When I intend for it. But I wasn't projecting." Cullen's voice was overly serious.

"Is it a problem?" Aislinn asked. Her beast retreated into the back of her mind, grudgingly giving way to the serious conversation.

"Not a problem exactly. Just strange. Is it something druids do?" Cullen asked, trying to make his voice less serious.

"I don't really know," Aislinn said and her mind drifted toward her grandmother again.

Cullen sighed sympathetically and walked up to her. She had been through far too much lately, and he wasn't helping. He could feel that the only thing keeping her smiling was the fact that she was completely ignoring everything that had happened the last couple days. "Mo piseagan," he said softly as he wrapped his arms around her. "I'm sorry," he said softly, hugging her close. "I wish I could give her back to you."

She rubbed her tears on his shoulder and then pushed him away. "I'll be okay. Eventually." Cullen could feel that she didn't want to think or talk about it, so he let it go. "Anyway," she added, getting a grip on herself. "I guess if we can pick up on more than we should from each other we'll just have to get used to it."

Cullen was struck by how strong she could be when she wanted to be. He could feel how much pain she was in over her grandmother's death, but that last statement didn't hold a hint of it. "Don't sound like it's such a burden," he teased.

She flashed him a visually convincing fake smile. If he couldn't feel the turmoil from her, Cullen would have believed Aislinn to be happy and fine. "We'll figure it out. When I was told 'bond' I didn't really know what it meant, until now. You know, you and everyone else I've talked to have a nasty tendency to explain things to me with terms that you get and I don't. I never know what to ask more about."

They went back to trying to get their clothes on. Aislinn pulled up her jeans and fiddled with the destroyed button and zipper. That helped to improve her mood, as she thought about how he had torn her clothes off, literally. "Hey, you still didn't tell me why I'm back to normal."

"Okay, first," he laughed, "you're not back to 'normal.' You have three forms, all of which are 'normal.' Watch who you say that to, or you'll start a fight," he said in amusement. He was staring at his own jeans. The seams were pretty much gone. Really, he was holding some pieces of what used to be jeans. There'd be no wearing them. He desperately wanted to make a pretense of decorum, when he walked back into the cabin. *Oh well.* "I'm just going to have to take the pieces back. And as far as being in your human form right now, we had a quite pleasant nap."

He sounded so off-hand about it that Aislinn found it infuriating. *Is it so impossible for someone to just give me a straight detailed answer?* "Okay, but I was still *hybrid*," she said with excessive stress, "when I woke up this morning in the cabin."

He cocked an eyebrow at the thought he picked up on. In conjunction with the obvious frustration, he couldn't help but find her cute. He hadn't realized how frustrated she was getting. It implied that she was looking for a great deal more information than she had actually asked him about, and he wondered who she was talking to. "Yeah, but how did you feel?" he returned smugly.

"I guess I was still pretty upset."

"You'll have to learn to control how much you feel. It's an over simplification of the real explanation, but emotion affects the change quite a bit. Really, it's about who's in charge at any point in time. The beast or the human. It's like there's two voices in your head. There's one who doesn't care much for logic or reason and just wants what it wants, and one who is patient and considering and can deal with what life throws at you and move on. When you start to let things get to you, it makes it easier for the beast to have its way. Anger, lust," he said with a smirk, "even happiness. Anything in an extreme can let the beast have more control than might be appropriate. You can also call it to you when you need it. Anyway it happens, there's a moment of conflict and submission. Where the two halves of you decide who gets to be in charge for the moment. Human and wolf or cat are pretty straight forward. But the hybrid, well he can sorta go either way. It all depends what the situation is."

Aislinn nodded seriously, obviously thinking about everything he said. "You'll have to give me some lessons I think. I kinda get it. But understanding the explanation and controlling or experiencing it, I think, will be two different things."

Cullen walked over to her and pulled the neck of her shirt over the bite he'd left. It would need to be cleaned. "I intended to give you some lessons. The bond will help. Keep that covered up for now. When it's healed a bit more it won't be so obvious." He smiled. It would scar pretty badly. He hadn't intended to be quite that thorough. His wolf probably would have been worse, if given the chance.

"What are we going to do? About telling the pack I mean."

"I'll have the arrangements set for us to have a mating ceremony." His smile broadened. "And for you to get a lesson on what exactly will happen with that as well. I don't know when it will be yet. Don't worry about it. There are still a number of problems waiting back at the den to be dealt with. We won't have the ability to have the ceremony until after we clean up the mess."

"So when everything is said and done, do I go back to sitting in the library bored to tears," Aislinn asked. "You know, I'm going to need a job or something to do. I can't just sit around all the time waiting to have sex with you," she grinned at him, and he grinned right back.

"You sure?" he teased. Cullen thought about it. "Well, there are any number of things you could do, now that Rafe isn't a threat. There are some limitations, seeing as you're mine. Liam probably won't let you wait tables," he added, reading her mind and smiling at her. Cullen nodded in the direction of the cabin. "We'll figure something out if you're determined to do something other than hang out at the den. Maybe you can help Sarah out. That would probably be the most fitting job for you."

They started walking toward the cabin. "I just don't want it to look like I'm not pulling my weight."

"When we run into Keith again, you should ask him what he thinks your job in the pack is now," Cullen smirked.

"What's that supposed to mean?" Aislinn asked in bemused concern. He chuckled at her. The walk to the cabin wasn't long. Aislinn spent the entire time contemplating how to get Cullen to play a bit more before he went to work and smiling innocently at him when a frustrated growl told her that he knew what she was up to. When they got to the cabin Cullen opened the front door for her, and they stepped inside.

To look around the front room, you'd never know that there had been a battle there the day before, save the bloody spots on the floor. Cullen had her by the hand as they walked through the room. Aislinn hadn't actually looked around before. There had been too much else going through her head.

The front doors opened into a large main room with a vaulted ceiling three floors high. There were doors on all the walls of the huge room and stairs that led to a balcony which circled the room and to the second and third floors. There were lots of overstuffed couches and chairs arranged around the room, so that several groups of people could sit and talk with each other in separate little areas. There was a gigantic fireplace on the far wall and the room as a whole was decorated with a lived-in, worn, comfortable, antique feel.

As Cullen and Aislinn walked through the room to the stairs, there was a lot of staring, but no one said anything. Aislinn noticed that everyone seemed to be in jeans and plain t-shirts. It almost looked like they were wearing uniforms. She supposed that no one had time to pack a bag before coming out here for the fight.

They were all wearing clothes from the closet storeroom.

Cullen guided Aislinn up the stairs, along the third floor balcony, and through another set of doors at the end of the hall. Walking into his rooms, Aislinn smiled. The rooms could almost be a replica of his bedroom back at the Madadh-Allaidh Saobhaidh. There was a lot of dark blue. The first room they walked into had a desk, a couple book shelves, and a sitting area with a television and a couch, similar to the ones downstairs. There were a two doors on opposite walls. One led to the bathroom and the other to the bedroom.

Cullen went into the bedroom and over to his dresser to pull out some clothes. "I'm gonna get a shower. I'd bring you along," he smiled at her, "but I don't think we'd get out of here before next week if I did."

Aislinn smiled back and stretched out on his bed. His eyes followed her cat-like movements and he had to force himself to head for the bathroom. She was so comfortable lying on his bed and cuddling with the pillows that smelled so much like him that she fell asleep the instant Cullen was out the door.

* * * *

Aislinn knew the minute the dream turned from a simple walk through her imagination to a nightmare of a premonition. She didn't know if she should be proud of herself for coming to the point where she could consciously recognize it ,or if she should be terrified. The battle wasn't over yet. She was padding on four feet through the Tairneach manor. The rooms were all dark. Aislinn felt drawn through the building. She was compelled to keep going. The stairwell seemed to be ten times longer than it had looked when she was there.

The white marble floors were ice under her feet. When she reached the top of the stairs, there was a long hallway. Again the hall seemed longer than it should have been. By the time she reached the open door at the end of the hall, she knew she was too late. *Too late for what?*

Aislinn walked into the room, and she felt as though she was shrinking. Or the room was getting bigger. There was a desk against a wall, and a light on it. She had to jump to get into the chair and then again to get onto the desk. She felt as though she was being watched. She slunk against the desk, flat on her belly, toward the light. It was shining down on a book.

Aislinn jumped up onto the book and walked across the Gaelic writing. It was hand written. She stared down at the scrawl, trying to make out what it said.

* * * *

As Cullen showered, a strange feeling of fear and fascination filled the back of his mind. He didn't think that Aislinn was in trouble, but he knew that something was happening. He cut his shower short and went back to the bedroom, toweling himself off as he walked.

In his bedroom, Cullen smiled uncertainly at the sight of Aislinn curled around one of his pillows. He padded over to the bed and stood there watching her. Something was upsetting her in her sleep. Even knowing that she wasn't really in danger his wolf was feeling rather protective, wanting to keep her safe even in her dreams. He didn't know if he should wake her or not. Finally he decided that holding her might drive away whatever was bothering her. Cullen was in the process of dropping the towel and joining her in the bed, when a knock on the door tore through his thoughts.

I'm gonna kill him, Cullen thought angrily, as his wolf took over his senses. Aislinn's fear had brought Cullen's other half close enough to the surface that the thought was much more real than Cullen intend. The violent shift in Cullen's mood shot through Aislinn, waking her.

She turned groggily to see what was going on, just in time to hear a door crash and then a body slamming against a hard surface. It took a moment for her mind to clear. She had been trying to read the book and was attempting to bring the image of the words back to her mind, but nothing was coming.

Cullen's anger seemed to call to her, and she hurried out of the bedroom. When Aislinn got to the door she saw Cullen, in his hybrid form. He had Keith by the shirt, back against the wall. Keith's eyes were submissively lowered, as Cullen growled menacingly at his friend. *Do I need to give you a reminder lesson about how I ended up in charge around here?*

Keith bowed his head and raised his hands apologetically. "Cul, I just came up to tell you about the sat-phone call I made. I didn't mean to barge in."

Aislinn could feel Cullen's common sense warring with his wolf. Seeing her at the doorway, Keith looked up with a warning, as if to tell her to stay back. Cullen picked him up higher and bashed him against the wall, regaining Keith's full attention, and making him wince as his head cracked against the wall. "Cul, I'll leave. Really. Just put me down."

Disregarding Keith's warning, Aislinn walked up to them and put her hand on Cullen's arm. "Cullen," she asked in confusion. Keith seemed to brace himself for something awful to happen. To his surprise Cullen calmed immediately and lowered him to the floor, but had yet to let go.

Aislinn leaned in and nuzzled against his arm. "Are you okay," she asked softly. She could feel that he wasn't.

It took Cullen a moment to force the wolf back, but even his wolf seemed to be responsive to Aislinn. Cullen felt his wolf backing down like a little kid who'd gotten caught doing something bad. When he regained his human form, Cullen looked at Keith and released his friend's shirt. He shot Keith an apologetic look, and Keith nodded back indignantly.

"Like I said before," Keith growled. "You need to get the ceremony dealt with. And with how worked up you are, you may need a month off instead of a week."

Cullen nodded, taking Keith's joke serious enough that his friend drew in a deep breath and shook his head uncertainly.

Rubbing his face with both hands, Cullen tried to regain his composure. "You'd better watch how you come in here for a while. Maybe we should just announce it. If I'm going to start going off on people like that, it could be dangerous."

Aislinn was wide eyed. "You don't mean that was normal?"

Cullen growled. "Only if you don't let it run its course. Technically, I should only get like that when you're in heat."

Aislinn shook her head. "Maybe I should sit in on that elementary class that Sarah was talking about before."

Cullen smiled, then chuckled and kissed her forehead. "If you like. But Keith is a big boy. He could have handled a pummeling. He probably did something recently that deserved it anyway."

Keith grumbled at that. "Thanks," he said angrily. "You do realize Aislinn, he can turn on you when he gets like that, and unless you like it really rough then that little move you pulled, as grateful as I am, could get you hurt."

Cullen took a deep breath, and Aislinn could tell that he agreed with Keith.

She smiled at Cullen. "No. He wouldn't hurt me," she said with an air of confidence that made both of them stare at her. "Anyway. I'm going to get a shower now, if there's enough time before we need to leave?"

"Yeah, go ahead. I'll get some clothes brought up for you." He leaned in and nuzzled her neck. "Make sure you clean up that bite so it doesn't get infected."

Aislinn kissed him on the cheek and disappeared into the bathroom. Watching her go, his eyes flashed, as the wolf tried to surface again. "I've got a problem," he said after the door closed.

"That appears to be an understatement. I wouldn't have expected you to attack me. Are you sure you can hold out? I mean maybe you two need to disappear for a while."

Cullen seriously considered Keith's suggestion, as he walked into his bedroom with Keith on his heels. "That'd be too obvious. Besides," he said contemplatively, "Aislinn seems to be in control of herself pretty well, and apparently she can bring me back to earth. I'll just make sure to get to bed early and sleep late. I've caused enough upheaval for the time being. If I were to announce that I took Aislinn as a mate without going through the steps, then I'd be risking loyalty issues. The people who've been moaning about her being like Rafe or non-lycan would be all about her having screwed with my head. They'd make everyone else start doubting my actions, especially with that charge to her rescue I pulled. I realize he was threatening our territory, and I would have dealt with him even if Aislinn hadn't been involved, but it would have gone differently. All my decisions are starting to get questioned. Not to mention they'd be all over Aislinn, and she's having a hard enough time fitting in and dealing with all the changes she's gone through as it is." Cullen pulled his shirt over his head. "I need everyone to keep following my lead without question. Same as they always have. I have to admit that I'm a little pissed that there's so much random doubt about me right now. Decades of consistent leadership and one lousy detour from the road I paved for them and they're all acting as if I'm a different lycan. On top of that, Jenna is still questionable, and the feds are watching us. The last thing I need is being questioned and doubted. Hell, they've all fallen out of shape. Do you realize that it took all muin day to mobilize? Thirty years ago it would have been an hour, tops. This may sound ignorant but I'm starting to think that all these years of peace and quiet have been too much. Without a threat outside the pack, we apparently aren't strong enough to hold together." Cullen's voice got increasingly more agitated as he spoke.

Keith nodded, knowing better than to interrupt and waited patiently for a Cullen to pause in his tirade. "I know what you're saying. That's why nations love war so much. United in a common cause. Blah blah blah. Everyone says that they want peace. Then they get bored. So they turn on each other. So what do you suggest?" Keith leaned against the door frame and waited.

"As far as the unplanned mating goes. We keep it quiet. Not even innuendo about it in public," he said with a hard look at Keith, who put his hands up as if he was giving in. "We'll start with arranging as much time, uninterrupted, alone with Aislinn as I can manage. And you'll actually wait to be let in after you knock. Beyond that, we're going to have to play it by ear. We need to set up some drills for the troops and lay into them about the lousy show they made yesterday. Not to mention the fact that I wasn't taken seriously. That pisses me off more than anything else. I say there are people we need to watch for in our own pack and no one really believed it. What? Was I just talking out my ass? They ignore my warnings and question my ability to lead?" Cullen finished by violently tying his shoes and standing up. His hair was still wet, and he shook his head like a dog, splattering Keith.

"Funny," Keith groused. "At least it was just water and not getting slammed into the wall. I'm thinking that I need to get out of here before she's out of the shower."

"Oh come on. I wouldn't have killed you." The two men headed for the hall, knowing that Keith was right about how Cullen may react to Aislinn being wet and naked with Keith in the room. Cullen called an omega over to send for clothes for Aislinn, then turned back to Keith. "Anyway, the sat-phone call."

"Hell, I nearly forgot. Right. Liam has everything under control for the most part. Ranaild and Elise showed up at the den this morning. Ranaild is apparently his own jailer, and Elise spent the morning telling Liam what happened to her and trying to convince him to advocate for Ranaild when you get back. Apparently, when Elise was being held, there were a significant number of others being held as well. I'm gonna guess that there's a scary correspondence between the guys you dungeoned before we left and the women who Elise has reported as being held."

Cullen nodded gravely. "Maybe I can talk to Jenna. Who knows. We might be able to reach an amiable solution and get Jenna to let them all go. It appears as though the Tairneach have allowed her to step in as alpha without too much complaint. With Gregor dead that gets her main opponent out of the way. She may be willing to back off and just be happy about being able to follow in Brennus' footsteps. As far as Ranaild goes," Cullen growled. "I better spend some time with Aislinn before dealing with him. He's lucky things worked out. If she had been permanently hurt or had left me, I don't know if I'd be able to reason my way around a very painful death for him. As it is…" Cullen had to stop what he was saying. His wolf was pacing in his mind like a caged beast and wanted to go charging back to the den.

Keith nodded. "Who all is going back to Madadh-Allaidh Saobhaidh now?"

Cullen leaned against the wall. He was watching for the omega to return with clothes for Aislinn. "If we're going to have to go on a rescue mission, then we'll need all the betas. But I'm still thinking I may be able to talk Jenna out of having another fight right now. Let's leave it as me and Aislinn, and I'll take Sarah along. You stay here and get things ready in case we have to go charging in to get the rest of ours out of there. I want to try talking first. If we leave within the

- 343 -

next half hour we can be back at the den by dinner. Taigh-O\sda," Cullen said with a nod. He was in the mood for steak. Keith shook his head and laughed. "If you want to get the sat-phone out and call the den around 10 tonight I'll make sure that either myself or Sarah is able to answer."

"Yeah, I'll call Sarah."

With that, the omega came back carrying jeans and a t-shirt similar to the ones Cullen shredded earlier. The omega bowed her head and disappeared down the hall. Keith watched the girl walk away intently. "I wonder how Jay's doing. I hate not being there, but she's been getting so bitchy the closer she gets to having the litter. I swear she's gonna kill me for nothing. And," he stared at the omega's butt as she turned down the stairs. "I'm so damn deprived right now, it's not funny." He looked back at Cullen who was grinning and laughing to himself. "Yuck it up now alpha boy. Just wait 'til Ais is pregnant, and you're not getting any. We may have to clear the den, if your behavior now is any indication."

* * * *

Sarah was waiting in the great room as Cullen and Aislinn came down the stairwell. Keith had let her know that she'd be leaving with them to head back to the den. She would have to deal with the reorganization of room assignments depending on what Cullen decided to do with the traitors. He still wasn't sure. Every time he thought about it a pain hit him in the stomach, and he thought about grabbing Aislinn, taking off and not dealing with it at all.

As Cullen walked up to Sarah to see if she was ready to go, Gaven and Hagan approached them. The two men looked cowed and miserable. They were both bowing more than usual and Cullen instantly got a bad feeling about it. *How many of my men did he get to!*

"We were hoping that we'd be able to go back to the den with you. We'll accept whatever punishment you intended for the others. We're the last of the men in the pack that you've been looking for." Cullen's jaw tightened. The gaze he leveled on the men was pure death. "We just want to be there when you bring the others home." There was a tear in Gaven's eye that overflowed and ran down his cheek.

Aislinn could almost feel Gaven's misery, and she was the only one present who knew how hurt Cullen was by what was happening in his pack. Between how unhappy the traitors were about failing their leader, and how unhappy Cullen was about believing the pack didn't trust or want to follow him, Aislinn was feeling inundated by miserable emotion from all angles. Considering she had her own lot to carry, the last thing she needed was additional outside baggage. She sighed. *Cullen, this isn't your fault. Rafe did this. It doesn't mean-*

Don't, Cullen violently thought back at her. *You said that he couldn't do things to them that they weren't inclined to do.* Cullen's eyes never left Gaven, and everyone in the room was holding their collective breath to see what would happen. The alpha's eyes flashed with fury.

Aislinn butted her head into his shoulder and reached for his arm. Her actions, in the face of Cullen's stance, caused a murmur of amazement through the room. The consensus was that she was either incredibly brave or very stupid.

Aislinn tried to send comfort to Cullen. *Rafe had their mates and loved ones. Everyone is this pack is very close. They're all inclined to save their lovers. You came after me. It doesn't mean that they were inclined to turn against you. It means they were inclined to do anything they needed to in order to save their mates. You've made this pack to be close and caring of each other, as well as loyal. Are you really going to hold that against them and berate yourself for it?*

You're not going to turn this around, came a growling thought. Aislinn knew which half of Cullen was talking.

She closed her eyes and took a deep breath. *Do you really expect your men to behave differently than you do? You set quite the example Lord Arnauk. Drag your entire pack out here, knowing you were outnumbered, no plan, and all because Rafe had someone you loved. How many bodies are on the pyre?*

Cullen growled and ripped his arm away from her. She could feel how deep her comment had stung him. His glare shifted from Gaven to Aislinn, and there was more than one elder in the room that took note of the far too meaningful eye contact between the two.

Aislinn didn't even flinch. She released him. *I wasn't trying to hurt you. Just make a point. I love you Cullen. I may well have done the same thing. And each of the so-called traitors were doing exactly what you did. You're hurt because you were left out of the secret, and they are all your friends. But who do you expect them to love more? You or their mates?*

You don't know how a lycan pack works, Cullen growled.

Maybe not. But we're dealing with hearts here. Not packs or logic.

Cullen was pacing back and forth. There was a strong part of him that agreed with her. That left them where? He couldn't just let it go. The wolf would never be able to let Ranaild go. He had to do something. He was just so pissed.

Sarah came over to Aislinn. She spoke very softly. "You two are being watched."

Aislinn looked over at Sarah and then around the room. "He was going to tear them apart where they stand," she whispered.

"That may be so. But as it is, all anyone saw was you both sharing an intense gaze and Cullen acting strangely. With all the mind control stuff going on with Rafe, and you being an unknown around here, do you know what that looked like?" Sarah was speaking cautiously. She didn't want anyone standing by to overhear. If they weren't already thinking it, she didn't want to give them ideas.

"I'm sorry. I just wanted to help," Aislinn said softly and lowered her eyes.

Sarah shook her head, and looked over at Cullen. She could see that he was overwrought. It wasn't like him at all. He always kept his emotions in check. Aislinn was having quite the effect on him. "What's going on between you two," she asked confidentially.

Aislinn looked over at Cullen. He walked to a large window and was standing with his arms crossed staring out. She could feel the war inside him. His human half was trying to convince his wolf that Aislinn was right. Aislinn was uncertain as well. She needed to be trusted by Sarah. She was logical enough to understand that Sarah was the alpha female, and if Aislinn wanted to fit in she was going to have to be friends with her. Besides, Cullen trusted Sarah, and someone was going to have to help Aislinn understand and fit in with the women. Cullen obviously didn't have the knack for that.

Sarah's patience was waning. She didn't know what was going on but she knew what it looked like, and so did the rest of the elders.

Aislinn finally leaned in to talk to Sarah. There was a suspicious murmur that ran through the hall, when Aislinn spoke softly into Sarah's ear. The whispers were suggestions that the druid already had the alpha male and was now out to control the female alpha as well.

"Cullen and I," Aislinn took a deep breath. She couldn't believe how nervous she was. She pressed her hand to her stomach to try and stop the butterflies from bursting out. "We mated," she said so softly that Sarah almost missed it. "We just couldn't stop. It started as an apology and ended well... Now he's so worked up about everything. And we can hear each other's thoughts. It's amazing and scary. I don't really know what to do."

Sarah pulled back and looked into Aislinn's pleading eyes. She smiled gently, but wasn't sure what to think. She was torn between hating Aislinn and being happy for Cullen. Sarah was positive that none of the other women he had been interested in could have threatened her position as alpha female the way Aislinn could. The girl may not be there yet, but she would be. Sarah could see it. *Well, I've been Cullen's sister for so long. Maybe it's time.*

Sarah reached out, pulled Aislinn close, and hugged her. That sent another murmur through the room, before she stepped back. "Cullen, we need to go. Are they coming or do you want them penned up here?"

Cullen turned around to see Aislinn and Sarah standing together while Gaven and Hagan waited for sentence to be passed. "Bring them with us. They can join all the others." Cullen looked around the room. Everyone was staring uneasily. It didn't take a genius to understand the uncertainty. They had never faced an enemy like Rafe before. It was going to haunt them all for a long time.

Aislinn felt a strange calm come over Cullen, and his face seemed to relax. He made eye contact with each of the men and women staring at him in turn, as he spoke. "I know we've been through a great deal recently. You all have doubts and concerns. Some of those concerns involve me. I can tell you that the battle with the unseen enemy is over. The inside threat is under control. I would not say that if it wasn't true. Remember, it wasn't your family that caused the betrayal, it was Rafe. That beast is dead."

Gaven and Hagan were virtually shaking. Compassion and a strange compulsion flowed through Aislinn. She stepped up to the man and reached out to brush the tears from his face. When she touched his skin, a lightning shock seared through her, and she fell to her knees with a cry. Her eyes were wide, and she was staring up at Gaven in tears, trembling. Gaven stepped back with his hands in the air, as the alpha growled a warning that sent fear through all those assembled. "I didn't touch her," he pleaded in terror.

Cullen ran to Aislinn, vaulting the couch and stared into her face. The feeling he was getting from her was nothing like when she had been attacked. She had the same look she'd gotten at the Taigh-O\sda when she had the vision about the mating ceremony. His wolf retreated, knowing that he could be of no help, and

Cullen was torn between trying to get her attention and waiting for the vision to run its course.

* * * *

Aislinn couldn't help wonder why the visions were suddenly so strong and so frequent. She was standing inside the Tairneach manor again. This time she was human. The room was cold, and she was naked. She wrapped her arms around herself. Details of the room faded into view slowly, as she looked around. There was dim light and shadows spread eerily across the bloodstained floor. There were no windows. People were chained to the walls. All of them were women, naked, bruised, and bleeding. Aislinn could feel fear and determination throughout the room. One woman drew her attention. She was heavily pregnant and lie on the floor whimpering, holding her stomach. Aislinn knew, when the woman returned to the Arnauk, she would no longer be pregnant. A terrible sadness over came her, and Aislinn began to cry for the woman.

As she watched, the women disappeared and were replaced by others. These people weren't weres. They were at least allowed to remain in their clothes. One of them stood up, looked directly at her and reached for her. The people in her visions had never interacted with her before. Aislinn stared at the man with amazed uncertainty. He was tall and lean. He had icy blue eyes, a pale complexion, and brown hair. "Who are you," she asked.

* * * *

Cullen couldn't handle it any longer. When the tears began to pour from Aislinn's blank eyes and roll in streams down her face, he reached out and touched her cheek. "Aislinn?" he said softly, but insistently.

Her eyes swirled amber and the trembling grew worse. *Aislinn,* he insisted, into her mind.

Aislinn blinked. Tears forced from her eyes, and she reached for Cullen. She wrapped her arms around him and held on as if he was going to vanish, and her breath caught in her throat.

The lycans in the room watched in confused silence, as Cullen held her tightly. It was a rare show, seeing as Cullen usually took Aislinn into private to interact with her, aside from that afternoon in the library.

"It's all right. I've got you," he said gently, stroking her hair.

When Aislinn looked up her eyes focused on Gaven, and the tears came back. She shook her head, trying to decide if she should tell him. Finally, she pushed Cullen away and stood up, walking to Gaven. "I'm so sorry," she whimpered. "When you get her back," Aislinn couldn't continue.

Gaven seemed to know what she was saying. He had been feeling it in the back of his mind for some time. "How do you know?"

"I just saw it," she said softly. "But you'll get her back. They're all coming back," she added, as she looked up at Hagan.

Cullen saw the relief on the men's faces, even mixed with the pain. He stood up and went to Aislinn. "That's enough. I think we need to get going."

Chapter 17

Some people make things happen, some watch things
happen, while others wonder what has happened.
-Gaelic Proverb

The group loaded silently into the large black SUV,
and Cullen began driving back to Madadh-Allaidh
Saobhaidh.   Gaven and Hagan were afraid to speak.
They didn't know what to say to Cullen after
everything that had happened.   They looked at each
other with hope, as they felt some of the muffled fear
in the back of their minds ebb away.   Something was
happening with their mates that was making them less
frightened.   The men didn't know what it could be.
Their bonds weren't strong enough to project thoughts
over this kind of distance.   But there was hope now.
The two men sat impatiently in the back seat, as the
SUV sped down the highway.

Sarah seethed palpably, and cast annoyed glares at
Cullen that he could feel on the back of his head as he
drove.   She had about a million questions she wanted
answered, however she wasn't able to ask Cullen about
his mating with Aislinn while Gaven and Hagan were
present.

he only positive thing Cullen could get, from
having all the upset and conflict before leaving, was
that he didn't feel harassed by his wolf to pull over and
play with Aislinn on the way back to the den.   Now
that he knew Aislinn was all right he had gone back to
dwelling on the things she had said to him.   He still
didn't know what to do about the traitors.

"I think we have another problem," Aislinn said, trying to ignore the upset radiating from him that she knew she had helped to cause.

"Just what I need," Cullen growled. "What now?"

"When I was sleeping in your room, during your shower, I had a premonition, and then another one when I touched Gaven. There was more to that one than just the stuff it told me about the captured people."

"Okay," he said shortly. "Again I say what now?"

"You don't have to be so snippy. I'm sorry," she snapped back. "But I'm not taking back what I said. I'm just sorry you're being so upset by it."

Cullen growled and everyone felt the SUV speed up. "What did you see?" he said impatiently.

"I don't know exactly yet. I'm you'll be pissed though, if three days from now I figure it out and tell you, but have to admit that it started today." Aislinn was staring out the window.

Sarah sat forward at that point and snapped at both of them. "The two of you need to stop blowing so hot and cold. Get over it. Aislinn if you have something to say just say it."

Aislinn glared at Sarah over her shoulder but continued anyway. "I saw the Tairneach manor in both visions. The first time, I ended up looking at a book with Gaelic writing in it. The second time, I was in a kind of dungeon. First, it was full of your missing people, then they all disappeared, and a bunch of new people appeared. They weren't weres though. I don't know who they were. One of them tried to talk to me. That's weird because my visions have never interacted with me before."

Aislinn felt Cullen's anger ease, as his brain began to work on what she said. "So what do you think it means," he asked, in a relatively decent tone.

"Like I said, I don't know. The fates must think that the book was important. Wasn't Rafe stealing books and burning buildings? I don't know what he was stealing the books for. As far as the people go..." Aislinn thought about it all. "I know that the first vision already happened, and I was too late. I don't know what that means. The second vision hasn't happened yet. The man seemed to be reaching for me, like he wanted me to help him."

Sarah stared out the front window of the SUV. "Well, Rafe was stealing the books from druids. He was after the stone circle, and he was out to turn himself into the biggest baddest thing he could mix together. The books could be maps, could be recipe books, could be something he was planning to do next that we don't know about, or could be nothing. Any way you look at it Rafe is dead, so he can't be using the books. But if they're at Tairneach manor, then Jenna or someone else there must have them."

Cullen let his brain process everything Sarah said before responding. "So even if she has a bunch of books, and she turns the basement into a prison for some people who don't deserve to be in prison, it's not like that has anything to do with us. We're going to get our own back, but I'm sorry Aislinn, I'm not going to start a war over books or some unknown prisoners. I can let the feds know that Jenna's up to something, but that's it."

Aislinn sighed. "I understand what you're saying. Except, I've yet to have a premonition that didn't apply to me in some way. Even when I had the vision at the

Taigh-Olsda, I knew that I needed to tell you, but it was still Rafe, and I was drawn into it. In the end, whatever these premonitions mean, it's going to catch up to me. They always do."

Cullen's brow furrowed. "Well, we'll deal with it when it happens. For now, we have enough going on."

Aislinn knew she was being dismissed. *I can tell that this feeling sharing shit isn't going to be all fun.*

Cullen growled back angrily.

Leaning back in her seat, Aislinn watched out the window. Between the blurring scenery they were passing and the silence in the car, she fell asleep, trying to direct her dream back to the premonition from before, hoping to get another look at that book. As she slept, she felt more conscious in some ways than, she felt when she was awake. It was an odd sensation. She had never tried to direct her premonitions before. They had always just happened. When Aislinn was a child her grandmother always discouraged exploring the talent. Then there was college, and Aislinn believed she had more important things to learn, especially since the visions were never significant until Rafe came along. Then there was Rafe. He made her frightened of what she could do, and all her energy was spent trying to avoid it or unsuccessfully block him. It wasn't until Cullen came along, and she felt safe, that Aislinn began to think about using it to her own advantage. She felt like he gave her strength somehow.

Aislinn found herself drifting. There was something odd pulling at her. She felt as though she wanted to go back to the reservation, but she wasn't sure why. The harder she tried to bring back the book, the farther away it seemed to get. She was able to summon fleeting images and feelings of fear and acceptance that she knew didn't belong to her. There was also a floating feeling of evil, angry, determination. While it reminded her of Rafe, there was something different in it. Rafe had been scary crazy. This feeling was more cold and lost. It wanted something and Aislinn knew that it would never find what it wanted.

No matter how hard she tried to bring the premonition, throughout all of the strange feelings and flashing indistinguishable pictures, she wasn't quite able to summon up a vision like the ones that just happened. Aislinn felt like she was barely missing something, and if she just tried hard enough to focus she could make it all come clear.

* * * *

Cullen looked over at Aislinn several times. He was getting the strangest sensations from her. He knew that she was concentrating very hard on something. There was curiosity and sometimes a little fear. Every time he felt the fear start, he reached out and touched her hand or leg. She would stir in her sleep a bit and then settle, and the fear would fade away. He just felt like she needed him.

By the time they pulled into the private garage attached to the Madadh-Allaidh Saobhaidh, Cullen's stomach was growling as was his wolf. The few times he touched her, combined with Aislinn's scent in the enclosed space of the car was starting to get to his wolf, no matter how annoyed his human half might have been.

As the others got out of the car and started slamming doors, Aislinn was shaken awake. Gaven and Hagan were still holding their tongues, but they could feel their mates nearby, and they were doing their best to be patient.

Aislinn's mind was exhausted. It took her a moment to come to herself. She saw Cullen slam his door as he got out of the car, and she sighed. *How long is he going to stay angry?* She turned to get out of the car and found her door already opening for her. Cullen was standing there waiting, with his hand out to her. The look on his face was a combination of still unhappy and getting over it.

She smiled at him wanly and took his hand, as she slid from the car. He pulled her into his arms and buried his face in her hair, taking in her scent. *There's nothing quite as frustrating as being annoyed with the one person who always seems to make you feel better,* he thought at her.

She smiled and cuddled against him. *I am sorry. Maybe next time I won't be quite as direct.*

Then you wouldn't be you, he smiled back as they parted. *I'd rather have honesty.*

When they started kissing, a concerned, "Ahem," caught their attention.

The kiss ended reluctantly. Cullen let his head fall back onto his shoulders, and his neck cracked before he looked to see who had interrupted. The impression was obvious annoyance. Cullen knew that he was going to have to spend some time alone with Aislinn and he needed to get something to eat or he'd just kill everyone and be done with it.

"I am sorry to interrupt, General," came the voice.

Cullen finally turned to see who it was and released Aislinn from his grip. Tad was watching with a mix of uncertain fear and determination. He was Liam's middle son, and had been left behind with Liam to help with keeping a handle on things at the den. He was smaller than most men, but took after his father in his intelligence. He had brown hair and dark brown eyes, like the rest of the Arnauk. Like all the younger men, he tended to dress like a punk, in his baggy pants, oversized t-shirts and backward ball caps. He was a good kid though.

Tad lowered his eyes and bowed his head submissively, before looking up again. Cullen growled possessively, when Tad smiled as his eyes fell on Aislinn. She touched Cullen's arm. She felt him force his wolf under control, as Tad's eyes went wide. "What do you need Tad?" Cullen asked in a strained voice.

"Uh, Dad, sent me to tell you that everyone's in the holding area in the basement, and you need to come down as soon as possible." He was shifting uncomfortably. Tad was smart enough to see the danger he was in, even if he didn't know why exactly.

Cullen cleared his voice and took a deep breath. "Tell Liam that there's no way I can deal with that immediately. I'm going for dinner, some sleep, and then I'll take care of the mess in the basement. If Liam is interested, I'd say the next hour I'll be in the Taigh-O\sda. You can take Gaven and Hagan down to join the others. I don't think they'll give you any trouble." Cullen indicated the two cowed men who were standing with Sarah and waiting.

Tad nodded, though he still looked confused. "There is one thing you should probably know. About an hour ago a caravan arrived from the Tairneach, and our missing people were returned."

Gaven and Hagan suddenly looked relieved and excited. Cullen asked the question they were restraining themselves from shouting out. "Where are they all?"

Tad looked over at the two men sympathetically. He hadn't taken account of all the women who had been returned, but he had seen the injuries on a number of them. "They're all downstairs with the others. There really wasn't any keeping them apart."

Cullen nodded. "Then you better get going. Sarah are you coming with us? Dinner?"

Sarah walked over to Cullen and Aislinn, allowing Tad to take responsibility for Gaven and Hagan. "As long as you promise to keep the touchy feely stuff to a minimum."

Cullen threw Sarah a glare and took Aislinn's hand, dragging her along with him as he headed toward the Taigh-O\sda.

* * * *

The atmosphere in the Taigh-O\sda was more sober than usual. All the waiting staff were uncertain. They had heard about the body count and the rumors about Aislinn were disturbing. Everyone had only met her within the past month. Aislinn wasn't forthcoming about herself, and Rissa had been the only one she seemed to get close to. When Cullen and Sarah came in with Aislinn the weres all stared suspiciously, looking for signs that Aislinn was doing something to the two pack alphas. The looks were far from subtle.

They sat down and a young woman, who Aislinn knew as Marta, came over with menus. She was nervous, as she bowed her head to the three of them. She didn't know how to respond to Aislinn. No one did. She wasn't officially part of the pack, as far as anyone knew. But her status with Cullen was uncontested, and those who had tried to question the situation had been dealt with. No one knew if that qualified her for beta status or not. She had beaten a beta, but there was no formal challenge for her position. Meredith was still doing her job as beta and hadn't been replaced.

Marta settled on an overall head bow. She was just an omega, after all. It was the betas who were really grousing about the situation. Their ranks seemed to be getting infiltrated. Current rumor had it that Meredith hadn't actually lost that fight. Aislinn had used some kind of mass hypnosis to beat her, and that was why none of the normal protocol had been followed.

Cullen ordered his usual without thinking about it. Aislinn ordered a smaller version of what Cullen asked for, and Sarah opted for the steak as well. Pretty standard fare at the Taigh-Oˋsda, it was a steak house, after all. Marta bowed again and left to bring back drinks and to place the order. The relief on her face to be leaving the table was obvious.

Aislinn shifted uncomfortably in the booth. "Rafe's influence seems to have gotten to everyone," she said sadly.

Cullen had been hoping that she wouldn't catch everyone's looks or at least not interpret it all so well.

Aislinn glared at him. "I'm not blind," she said to his train of thought.

"Okay," he said gently. "You need to start being a little less obvious about answering me when you catch things like that. We're going to have a little talk about exactly how much you're really picking up on."

Sarah looked around to see how confidential a conversation was possible. There were only a few full tables this late in the evening on a week night. The restaurant had just closed. Not that it mattered when the alpha wanted a table and dinner. He didn't usually take advantage, but he was hungry and left-overs up stairs weren't going to hack it.

Sarah made sure to watch for the approach of Marta or anyone else for that matter. Then she shot Cullen the disapproving stare she had been hanging onto all night. "What were you thinking?"

"I wasn't. It's done. Let it go, and help me figure a way to deal with it now." His tone said that in no uncertain terms would he allow Sarah to berate him. "Besides, mom, dad already gave me that lecture. You and Keith seem to have forgotten that I'm in charge." He felt like he was reminding people of that an awful lot lately.

"Oh I am sorry, Lord Arnauk," Sarah said dripping with sarcasm. "I will try and remember more clearly who's in charge in the future."

Sarah cut the conversation as Marta appeared with water and the drinks they had ordered, beer for Cullen and red wine for the ladies. She placed the drinks uncomfortably. Marta felt the conversation stop as she approached. That would go over well in the kitchen. Aislinn watched her retreat. Marta glanced over her shoulder at the table, saw Aislinn watching her, and seemed to flinch, hurrying her steps.

"They're all afraid of me," Aislinn said softly. Her head was throbbing, and she wasn't sure if it was from trying to force the premonition to come back or from the fact that she was getting so upset about the way everyone was looking at her.

"They'll get over it, if you both stop spending so much time alone." Then Sarah's sarcasm returned. "Oh, but you can't do that because you went and mated without elder approval or ceremony, and now you'll be wanting *more* time alone. I almost forgot. All we need now is for Aislinn to go into heat."

Cullen growled at Sarah. "Enough. I've got plenty to worry about. You're supposed to be support. If you can't handle the job--"

"I'll be replaced?" Sarah offered, cutting him off. She sat back in her seat and stared into Cullen's eyes, trying to read him.

Realization overcame him. It had never even occurred to him that Aislinn might replace Sarah as alpha female. Not that Sarah had anything to worry about; Cullen could feel the lack of ambition in Aislinn. All the same, it wasn't as if he could convey that to Sarah. She was already concerned about the situation and probably had reason. No one knew how strong Aislinn had been before the change was finished. From the looks of what Rafe mixed together, Cullen was guessing tiger and leopard of some kind, Aislinn was probably more formidable than she had been before. If he took into account that she had thrashed Meredith, a beta, and wasn't concerned in the least about dealing with Celia, then it wasn't a far guess that she might be comparable to Sarah. With all that in mind, Cullen made a mental note to take Aislinn down to the gym and find out exactly what she was capable of. For now he just needed to come up with something to say to Sarah.

Aislinn was the one who interrupted the glaring contest. "I don't want your job Sarah. I've never been the type of person who could run things. I don't even know what you do. I'd be happy to help out and make myself more visible if that would help things. But I don't want to have to be in charge of anything. Besides, I think that would make things worse."

Sarah looked at Aislinn as she spoke, listening to the sincerity in her voice. Sarah sighed. She still was wavering between moments of annoyance at being replaced after all this time and moments of acceptance and thinking she should have been replaced by Cullen's mate long ago. It wasn't his fault that he had taken so long finding one. Her voice softened. "Aislinn, you may not want it. The best leaders never do. Whether you give yourself credit for it or not, I can see you stepping up to handle my job fairly well. There's not as much to it as you may think. By keeping Cul on a short leash, you're already doing part of it." Sarah took a sip of the wine in front of her. "It's really only a matter of time, and Cullen knows it. He never would have mated with a woman who couldn't match him. He's too smart for that, or at least his wolf is."

Cullen smiled and picked up his beer. He was glad that Sarah was handling this so well, even if her reassuring lecture wasn't sitting well with Aislinn.

Aislinn could feel his agreement with Sarah. "No. I don't want to," she said looking concerned. "If they all hate me now, what do you think would happen then. They can't stand the idea that I beat up Meredith. Hell they probably think that I did something to her brain to make it possible. How do you think--"

Cullen cut her off. "Calm down. You don't have to do anything you don't want to do. I'm sure Sarah would be more than happy to just have help for a while. It's not necessary for you to be alpha. I could have mated with an omega if I wanted."

Aislinn's eyes narrowed. "Then just have a toy in your bedroom all the time. Totally useless except when you get horny."

"If that's the job you want," he teased.

"I don't think so. I want to do something, but that's not something I want people seeing as my *job*. I can already hear everyone calling me your *pussy* cat," she groused. Sarah started laughing at that, and Cullen grinned, trying not to be amused. Their reactions earned them both deadly glares.

"All right," Sarah said. "Now that I've established that I'm still in charge for the time being, what are my current orders?" The relief in her voice and her obviously relaxed demeanor brought a new calm to Cullen as well.

"I think that first order of business is that I'll get a hold of Jenna and thank her for the return of our people. Then I'll call the feds and check up on the weres that were handed over to them. I want you and Keith to get a feel on the atmosphere around here. Arrange something to improve moral and includes dealing with pack doubt about Aislinn. I'll do my best to try and keep things more public, but if they think she's messing with my head I don't know how much that will help. I'm going to set up a meeting with the elders for after the funeral, and I'll deal with the mating ceremony issues. I think the only other thing would be assigning Aislinn to work with some of the others. They'll get more comfortable with her if they meet her. Finally, as much as I hate to bring this up," he looked at Aislinn apologetically. "Make sure everyone knows that Brinah was a druid from the same order as Rafe and, she gave her life to help us. That might help." Cullen took another drink of his beer.

Aislinn was playing with her cup, staring at it. Feeling a strange uncertainty, Cullen watched her expectantly. "Whatever it is just ask it," he said.

"Now who's over-reading whom," she snapped.

"I could have read that from anyone. Stop playing with your drink, and say whatever it is."

There was a long pause. Sarah watched the two of them, smiling in amusement. "How strong is your bond anyway?"

Nearly choking on his beer, Cullen swallowed and wiped his mouth. "That has yet to be completely determined." He was still wondering what Aislinn was afraid to ask. "How strong is yours? It's been a long time since I had that part of my lycan education," he clarified when Sarah chuckled.

"Well," she said thinking about it. "It's been so long since I was without Drake. I don't really remember what it's like to feel by myself." She sat contemplative a moment. Both Cullen and Aislinn stared at her attentively. "We seem to have a connection that's good for most of the territory. I can still sense him even at the reservation, but it's weak from here. I know a couple people who have stronger links than that. I don't know really what determines the distance allotment. Uh," she thought some more about what he might be trying to find out. "Sometimes I pick up things that he didn't mean to project at me, but that's usually only when he's projecting at someone else and angry. From the sounds of things," she smiled, "you two go a bit beyond that."

Cullen glared at her. He wasn't finding it funny.

Aislinn growled. "You know, if it bothers you so much, I could always try and teach you how I blocked Rafe out. Then you could shut me off whenever you wanted." Sarah suddenly felt like she was about to become the third wheel in a dangerous argument.

Cullen could feel the hurt coming from Aislinn. He hadn't meant to hurt her feelings. "That's not it," he said gently.

"It just seems to me that everyone else around here accepts this part of mating. If you didn't want it you shouldn't have done it. Logically, considering that I'm the outsider here and the one who didn't see it coming, I would have thought that I'd be the one having such a hard time adjusting." Aislinn almost started to cry. She wanted out of here. Her head was throbbing.

Cullen breathed out heavily. This was not a conversation that should be happening in front of Sarah. It didn't take any kind of bond for Sarah to sense the need for privacy. She shot Aislinn sympathetically and excused herself to go to the lady's room.

Cullen reached across the table and took Aislinn's hands. She glared at him and tried to pull them back, but he wasn't about to let her have access to running away from him again. He knew she wanted to. Speaking very softly, he was trying to coax her into looking at him. "Piseagan, it's not that I don't want it. I love you with all I am. You can feel that can't you?"

Aislinn stopped trying to pull away from him, but still wasn't looking into his eyes. He decided a different tactic might be better. "Do you really feel so sure of yourself that you have no problem with me knowing everything that goes through your head?" Aislinn didn't answer. Cullen smiled, knowing that she caught his point, and her answer would have been 'no' if she were speaking to him. "Now add to that the fact that you seem to pick up far more from me than I get from you." She looked up at him when he said that. There was confusion in her features and he continued. "I know that I'm picking up more from you than normal bonds give the others. I can feel more reasoning behind your emotions than the others get from their mates. I know most of the others only know if their mate is happy or sad or whatever. I know you're upset now and somehow get why you're upset too. If that were all you were getting from me, then I don't think I would be nearly so concerned. But you also seem to pick up on thought process as well. You answer me like I was talking. I've never had to censor my own head before, and I don't think any of the others do either. How happy would you be with the situation, if our positions were reversed? You only get to know feeling and why, but I could hear you thinking."

"I don't know why it's like that," Aislinn said. "I can try not to listen," she offered. "I mean, I could probably block it out the way I did with Rafe. But," Aislinn hesitated, "I kind of like knowing you this well."

"It's certainly adding to your confidence level," he said with raised eyebrows, thinking about how she was carrying herself, and the way she was talking to Sarah.

"Is there anything else weird with us that isn't there with the others that might be my druid fault?"

Realizing that it would take time for him to convince her that she wasn't the cause of all the world's problems, Cullen sighed. "Not your fault. It pleases me to think that we were meant to be together like this. The stronger the bond, the more compatible the couple. At least that's what they teach. There's the projecting in human form. That only happens with really strong bonds. Most lycans can only project thoughts in hybrid or wolven forms. That is part of lycan lore, so it's not your *druid* fault. I've even heard of partial bonds that ended up with the couple having the ability to project or sense each other without completely finishing the mating. That's incredibly rare."

"I don't want you to start feeling like I'm invading." She looked around. "Technically I seem to be able to get into anyone's head if I try to. I've done it while people were sleeping." Her eyes started to tear. It frightened her. "Before we mated, I thought about trying to read your thoughts about me. I never did," she said quickly. "I don't want to be like Rafe. I don't know how to make it stop. The more things I try, the more things I seem to be able to do. What's worse is that there isn't anyone for me to ask about it. Not now." Aislinn's mind was overwhelmed by a feeling of her grandmother watching her. It only made her more upset.

Cullen felt her hands trembling in his. "If it makes you more comfortable to be inside my head, piseagan, then it's okay. Don't worry so much about what you can do. You'll never be like Rafe. It's not your capabilities; it's what you do with them that make a person. Just be more selective about what you choose to answer when you catch what's going on in my head, especially if there are other people around." He smiled at her and his thoughts turned toward what he'd like to do with her after dinner. "Although there are times that a man could grow to love having a mind reader around." His eyes sparkled, and he could feel her upset fading away.

The image she was getting was pretty graphic and Aislinn blushed. "I love you," she said softly.

Just then Marta appeared with their dinner, Sarah came back from the restroom, and Liam came walking in with a storm cloud over his head promising to rain on their plates. It was as if they all decided to descend upon the table at once. Aislinn felt a resigned annoyance take over Cullen. She sat back as he reluctantly released her hands. Choosing to ignore Liam's approach, Cullen ravenously dug into the rare meat on his plate.

Liam grabbed a chair from a nearby table, spun it around and seated himself at the end of their booth, glaring at Cullen. Marta was nearly shoved out of the way, and she had to reach over him to distribute the rest of the plates. Liam watched Cullen chew and glared some more, though it was accompanied by a reluctant head bow. "I must ask why exactly dinner has taken precedence over a room full of battered, abused, tired, cold, frightened people."

Cullen slammed a fist holding a knife down on the table. His eyes blazed with anger at Liam, and the man immediately backed down. Liam re-bowed his head, this time with submissive intent as an apology.

"Because," Cullen strained. "I'm more likely to do something drastic and unfortunate to the tired, cold, frightened *traitors*, if I don't get a grip on my wolf first."

Liam cleared his throat. "I guess that after the stories I've heard, I've become a bit more sympathetic to their situation. I'm sorry Cullen. I didn't mean disrespect."

Cullen sat back and poked at his steak, mulling over what Liam had said. "Okay, so tell me."

With that, Cullen sat forward and ate as Liam gave him the full report on what Rafe had done to the women, how he had gotten a hold of them, and the different threats that had been made. "Actually, the worst of it was Peter. Apparently, he had been one of the first. When he decided that Zoe would rather die than help betray the pack, he tried to go to you. Rafe threatened the others that if Peter managed to let you know what was going on, then he'd kill three women for every one thing you found out. So it was our own men who stopped Peter from confessing. Then Rafe tortured and killed Zoe anyway. She's the only one who didn't come back, but Peter knew she was dead days ago. He's been sitting in a corner of a room in the basement ever since."

Aislinn lost her appetite, and a tear streaked down her face in sympathy. Liam looked at her curiously. "You didn't even know Zoe," he said.

"Does it matter?" Aislinn looked at him with a glassy expression. "I'd have to be pretty cold hearted to not feel how much this has affected everyone here."

Liam nodded. He watched her contemplatively for a moment. When Cullen growled a warning, it got his attention and Liam shifted his eyes to Cullen questioningly. Cullen rubbed his face. His wolf was in high gear. Nothing was sating the beast this evening. He was far too worked up. Right then, he only wanted to forget what was happening, and that would involve Aislinn naked, on all fours. The image brought some small calm to his demeanor.

Liam cleared his throat and shifted in discomfort at Cullen's strange behavior. "I don't want to add to your upset Cullen. I would point out that I have a mate, and you know that I have no intentions toward Aislinn. You've been acting so strangely with her. It's one of the things causing so much talk."

Cullen stabbed at another piece of meat on his plate. "I've heard all about the talk. I think what's pissing me off is that everyone seems to assume that I'm supposed to have this magical ability to turn my wolf off whenever I want. Am I not supposed to be possessive of a woman when I finally decide that I want to take a mate?"

Liam raised his eyebrows. "So you're making it official then?"

Cullen nodded at Aislinn. "She's agreed to it. I don't see a reason to hide my intentions. I don't intend to make anything formal until after the funeral. So don't go advertising."

Liam nodded. "You know I wouldn't. Congratulations," he said tentatively.

"Don't sound so happy about it Liam," Cullen growled.

"I'm sorry. I've always been honest with you. I agree. When I first met Lizbeth, okay, I acted similarly to what you've been doing lately. But you have to admit that with Rafe and the mind control crap and it being so unlike you, it's not so strange that some of us would question the situation."

Cullen glared at him. "You know, it's rather insulting to think that the whole of my pack thinks my mind could be so easily manipulated."

"Cullen, I didn't mean-"

"I know what you meant. You and the rest of the elders can just suck it up," he said violently.

Liam stiffened. "Things have just been so strange lately. I'm concerned."

"The implication in that statement seems farther reaching than my mating choice," Cullen said, staring at the man.

"Just watch your back, my friend. You know that you have my loyalty. Regardless of your choices."

Sarah sat forward at that. "Liam, why exactly would Cullen need to watch his back?"

"I'm just saying that some of the rumors are going pretty far. I've heard about a pack split. There are people claiming that she's neutering him. I don't know what the general private thought process is, however the public talk is disturbing."

Cullen started growling again, a low angry rumble.

Aislinn knew that if the conversation went too much farther he was going to lose it. "Well, hopefully, if I start spending more time trying to be social, they'll all figure out that I'm just a normal person and not trying anything. Cullen are you sure I couldn't just go back to waiting tables here," she asked hopefully. "I mean if I don't look like I'm trying to be in charge of anything, and I'm willing to do my part maybe it'll stop."

Liam looked at her again. He was trying to read her. He had never had too much contact with her, but this didn't strike him as a girl trying to take over a pack, mentally or any other way. Cullen shook his head at her. Liam cleared his throat before Aislinn could argue some more. "Aislinn," he said, "it's not appropriate for the alpha's mistress to be doing things like waiting tables down here. Even if you were an omega it wouldn't be allowed, and from what I've heard, you could qualify as a beta if you wanted to. You don't want to, do you?"

Aislinn nodded and shrugged. Liam just stared into her eyes. He nodded back and sighed. "You are quite the enigma. I think that you'll win them all over eventually. Just keep being you and you'll be fine.

That is, after Cullen stops carrying you upstairs so often."

Sarah grinned and flashed Cullen an I-told-you-so expression. At which point, Cullen got out of the booth and held his hand out to Aislinn. Sarah had to move in order to let her out. "I'll do as I like," he said, grabbing Aislinn as she stood. She squealed, when he tossed her over his shoulder and headed out of the Taigh-O\sda toward the elevator.

"Cullen put me down," she growled and pounded on his back. "This is not dignified."

Her protests drew quite a bit of attention and resulted in amused smiles and giggling from the few waitresses who were left in the restaurant. Liam looked over at Sarah, who sat back down and smiled to herself.

"He is the alpha," she said. "You tell him to stop something…"

Liam started to laugh. "I guess I should be happy for him. I just wish he had better timing."

* * * *

Cullen set Aislinn down once they were in the elevator. Immediately, he pinned her against the wall, kissing her roughly and deeply. The doors slid closed, but the elevator went nowhere since Cullen hadn't pushed any buttons. His hands were far too busy.

Aislinn started to protest again as the elevator went up a floor, and the doors slid apart to reveal an elderly couple headed down to the casino. The older couple stepped into the elevator as if there was nothing going on, and Cullen watched Aislinn blush strawberry red. Amusement sparkled in his eyes as he smiled at her. Leaning in for another deep kiss amidst unspoken protests, Cullen pinned Aislinn's arms, as she tried to push him off of her. He was having far too much fun with this distraction to allow for her to win. He grabbed her hands and wrapped her arms around his back as he kissed her again, trying to slide his tongue into her mouth, amidst soft pleading for him to behave.

The doors opened again on the lobby and the couple got out, still pretending to not notice the young lovers. Though, Aislinn heard the woman comment, "Remember when we were like that?" to her companion. As Cullen let Aislinn loose, so that he could put his key in the panel and push the button for the penthouse, he saw the old man reach over and grab his wife's butt. She giggled, and the two of them headed for the casino across the lobby.

Cullen chuckled. When he had the elevator on its way, he turned around and his eyes shifted to swirling amber as he refocused on Aislinn. She smiled back at him widely and bit her bottom lip. "Where was I," he asked. "Oh, I was just about to do this," he said, as if he remembered something brilliant. Before Aislinn could move, he pounced on her and ripped her t-shirt down the back as he smashed his mouth against hers.

Finally, Aislinn gave in. She knew there was no fighting him on this. He wanted her, and she wasn't far behind him. She could feel her cat growling in the back of her mind and totally eradicating any embarrassment factor that might have been created by being caught by the older couple. When the elevator opened on the penthouse Aislinn was already naked. Her clothes were left in shredded piles in the elevator, as they tumbled out and onto the floor.

Cullen started pulling at his own clothes in annoyance, as if he was put out by having to wear them at all. Taking advantage of his momentary distraction,

Aislinn giggled and ran from him into the main room. His shirt and pants hit the floor in short order and he stalked toward her. She grinned wickedly at him. Suddenly strange sensations began running through her body. Cullen could see her cat fighting to take over as her eyes swam in amber and blue, shifting to an incredible iridescent green.

He lunged to grab her, and she managed to duck under his arms. Aislinn giggled again and circled round to hide behind his desk. Cullen growled at her as his wolf took over, turning him to his hybrid form. He couldn't hold it down with her teasing him like this. *You play games and you're going to get me more worked up.* He warned. *It's not smart to run from a wolf.*

Aislinn could feel how much he was enjoying it, so she decided that she wasn't going to go easily. "I think you're going to have to work for it if you want it tonight." Grinning, she ducked out of reach again as he came over the desk after her.

Cullen knocked everything on his desk off onto the floor. The lamp almost tripped him as he tried to grab her trailing hand. Aislinn was too quick, and she managed to escape him again. His growling was getting louder, and as he wheeled to see where she was, he almost howled his amusement. *I'd never make the mistake of thinking you were easy, mo piseagan.*

Aislinn missed the lunge as he came after her, and he managed to get her just around the waist. Cullen twisted so that his shoulder would hit the floor, and she wouldn't take his weight, but the consideration cost him. Aislinn's cat wasn't about to let her lose like that. She felt the beast force its way free, and she shifted into her hybrid form to match Cullen. It was as though some part of herself had pushed her farther back in her own mind. She felt almost lightheaded as the fur grew instantaneously, and her body changed. When they hit the floor, Cullen's grip loosened just enough for her to twist free of his grip.

Aislinn seemed to fly across the room and through the bedroom door. Cullen only barely caught the change, it happened so quickly. He was more than a little impressed, considering how much trouble she was having with it. *I guess given the right situation you've got enough control over that beast of yours*, he threw at her as he charged toward the door, only barely stopping himself from barreling through it after her.

I didn't do it on purpose. It just slipped out, she thought back.

Cullen could feel the concern tinting her thought. At the same time, it was overridden by the desire to continue their game. When he opened the door, she was nowhere to be seen. He smiled and raised his nose to the air. *There aren't that many places to hide in here, piseagan. And I could find your scent anywhere.* By the time he finished the thought, he had already honed in on her. She had gone out onto the balcony. He pushed the curtains aside and headed slowly through the doors onto the balcony.

Perched on the ledge just above the door, Aislinn waited with a mischievous grin on her lips. When he walked out toward the railing, she jumped lithely down from her perch. Cullen turned barely in time to see her dash inside and slide the glass door closed. She turned the latch and grinned at him through the glass.

Cullen's wolf was raging with lustful intent as he watched her through the glass. It took all of his control to not break through the door. *Enough piseagan, let me in.*

Aislinn eyed him. His cock stood out from him in a tempting display, and she almost gave in, except for the fact that there was too much fun to still be had. *Mmm, you fell into my trap. The piseagan has caught the big bad wolf.* Aislinn's eyes gleamed, and she began stroking her breast absentmindedly with one stray finger as she watched him pace back and forth on the balcony.

I don't like being caged. When I get my claws on you...

I can't wait, she thought back. *For now, I'm thoroughly enjoying my moment of triumph.* Aislinn pinched her nipple and watched his eyes follow her fingers as they danced over her body.

Cullen's cock bobbed in response to Aislinn's hand on her breast. She bit her lip and stepped in close to the window, so he could watch as one of her hands pinched and teased her nipple while the other hand traveled the length of her stomach and her fingers dipped into her wet slit. She moaned softly in that purring cat-like way that drove him mad.

Cullen didn't know how long he could handle watching her through the glass. He looked around for a way in, knowing that there was only the one door to the balcony. He growled in frustration, and Aislinn could feel the amusement in his mind waning as she tortured him.

She pulled her fingers from her wet cunt. She was getting to the point where she needed him more than she wanted to play games with him anyway. She put her wet fingers in her mouth to lick her juices off of her fingers and walked toward the door to let him in.

Cullen couldn't wait any longer. He stepped up to the door and grabbed the handle. With a sharp tug he heard a crack and a spider web traveled through the glass from near the handle. Aislinn stopped, her eyes wide, and she realized she had pushed him too far. Another sharp tug and the door flew open. The glass shattered as it rammed into the wall at the far end of the track.

There was nowhere to run this time. Cullen managed to tackle Aislinn and drag her to the bed. The rest of that night was sweating, moaning, and wrestling. By the time they got to sleep it was already near dawn.

Chapter 18

Cha do bhrist fear riamh a bhogha nach d'fheum
fear eile 'n t-sreang.
No man ever broke his bow but another man found a
use for the string.
-Gaelic Proverb

Cullen woke up early in the morning. The sun was just beginning to peek over the balcony. A nosy pigeon had noticed that the sliding door was no longer blocking his entrance and was poking around the glass. Cullen threw a pillow across the room at it and scared it out the window. Stretching, he moved away from Aislinn before he got anymore ideas, although she had pretty well exhausted most of those last night. He smiled at the memory.

"Stop thinking like that or you'll not be allowed out of this bed," Aislinn said, without moving or opening her eyes.

Cullen chuckled and leaned down, placed a kiss on her check and then jumped out of bed. "By the way," he said, as he headed for the bathroom, "I'm leaving it to you to call maintenance and explain to them why they need to come up here and replace the door."

"I didn't break it!" she called after him.

Cullen laughed some more and closed the bathroom door. It didn't take him long to clean up, and as he headed out of the bathroom, Aislinn pulled herself out of bed and limped toward it. "Are you okay," he asked with concern, watching her walk.

She looked over her shoulder at him with a broad smile. "I'm fine. Just a little sore." She stretched deliciously in front of him. "And I'll probably harass you into doing it again sometime soon. Maybe not tonight," she added. "But soon," she said, as she limped into the bathroom for her turn in the shower.

That comment almost had Cullen delaying his morning plans. Gods, sometimes she amazed him. He growled to himself and rubbed his face with both hands, getting control of his wolf again. By the time Aislinn was out of the bathroom, Cullen was dressed and headed for the elevator. He knew too well that if he stuck around he'd get to see her dry off and then it'd be all over.

He stopped her in the main room and pulled her close to plant a kiss on her lips. After a long moment that left her breathless, he pulled away. "Good morning beautiful," he said with a smile. "I'm going downstairs to deal with the others before my good mood fails. Then I've got some phone calls to make. I'm probably going to have breakfast in my office. I suggest you take some time to mingle with the masses, find Sarah and see if she needs anything done. Maybe get yourself something to eat. I plan on herding us all back to the reservation this evening. Good?"

Aislinn nodded. She felt like she had just been bowled over by the lengthy instructions. He smiled at her again and released her as he stepped toward the elevator. Cullen hit the button for the basement. The elevator seemed to take forever to finish the descent. He had finally decided what to do with everyone. He was still bothered by the fact that they had turned, but he did understand why. As much as it galled him to admit it, Aislinn had made a very good point. He had built this pack on family and caring as well as loyalty. He wasn't about to destroy all that because a handful, well more than a handful, of his men had betrayed him to protect their mates.

Cullen walked out of the elevator. The basement was actually several floors deep. There were underground living quarters, just in case they were needed for security purposes. Cullen hoped that they'd never have to be used. There was an extensive gym, with a pool, track, basketball court, and training facilities. That room was always in use. There were the security suites and the holding area. It had never been used to hold his own men before. He growled at that. Then there were the tunnels that gave access to the local subway system. Most of the pack was unaware that the den had an escape route in the basement. Again, Cullen hoped it would never have to be used. In any case, he didn't become alpha without having a mind for the future and all contingencies. Though he had to admit he never saw this coming.

The elevator only went as far as the first level. That was the floor the gym was on. Cullen walked down the hall toward the stairwell that led to the security suites and the holding area in sub-basement level 2. The cameras caught his approach, and Liam met him at the door when he came into the main entry way. The two men clasped hands, and Liam nodded his head in greeting.

"Glad to see you early. The men are getting antsy. They all think they're as good as dead," Liam said soberly, looking for Cullen's response. He obviously wanted to know what was going to happen.

Cullen nodded. "I'm not killing anyone. Though I did consider it," he added.

Liam's relief was evident. The two men headed through the security door and back to the holding pens.

Liam had allowed the doors beyond the main one to be left open. The rooms were mostly small cells down a long hallway. He had allowed the men to move amongst each other, especially after the women had insisted on joining them in the cells.

Cullen looked around at all the distraught faces. "Does anyone have anything to say," he asked in a hard tone.

Ranaild stepped forward. He was the only beta in the group, though there were quite a few thetas present. The rest all had lower ranks, so Ranaild was the spokesman. "We've all agreed that we deserve the worst of what you could do." That comment had half the women sniffling and the other half bowing their heads in shame. "But we ask that you spare Pete. He's lost enough, and he tried to tell you what was going on. We stopped him to save our own. I would say that if we had it to do over again, if it meant getting our women back safely, I am sorry Cullen, we would." There was more crying.

Cullen looked around. His brow was furrowed. "I would be lying if I said that I didn't spend a great deal of time thinking about how nice it would feel to rip your throats our personally." The men in the room flinched. If he asked, they would line up and offer their necks to him one by one, watching as each of their fellows went before them. "But, to your incredible benefit, Aislinn has managed to convince me that there was more to consider than the fact that you betrayed me." Every man and woman looked up at him, the women with hope in their eyes and the men with shame. "Rafe has caused my pack, my family, a great deal of pain. I don't intend to perpetuate it. As Aislinn put it, I intended for our family to mean as much to us as our loyalty to the pack. If I punish all of you for your behavior, then I have to consider my own actions when I was trying to save her. The woman is far too logical for my tastes sometimes." The last comment had a number of the women smiling. "Not that I intend to let you all off. I still believe that the better course of action would have been for you to tell me what happened. In as much, I intend to demote the lot of you." There was a murmur of uncertainty that ran through the room. Demotion was only a step above death. "For the next year, every man who betrayed this pack will be given the rank of omega with no opportunity to earn his rank back until the completion of the year. At that point, you may attempt to regain your position. And expect to be watched as well. You all know what's expected of omegas. If you don't embrace your new duties, I'll find another sentence for you."

The relief was accompanied by understood upset. It would be hardest on Ranaild. A beta forced to live as an omega would be miserable. Cullen thought it fitting. More was expected of a beta, so his punishment should rightly be more severe.

Cullen looked around. "Peter," he said. A pale looking young man stood from where he was sitting against the wall. He didn't care what happened. Peter would have preferred death as a sentence, and that was evident in his eyes as he approached Cullen. "I am sorry for your loss, my friend. I have no reward for your loyalty that could possibly compensate for that. You are not being counted with the others." The room murmured agreement. "Return to your life as best you can. When you are ready for further duties, come see me."

Peter nodded. He looked to Cullen with an empty blank stare. "There are old stories that druids can talk to the dead," he said hopefully.

Cullen could see where that was going. He shook his head sadly. "That I know of, Aislinn has no such talent. She sees dreams. That's all. She was never trained as a druid." In his mind, Cullen was thinking that this was an excellent opportunity to get rid of some of the bad rumors about her and seem open to talking in front of others. "You're welcome to ask her about it. I would caution you to give her some time. Her grandmother died in the fight at the reservation, and she isn't dealing with it well."

Peter nodded. "Maybe after the funeral then," he said flatly.

"That would probably be best," Cullen answered. He looked around the room. They had all been listening intently, as had Liam. *Good, that's a start,* he thought. "As for the rest of you, after the funeral make arrangements to speak to Sarah about your new assignments." Cullen looked over at Liam. "Is there any further business here?"

"No, not that I know of. Thank you, General. I'm sure that your understanding and lenience has been appreciated." There were a number of women who made to approach Cullen out of gratitude, but the look on Cullen's face had them backing down.

Leaving the room, Cullen could hear the relief being expressed. He felt good about his decision. It was a tough punishment, but it would be viewed well across the board. He didn't let any of them off easy, at the same time he didn't shed any more blood.

* * * *

There was no way that Aislinn was going to stay in their room all day. Except that she was nervous about dealing with all the people who were so intimidated by her now. *Staying in your room and hiding will do nothing to help resolve that situation*, she told herself. So she got dressed and went down to the great room.

When the elevator doors opened she headed into the main TV room to look for Rissa. Usually if the Taigh-O\sda was closed Rissa could be found in the great room. Since the restaurant wouldn't be open for some time yet, Aislinn figured that there was a good chance that Rissa might be around. There was also the possibility of finding Sarah and getting that assignment Cullen talked about.

Unfortunately, Meredith was the first person she ran into that she recognized by name. The woman narrowed her gaze on Aislinn and smiled beautifully. The effect was disturbing. Aislinn rolled her eyes and moved to find a different group of people, but Meredith was having none of that. "Are you afraid to stop in and say hi, Mistress," came the sarcastic call.

Aislinn stood still for a moment. She couldn't decide if she wanted to deal with Meredith or not.

There was a good deal of laughter in the room. Aislinn hadn't caught the comment that initiated the laughter, but there was something about it that wouldn't let her walk away. "Okay Meredith. You have my attention. What? Are you looking for another thrashing?" At that Meredith looked concerned. This wasn't the same uninformed and uncertain woman as before. "Or should I formally challenge you this time and shut you up permanently?"

"Why would you want to do that now? You've avoided it for so long, I have my doubts that you're actually capable." The look in Meredith's eyes told Aislinn that she didn't really believe what was coming out of her own mouth. Her arm was still in a cast, and the group surrounding her at the moment was all pregnant women who had been kept out of the fight.

Aislinn smiled knowingly. "Say what you like to impress the others. You know what happened in that fight. You also know that Cullen is done with you and the others. Get over it and move on."

Meredith growled. The other women were staring on to see who would win the verbal skirmish, and Meredith wasn't doing well. "How, I wonder, did you talk him into that?"

Aislinn flinched, and Meredith smiled. "I can't do what you're implying. Druids have varying abilities. Although I could give you the worst nightmare of your life, that would be the extent of it. I'm sorry to inform you Meredith, but Cullen chose me over you of his own volition. I have to tell you that I don't think it was a tough choice for him." Aislinn smiled, confident in the fact that her response seemed to have gotten to Meredith quite badly.

Meredith was furious and the women were chuckling amongst themselves.

"In any case," Aislinn said off hand. "I don't have time to banter with you. Cullen told me to report to Sarah for some kind of assignment, so I was wondering if anyone had seen her." Aislinn looked around at all of them in turn.

The women looked uncertain about that. Talking to Aislinn was totally different from hearing or talking about Aislinn. She was confident and attractive, and she didn't appear to be doing anything underhanded. One of the women who was more heavily pregnant spoke up. "Sarah is probably in her office. It's just down from Lord Arnauk's office and the library. You know where the library is," she added with a knowing smile.

Aislinn smiled right back. "Yes, I'm very familiar with the library. Thanks." Then she headed out of the room and down the hall, satisfied that she had made the right decision in dealing with Meredith.

It didn't take much to find Sarah's office. She was sitting in a room strikingly similar to Cullen's office. Her door was open, inviting anyone to come in. That differed from Cullen's usually closed door. Aislinn figured that the invitation was for someone to bother Sarah before bothering Cullen, and then Sarah would decide if the problem was worthy of the real boss. Aislinn smiled to herself. That was certainly one job she knew she didn't want.

"You guys don't have much variation in your decorating from room to room do you?" Aislinn joked as she poked her head in the doorway and waited to be invited in.

Sarah looked up. Her brow was furrowed, but she smiled at Aislinn just the same and waved her in. Aislinn walked across the room and sat down in the chair across from Sarah at the desk. "So, Cullen suggested that I come to you for some kind of assignment. You look worried about something. Is this a bad time?"

"No," Sarah sighed and pushed the papers in front of her away. "I was just looking over the room assignments. Cullen apparently chose to demote everyone instead of killing them. Good for them. A lot of work for me. Omegas don't get to live on the same floors as the others. That means moving everyone around. It'll be easier to deal with if it's done before we all come back from the reservation. That way they'll all be moved before the place fills up again, and they have to face the embarrassment of moving downstairs with people watching."

Aislinn nodded through the explanation. "So what can I do to help?"

Sarah smiled at her. "Yeah, why don't you go recruit a few omegas to help the others with the move. By the time you get back, I might have the new room assignments figured out. Then you can help me get the rest organized before we leave."

Aislinn nodded and left to take care of the job.

* * * *

Jenna ran her hand up Maon's chest. His eyes swirled molten Amber as he looked down at her. He had wanted her as his own since they were very young. He blamed the fact that they weren't mated now on Brennus and his ridiculous expectations of her. He also blamed her blind ambition on her father. He knew full well that the pack followed her for now because her decision at the battle with the Arnauk had paid off. But it was only a matter of time before someone large enough to rip her apart took control. That was, unless someone like Maon protected her and kept her in power. She needed him. She knew it, and he knew it. Now he was just waiting for a point when he could force his hand with her. She had too many alliances that she could use against him at the moment, but he had his own ambition. If he could convince her to mate with him, and he could take the alpha position with her at his side, so be it. He didn't want to have to kill her. However, Jenna had designs on being the sole alpha and didn't want to share power. For now, Maon would hold his position and see what would happen. The more time that passed between her show at the battle and his move, the better off he would be. Each moment brought doubt into the Tairneach minds that Jenna would be capable of remaining alpha.

Jenna's eyes gleamed with pleasure as she looked up at Maon. He towered over her, and his size gave her a feeling of ultimate power, knowing that he would do anything she asked without question. He hadn't slept since she started to send him on her little trips He was perfect. "What present have you brought me," she asked sweetly.

Jenna's eyes left Maon and traveled over the man who was on his knees in the middle of her great room. He looked a great deal like the last one that Maon brought in. Rafe's list wasn't very detailed. There was a column of names with several crossed off and several others with check marks next to them. What Jenna found out, that afternoon, after having her teams bring in several of the men and women on the list, was that no two druids could do the same two things.

It was getting very frustrating. She hadn't believed the first druid when he said that he couldn't reproduce the formula Rafe was using. Jenna had him beaten several times before working on the woman. The second druid told her the same thing. That only made her pissed off. When the third druid hadn't panned out she brought the three of them the list and told them that they had a choice. The first person who could tell her which druids on the list had the same skills as Rafe could have a hot meal and a real bed. That was when she was told that the people on the list most likely to be able to help her were all crossed off or had checks next to their names. A little more investigation revealed that the crossed out names had been killed and the checked names were missing. Her life was getting infuriatingly complex. The only bright spot seemed to be that these druids were very willing to cooperate. They bent to logic or threats very easily.

This new druid had been very difficult to find. His name was one of the ones with a check. He was tall and thin, with Aislinn's bright blue eyes. That only made Jenna dislike him, from the beginning. She smiled at him winningly, but the man didn't seem to be affected by her looks. She walked around him. He was wearing jeans and a white polo shirt. Maon had found him boarding a train. He had made the mistake of being the first name on the list to use a credit card while Maon had a man monitoring the names on the list through a connection at a local government office.

Jacob Senach was young, but exceedingly intelligent, as were most of the members of the Senach. When he received word that Rafe had been killed, he was the first to come out of hiding. He'd been waiting for the news because his mother was sick and had been taken to the hospital while he was in hiding. The minute the phone call came that morning and his cousin said that the council had felt Rafe's force eliminated from the Circle, he jumped to take the next train home. If he'd only had cash left.

Jacob knelt on the floor, resigned to his situation. He already knew vaguely what she wanted. Rafe had been doing something with alchemy. He'd been killing off all the Senach with alchemical abilities. He'd been after books with old information about were creation and maps to the Circle located on Arnauk territory. Now Jacob was on his knees in front of the lycan who had been used by Rafe to attempt to build an army large enough to take the Arnauk territory. Jacob knew that Jenna Tairneach was dangerously ambitious and that, at last count, the Circle had been undecided about whether they thought she was cooperating with Rafe or planning against him. Jacob deducted, that if she was hunting down the druids where Rafe left off, that she wanted him to make something. Jenna probably wanted whatever Rafe had been trying to make. He figured that his main advantage in this situation would be that she had no way of knowing how much he knew about her, this situation, or what he was actually capable of. There were advantages to being a member of the Senach. It was very difficult to keep information from a group of druids who had talents toward premonition and mind reading.

Jenna was about to begin the questioning process, confident in the fact that she had the right one this time, when an omega came in and notified her that there was a phone call for her.

* * * *

Cullen sat in his office with his phone in hand. The sooner he got through the small pieces of business he had left, the sooner he could get the pack on the road back to the reservation. He had a plan in mind for working with Aislinn on her ability to change. He hoped it would be easier than most, since she could read him so well. He'd start with explaining it, then show her. Smiling to himself, he searched through the numbers on his speed dial and located Brennus Tairneach. With some regret, he changed the number to Jenna's name. No matter what had happened in the end, Brennus and Cullen had spent too many years as friends to hold a grudge against the dead.

Jenna kept him waiting on the line for some time. He half expected it. Besides, he was in a good mood and not even Jenna's ego could spoil that now.

Her voice was honey dripping through the line. "Hello love. Calling for me so soon? Have you decided you don't like used toys and want to trade up already?"

Well he *thought* nothing could spoil his mood. It amazed him how easily Jenna could rub him the wrong way. "I think I liked you better when you were set on winning me over," he said flatly.

"Mmhmm, that doesn't surprise me. To what can I attribute the pleasure of this call?"

"I wanted to thank you for returning my people," he said honestly.

"I may be many things," she said with a sincere tone that got to him. "But I'm not quite as nasty as that druid was. Not quite," she added, and Cullen could almost see the plotting smile slide across her face.

"Can I ask what your intent for Arnauk/Tairneach relations is to be in our near future?"

"Oh, Cullen, I was only kidding when I asked if you were looking to trade in your toy."

"Jenna, you know that's not what I mean. From what I hear you're sitting pretty good as alpha over there at the moment. It's standard policy for me to attempt to figure out where the minds of my borders lie."

Jenna knew from experience not to underestimate Cullen Arnauk. "At the moment, Lord Arnauk, I have no intention of trying to cause direct trouble on Arnauk territory," she replied in an official tone.

Cullen read the tone with the exact the intent behind it. He heard the 'at the moment' loud and clear.

"Understood. We're having a memorial service for the lives lost, tomorrow at the reservation. I'm inviting you and your men, since our tentative alliance is what saved us from having much larger pyres."

Jenna was taken aback by that. After all this, he was still trying to be friends. A small voice inside her head suggested that she take his peace offering. "I'm sorry, but we've planned a service of our own," she lied, deciding that it would be a good idea to add it to the agenda as a way to further ingratiate herself to her people.

"Shame," Cullen answered honestly. "I truly hoped that the bond the Arnauk and Tairneach have shared for all these years would continue."

"Hmm, it would be a terrible loss, if that were to change," Jenna replied.

Cullen shook his head. He didn't need any more of this. He growled inwardly. *I should have called the feds first*, he thought. They wrapped up the conversation, and Cullen added Jenna's name to the list of people he'd have to keep a close watch on. They could move some of the spies and start getting more frequent reports from their Tairneach contacts.

Cullen paged through his list of contacts again and hit the button to call Stevens. The federal agent answered the phone on the first ring. He was always overly efficient.

"Stevens here," came the official voice through the phone.

"Arnauk," Cullen replied.

"Checking in, I assume."

"You could say that. I was wondering what had happened to our friends that you picked up," Cullen asked. He didn't want to admit his fear of the

- 393 -

government turning the weres into the next super soldier project, when they found out that they were all created recently. The belief, to date, that weres had to be born had kept the scientific experiments to a minimum. Cullen couldn't help considering what would happen when the word got to the fools who ran the government that they could mix up a batch of whatever they wanted.

"For now, the weres you turned in are being held in protective custody, pending interrogation and relocation. That will also be dependent on the review of the report completed by your second. It may help if we received a report from you as well."

Cullen nodded. He wasn't going to get anything helpful. "I'll see to that you get a detailed account as soon as possible."

"We'd appreciate that. I'd also like to know if the conflict between the Arnauk and the Tairneach is still a threat to the human population on your territory."

Cullen growled inwardly, but answered honestly. "That has yet to be determined. Jenna still seems to be planning something, though she's yet to declare what."

There was that tell--tale silence on the other end of the line that told Cullen Stevens didn't like what he heard. "So can I take it, from the fact that you're informing me of this, that the Pack Council is allowing government intervention on the matter?"

"No. I haven't discussed it with them as of yet. You can take it that I'm being up front about the situation, and I don't know if the human population is under threat from Jenna's intentions or not," Cullen answered. "I don't think the Pack Council would see this as reason for government intervention. I would like a report on your part to give to the Pack Council covering what happens to the weres we handed over."

"Understood. I'll get that to you as soon as possible. Anything else?" Stevens answered.

"No."

With that, both men hung up the phones. Cullen sat grousing for a moment. The only things that kept the government in line were the fact that the human population was clueless, and the were population was large enough to cause serious damage worldwide if they chose to attack. That didn't stop the feds from poking their noses into pack business on a regular basis. At the same time, the pack wasn't above using the government for their dirty work, if they didn't feel like leaving their dens to take care of someone messing with the human population. Cullen didn't know who the people that Aislinn saw in the Tairneach manor had been, but if they weren't Arnauk and they weren't weres, then Cullen figured that the human government was welcome to deal with Jenna if it came down to it.

Cullen finished his business by spending the rest of the afternoon writing up the reports he needed to send. One was for Stevens, to encourage that the weres be handed over to the Pack Council as soon as possible. After all, it was pack business. If there had been any other way of dealing with the weres after the battle, Keith wouldn't have handed them over. But the reservation had no facilities to hold the weres, and there had been too many of them for the Arnauk to control with guards for long. When the feds showed up and Keith was given the opportunity to get rid of the problem, he did. Cullen couldn't blame him for that. He may have done the same thing.

The second report was to the Pack Council, to explain what had happened over the past few weeks, why, and where the weres that had been taken prisoner ended up. He encouraged the Pack Council to seek out the proper government contact to get the weres turned over. He also suggested that the Pack Council look into the possibility of the existence of a large population of druids underground that could pose a threat to were society.

The last of his reports finished, Cullen pushed his chair back from his desk, stood up and went to find Aislinn. He grinned as he thought about her, wondering if there was time for another game of tag before they headed back to the reservation. He looked at the clock and sighed, realizing that it was late enough for dinner. He hoped that Sarah had all her business with the new omegas wrapped up so that they could just eat and get out of here. He wanted to be there for the last of the funeral arrangements.

Chapter 19

Neither seek nor shun the fight.
-Gaelic Proverb

Cullen drove back toward the reservation with a full belly and his wolf growling in his ear for not having spent some time alone with Aislinn before getting into the car. Her scent was driving him nuts. Everyone attending the funeral would be caravanning to the reservation that evening and the next morning.

Cullen listened to Aislinn and Sarah discussing the fact the new omegas had been overly friendly to her. Though Ranaild had avoided her like the plague, Elise had hugged her and then spent the rest of the afternoon following Aislinn around and trying to do all her work. Cullen smiled, figuring that his little comment about Aislinn changing his mind made her a few friends. Aislinn was so engrossed in her conversation with Sarah that she missed his thoughts about it. He noted that the next time he wanted to have his mind to himself he'd just get her involved in a conversation with one of the other women.

"I caught that one," Aislinn said and shot him a look that made him chuckle as he drove. If not for the fact that they were headed to a funeral, they would have been in great spirits.

They arrived at the reservation in good time. Cullen decided, 10 minutes into the car ride, that as soon as they got there he was going straight to bed with Aislinn. For the last hour of the trip he kept sending her images of what he intended to do to her. Aislinn countered with her own ideas of what would be fun, and it was working them both up so much that Sarah commented on the rapidly rising pheromone level in the car.

When they finally arrived at the reservation, the hour was late. Even so, most of the lights in the cabin were still on. It was a sign of the pack's upset that so many people were still up. Cullen looked up at the building, wondering if he would even be capable of making it to their room. He growled, knowing full well he didn't want to wait to have her at this point. Cullen shot Aislinn a predatory grin and nodded back toward the woods. "There probably aren't any glass doors for you to hide behind that way," he suggested.

Aislinn grinned and her eyes shifted. "No, probably not. But, I don't need to hide if you can't catch me." She started to back away from the car toward the woods.

When Cullen started to follow her Sarah growled at both of them. "This won't go over well. You're supposed to be more public. If this isn't running and hiding, I don't know what is. What the hell am I supposed to tell them when I walk in alone?"

Cullen pulled his shirt off and tossed it at Sarah. He had no intention of going inside yet. "I don't care. Tell them to come out and join us if they like. I'm guessing that I'm not the only one who could use a run in the moonlight."

Sarah watched Cullen take off the rest of his clothes, shift, and then take off in the direction Aislinn had gone. She yelled after him that he was acting like a teenage idiot, but the last thing she got from him was a howl crying at the moon, telling her that he'd found Aislinn's scent and was on the hunt.

Sarah threw the clothes she was still holding on the ground. She couldn't believe he left her to deal with the pack tonight. "Why exactly did I not want to give this job to Aislinn," she grumbled. "I hope she manages to completely snow your ass," Sarah added as she stomped toward the cabin. *It would be great if she managed to get away from the mighty hunter. Gods, he'd be frustrated if that happened.* Sarah snickered at the thought. If anyone could manage to get away from him it would be Aislinn.

When Sarah walked into the cabin, the atmosphere was frigid. Keith approached her, and the first thing out of his mouth was, "So where's Cullen?"

"Playing hide and seek," Sarah groused. "What's wrong?"

"Hide and seek," Keith asked incredulously.

"Yeah, hide and seek. They're getting worse. He actually carried her out of the Taigh-Olsda on his shoulder when I told him to start controlling himself." Sarah was watching the onlookers. The room was full of elders, and Terrick was glaring in her direction. "What exactly is going on here Keith," Sarah said, growing increasingly more concerned.

Keith leaned in and spoke softly to Sarah. "Terrick's instigating a pack split. He's trying to convince everyone that Aislinn is currently running the pack, and we don't know it. He doesn't have many men on his side, but enough, and the others are listening. Cullen needs to get in here now."

Sarah nodded. Her brain was scrambling for a way to diffuse the situation. "Leave it to Terrick to cause problems on the eve of funeral," she growled angrily, eyeing Terrick.

He smiled at her. "Has the druid gotten to you as well then," Terrick asked loudly.

Sarah knew that he was setting her up to lose credibility. "Terrick, firstly Aislinn isn't capable of what you're suggesting. You don't know enough about druids to be able to talk on it. Secondly, what kind of caoch goes and starts trouble the night before a funeral? I realize you've always been out to displace Cullen, but this is low even for you." That comment had a soft murmur rumbling through the room. Everyone knew that Terrick had designs on being the alpha. Now they were wondering if Terrick's talk while Cullen was out was really him being overly ambitious and trying to stir up discontent, since he saw an opening.

Terrick noticed the turn in his tide. It had taken him quite a bit of work to set this up. He wasn't about to let it go this easily. "Then where is our alpha? If there truly isn't anything to be concerned about with this woman, then why does he spend so much time keeping her to himself? Every time we've seen him lately, they act strangely."

Sarah rolled her eyes. "Everyone acts strangely when they meet the one they want to mate with." That sent another wave of murmuring around the room. "You just think it's weird from Cullen because he's been so long in the choosing. He's keeping her to himself because she was raised as human and doesn't really understand what's going on most of the time. You're turning it into more than it is. You want to see Cullen and Aislinn. They're having a run." She pointed out the window, chuckling to herself. *Well, he did say to invite them all to join him.* "I think that we could all use an outlet. There's been too much upset of late. You want to see what Aislinn is up to with Cullen? I suggest you go hunt them down for yourself.

I'm done playing babysitter. But I'll warn you not to interrupt. He wants to mate with her and he's getting more and more possessive the longer he's being forced to wait."

Terrick looked distraught as his audience started to filter out the door. Sarah smiled at him triumphantly. She knew that it wasn't over, but she had won this battle. Keith looked at her. "Do you really think that was a good idea," he asked nervously, as he watched the rest of the pack heading out after the alpha.

"Well, he did say to invite them out," Sarah said with a vengeful look. "But you're probably right. Come on. We'll catch him first and warn him that he's got an audience. That's if he's even managed to get his claws on her yet." Sarah smiled at Drake as he approached her. He always had a look of pride on his face when he caught up with her after something like this. Sarah counted herself incredibly lucky that she had found a mate who could handle the fact that she acted as alpha in the pack. Drake was her support. He was always there when she needed him and never minded standing in the shadows of her spotlight.

Keith saw the looks on their faces and knew that he was no longer needed. Jaylyn was her way, but wouldn't arrive until later that evening, and he knew that he wouldn't be getting any from her. Maybe if she was there she'd let him take out some of his pent up aggression on an omega. He thought back to the one who had brought Cullen clothes for Aislinn the day before. She had an awfully nice ass.

Sarah, Drake, and Keith ran out into the night, shedding clothes as they went. Keith and Drake actually had the best chance of finding Cullen, considering they had hunted together for so long. They knew his tactics. They shifted into wolves and headed for the woods, howling into the night as they went and hoping that Cullen wasn't too far gone to notice the noise the pack was making.

* * * *

Aislinn threw her clothes in various directions as she ran through the woods, hoping it might confuse her scent a little. She didn't have enough of a head start to actually do anything clever, and she wasn't exactly positive what she should do to throw him off. She wasn't familiar with tracking or hunting. Right now she was just trying to stay ahead of him.

Her heart raced. She heard him howl, and she spared a look in that direction, her eyes searching the shadows for her lover. She stifled a laugh, knowing how good his hearing was and ran deeper into the woods. She didn't know the territory or where she was going. Those were both disadvantages. She felt her cat trying to take control. When she heard Cullen howl again and could tell that he was still a ways off, she stopped and stood still. Closing her eyes, she tried to feel her beast like he had told her. She took some deep breaths and reached into herself, but there wasn't anything that she could get a grip on. When she heard a rustle in the bushes she stopped trying and bolted.

Cullen knew he could find her easily enough. Her scent was a part of him, and he could feel her excitement. He was moving slowly, so that she could get a bit of head start. That would make it more fun. When he found her bra in a bush, he rumbled in his chest and pushed his nose into the clothing, taking in her scent on the fabric and howling again, before following the trail after her.

Aislinn felt him coming. She knew he was close behind. She could feel the cat, but she couldn't quite let it slip through. She didn't understand what she was doing wrong. *If I didn't want it to happen it would already have taken over by now,* she thought angrily.

Cullen could feel her frustration. If he could have smiled and laughed as a wolf, he would have. No wonder he was catching up so quickly.

Aislinn sent a mental growl at him for his amusement at her predicament. *It doesn't matter,* she told him. *I can still out smart you.*

Only if you can change your scent mo piseagan. Keep getting mouthy and I'll come after you right now, and end the little fun I'm letting you have.

You are such a smug bastard. Just wait! Aislinn ducked under some branches and looked around for something brilliant, but she wasn't seeing anything. She knew that if she didn't get her cat to help, then he was right. Even with her cat she didn't know if she could win this. He had too many advantages, not that she didn't want to get caught in the end. She just wanted to at least make him work for it.

Aislinn didn't know where she was going, but Cullen did. He knew the territory too well. She was heading straight toward the stones. He wondered briefly if he should work his way around and herd her off in a different direction or not. Aislinn was so caught up in finding a way to outsmart him that she didn't notice the stones until she had stumbled into the clearing outside the Circle. She didn't think much about it other than the fact that it allowed her some bearings. She ran straight for the stones. As she stepped into the Circle, however, she felt like she was grabbed by the wind and wrestled to the ground.

Cullen sensed the fear the minute she was caught, and he charged headlong through the bushes toward the stones. She was confused and frightened. Then suddenly the emotion was muted. It was as if he was feeling her through a fog of some kind. That only drove him on harder. Cullen didn't know what could possibly be attacking her, but there was no way he was going to let harm come to her again. When he barreled into the clearing she was gone. He could still feel her, barely. He knew that she had to be here somewhere. He followed her scent into the middle of the stones to the point where it stopped. Cullen whirled about trying to find whatever or whoever had taken her, but there was nothing. no scent, no footprints.

* * * *

Aislinn felt like she was in one of her visions. She was staring around at the stones, and there seemed to be a timeless sense about the place that wasn't there before. It was as if everything had stopped. The trees were still, and there were no animal sounds as there had been before. She stood looking around and a terrible foreboding came to her. The bond she shared with Cullen felt weaker. She knew he was panicking, but there was something missing or blocking most of him from her. That terrified her.

Aislinn walked to the stone that had fallen over during the fight. Someone had stood it upright again. Suddenly there was a sound behind her. Aislinn turned hoping that it would be Cullen. When her eyes fell on her grandmother standing there and smiling gently, she burst into tears.

"What is this place," she cried, almost hysterical. Her legs wouldn't work. She just stared at Brinah's ghostly figure in disbelief.

Brinah walked up to Aislinn slowly. It was obvious that she hadn't been ready for this, but there wasn't enough time to do it gently. "Calm down child. You're perfectly sane. I'm here."

"You're dead," Aislinn responded through the tears.

Brinah reached out to touch her and her hand passed through Aislinn's cheek, leaving a cooling sensation, but no tangible touch. "You're right," she said softly. "However, the way I died bound me to this place. I didn't know that it would happen, but here I am."

"Grandma, I'm so sorry." Aislinn couldn't stop the pain. She felt as though her chest was going to explode. "I never should have involved you. I can't believe you're trapped here now."

Brinah smiled at Aislinn. "You've a great deal to learn. That's my fault. I never allowed you to be taught. How could I have known that the fates would draw you back into this life? Don't cry for me child. I knew what I did each step that I took, and I would do it again to help you if need be. Besides, everyone who dies must go somewhere. The clearing is beautiful, and the ley lines allow me some small existence beyond death. That's a great deal more than some."

Aislinn shook her head. She didn't know how to take all this. "Grandma--"

"Hush," Brinah cut her off. "Your mate grows anxious and will tear about the clearing, if I don't return you soon. I have some important things to tell you. First, when you need me you now know where to find me," she smiled at Brinah. "I encourage you to take advantage of that in the near future. For now it will suffice that you know where to go. Second, the books that are missing hold dangerous information. You need to convince Cullen that something must be done about it. Jenna is bad enough. But, if they pass into the hands of the men Cullen has sent to deal with Jenna, that will be much worse. You need to find them and destroy them. The rest will fall into place as that goal is accomplished. I think our people were much smarter in ancient times. Never write down something you don't want others to know."

* * * *

Jenna stood over Jacob. He was doing a great deal of reading and rereading. She had provided him with all the books and notes that Rafe left behind and was insisting that he learn how Rafe was turning people into weres. When Jacob asked why, he was beaten. That was a quick lesson learned. Do as you're told and ask no questions.

Then there was the fact that he was shown the other prisoners that Jenna had in the basement. She also spent some time telling him to work faster, or she'd harm them.

"As motivating as that is, Mistress," Jacob said. "The man you're asking me to emulate spent a lifetime learning these things. I cannot assimilate the information over night. I'm doing my best. Perhaps if I knew your goal, it would allow me to pick and choose the information that would be most helpful and gloss over the parts that I do not need. Especially if your goal is not to create a mixed were from a human base. That seems to be what all of this information pertains to."

Jenna scowled at him. She was tempted to have him beaten again for being so insolent, except that she could see his point. "How long do you think it would take for you to be capable of doing what he did? Do you at least have an estimate on time? I can't believe that following a recipe should be as difficult as making it."

"Technically, I suppose you're right there. But my predecessor," Jacob didn't even like thinking Rafe's name, "didn't trust anyone. He wrote a great deal of this in various languages, so as to confuse the reader. Gaelic I know, and English. There is also another here and I can't quite catch what it is. I've been reading around those bits. I don't know how dangerous that will end up being. I'll need to spend some time translating it, after I figure out what language it is. Then there is the fact that these recipes are specifically for creating werecats of various types and one that appears to be elephant, boar, and bear. That one appears to have been abandoned in mid creation. The rest of these notes and information are ancient and contain the basic knowledge needed to create the recipes. The older notes will take me a great deal of time. The ancients wrote in riddles, so as to disguise their intent. I'm sorry. I don't know how long it would take to decipher that."

Jenna growled impatiently. "Fine, I will tell you my intent. I need you to create a formula that will allow me to mix this," Jenna produced a large canine tooth from her pocket, "with existing lycan bloodlines."

Jacob looked at the fossil she placed on the table in front of him. "I'm sorry. All of these notes involve blood. I don't know what you expect me to do with a fossilized tooth. What is it?"

Jenna was getting angry. "I won't accept excuses. I'm sure you can figure it out. That," she said indicating the tooth, "is from canis dirus. My father has a small museum dedicated to the dire wolf. We consider the species to be an ancestor. A slightly larger, more powerful ancestor. Find a way to use it. I can get you more if need be."

"I think you are going beyond me with this assignment, mistress," Jacob said as he stared at the tooth, awe and concerned understanding in his voice. "You need DNA specialists or something. If you can find a way to make blood from fossilized bone, okay. Or you can find a druid with enough knowledge of ancient ritual to be capable of changing the formula provided here from blood to bone. How would you ingest bone? I suppose it could be ground down?" Jacob was torn between being frightened and refusing to help and being fascinated by the prospect and wanting to find the solution.

Jenna was a little pleased with the fact that she seemed to have caught Jacob's attention. "I'll see what I can do to bring you one or both of those options. For now, continue your studies," she said. She left the tooth with him as she went to find Maon. She needed him to bring her some more people.

* * * *

Cullen was going mad. He could feel her utter despair. The fear was gone, and now something was hurting her terribly. He was pacing back and forth. It had to do with the muin stone circle. He was getting close to having the whole muin thing destroyed.

Suddenly Cullen heard howling and shortly thereafter three wolves appeared in the clearing. When Sarah, Drake, and Keith saw Cullen pacing, they knew that something was wrong. At first, they thought it was funny.

Sarah was the one to mistakenly speak first. *Did she get away from you, Cul?*

Cullen growled angrily, and they all backed up. *Something here has her. She's vanished!*

No one knew what to make of that. They shifted into their human forms and walked toward the stones. Cullen was too worked up to be capable of shifting into human. They others looked around. Her trail ended at the stones. Cullen was right. She just vanished.

"Cul, there has to be some explanation. People don't just disappear. She's here. We'll find her," Keith said.

Others were starting to gather about. They were curious as to what was happening. With all the fuss Terrick had made, it was looking bad that Cullen would be so worked up that he couldn't shift back into his human form. All they saw was Cullen pacing about the stones, ready to kill. When it hit everyone that she was gone again, there were some annoyed comments about what Cullen might do this time.

* * * *

"As much as I don't want to send you back, you need to go now," Brinah said softly. She kissed Aislinn's cheek.

Aislinn could feel that cool sensation on her face as Brinah pulled away from her. "How do I go back?"

"Leave the Circle," Brinah said.

"Will this happen every time I come here," Aislinn asked.

"Only when you need it to."

Aislinn could feel Cullen's need to have her with him. She knew that he was near hurting someone. She walked through the stones and watched as her grandmother's ghostly figure vanished from sight.

Suddenly the clearing blinked into normal time again. All around her people seemed to appear out of nowhere.

When Cullen felt the fog lift from his mind it was like being slammed with a sledge hammer of hurt and despair all of a sudden. Then Aislinn walked into the Circle, as if she had never left.

Before Aislinn could get her wits about her, she felt a large furry beast barrel into her and knock her to the ground. She was just cognizant enough to know that it was Cullen, and that he was trying to see if she was all right. A cold wet nose was examining her closely, nuzzling into her neck and along her shoulders and back. Aislinn let him do as he liked. She was still trying to understand what happened.

Everyone else stood around watching. Aislinn was obviously out of it. She looked drunk or drugged or something. Her face was more pale than usual, and there were tears streaming down her cheeks. Everyone watching could almost feel the hurt radiating from her and mates drew closer together as they watched Cullen examine her to try and figure out what had happened.

As Aislinn realized where she was, she reached out and wrapped her arms around the large black wolf that was fussing about her. He let her grab onto him and sat down as she rubbed her face into his fur and started crying again. He could smell Brinah all over her.

Sarah, Keith, am I losing my mind or does she smell like Brinah, Cullen projected ,not caring who overheard the conversation. His friends moved in and didn't even have to get close to catch the scent. They all looked at each other in confusion.

Sarah sat down next to them and stroked Aislinn's hair gently. "What happened?"

Aislinn took a deep breath and got a hold of herself. When she finally let Cullen go, he managed to take his human form again. Everyone in the clearing was moving in closer to try and hear what was going on. "I saw my grandmother," she said. Cullen could feel the pain surge through her again. "She's dead," Aislinn said, answering the confusion on their faces before anyone could say it. "I know. Her spirit is here."

They all looked around as if Brinah was going to magically appear out of nowhere. "Okay," Sarah said. "What did she want?"

"To tell me that Jenna has the books Rafe stole and is doing something dangerous with them."

Cullen growled, "We kind of already know that."

Sarah gave him a hard look when Aislinn's head fell with his tone. "Is there anything more than what you already knew though?"

"If I don't get the books away from Jenna before someone else gets them, something terrible will happen," Aislinn said, knowing that it didn't sound very convincing or powerful.

Cullen growled again and shook his head. "We already discussed this. It doesn't have to do with this pack. We're not starting another fight so soon after the last one." There was an approving murmur through the crowd surrounding them that caught Cullen's attention and made him realize that they were being watched by half the pack. This wasn't a conversation that should be public.

He reached out and lifted her chin to make her look at him. "Are you all right?"

She nodded.

"Then that's it for now. We can discuss it more after the funeral."

Aislinn nodded again and leaned into him. He wrapped his arms around her, even with the crowd watched. Terrick was losing more ground. This didn't look like Aislinn was running anyone. She looked more like a scared child than anything else, as she huddled in Cullen's arms. Terrick watched from the shadows. It didn't take a genius to see that he was going to need to try a different tactic.

* * * *

Celia and Mack had pretty much missed the major excitement. By the time they arrived, arguing, at the stones Cullen and Aislinn were standing up, and most of the conversation involved whether or not the pack was going to have that run they were promised. Cullen and Aislinn were inclined to go in to their room after what had just happened, but Sarah was trying to convince them that it would be a good idea to take advantage of the situation to improve morale.

Celia was trying to talk to Mack. It was a strange change in dynamic for them. Celia had done her best to try and ignore what happened between them. She even tried to be happy about not being chased by him any longer. But her heart just couldn't take it.

"Cel, if you think that I don't know you'll say anything to get things the way you want them, you're wrong. I'm sorry love, but you fucked this one too hard. I'm done." Mack was pissed because he had been in the process of a very pleasant game of hide and seek with a pretty little omega when Celia interrupted.

"Mack please, just listen." The unnatural sound of pleading coming from her mouth was enough to draw the attention of the group in the stones which had grown very used to Celia's own personal brand of arrogance.

"I think I've heard enough from you," Mack said, stopping near the others and turning to glare at her. The anger in his voice was just as unnatural as the desperation from Celia. "Unless you care to tell Aislinn and the General about what happened the other night?"

Celia blushed, and the red ran all the way down her chest and across her breasts.

Cullen growled with annoyance. "What's the problem?" Mack was implying that it had something to do with Cullen and Aislinn, and Cullen couldn't ignore that.

"Oh nothing, apparently," Mack said sarcastically. Celia came walking up to him with a fearful pleading look in her eyes. He was too angry to take pity on her and not embarrass her front of the whole of the pack. "Celia seems to think that I should not be bothered, if she calls out your name while I'm fucking her instead of mine."

Celia was close to tears, and her pride started to take over, when Mack told Cullen what happened, especially when several groups of people started laughing.

Keith chuckled with amusement. "This is turning out to be a more entertaining night than I had thought it would be," he grinned.

Sarah elbowed him to shut him up. This wasn't his business, not that it ever stopped Keith.

Aislinn felt bad for Celia. It looked like she screwed up pretty bad. Celia reached out to Mack and he shoved her away, toward Cullen and Aislinn. When Celia tripped and fell into Aislinn, the entire incident between Mack and Celia flashed before Aislinn's eyes. She found herself on her knees on the ground again.

Cullen swore as he knelt down to see why Aislinn didn't stand back up and saw the glazed over look on her face. He growled, "Enough." He stood back up. He could feel Aislinn's fascination and knew she was all right. He was currently more concerned with putting an end to the stupidity that was playing out for the whole pack to see.

Aislinn could hear the angry tones in the background and knew that there was more arguing going on between the people around her. What had her attention however, was that she seemed to be seeing through Celia's eyes as she had sex with Mack. Aislinn smiled to herself, as she felt that same amazing need and pleasure surging through them that she felt with Cullen. Aislinn was looking through Celia's eyes as she looked down at Mack and fucked him wildly. Aislinn could feel Mack's cock swelling inside Celia's body, and she knew they were mating. Sensations of pleasure coursed through Celia and vicariously through Aislinn.

Cullen looked over at Aislinn. He grinned. He didn't know what she was seeing, but whatever it was it must be good. She was getting amazingly worked up, and he was feeling it though their connection.

Aislinn felt Celia's orgasm approaching and then the fear. It was as though up to that point Celia hadn't cared what she was doing. Then all of a sudden she realized that if she mated with Mack she was completely done with Cullen. That was when she said Cullen's name. In an instant, Aislinn felt the pain sear through her body as Celia was thrown from Mack onto the floor. Then came the even more intense pain centered in her chest as she realized that he wasn't going to come back. Celia's heart was racing, and she couldn't breathe. For the first time since she met Mack, she finally realized what she really wanted. Now she didn't know how to fix it. She was scared and lonely. She could feel how much Mack hated her through the bond. Aislinn started to cry again. It had been hard enough feeling Cullen upset with her, but to feel him hating her would destroy her. What was worse was that Celia was pregnant. She didn't know it yet though. For once, Aislinn wished that those extra pieces of information she randomly picked up in her visions didn't happen.

It was one thing to let her keep staring off into nothing, if she was enjoying it. When Cullen felt Aislinn's heart breaking though, he had enough. *Aislinn,* he called to her, as he knelt down to try and bring her back to reality.

Aislinn blinked a couple times and looked around. When her vision cleared she bypassed Cullen entirely, went to Celia and wrapped her arms around her. Confuses as Celia was, she accepted the comfort. Mack stared questioningly over at Cullen who just shrugged. He didn't have any idea what she had seen that time. "Sometimes, I think it would be easier if she could mess with heads instead of this vision caoch," Cullen said, crossing his arms over his chest as he waited for an explanation.

"Whatever. I'm getting out of here before she stops distracting Celia," Mack said and headed for the woods.

Aislinn turned on him. "Mack, I can't believe you'd put so much effort into trying to get her attention, and then when you have it, you'd turn into a creep."

Cullen raised his eyebrows. He didn't know what was possessing Aislinn, but the sense he was getting from her now told him to just keep out of it. There was more chuckling from the assembled crowd when Aislinn called Mack a creep, and Keith was looking as though he had been given an early Christmas present.

"This is none of your business, Aislinn," Mack growled, turning on her. Cullen growled back and stood behind Aislinn in warning, to let Mack know that he'd better watch it.

Aislinn leveled an impressive glare of her own on Mack that had an impact only an alpha could give. The assembled pack wasn't sure if it was all Aislinn, or if Cullen standing behind her added to the impression. "You made it everyone's business the minute you walked over here and declared what happened," she growled back. "So she made a mistake. Don't be stupid enough to throw away what you've already done," Aislinn said, with an emphasis that told him she knew they had bonded already, "when you know she didn't mean it."

Celia wasn't sure what to do. The idea that Aislinn would be defending her after everything that happened between them was mind boggling. At the same time, Aislinn seemed to be reaching Mack in a way that Celia couldn't. So she wasn't about to interrupt.

Aislinn took Celia's hand and led her over to Mack. He growled a warning to keep the distance, but Aislinn ignored him. "If Cullen's growling doesn't intimidate me, what makes you think yours will?" There was more laughter from the audience. Even Cullen had to grin at that.

When Aislinn had them close enough that she could speak without having the whole of the gathered pack hear what she said, she looked at them both. "Besides, she said softly. The litter will need two people who care about each other. You'll be better off making up now, because in a few months, good makeup sex will be impossible." With that, she left the shocked pair to stare after her and walked back to Cullen.

Aislinn stepped up to Cullen and wrapped her arms around his waist, hugging him and smiling to herself as she lay her head against his chest.

He hugged her back as he watched Celia and Mack go from glaring and uncertain angry tones to tentative friendly ones. Then they ended up kissing. There was more murmuring from the gathered group.

Keith came over to Cullen and Aislinn. "What did you say to them?"

"I told them that Celia's pregnant and if they didn't makeup now in a couple months the makeup sex wouldn't be nearly as much fun," she grinned.

Keith burst out laughing, and Cullen smiled at her shaking his head. "So," Cullen said softly, "do we take Sarah's advice, or do we go back to our room?"

Aislinn smiled at him and leaned in for a kiss. Around them, people began to follow their lead. Cullen's hands traveled down her skin. *We have to keep this low key,* he sent to her.

Aislinn moaned into his mouth as he picked her up, and she wrapped her legs around him. *I'll be fine. But are you sure you can handle that?* She felt his cock harden against her as he carried her out of the Circle and toward the woods.

Cullen wasn't taking the chance that she would have another vision or whatever happened before that. He put her down on the ground just outside the trees.

There were quite a few people watching as he grinned at her, and his eyes swirled. "I'm going to count to ten," he said. *Let's finish what we started.*

Aislinn grinned back. She had a plan this time.

"One," he said. The couples that heard his suggestion were readying themselves to join the chase.

Aislinn turned and ran, followed by half the pack of men and women into the trees. All around her, people were turning into wolves. Aislinn kept her mind focused on Cullen. She waited as he counted. Running as fast as she could though the trees without letting go of his mind, she waited. Finally he turned. She let the strange sensations run through her body. She felt Cullen call up his wolf. It wasn't difficult, seeing as the beast had been waiting for his chance all day. Aislinn felt Cullen give over to his wolf. As he did, she realized what she had done wrong. She never really accepted that she had to let go completely.

Aislinn stopped and looked behind her. The others were all passing by as their mates and lovers came bursting through the underbrush. Aislinn closed her eyes and reached for her cat. It all happened in a rush of adrenalin. Aislinn let her mind go to the animal half of herself, and the entire world shifted around her. She could see more clearly, smell and hear more clearly. She looked down at the fur on her body, the claws on her feet where there used to be hands, and she started to run. It was strange going on four legs instead of two. It took her a minute to get the hang of it. She looked around for Cullen. She knew he was nearby.

The sound of howling filled the night as lycans caught up with their counterparts. The rutting was wild. Aislinn took to the trees. She knew he would have a harder time chasing her since wolves were ground bound. She paced herself as she jumped from one tree into the next.

Cullen caught up with her some time before she managed to change. He watched her turn with pride. She certainly deserved credit for creative thinking. He felt her in his mind as he shifted. It took most cubs weeks to totally master the shift. Cullen decided that there was an obvious advantage for Aislinn in being bonded with someone and capable of feeling it, instead of having it explained to her verbally. He watched her try to get the hang of running on four feet and stalked her as she jumped through the tree branches. He was patient. She would have to come down eventually.

She was difficult to see, as she jumped through the trees. Her coloring blended well with the shadows in the branches. Aislinn looked down into the bushes, and Cullen ducked to try and keep out of sight. Aislinn wasn't trained for this, so she didn't quite manage to catch a glimpse him. She did, however, manage to get herself stuck in a position where there wasn't another tree close enough and strong enough for her to jump to. She scanned the ground for Cullen. Not seeing him, she jumped down.

The minute her feet hit the ground he howled in triumph, leaping from his cover and pouncing. He rolled her to a stop in the shadow of a particularly large tree. Pinning her to the ground and growling at her for submission. She struggled a moment, and he watched her with immense pleasure.

Finally she lay still. He was nuzzling her neck and moving down against her with his erection. She didn't want to fight him. She wanted him inside her. Aislinn shifted beneath him in frustration. She didn't realize why this was so complex. Cullen rumbled in amusement, *Move your tail.*

Aislinn growled appreciatively as she finally felt him push into her sex. He started slowly, driving into her and trying to hold back enough that he'd be able to pull out before they got stuck together. There were too many possible witnesses to it out here tonight. He didn't even bother to check the shadows. He knew someone was watching from somewhere.

Aislinn shook with the pleasure of each stroke. Everything felt different and new in this strange form. She felt her fur rub against him, and his legs wrapped around her as she dug her claws into the ground to hold herself still.

When Cullen pulled out she whimpered and looked back at him, pleading for him to continue. Cullen licked her dripping sex. His tongue delved into her, and she purred with the shivers it sent through her body. *We can't finish like this,* he told her. *Change back with me.*

It was all Aislinn could do to calm down enough to concentrate on Cullen's mind. *I don't know if I can,* she moaned. *Please Cullen, take me like this*, she said and raised her butt toward him enticingly.

Cullen growled and licked her sex again. His tongue slowly stroked her. *We're being watched. I need you to try, or we'll have to be done.*

The threat was enough to get Aislinn to pay attention. She lay down and panted hard as she closed her eyes and reached out for Cullen with her mind. Cullen went slowly, forcing his wolf to retreat into the back of his mind and allow his human side to take over. Aislinn felt him promising his wolf a much heavier love making session when they returned to their room and closed the door. There was a great deal of protesting.

Aislinn found her cat in her mind and followed Cullen's example, bargaining with the beast to get it to back down. After an extensive bout of arguing, Cullen pulled Aislinn into his arms, both of them human. Cullen pressed her legs apart and plunged his cock into her wet pussy eagerly. He didn't have the patience to wait for permission at the moment. She growled in delight as she felt him begin to thrust into her over and over again. They kissed, and as their tongues danced together, she had to admit that although there was lost intensity the kissing made up for it and paws were no replacement for hands. He pinched her nipples roughly as he caught the thought in her mind about hands and listened to her moan with delight.

Aislinn heard the sounds of others around them. Cullen was right. They were definitely being watched. Aislinn turned her head and saw several couples who had come out of hiding. Aislinn's eyes met those of a woman who was on all fours as a large grey wolf pounded into her from behind. The woman smiled at Aislinn, then closed her eyes. Her head fell forward, allowing the wolf to bite her neck. Her arms collapsed beneath her as an orgasm shook her body.

Aislinn felt her own building. When she looked back to Cullen, she found that he had been watching her watch the others. He smiled knowingly, and Aislinn blushed, but smiled back. As she stared into Cullen's amber swirling eyes, she felt her body begin to tremble. It built down low in her stomach and flowed in waves through her. Her breath caught in her chest, and her pussy spasmed around his cock. Cullen gritted his teeth and growled. When he felt her walls clamping down on him, he couldn't hold back any longer. He came into her as they stared into each other's eyes.

Tá grá agam duit, Cullen, she thought, in lieu of breath to say it out loud.

He pulled her close to himself and hugged her tightly, rolling them over so that he was on the bottom. He kissed her passionately. *Tá grá agam duit, Aislinn.*

Chapter 20

Life is the fire that burns and the sun that gives
light. Life is the wind and the rain and the thunder in
the sky. Life is matter and is earth, what is and what
is not, and what beyond is in Eternity.
-Lucius Annaeus Seneca

The pyres burned high into the night sky. All around the reservation, wolves raised their faces to the heavens and howled their mournful song into the night. There were only a few Arnauk not present. Too many lives had been lost for there to be a single person unaffected by the deaths. The only ones who weren't there were those that had to run the Madadh-Allaidh Saobhaidh and the Taigh-Olsda. A minimal staff had been left behind. The restaurant and hotel were mostly being run by the human hires tonight.

Aislinn stared at the enormous pyres. The yellow and orange flames licked the sky and sent shadows dancing about the trees. It was a sharp contrast to the howls of pleasure, and the bodies dancing amongst the trees the night before. There was very little talking. That morning they had found two suicides. It was expected. With so many mated losses, it wasn't unusual for the one left behind, especially if there were no children, to take his or her own life.

The day had been long and hard. Aislinn had seen very little of Cullen, and it was getting harder and harder on both of them. He had spent the entire day being diplomatic and sympathetic to all the families that arrived to attend the funeral. Aislinn had spent the day trailing after Sarah and taking on odd duties that

Sarah suggested. Mostly it was to show the rest of the pack that Aislinn was taking orders from them and not the other way around. Sarah hadn't assigned her anything difficult. She would deliver a message to one person or another. She helped with carrying things in when more important people arrived. She smiled and spoke when spoken too. The only difficult part was answering a lot of questions about herself. In the end she was mentally exhausted.

Aislinn watched Brinah's body burn, and tears slid down her cheeks. Knowing that her grandmother's soul existed, but was tied to this place was little comfort. She had questions. Aislinn leaned against Cullen, her arm entangling his. It was the first time the two of them managed to be standing next to each other all day. He knew what she wanted, and she knew that he was uncomfortable with the idea.

"I'll be fine," she said. "It scared me the first time because I didn't understand what was happening or why. I need to talk to her."

Cullen shook his head. "People will notice if you go missing right now."

"We're leaving for the Madadh-Allaidh Saobhaidh in the morning. I won't have another chance."

Cullen growled. "Aislinn I don't like it."

"I know. I'm sorry. But I have to." She kissed him on the cheek and then walked away from the pyres, and down the path in the woods, toward the stone circle. He watched her walk away, knowing he couldn't stop her.

Aislinn felt him nearby, knowing that he wouldn't stray far from the stones. There wasn't anything he would be able to do, if something happened. Still, he didn't care about that. He would try if something went wrong.

Aislinn stepped through the perimeter of the stone circle, with the firm intention of finding there, and to her surprise it worked. Everything went still. No breeze, no sounds, just black and the stones, and there in the middle of the Circle stood the ghostly figure of her grandmother.

Brinah smiled with pride, and her blue eyes sparkled an unworldly glow. "You have no idea how difficult what you just did should have been. It took a great deal of energy for me to bring you here that first time. You plane walk as though you were born to it." Brinah walked over to her granddaughter. "I never dreamed I would regret keeping you from the Circle. Now, I can't help wondering if I held you back."

"Why did you leave them? Did they do something to you or something wrong? I know you said you wanted to marry grandpa, but did that require leaving?"

"Straight to the point. You remind me of myself some times. You know that is not a characteristic of the Circle. They are much more... diplomatic." She smiled. "No it wasn't a requirement. Except, your grandfather didn't know about the Circle, and I didn't know how to tell him. He was very Christian. Traditionally that isn't a religion accepting of the types of things and beliefs the Circle represents. It was easier for me to hide it, than for me to try and explain it. The Circle itself wasn't at fault for my leaving. It was my choice, and they let me go."

"Should I be concerned about the things that I can do? Should I try and learn about it?"

"That's up to you, child. You can ignore it all if you want, though the fates don't seem to be willing to let you. Now that you've bound yourself to a lycan, it will be even harder if you want to attempt to ignore that side of yourself. The more you use it, the stronger it will become."

Aislinn nodded. "Then the visions. They've been happening more and more recently."

Brinah tilted her head and stared into her granddaughter's eyes. "That should only happen if you're willing to let it happen. You must be becoming more accepting and open to it. Premonitions come when you allow them to."

"What about controlling it? Can I have one when I want one?"

Brinah suddenly understood, and smiled knowingly. "That's why they're increasing. You're trying to use them." She shook her head. "That's more complex an accomplishment than you might think. The fates control the premonitions, and they'll not let you have influence over them. It takes a powerful druid for that. The best you can do is will yourself to be open to allowing one to come to you. You control them by accepting that one might come. You don't control the content or influence them. The harder you try the less you will get. It's kind of like your shifting from one form to another. To have a premonition, you have to surrender your control to the fates, and hope they give you what you want."

"It seems that the druids are big on stepping back and allowing the fates to control them."

"Traditionally we're observers, philosophers, and teachers." Brinah's voice was soft and reflective as she spoke. "The people who seek to control things usually get replaced by time or someone else out to control. We move with the fates like the oceans and the tides."

"What else am I capable of?"

"Now that is a very complex question. Everyone is capable of whatever they like. It all comes down to what you apply yourself to, and if you choose to use your natural talents or seek to develop an ability that may be more difficult to come by, but may be more helpful to you."

Aislinn stared at her. "No straight answers then?"

"You have the answers. You just don't know it yet. They'll come to you as you need it. I've given you advice that is more helpful than you may think. Is there anything else?"

Aislinn nodded. "I can't convince Cullen to deal with Jenna and the books. He doesn't believe it's a pack matter. With the recent deaths and the pack dissension as it is, he doesn't want to risk giving them a reason to doubt his leadership. I'm a big enough problem for him to justify. If he goes chasing down other packs based solely on my word, he risks loyalty issues."

Brinah's face fell a bit. "It will become pack business shortly. If he ignores it long enough, it will come looking for him. It would be easier dealt with now than later. The fates will play out as they wish."

"Can't you tell me what the problem is? What does Jenna want with the books?"

"I'm sorry. I don't know everything. I only get impressions of paths that could be taken. It's like when you have a premonition, and you walk in knowing whether it's the future or the past. You don't know how you know. It's just a feeling the fates have allowed. A hint to help you find your way. Perhaps the warning I have given you is enough all by itself to help you survive your path, even if you do nothing other than wait for it to come."

Aislinn sighed. "I don't do well with just allowing things to happen. I'd rather do something about it."

"That's because you were raised human. Different philosophies. I suggest you do what you believe you need to."

Aislinn could feel Cullen's impatience at her absence. "I should go back."

"I understand. Lycans can be very possessive. And the alpha is very controlling. If anyone is going to be able to handle him, I believe you can." Brinah stepped closer to Aislinn, kissed her cheek, and vanished into a fog of sparkling silver blue dust.

Aislinn looked around for Brinah, but she was nowhere to be seen. As Aislinn stared into the shadows of the dark, silent stones she felt a presence beyond Brinah. Or more precisely, many presences. It was only then that it occurred to her that the stones had been here for a very long time. At one point they were used regularly for rituals and spells. If Brinah's soul could be trapped here, what was there to stop other souls from being trapped here as well? The uneasy feeling grew as she turned and left the Circle. She decided that she would definitely need to be very careful about who she was thinking of when she entered the stones.

Cullen was waiting for her when she stepped through the border of the stones. He was leaning against a tree with his arms crossed. Aislinn smiled at him as she felt the fog blocking her mind from him clear. There was a strong sense of concern coming from him. It ranged from concern about the pack seeing Aislinn's pursuit of her druid abilities as a threat to them, to her pursuit of her abilities taking her away from him. Aislinn approached him, walking straight into his arms.

Holding her close, he took in her scent. "I don't like the fact that you're blocked from when you walk into those stones even a little bit."

"I know. I'm sorry," she said and hugged him harder.

He growled. "Did you find what you wanted?"

"Some yes. Some no. Druids can be very enigmatic," she said and grinned at him.

He grinned back and shook his head. Then leaned down and kissed her. His tongue slid over her lips, and she opened her mouth to let him in. It only took moments for the kiss to grow heated. *Let's go back to our room,* he suggested.

Aislinn broke the kiss and nuzzled into his neck, biting him gently. "Okay," she said, and they headed back up to the cabin.

* * * *

The next day was a great deal like the previous day, except that it involved saying goodbye to everyone diplomatically instead of saying hello. Cullen, Aislinn, Sarah, Drake, Keith, and Jaylyn, as well as the rest of the main group of betas from the den, were the last ones to leave that day. The plan was to arrive at the Madadh-Allaidh Saobhaidh, have dinner at the Taigh-O\sda, do the last of the mourning and then sleep. The next day would return everyone to business as usual.

The first thing Cullen said when they all got in the car was, "By all the Gods I'll be glad when this is done. Now I remember why I worked so hard to stop this kind of crap." Aislinn decided to save her discussion about Brinah's warning for a later date. She sat uncomfortably throughout the car ride. His scent was getting to her more than usual. All she wanted was to be alone with him.

When they managed to walk into the penthouse without further incident, Cullen smiled and laughed wondering how long it would take for the next natural disaster to hit. Aislinn was torn between attacking Cullen and cleaning up. She finally decided that one would make the other more pleasant, so she started dropping clothes on the floor and walking toward the bathroom. She felt guilty that she had just come from a funeral, and all she could think of was sex. But she couldn't help herself.

Cullen watched Aislinn undress and head for the shower. He could feel her upset over everything that had been happening. She'd been dwelling all day, in between thoughts about getting him naked and alone. More than willingly, he undressed and followed her.

Aislinn heard the curtain slide and then felt Cullen's hands across her body. "Stop it," he said.

She scoffed, "What? You got something against me showering?"

"I know what you're thinking remember?"

"No you don't. You said you only know what I'm feeling. I could be upset about anything."

"Smart ass. I know why too. None of this is your fault. You didn't bring it here. Rafe would have come looking for the stones whether I'd fallen in love with you or not. At least that's what people keep telling me. If I can come to terms with it all so can you." He took the soap from her and started rubbing her body in way that had nothing to do with cleaning. "Besides," he said softly, "you're worth it."

Aislinn felt him slide his erection against her butt, and then he pressed her forward, away from him, and into the stream of water. His hand slid down the center of her back, along her spine, over her butt, and between her legs. Aislinn bent over and braced herself against the wall as water pounded on her back. Between the heat of the shower and the heat that Cullen was creating, she felt like she was on fire.

Cullen slid his fingers into her slit and felt her coat them. He growled his pleasure at that. She was always ready for him. He pulled his hand from her and listened to her whimper, wanting his fingers back. He chuckled and brought his fingers to his mouth. Suddenly his wolf roared into his mind and seized control of the situation.

Aislinn felt the rush and was more than a little shocked, when she felt him grab her roughly and force her out of the shower. Before she knew what was happening, she was on her hands and knees on the bathroom floor, and he was fucking her hard from behind. She tried to get away at first, but he was far too strong and determined. It took some time for the forceful thrusts to become pleasurable. Aislinn gave over to her cat, knowing that she'd be more capable of handling it that way.

As the cat took control, her confusion gave way to primal need. Aislinn began growling and pushing back into his thrusts. Cullen wasn't concerned in the least with her pleasure this time. He was going to come inside her, and then he was going to do it again. He swelled inside her and forced himself as deep as he could into her sopping cunt. He came hard, and Aislinn shook with her own orgasm as she felt his seed fill her. She growled happily as they collapsed to the floor.

After some time and some internal struggle, Cullen was able to force his wolf down. Aislinn had already returned to her human self. She could feel the soreness already starting. She stretched a bit. He was lodged inside her more solidly than usual. With a great deal of amusement, she wiggled her butt against him. They were still wet from the shower and sweat.

"I'm going to need another shower," she said with a satisfied sigh.

Cullen wasn't amused though. "I didn't hurt you did I," he asked.

She looked back over her shoulder. "My knees a little," she chuckled. "But I'll get over it. What's wrong?"

Cullen cleared his throat. "You're going into heat," he said flatly. "By morning I'm not going to be able to stop."

She could feel how serious he was. "How long will that last?"

"Couple days, a week? Hard to say."

"You're worried."

"Yeah. I've got meetings scheduled. This isn't going to look good, but judging from how I reacted to the preliminary, there isn't going to be any fighting it once you really start. We're not going to be able to go out into public."

Aislinn giggled and cuddled against him. She felt his annoyance at her amusement. "I'm sorry. I kinda like the idea that you want me so badly that you literally can't keep your hands off me."

Cullen smiled smugly. "You do realize that I'm trying to get you pregnant right?"

That stopped the giggling. "Okay, so you want to have kids," she realized suddenly.

"Now," he said harshly. He could feel his wolf growling to take her again.

"On the bed," Aislinn said, knowing there was no stopping him and unsure how she felt about being pregnant. "And the shower needs turned off," she added.

* * * *

Terrick was in his room grousing. He was doing his best to sow seeds of doubt in everyone's minds about Cullen. The new omegas being in love with Aislinn, was destroying that route. Every time he said anything against the missing couple someone else would come along and suggest that the problem was Terrick's interpretation. He was getting frustrated with the fact that he seemed to have miss played the best chance he'd been giving for ousting Cullen in centuries.

No one even seemed to care that he had probably already mated with Aislinn and was lying about it. Ranaild, Elise, Celia, and Mack were the ones who were pointing out to people that they were expecting more of Cullen than themselves. At least a third of the pack had 'accidentally' skipped the dumb ceremony. If Cullen fell short on that one, well maybe he had earned a reprieve from their expectations. That mixed with the omegas spouting how wonderful Aislinn was and how dead half of them would be if she hadn't talked Cullen down, had the pack pretty much over the whole situation.

Terrick only had a select few people on his side. Luckily the few he had were elders, and they agreed that Cullen shouldn't be skipping protocol. More was expected of the alpha for a specific reason. And the elders certainly didn't like being lied to. Terrick's support was less than Cullen's, but he still had some.

When his phone rang he answered it angrily, "What?"

"Hmm, something certainly does have you in a foul mood," came the honey sweet voice of Jenna Tairneach.

"What do you want, Jenna?"

"The same thing I wanted last time, Terrick. I'm just trying to find out if you're still stubbornly holding out against me," she cooed.

"Remind me what you think our mating will accomplish?"

"Well, you would at very least get to be alpha with the Tairneach. Once you have a pack maybe then you can get what you truly want."

"Jenna if I mate with you I'll never get what I truly want. Although I may despise Cullen Arnauk, my loyalty to this pack is true. I want Cullen gone and the Arnauk hailing me as alpha. Your way won't do that. I'll not risk any of our own lives. There isn't a single lycan here who would trust and follow me with real loyalty, if I left the pack only to start a war so that I could take it over. If I can't beat Cullen in a one on one fight, it's pointless. We've already had this discussion. So why the hell are you really calling?"

Jenna was annoyed. Even the Arnauk who wanted to get rid of Cullen were difficult to get to. She may have to have the druids teach her how Rafe played the mind games he did. "How about just making him look bad for now? Would you be interested in helping me with that?"

"I'm listening," Terrick said, his tone less annoyed.

"The Pack Council is sending a message to him. There's going to be a meeting. Just intercept the message," she cooed. "The council will get mad, and he'll look like a fool."

Terrick thought about it. Making Cullen look the part of the fool was always a good idea to him, but there was one thing bothering him. "What's in it for you Jenna?"

She growled to herself. Terrick was a thoin, but he wasn't stupid. "Time," she said. "Just time."

"For what?"

"That's not your concern. Do it or not. I don't care. I was just trying to be helpful." With that, she hung up on Terrick.

* * * *

Keith and Sarah were pissed. They'd been running interference all week. "How much longer do you think she's going to be in heat," he asked angrily, as he slammed into Sarah's office and sat down in the chair across from her desk.

Sarah shrugged and shook her head. "Terrick knows what's going on. Most of the others are suspicious. That's making Terrick's stupidity easier for them to stomach. I'm tired of lying to everyone."

Keith nodded in agreement. "He better name all the boys after me and all the girls after you," he said only half joking.

"Speaking of names, do you and Jay know what you're naming yours yet," Sarah asked.

"No. I leave it to Jay. It's her first litter. There's only the two. Thank the Gods. She has a list a mile long to pick from. As long as she's happy, and I'm finally allowed to touch her again, I don't care what they're named."

Sarah smiled. She had been trying to have a litter with Drake for a while. It didn't matter how much sex they had while she was in heat, she just wasn't pregnant yet. It wasn't uncommon for it to take years for a lycan to get pregnant. They went into heat so rarely. At least when they finally did get pregnant, they had several at once. Sarah didn't mind at all when Keith interrupted her thoughts. She was more than a little jealous of Jaylyn at the moment.

"How are the arrangements for their mating coming along," Keith asked.

"It's set. We only need the couple to come out of hiding. Then we get to put up with them disappearing again," she groused.

"Oh well," he said, in resignation. "It's not like he doesn't deserve to get something good. At the moment there's nothing pressing to stop it. I've got the retraining of the out of shape troops dealt with. You've got the new quasi-omegas relocated and assigned only semi-demeaning duties. Jenna's been quiet, and there's no new info on that front. Even the southern border's quiet. Terrick's the only problem, and he's always been a problem."

Sarah growled. "I don't know. Terrick's really pushing it this time. Cullen's going to have a lot of explaining to do."

The phone rang and Sarah grabbed it. "Sarah, what?"

"Cadifor," the voice said. "Where's Arnauk?"

Caoch, Sarah swore to herself. *Muin Pack Council.* "He's indisposed. Can I get him and have him call you back?"

"It better be soon," came the angry voice. Then there was a click.

Keith raised his eyebrows. "Who could that have been that you would be willing to go get Cullen?"

"Pack council."

"You've got to be kidding. That was too short for him to have told you what he wanted."

Sarah nodded. "It must be important. He didn't even offer to tell me. Obviously I'm not good enough to know what it was about." She stared at the phone with concern. "You never should have said that we didn't have any problems at the moment. You jinxed it." Sarah stood up to head for the door.

Keith jumped to go with her. "I'm coming too. I'm suspicious. I think he's dragging it out for the fun of it."

"If he isn't, there's a chance we'll get attacked," Sarah said off handedly, as they walked down the hall for the elevator.

"Yeah, then it would be better if there's two of us anyway. Don't know about you, but last I checked I couldn't take him one on one," Keith said with a grin. There was more than one reason Cullen was the alpha. "He did manage to bring down a were-bear-lion-thing recently. I guess he's been keeping up on his training, even if the rest of us weren't overly concerned for it."

Sarah nodded. "Well hopefully he worked out enough aggression that he'll at least listen before attacking. Doesn't matter," she said as they walked into the elevator, and she inserted the key. "He's got to know that Cadifor is looking for him. This isn't one he can ignore until he's done fucking Aislinn."

Keith chuckled.

"You've been waiting for a reason to interrupt. Why do you get so much pleasure out of this?" Sarah was only letting him come along because he was right about the possibility of getting attacked.   "Because I haven't been getting any, and I don't like knowing how much he's getting," Keith chuckled some more.

Sarah shook her head. Her stomach was turning as the elevator headed for the penthouse. She didn't relish dealing with Cullen if he was going to attack her. *Why the hell did it have to be Cadifor? Couldn't have been any of the others could it?*

* * * *

Aislinn lay across the bed, exhausted. Cullen hadn't let up since that evening in the shower nearly a week earlier. The routine had developed rather quickly. Sex, sleep, sex, eat, sex, sex, sleep. Once in a while, he let her get to the bathroom. At least two of those trips involved Aislinn running from him. That resulted in a broken bathroom door. Cullen was completely unreasonable, and it annoyed him that Aislinn was able to remain partially reasonable. In one of his brief moments of clarity, he figured that it was the druid half. For as much as lycan's were instinct driven, druids were always portrayed as logic driven. If Cullen was more rational at the moment, he may have thought that it was a good balance. Right now though, it was bothering him that she was able to apparently turn it all off when she wanted.

He was in the main room pacing. Aislinn was finally coming out of heat, and she managed to convince him that a shower would be a good idea. She also worked into that a need for her to shower alone. After about 5 minutes of her being in the bathroom, door or not, he was considering dragging her out. This was a vast improvement from the day before. She never would have gotten the water on.

Aislinn giggled, feeling his frustration. *Five more minutes,* she reassured him, knowing it would take longer than that, and was rewarded with a mental growl. She laughed. She was just as happy to let the omegas come in, clean the place up, and change the bed sheets at this point. *How much longer is this going to keep you worked up like this?*

Cullen forced himself to be rational for a moment. *You're almost done. I wouldn't be capable of waiting impatiently if you weren't. Probably by tomorrow, maybe tonight.* He sighed heavily. He was torn between being relieved and disappointed.

Aislinn smiled again. *Haven't you had enough yet?*

Mo mhúirnín bán I don't think I can ever get enough of you, he responded sweetly.

That was enough to get Aislinn to cut her shower short. She felt much better having been allowed to clean up a bit. She was dying to shave her legs and put deodorant on, even if she knew he was just going to mess her up again. The minute she came out of the bathroom, toweling off, Cullen grabbed her around the waist, threw her over his shoulder, dropping the towel, carried her across the room, and then dumped her onto the back of the couch.

Aislinn giggled. She had to admit that she was still feeling a need for him even through the soreness that seemed to be a perpetual state of being at the moment. Her hands were on the couch seat cushions, and her rear was up in the air, with her feet dangling above the floor behind the couch.

"Perfect," Cullen said, and his eyes shifted to molten amber. His body shifted into hybrid form as he fell to his knees behind her. He stared at her sex for a moment. He could still smell the soap she had cleaned herself with. He leaned in close to her sex and he could smell himself on her.

Cullen growled his excitement, and Aislinn could feel his breath on her pussy. She couldn't see what he was doing, and the waiting for him to make his move was driving her crazy. She could feel her cat clawing at her mind, and she forced it to be patient. She was enjoying her moment of control. It had been a rare thing this week.

Cullen watched her shiver as she waiting for him to do something to her. He growled again. His ability to take his time and torture her like this was a testament to the fact that her heat was ending. He reached up and stroked her thighs gently, letting his claws draw white lines down her damp skin. Aislinn sucked in a sharp breath and adjusted her position on the couch to keep her balance.

Cullen's eyes were focused on her sex. He watched her move and leaned in to smell her again, delighting in her whimpering as she felt his breath on her skin. He was so close. She wanted to push back so that he would touch her, but there was no way with the position she was in.

He was pleased with her need and frustration. He stared at her neatly shaved pussy. The outer lips were bare except for a patch she left on her mound. His tongue snake out and lick at the crease between her inner thigh and her outer lips. She whimpered some more and tried to wiggle so that his tongue would touch the parts she wanted touched.

He took his time, working his tongue over her smooth outer lips. *You made me wait. Turn about it fair play,* he teased. He dragged his tongue up to her butt and nibbled at each cheek, causing her to giggle and wiggle as he watched. He was enjoying his game, but watching her was getting to him. Finally he leaned in close and let his tongue stroke her swollen pink inner lips.

Aislinn moaned appreciatively at the touch, hoping that would spur him on. Cullen managed to hold himself back. He gently ran his tongue over her pussy, lapping at the outside and working his tongue into the groove between the inner and outer lips of her sex, being careful to avoid her clit.

Aislinn was going crazy. Cullen watched her wiggle and listened to her needy moaning and whimpering. "Cullen!" she demanded, trying to get herself off the couch, so that she could be more active in what was happening.

No you don't, he growled into her mind and gripped her thighs tightly, keeping her from getting enough leverage to move. Mercifully, he gave her a little more attention in return for behaving. Cullen pushed his nose into her slit and parted her inner lips as he breathed in her scent and his own.

"Cullen, please…"

Finally, she felt his tongue stoke her clit. It was agonizingly slow and only gently grazed her, sending waves of pleasure shooting through her body. Aislinn was shaking with need as Cullen lapped tentatively at her clit and ran his tongue along her slit to her weeping opening, before dipping inside and causing more moaning.

He was getting to a point where he wasn't going to be able to keep torturing her, no matter how much he was enjoying the view and the sounds. Cullen stood up and took his cock in one hand as he lined up for what he really wanted.

The knot at the base was already hard and large and would hurt a little as he pushed into her. But he had learned this week that she didn't mind a little pain, if he did it right. Aislinn wiggled some more, looking back over her shoulder, and she could see him standing behind her. The waiting was driving her crazy and her cat had gotten a little more of a hold on her. Cullen could see the amber and blue swirling together, and there were dark lines and spots starting to bleed onto her pale skin. He was amused at how hard she was trying to keep her control.

He ran the head of his cock up and down her wet slit, and this time the moan was tinged with jungle cat. Cullen growled his pleasure right back. Aislinn's head fell forward as Cullen took hold of her hips and lined himself up behind her. With one solid thrust he forced himself into her. Aislinn winced and groaned. She felt like he had shoved his fist into her pussy. The pain and pleasure mixed deliciously and flowed through her body in alternating waves of bliss and torture. Cullen gave her a moment, before he began to move.

Aislinn felt him swelling more as he thrust over and over into her. She leaned further down the couch so that he would press against her clit with each stroke. Cullen dragged it out, listening to her and feeling her cunt squeeze his cock as he humped her relentlessly. He loved hearing her call his name. As they neared the end, he grabbed her from the odd angle she was in and pulled her up against him so that her back was pressed against his chest. She pulled her hair to the side for him. She knew what he wanted. He had bitten her again several times over the week and she had returned the gesture twice.

Cullen brought them both to their knees on the carpet. He thrust up into her, waiting for her to give in and come. He put his mouth on the join between her shoulder and neck and growled hungrily, knowing how close she was. His clawed hand ran down her stomach, and he pressed his fingers roughly against her swollen clit. Aislinn's body jerked in his grip and she came hard, crying out as he sank his teeth, and allowed his own release to surge through his body.

Neither of them noticed the audience, waiting quietly for them to finish. Keith and Sarah stared around the destroyed penthouse in amused awe. They had never seen Cullen's room quite this trashed. The furniture was all askew. Everything, normally neatly arranged on his desk, was scattered about the floor. Pillows, from the couch, were thrown around the room. The bathroom door was on its hinges and hanging to the side. There were two broken lamps, and the bookcase was missing one shelf. The contents were on the floor in front of it. They were afraid to look in the bedroom.

Cullen collapsed onto his side, taking Aislinn with him. Then he rolled slightly onto his back, or at least as much as he could with his member lodged firmly in Aislinn's limp body. The wolf retreated again, temporarily. Keith and Sarah actually couldn't have asked for better timing. If they were going to get him in a moment of lucidity it would be right after he had sated the beast.

"Whatever it is, it had better be good," Cullen said without looking at Keith or Sarah. He took a deep breath and let it out, as he closed his eyes, lying on the floor.

Aislinn was confused at first. When she looked up and saw Keith and Sarah standing there, looking at them she blushed furiously and pulled a stray pillow to herself.

Cullen laughed and tightened his grip on her hip to stop her from trying to escape. *You're really going to have to get over this embarrassment issue. Just wait until we have the ceremony. If you can't handle people looking, what are you going to do when they want to touch as well?* Aislinn growled at him.

Sarah cleared her throat. "What do think the omegas are going to think of this mess? I don't know if you could have made it any more apparent what's going on up here, aside from making a general announcement," she said with annoyance, partially testing the waters to see how reasonable he was going to be.

Keith held his breath waiting for a response.

"So don't have them come for the clean up until after the mating ceremony," he said. "Why are you up here? I didn't call down with the all clear, so it must be urgent. Terrick?"

"You're sounding all right," Keith said grinning, figuring he could get away with a comment or two.

Cullen stretched and looked over at them. His eyes narrowed as he focused on Sarah's concerned face. "I think we'll be done by this evening or morning. What's wrong," he said much more insistently. He didn't like the fact that it was the third time he asked. They were avoiding telling him.

"Cadifor," she said. That was all she said.

Cullen groaned and let his head fall back onto the floor with a thud. "When?"

"About ten minutes ago," Sarah said.

Keith grinned widely. "You guys really have trashed this place," he said enthusiastically. "Can't wait 'til the mating ceremony. This is going to be good."

Aislinn pulled the pillow over her face, Keith chuckled, and Cullen and Sarah glared at Keith. "Enough," Cullen growled. He sighed heavily. "All good things," he said contemplatively. "Did he say what he wanted?"

"No."

Cullen growled. "Fine. Give me my phone."

Aislinn turned and glared at him. "You can't be serious," she said in disbelief.

Cullen looked at her like she was being ridiculous. "It's not like he can see us. I have to find out what he wants."

Sarah and Keith rooted through the mess on the floor until Keith started laughing. "Where is your phone?"

Aislinn growled. "It's probably in the bedroom."

"Temper, temper," Keith snickered. "I bet you didn't complain while you were helping to make the mess."

Cullen smiled at that, and Aislinn elbowed him for the thought. "All right," he said holding his side where she got him.

Finally, Sarah managed to find the phone on one of the end stands next to the bed. Actually, it was the only one still standing. She grabbed the phone and a blanket from the floor. Aislinn gave her a grateful smile as Sarah handed her the blanket and Cullen his phone.

"How are you going to handle--" Sarah started.

"I know, the mating ceremony," Aislinn interrupted.

"Well at least he told you about it," Sarah said a bit relieved.

Aislinn shook her head. "No, he's just implied. He hasn't explained. Chances are, I'm imagining something worse than it will actually be," she asked hopefully.

Sarah looked thoughtful. "I don't know about that."

"Shh," Cullen growled as he finished paging through the numbers and found Cadifor's name in the contacts list. He hit the button and the phone only rang once before an angry voice picked up. Aislinn felt concern surge through Cullen. "Arnauk," he said to the silence on Cadifor's end.

"Where the hell are you," Cadifor growled.

"Where I always am. Why?"

"Cullen you were summoned to a meeting three days ago. No word. No appearance. You better have a damn good explanation."

"I can honestly say I never received word that I was due at a meeting." Cullen looked at Keith and Sarah and they both shook their heads uncertainly.

"We called the pack heads for a council. The government is on our asses. For the first time in centuries, we've been contacted by the Circle. You wrote the reports that instigated all of it, and you never received our message," Cadifor ranted. "Fine. I'll accept that. I'm going to have the messenger tracked down and find out who did receive the message. You need to find out why all the calls from anyone less than me have been intercepted and rerouted to avoid getting a hold of you for three days. In the mean time, get your ass here."

"By nightfall," Cullen said gravely and heard the other end of the line click.

"Well," Keith said as Cullen let the phone fall away from his head. "Don't keep us in suspense."

"The government and the Circle. And a missing message." Cullen didn't have to track down why the lackey's phone calls were intercepted. He'd told them not to disturb him. "Keith, find out why I didn't get it. Sarah what's going to happen when I go downstairs?"

"Honestly, if you're referring to you and Aislinn and all this, I don't really think there's much to worry about. Most of the pack is okay with us pretending you're behaving. There are just a few elders who are siding with Terrick and think you should have shown Godlike restraint and waited until it was appropriately condoned by the elder council. It won't be too bad. But don't expect them to not be suspicious," she said. "And I'd like to point out that you've used up your allotment of me taking the fall for you for quite some time."

Cullen looked over at Sarah gratefully. "Thank you," he said.

Instantly her anger faded. It was kind of hard to glare and stay angry at the guy when he was in such a compromised position on the floor and thanking her for helping him get there. "I'll survive. Besides, I'm assuming Aislinn doesn't get to go with you to the Pack Council. At which point the heat will all be on her once you're gone."

Keith started laughing. "Did you say it that way on purpose," he chuckled, knowing that she didn't.

"That wasn't that funny," Cullen growled at him, and Sarah rolled her eyes. "Both of you get out of here. I need a car ready to leave within the hour. I'll be down as soon as possible."

Luckily Aislinn's heat was so close to being over. He didn't really know what he would have done, if he'd gotten the message when it was originally sent.

Chapter 21

Cha sgeul-rùin e 's fios aig triùir air.
It's no secret if three know it.
-Gaelic Proverb

Aislinn crawled onto the disheveled bed, dragging a blanket with her. The pillows were strewn across the floor, but she didn't care. She just wanted to get some sleep. She could hear the shower running and knew that Cullen would be leaving the minute he got out. She couldn't decide if she was happy or upset about that. Her body desperately needed a break and at the very same time didn't want one. Aislinn closed her eyes and instantly fell into a sleep that could only be induced by days of sex and exhaustion.

Cullen knew the minute she fell asleep. The soft murmur in the back of his mind, telling him she was concerned about him, faded into a nondescript whisper of contentment. He smiled to himself. He didn't care how it happened. She was his, and he was pleased about it. The pack elders could go to hell, and he would tell them as much if they caused any trouble. The pack was technically only a democracy in as much as the alpha was willing to let it be.

Cullen snuck into the bedroom and pulled some clothes out of the closet. He didn't want to wake Aislinn. Cullen dressed in his standard black jeans and black shirt. Then he went over to the bed and placed a gentle kiss on Aislinn's forehead before sneaking out of the room. He ignored the mess that the place was in. He didn't even want to think about what the omegas would say to the rest of the pack when they got back from cleaning the mess up. He never pulled anything like this before. He grinned happily thinking about it. *It certainly has been a nice week.*

Cullen managed to get to the garage and on the road in short order. He spent the entire drive dwelling on Cadifor's phone call.

* * * *

Aislinn found herself walking through the Tairneach manor again. Sweating, it felt as if the place was on fire. The shadows bled along all the walls, as she looked around. She had no idea where she was going. Aislinn tried some doors, but none of them would open. Frustration grew. The more she tried the more the vision seemed to slip away from her.

Aislinn stopped and closed her eyes. *You're doing too much.* She told herself. *Just let it happen. Relax.* Aislinn opened her eyes, finding herself in a room with no windows, only a couple chairs, and several men and women who were standing over a large table. Bottles full of different colored liquids balanced on stands with burners under them. Several mortars and pestles contained herbs and various plants, as well as animal parts. Books and papers lay scattered about the tables. *The* books and papers. The place smelled absolutely foul and Aislinn covered her nose to mask the scent of burning flesh.

Aislinn waited for whatever brought here to reveal itself. She briefly considered going to look at the things on the table more closely, before deciding that it would be best to let the vision tell her what the fates thought she should know. She watched and waited.

One of the men turned and looked directly at her. He seemed relieved to see her. He looked beaten and bruised. A black eye and a swollen lip marred his features. Suddenly she realized that she was looking at the present. He walked toward Aislinn, but the others didn't seem to notice.

Taking a deep breath, he began to whisper. Aislinn couldn't understand what he was saying at first. She closed her eyes and tried to relax some more. Finally the words began to clear. He was speaking in Gaelic. *Tell Nora Senach that they're using the bone dust of a dire wolf*, he repeated over and over and over again.

Aislinn nodded when she finally understood. Relief and some admiration calmed his strained features. When Aislinn blinked, he was suddenly back at the table amongst the others, and they all continued to work diligently on whatever it was they were doing. The scene faded to black foreboding, and Aislinn feel into a fitful sleep.

* * * *

Frustration seethed through Jenna. The Pack Council insisted that all the alphas be present before holding the meeting. She had hoped that they would proceed without Cullen, but apparently she underestimated his importance. At least she knew that Terrick took her suggestion to heart. Cullen wouldn't have ignored a call to Council.

It pissed her off that the Council was acting as though Cullen Arnauk was an integral cog in the workings of the Pack Council. In addition to that, they showed her no respect whatsoever. All of the Council members apparently believed that she hadn't earned her position and were only allowing her presence based upon the fact that she was the 'current' Tairneach alpha. In secret, the quiet consensus, was that they believed she would be replaced in relatively short order. None of them were even being friendly toward her. Her father was always treated with friendly, mutual respect. It only made her more determined in her current plan.

Most everyone gathered in the great room. Lycan pack alphas from the neighboring areas lounged in various places about the room. Some of them spoke to each other. Some ignored each other. It was accepted that this was neutral ground and that there would be no fighting here. The lines were obvious between the alphas that got along and the ones that didn't. Jenna knew Stephen La Rayne, Neill Odgar, and Sean McDougal, but the others were new to her. Alone, in her corner of the room, Jenna watched them all. Mingling wasn't her priority tonight. She had more on her mind than remembering the names of lycans who ran packs too distant from her to be a concern at this point . Especially, when she considered that none of them appeared impressed by her or interested in speaking with her.

Cadifor stormed through the door, and everyone stood up. He was unmistakable. Jenna remembered her father taking Cadifor very seriously. Jenna never met him. However, when Cadifor summoned, Brennus Tairneach ran to answer. Her father's reaction impressed upon Jenna that this lycan was not to be messed with.

Cadifor looked almost albino. He was clean shaven and had short, white-blonde hair just turning silver, pale leathered skin, and frosty yellowish eyes, even in human form. He tended to wear a white collar shirt and suit jacket with jeans, in a way that only a man with power could manage. He was an ancient. Still he looked formidable. He was smaller than most of the men in the room, nevertheless he seemed to tower over everyone. No one knew how old Cadifor was. Rumors held that he had once been alpha of a pack that spanned the entire northern continent. But, rumors that old were often exaggerated. He supposedly gave the control of his pack to several sons and stepped down, when he grew so old as to not care for running the pack any longer. Jenna had a hard time believing that any alpha would choose to leave his position. Still, that was the rumor. Cadifor was one of the original members of the Pack Council and the lycan representative for North America.

Anger and annoyance radiated from him throughout the meeting. The longer it took for Cullen to show up, the angrier Cadifor became. Jenna smiled, more than a little amused at the situation.

Stepping into the middle of the room, Cadifor glared menacingly at the assemblage, commanding attention without saying a word. "Arnauk is on his way. The meeting will begin at nightfall." After silent nods of acknowledgement from all the gathered alphas, Cadifor left.

Jenna excused herself from the great room, rooting her cell phone out of her pocket as she went. She left Maon in charge of urging the druids to finish their job, and she wanted to know how far they had gotten. As far as Jenna was concerned, with four of them working on, there was no reason why it should take too much longer. When Jenna threatened the lives of the ones she was holding in the basement, the others promised that they would find her a solution to what she wanted.

Several rings and a deep male voice answered the phone. "Mistress."

Jenna smiled. She liked hearing him call her that. "How goes my project?"

"They've been working nonstop. Unfortunately, we can't tell if they're just making it look like they're doing something, or if they're actually making progress."

"I take it that they haven't offered a completed formula yet," she growled.

"No, mistress, but they claim they are close."

"Fine. Find a way to speed them up. Arnauk has finally surfaced. I should be back from this meeting tomorrow, unless it takes longer than one night to deal with whatever the council wants. Father was never gone that long."

"I'll attempt to have it for you upon your return," he said.

"I appreciate your efforts Maon. I'll find some appropriate reward for you," she purred.

Maon knew exactly what his reward would be, and that was more than enough motivation for him to make good on his promise.

* * * *

The drive to the manor always impressed Cullen. Paved roads stopped miles from the manor. Without an SUV or some kind of off road vehicle, getting to the manor was nearly impossible. A number of the alphas took motorcycles out in the summer, but the scenery was spectacular any time of the year. Over-grown dirt paths, which passed for roads, led up the side of the mountain. An incredible view, off the southern roads, looked out over forest and fields. Off the eastern roads you could see the lights of a nearby city. Either way, it was breath taking.

Immense and imposing, stone work made the manor look like it had been imported from some bad horror flick. Too new to look like a legitimate castle, it had all the trappings of modern society. From the heated stone floors to the Jacuzzis in the suite bathrooms, it was more like a luxury resort than anything else. Not that you could that from the outside.

Cullen pulled into the parking area, which was really just an open field, and walked up the stone pathway to the manor. The front doors opened for him, and he was ushered to Cadifor's office with a haste that virtually left his head spinning.

Cullen knocked on the heavy wooden door and waited.

"Come in," called an annoyed voice.

Cullen winced, knowing Cadifor's temper. He wasn't usually the one who pissed off Cadifor. *Ah well, a first time for everything.* He considered telling Cadifor what the delay had been. The thought brought on a smile as he walked through the door.

"I'm glad to see you're in such a good mood. Perhaps then this discussion won't upset you unduly," Cadifor growled. He waved at a chair on the other side of the desk.

"I'm sorry. I don't have an answer as to when or where the message was intercepted, yet," he said with emphasis. "I left before Keith was able to dig it up." Cullen nodded respectfully and sat down. Being friends for decades, most ceremony was long since dispensed with, when the two of them were in private. Cadifor had come to respect Cullen as one of the few lycan alphas in this era, who could run a pack as he did when he reigned, centuries ago.

"I already know. My messenger tells me that your favorite elder took the message, under orders that you were not to be disturbed. What, may I ask, was so

- 455 -

damned important that you were 'not to be disturbed' for days at a time?" Cadifor's eyes were on fire.

Anger this intense rarely surfaced on Cadifor's face. Even so mention of what Cullen had been doing had him grinning again. Cadifor's expression intensified, if that was even possible. Cullen decided that the truth was really the only excuse good enough to excuse his behavior, and there was no certainty that Cadifor would find it a good enough. "A bitch in heat that I intend to mate with. I don't know how much you've heard about the inner workings of my pack recently," he said seriously.

Cadifor sat back in his chair, and his face seemed to relax a bit. "I don't know whether to call you a complete fool or offer my congratulations. Either way, I've been down that road." He growled, thinking about the report and a few things that he read recently. "Who," he said and a knowing curious expression crossed his face.

"Her name is Aislinn. She was a victim of Rafe's little quest. She's got druid ancestry, but no formal training. She's in the reports." Cullen tried to sound off hand about it, but he knew that the reports were the reason for this meeting. So being involved with a prominent name in the report might not go over well.

Cadifor tapped his pen on the desk and shook his head. "Leave it to you to make even mating a complex endeavor."

Cullen smiled and nodded. None of his attempts at mating had gone without some incident. If this one went through, and he intended to make sure it did, then it would be the first. *And last,* he thought. At least the confession seemed to put Cadifor's fire out.

"So here's the situation. Shortly after your report, the Circle contacted us. I have been around as long as any living lycan, and I was shocked to find that not only do they exist, but they've been watching us since our inception." Cadifor growled. "I don't like finding out that there's been a force in play for the whole of our existence that we never knew about. So your report tells me that one of their own went rogue and tried to create a new species of were or several new species. He intended to use them as his own personal army and take control of a point of power on your territory."

"That's it." Cullen liked Cadifor's tendency to be concise and up front. It saved time. The two men were like minded in many respects.

"No that would have been it. Except your man Keith went and handed over the prisoners from Rafe's mismatch game to the feds. Not that I don't understand how that happened. But all of our attempts at recovering them and dealing with it ourselves have been sidelined. I don't know what the feds are doing with them, where they are being held, or if there is any real concern necessary. The last thing we need is the federal government pulling a Rafe and creating their own personal army."

"I did consider that after I found out what had happened. Unfortunately, there really was no way for us to hold them at the reservation, transport them to where we could hold them, or find another solution to the situation that wouldn't result in more deaths. I had enough bodies piled up from that night."

Cadifor let out a heavy sigh. "And what of the unrecovered book and notes? That's what the Circle wants."

"I've got no real proof of anything pertaining to those." Cullen growled, remembering Aislinn's warning. "Aislinn had a vision that they were in the Tairneach manor."

"No proof." Cadifor stared at Cullen with consideration. "Still, you believe she's right."

"She hasn't led me wrong to date."

"Any other visions that we should be concerned about?"

Cullen resigned himself to the idea that he was going to be paying more attention to Aislinn's visions in the future. "She saw a dungeon-like room at the Tairneach manor filled with people who wanted her help."

Cadifor pressed his fingers into the bridge of his nose and squinted his eyes as though he had a headache. "Are these the missing people you warned the feds to be on the lookout for?"

"Yeah."

"Did you know that there are a number of druids missing?"

"I knew that Rafe was killing Senach for some reason. We never got a chance to find out why. Rafe's dead. Even if the papers are at Tairneach manor, we had no reason to think that the Tairneach would pick up where he left off."

"Well," Cadifor said with a wicked grin. "Perhaps we need to ask Jenna what she's up to then. I have to admit that I wasn't happy the Tairneach allowed her to take the alpha position uncontested."

Cullen growled his agreement. "She did facilitate the overthrow of Rafe's power play that allowed us to kill him."

Cadifor smiled. "We'll take that into consideration." He pressed a button on an intercom and told the voice at the other end of the speaker to get Jenna and bring her to his office.

Cullen's face fell considerably. "I don't like where this is going. Jenna has books for creating weres and is doing something with druids capable of making use of them." The end of the comment was followed by a devilish grin.

"Can I ask what's amusing you this time? I'm guessing it must have a female name in it."

"Aislinn was right. Next time I'll take her more seriously. She tried to talk me into raiding the Tairneach manor over a week ago. I didn't want to risk the pack again so soon after such a large funeral. That's why I tried to sick the feds on it. I figured a few of them killed in the face of an unknown situation and danger wouldn't be a big loss."

"Sounds like the woman will be quite the asset."

"She already is."

A knock stopped their conversation and Cadifor called, "Come in."

Sauntering through the door, Jenna's face went from smug to suspicious in seconds. She thought that Cadifor summoned her in order to get to know his new alpha better. The minute she saw Cullen, she knew that wasn't the situation.

"Sit down," Cadifor said.

Immediately, Jenna smoothed over her features and gracefully eased into the chair.

Jenna's self-assured demeanor mildly impressed Cadifor. "Jenna I'll get straight to the point. The reason I called you to this meeting is because of some trouble your dead mate was causing. At the moment I have a number of concerned parties in the manor are giving me a bit of a hard time. I have to give them answers, so I have some questions to ask you. Perhaps you can fill in the blanks that Cullen couldn't."

Jenna's face went blank. Cadifor knew she wasn't going to work with him. "I'll do my best. I'm sure Cullen may have told you, Rafe was using mind control effects on the whole of my pack, including myself. I may not know as much as you might think. I spent a great deal of time asleep when he was in our manor."

Cadifor smiled at her sympathetically, but he didn't intend to go easy on her. "I understand that Rafe used books and notes to create the weres in his army. Do you know what happened to them?"

Jenna remained unreadable. "I assume that everything belonging to Rafe was removed from the manor with the few of his men who had been left behind when we went to the Arnauk reservation that night. I didn't find anything like what you're suggesting. Though, I do have one of his men in holding. I could have him interrogated."

Cadifor was amused at her attempt to sound cooperative. "Actually if you have one of them in custody, I'd like to have him turned over to the Council. They're curious about some of the things that they read in the report."

Jenna nodded. "Consider him yours."

"That brings me to the next question. The alphas who are were been brought in because there are people missing from each of their territories. Do you have anyone non-lycan in your custody?"

"No. What do you mean non-lycan? Humans?" Jenna asked innocently.

"The Circle recently made contact with the Pack Council and asked our assistance in the recovery of a number of druids. Many of them were found dead and were assumed to be the work of Rafe. However, since his death, quite a few more have come up missing. Since Rafe involved us in his attempt at creating his own little empire, they're seeking our help in resolving the issue of their missing people."

Jenna shook her head. "I can tell you that there were at least a dozen of them left at Tairneach manor during the battle on the Arnauk reservation. We captured one when we returned and killed a couple others. The rest got away. I suppose they could be continuing whatever he was doing. I suggest Cullen keep a close eye on that stone circle of his." She flashed him a winning smile.

Cullen hated to admit it, but if he didn't know she was lying, it would have been a fairly convincing story.

Cadifor stared at her measuringly. He didn't know if Aislinn's visions were more trustworthy than Jenna. She was supposed to be an alpha and loyal to the Council. "All right Jenna. Thank you for your help. You can return to the great room. The meeting should begin shortly."

With a respectful nod and an elegant flourish, Jenna got up and left. The pressure made her a little nervous, even if it didn't show. *Those damned druids had better be ready for me when I return.*

As the door closed, Cadifor's gaze slowly shifted to Cullen. "You don't believe her."

"I know Jenna. She's up to something. It can't be the same as what Rafe was doing. I don't know what she could possibly want with druids and a formula to create weres. Though, after hearing her story, I have to agree with you. I shouldn't have suggested the feds go after Jenna. We're going to have to get those books out of the Tairneach manor before someone else gets them."

"Not that simple. We can't just go raiding the Tairneach manor. It violates any number of laws we've laid out. The Pack Council cannot be involved. Since I've called this meeting and approached her already there is no way a raid wouldn't be seen as associated with the Council. We'll have to find another way."

Cullen growled. "The bitch has caused me headaches since she was old enough to spread her legs. I don't see why I couldn't deal with it and claim it was territory dispute."

Cadifor smiled at his friend. "Because you would never normally do that, and everyone knows it. For now, we'll hold the meeting. Deal with the feds, and wait and see what she does."

"What are you going to tell the others?"

"The same thing I originally intended to tell them. The same thing I told Jenna. The Circle is real and they want our help. I'll have them keeping an eye on the druids on their territory. That will make it harder for Jenna to take any more of them for whatever she's doing." Cadifor's mouth tilted deviously at the corners. "No to mention we'll be keeping an eye on the druids at the same time. Two birds, one nicely legitimate stone."

Cullen cleared his throat. "Now that the serious topic has been dealt with... Are you coming to the mating ceremony?"

"Of course. I wouldn't miss scenting the woman who managed to get her claws into you." He chuckled. "When?"

"Probably this week. I need to talk to Sarah. She's been arranging things. Since Aislinn was in heat last week, we're going to have to get the ceremony over with in relatively short order. Just in case." He was grinning again.

* * * *

Aislinn woke feeling incredibly uneasy, her head pounding as though she'd been hit with a sledgehammer. Looking around the dark room, she decided that it must be evening. The nightstand where the clock had been was lying on its side. The clock was probably somewhere on the floor, either under something or busted. Either option was a possibility.

She closed her eyes momentarily and tried to find Cullen. He was there, just quiet. She could feel him in her mind, but it reminded her of how it felt when she walked into the stone circle, fogged over. Save, this time, it was like he was calling to her from very far away. She wondered how far he could go from her before she'd lose him completely, and that thought bothered her a great deal. She tried to send her thoughts to him, but he didn't seem to hear her. She didn't like it at all.

Aislinn got up and made her way through the dark to the shower. Turning on the light, she ran the water. The bathroom, with the exception of the busted door, was the only room in the penthouse still in relative order. She stepped into the hot water, letting it cascade over her and feeling disappointed that Cullen wasn't there to present the possibility of help with scrubbing her back. Standing there she contemplated whether she should call him about the vision or wait until he returned.

There was no doubt in her mind that a great deal of trouble was going on. Aislinn knew that she was meant to convey a message, and it felt urgent. Finally, she decided to ask Sarah what to do. Cullen's concern about the meeting and this Cadifor guy, made Aislinn reluctant to add to his troubles. She didn't want to interrupt him, if it would cause trouble. He already told her that he didn't want anything to do with the people the Tairneach were holding.

When Aislinn left the bathroom and flipped on the light in the main room, she winced at the mess. That would be another thing she needed to ask Sarah about. She knew that she was supposed to have an omega deal with it, but figured it might be less embarrassing if she just cleaned it up herself. Picking her way through the debris, she managed to get to the bedroom, unsure how she got to the bathroom in the dark without breaking her neck. She fished some clothes out of the drawer, dressed, then headed for the elevator.

Aislinn got out of the elevator on the 13th floor. Some lycans lounged about, settled in for a quiet evening, but there were still quite a few people around, so she guessed it couldn't be too late. Much to her chagrin, as she passed the large open doors to the great room, someone spotted her.

"Aislinn," Rissa's voice called.

Aislinn winced and tried to keep going, but Rissa vaulted the couch, and was out the door grabbing Aislinn by the arm, before she could get away.

"Hey. You've been missed," she said with sparkling eyes and a smile almost too wide for her face.

"Hi Riss. I was just looking for Sarah. You seen her?" Aislinn hoped desperately that Rissa would let her go without a fuss.

"Sarah is currently in the middle of an argument with Terrick. Keith is in there too. So you'll probably have to wait in line. Something about a messenger. I don't really know exactly. It seemed serious." She smiled again. "Come in here, and we'll entertain you while you wait for her." Rissa beamed and started to pull Aislinn into the great room.   Just then one of the new omegas approached them, causing Rissa some obvious discomfort.

The man was a theta before the incident. It made a lot of the lower ranked lycans in the pack uncomfortable to see someone they respected having to act as an omega. The punishment was harsh, but at least they weren't dead.

He nodded respectfully to Aislinn as he spoke. "Excuse me."

Aislinn recognized the man as one she helped move the week before. "Yeah, whatcha need," she answered in a friendly voice, trying to offset the sudden tension.

He bowed his head and lowered his eyes, then cast a skewed glance at Rissa in a way that asked Aislinn for some confidence. Aislinn stepped aside with him to see what he wanted, and Rissa waited patiently. She wasn't letting Aislinn go for a second.

"Sarah asked a couple of us to take care of the penthouse when you appeared. Will you be downstairs for a time?"

"Uh, yeah, about that. I mean, I don't know if anyone should really go up there right now. What did Sarah tell you?"

He smiled knowingly at Aislinn. "She didn't tell us anything. Didn't have to. Most of us can guess. She chose a very specific few to deal with it. There's no need to worry," he said reassuringly.

"All right. I guess if Sarah said so," she answered nervously.

He nodded again.

"Yeah, I'll be here for a little while. I'm going to get something to eat and talk with Sarah."

His smile broadened. "There's not much left in the kitchens at the moment. We've had a lot of people around here lately. If you like I could get someone to bring you something from the Taigh-O\sda," he said eagerly.

Aislinn thought to refuse at first, except he looked so happy about it. "I hate to have people doing all this for me. Cullen may be used to it. I don't know if I like it."

"That's half the reason we don't mind. What would you like?"

"I guess just a steak and a salad. Medium rare," she answered reluctantly. It was going to take her some time to get used to stuff like this.

"I'll take care of it," he said and then headed off.

Aislinn walked over to Rissa, momentarily forgetting that she was trying to get away. "I feel so bad. He's trying to be helpful, and I still don't know everyone's names around here. Who was he?"

"Travis. His mate's name is Lisa. He's a good guy and sweet."

"I can tell," Aislinn said.

Rissa grabbed hold of her arm again and returned to dragging Aislinn into the great room. Reluctantly, Aislinn followed her into the great room and sank down onto the couch, in a seat that another woman happily vacated.

All Aislinn could think was that she didn't have the rank to be doing stuff like that. *Vicarious rank really sucks,* she thought. "You don't have to do that. I can sit-"

Rissa stopped her. "No you sit there. So," Rissa said with a grin and someone in the room turned the TV off, "where you been this week?"

It looked suspiciously like a conspiracy. Aislinn glanced around at all the expectant faces. She felt like a million eyes were boring straight through her head. She cleared her throat. "I wasn't really feeling well. I was in bed."

Rissa growled. "Come on. I believe you were in bed."

"Okay, so Cullen was there too once in a while," Aislinn said, suddenly deciding that she was not going to let Rissa play her. The minute she got the girl alone they were going to have a serious conversation about respect and rank. *Gods, maybe I am getting used to things around here.* "What are you getting at Rissa?"

"It's just weird for two people to disappear like that. I mean there are reasons for it," she said with raised intonation, as if the implication were obvious.

Aislinn sighed in exasperation. "I hate to disappoint you all, but I really wasn't feeling well. I was force fed some shit that turned me into a werecat, and then my grandmother was killed. I attended a funeral, and when I got back here all I wanted to do was crawl into bed and stay there. Cullen kept an eye on me."

Aislinn's tone was too convincing for Rissa's liking. In fact the entire scenario proposed was incredibly plausible. "That's no fun."

"No it isn't." Aislinn smiled to herself behind the serious look she gave Rissa. Technically she didn't say anything that wasn't true. She merely implied a different slant to it. "Now, can we all stop staring at me as if I've grown a third eye and go back to watching television?"

After a few head bows, as if Aislinn gave an order, the TV came back on, and Rissa apologized. "I don't really know what I was thinking Ais," she said.

Aislinn leaned over to Rissa speaking very quietly. "You don't seem to have any concept of correct timing or decorum. We're friends and I'd like to stay friends. You were the only person to give me the time of day for a long time. Even so, if you want to keep our friendship on the same level it was on, you need to start thinking about how to act with an alpha. Cause technically, I don't get to be an omega any more. At least that's what they tell me."

Rissa looked over at Aislinn wide eyed and nodded gravely.

"Now," Aislinn smiled and settled in for the movie, "what are we watching?"

* * * *

Cullen sat down at the heavy, round wooden table, in the middle of a room decorated with tapestries and stained glass. The ceiling vaulted high above them, and hanging from the wooden beams was a gaudy, supposedly antique, chandelier. It continued the way--too--new--to--be--a--real--castle motif nicely. The Pack Council couldn't be accused of not having their own special sense of humor. Cullen once asked

Cadifor who was supposed to be Arthur. The two of them laughed long and hard over that.

Jenna reclined comfortably in the seat next to Cullen. It once belonged to Brennus. Cullen watched the pretty blonde with a resigned sense of change. He stared at the back of her head and Aislinn felt a distinct sense of loss and sadness filter through their bond. Closing her eyes, Aislinn tried to let him know that she cared. Cullen was surprised to feel the sympathy returned and he smiled inwardly. The strength of their bond amazed him. He never thought she could catch his upset and then answer, at this distance. He was so wrapped up in his own thoughts that he nearly missed the beginning of the meeting.

The lycan alphas from his area sat at one side of the table and around the opposite side gathered Cadifor and the Pack Council leaders from around the world. In this room, the Council made sure that the human population never found out about the lycan population. The men and women didn't all get along, but they all agreed on one thing. A human--lycan war was out of the question.

Cadifor tossed a pile of paperwork onto the table that Cullen recognized as the reports he had sent in. "So here's the reason you're all here," Cadifor began.

* * * *

Slamming doors and loud insistent growling told Aislinn that movie night was over. The entire group in the great room saw Terrick storming toward the elevator. Anger radiated from his eyes. Amused glances were exchanged in the great room and they all settled back into their respective seats to finish watching the movie.

Aislinn put her take-out box from the Taigh-O\sda down on the table and got up to go to Sarah's office.

"Hey Aislinn," Christoff called after her. She turned around. He was a younger lycan. He had smiled at her with a more than friendly look a couple times that evening. But he was too smart to even consider hitting on the alpha's mistress. "You gonna finish that steak," he asked enthusiastically and one side of his mouth turned up in a half grin.

"No," she laughed. "It's all yours." Aislinn walked down the hall as Christoff and one of the other guys in the room descended on her leftovers like a couple of squabbling siblings.

Sarah's door was closed and Aislinn could hear venting coming from behind the door. She almost left, except she couldn't help the feeling that she needed advice now. So she tentatively knocked on the door causing the room to fall silent, before Sarah yelled to come in.

Aislinn cracked the door and poked her head around. "I don't mean to interrupt," she offered. "It's really just a quick question. I hope."

Sarah sighed. "Not a problem Aislinn. Come in. We've been dealing with one of the problems Cullen left behind. That always tends to result in arguing."

Keith growled. "I still say we throw his ass in the muin holding pen."

Sarah eyed him to shut him up. Aislinn was only sort of in the main group. Cullen didn't appear to have any reservations about talking in front of her, but her rank wasn't established yet. She wasn't an elder and she wasn't even technically a beta. As of yet, the Terrick info was still need to know. Keith rolled his eyes at her, and their conversation ended.

Aislinn glanced back and forth between them. "Okay?"

"Yeah Ais," Keith said. "What's up?"

"Another vision," she said despondently as she sat down in the chair next to Keith.

Both of them groaned. "Just what we needed," Sarah said. "What's going to explode now?"

"Well that's the problem. I still don't know. I was given a message to give to a druid named Nora. I can tell you that it's important that it be dealt with as soon as possible. But I personally don't know how to contact the Circle. The thing is that Cullen said there would be druids at that meeting he went to didn't he?"

Sarah considered the suggestion. "You want to call Cullen with the message."

"I don't know. I was hoping you could tell me if it was a bad idea."

Keith shook his head. "Pack Council meetings aren't something that should be interrupted, unless you're willing to risk your throat over the information. Do you think it's that important?"

"I feel like it is. Cullen didn't seem to think the last few visions were important, though." Aislinn sighed heavily. "I have a terrible feeling that we're going to be too late," Aislinn said.

"Too late for what," Sarah asked.

"I don't know. Just too late. The message was that I was to tell Nora Senach that they were using the bone dust of a dire wolf. The implication is that Nora will know what that means or be able to figure it out. I can't help imagining what a fight with a lycan who changes into a dire wolf thing would be like," she said softly and looked at Sarah. "I don't know what Jenna is doing with those men or the books. I don't know

- 471 -

when it's going to be too late to stop. Would you all rather take books and prisoners from her or get into a fight with an army of lycans that have been turned into whatever Jenna thinks is more dangerous than a normal lycan?"

Keith and Sarah exchanged uncertain, concerned looks. "So let's call Cullen," Keith said.

Sarah nodded her agreement.

Keith grinned. "I say we have Aislinn do it. He might not yell first if her name's on the caller ID."

* * * *

Maon leaned on the end of the table where the druids were working. He growled menacingly and smiled broadly at the same time. "Are you sure this will work?"

Jacob shrugged. "It's never been done. We believe it will do what your Mistress asked for. However, we won't know until someone tries it. That's why Rafe experimented so much before he used his formulas on himself."

Maon grinned. "I guess then we try it on someone." He stepped over to the door and looked out into the hall. Spotting a relatively puny omega carrying a try of food somewhere, he stepped up to the young man and knocked the tray out of his hand onto the floor. The blonde lycan dropped to his knees to start cleaning up the mess, apologizing for being clumsy.

Maon grabbed the kid by the collar of his shirt. "You'll work perfectly," he said with a chuckle and dragged him into the room with the druids.

Jacob eyed the young man sympathetically. There was nothing he could do about it. *At least it shouldn't kill him.*

Maon waited, glaring expectantly at the druids. "The whole thing?" He held up the bottle of foul smelling brown liquid that they gave him.

Jacob stepped up to Maon. "Actually I need to make some marking on him first. Then, yes he'll need to drink the whole thing if you want it to happen all at once. I have to warn you that it's painful and dangerous. If you want to do it right--"

"We don't have time for right," Maon said. "Just do it." He shoved Jacob toward the cowering boy on the floor.

Jacob walked past the boy to one of the other tables in the room. He picked up a jar of blue woad, and then walked to the boy kneeling on the floor. "You'll need to take your shirt off," he said sadly.

Trembling, the boy did as he was told. Maon was more than enough incentive for complete cooperation. Jacob knelt next to him and began writing in Gaelic script along the boy's back and chest.

* * * *

A deadly glare like nothing Cadifor ever focused on Cullen nearly stopped him from answering when his ringing cell interrupted the meeting. Silencing the ring as he pulled it out, Cullen considered that Sarah and Keith knew better. Cadifor was staring at him as he looked at the caller ID. Cullen hesitated. He thought Aislinn should know better than to make this call. If he didn't answer it and there was something wrong, he would be pissed. If he did answer it and it was nothing, then he would be pissed.

Silence in the room was deafening. Cadifor's glare turned sarcastic. "I don't believe I've ever seen Cullen Arnauk look so indecisive. You better answer it then."

Cadifor leaned on the table expectantly, and Cullen knew that he was about to be made an example of.

Aislinn felt a growl that shook her, and she shot Sarah an uncertain look as the phone continued to ring. "Maybe this wasn't a good idea," she said, wide eyed.

Flipping his phone open, Cullen felt on display as everyone in the room stared at him. *I'm gonna kill you when I get back,* he thought forcefully before he spoke. "What?"

"You know, I think I caught the threat," Aislinn said softly.

He closed his eyes and breathed out, trying to gather his patience. "What is it? I'm in the middle of the meeting."

"Cullen I'm sorry. I need to tell you to find a druid named Nora Senach and let her know that they're using dire wolf bone dust. The vision was blatant and urgent. You're the only one in a position to find a druid at the moment, so it has to be for you." Aislinn held her breath. She was praying that he would find it important enough to not kill her when he got back. His silence felt like an eternity.

"All right, calm down," he said gently. "Was there anything else?"

"No," Aislinn was relieved that he sounded less angry. "I got the impression that it took a great deal of effort for the man in the vision to send that much of a message. Like I said before, my visions usually don't interact with me. I think the men Jenna's holding prisoner must be druids."

Cullen stared at Cadifor with a meaningful look that had Cadifor standing straight again and looking less annoyed by the interruption. "Actually I know they are. All right. Wait for me to get back. We'll deal with it when I have the rest of the information."

"Okay," Aislinn smiled. "So I'm not getting killed when you get back?"

"Not this time," he said. "Goodbye." Then he hung up the phone.

Cadifor looked at Cullen as he replaced his phone in his pocket with the ring silenced. "Well," he said with a superior tone. All the others at the table were grumbling and growling.

"I'll tell you in private," Cullen responded. There was no other way to deal with it. Aislinn's timing had been lousy, even if the call was necessary.

Cadifor's eyes narrowed on Cullen. "Then I suggest we finish the meeting, and I'll deal with you afterward. I have to admit Arnauk, you're disappointing me." Cadifor's comment and tone had the other lycans looking at Cullen with delight. Most of them were tired of the favoritism. For once, Cullen was on the short end and they loved it.

Jenna chuckled inwardly. She batted her eyes at Cullen and licked her lips temptingly. Something about him being in trouble with Cadifor was turning her on. She felt her own cell vibrate, and she took it out of her pocket under the table. Cullen watched her glance down and read something from the face. She flipped it up and read something else. Then she closed it.

Jenna flashed Cullen another smile, as if to say, 'That's how you get a message while in a meeting.'

Cadifor took a good hour asking each lycan at the table questions about the possible druid population on their territory and describing what to look for. "They don't tend to interact in a significant way with

- 475 -

anything. They're there for gaining knowledge and sharing knowledge. They know a great deal more than any human you run into and tend to behave as such."

"That's not much to go on," Sean said. "It's not like we can read minds to know who knows the most, and then ask if they're druids."

"The Circle has instructed the ones who need assistance to approach the packs in their areas. They'll find you. I only want you to make sure you're helping the right people," Cadifor said as if that should have been understood. "There's to be no aggression toward them. The Pack Council wants to cultivate this relationship. Answer their questions; participate in the search for their people. Above all there is to be no government involvement with them. If the feds ask, send them in a different direction. Don't deny involvement or outright lie, but don't go leading them to the Circle either. They're set up similarly to us. They each have a 'family' unit that's referred to by a name in their areas and they each have a representative on a larger scale similar to our Pack Council. I'm told on some authority," Cadifor said sarcastically, "that we modeled our structure after theirs. So know that if you mess with one group," he looked at several lycans in the room in particular, "you're not only messing with that group, but with the whole of the Circle and, through our new relationship, the Pack Council. Don't do anything stupid. They've been in your territory for as long as it's been your territory. They're not a threat. They could be a powerful ally. Am I completely understood?"

Cadifor glared at each lycan at the table in turn. The rest of the Council sat with him showing silent support of his lecture. Cullen couldn't help thinking that the show Cadifor was playing out for Jenna was spectacular.

As Cadifor finished the other Pack Council members stood and walked out, leaving Cadifor to conduct any personal business with his group. Cullen wondered if he had ever heard another Council member speak during any of these meetings. Fortunately, Cadifor didn't have anything further to add to the lecture for his personal group this time. Everyone was dismissed from the room, except Cullen.

Cadifor leveled a fierce look on Cullen that was far from wasted on the men and women leaving the large room. As the last of them filtered out and the door closed behind them, Cullen smiled at Cadifor and shook his head. "I don't know if I should applaud the act or cower submissively in a corner."

Cadifor returned the smile. "Was I so transparent?"

"No," Cullen said. "None of them were present for our prior conversation. You even shook me a couple times. I do apologize for the phone call."

Cadifor nodded. "So what was it?" His curiosity was killing him.

"Aislinn had another vision. Do you know how to contact someone named Nora Senach?"

Cadifor's brow furrowed. "Where'd you get that name?"

"A man in Aislinn's vision told her to give a message to Nora Senach."

"Well, then let's go talk to Nora," Cadifor said. "She's upstairs."

Chapter 22

Patience is a poultice for all wounds.
-Irish Proverb

Jenna watched all the others disappear in different directions. She knew she wouldn't be missed. She wasn't wanted in the first place. Admiring herself in a large wall mirror, she studied her curves, her hips, her breasts. She looked at her eyes and her full lips. Her heart was racing with excitement. Glancing back in the direction that everyone had come from, she checked to see if anyone else was around.

Confident she wouldn't be seen, she turned for the front door. Jenna let herself out and couldn't help the little jog in her step as she found her jeep. Pulling out her phone while climbing in, she texted Maon to let him know to expect her before morning.

* * * *

Cullen and Cadifor mounted the stairs for the third floor. Cadifor led the way through the richly decorated halls to another wing of the manor, and Cullen nodded respectfully as they passed a couple Council members in the hall. The Council stayed in an area separate from the rest of the lycans who came to the meeting. It was nice seeing the men and woman acting like real people, talking to each other, and interacting as opposed to staring ominously down their noses in silence. Cullen was one of the few alphas invited back on occasion.

They all watched with interest as Cadifor led Cullen to a great room where a number of women were seated and talking quietly. Standing, Makeda walked over to them, eyeing Cadifor.

"Your meeting over," she asked, as she slid an arm around Cadifor's back and pressed against him. Every time Cullen saw her it was from a distance and always with a powerful lycan.

Makeda was incredibly beautiful. She had dark skin, long raven hair, and nearly solid black eyes. She was wearing a black sweater that clung to her ample breasts and was just short of her black jeans, so that her toned stomach showed in the gap. Gold rings decorated her toes. Almost intoxicating, she virtually radiated the scent of lycan. A strange Yin Yang impression came over Cullen, as he looked at the nearly albino Cadifor standing next to the raven beauty.

"Mmm," she cooed. "I like your friend." A strong African accent tined her words and she smiled winningly at Cullen. For one brief instant Cullen had to remind himself that he had his own beauty waiting back at the den.

Cadifor grinned. "Unfortunately for him, he is taken. Finally."

"Shame," Makeda said and winked at Cullen. "Perhaps you could ask permission." She placed a finger to the corner of her mouth and bit it gently, as she continued to eye Cullen. "Cadifor doesn't mind when I bring extra friends to bed." Soft, seductive amber swirled in the depths of her eyes.

He laughed as shook his head. "I already know the answer to that. Try me again in a few decades, once she's gotten used to the way of things in pack life. Even then I'll not guarantee she'll be willing to share."

Makeda pouted and looked back to Cadifor as if he should do something about the situation.

"I'll deal with you later," Cadifor promised. "I have business to complete. I need to speak with Nora."

Knowing the sound of dismissal, Makeda eyed him with annoyance then left to rejoin the others.

Cullen considered the group. "Council mates?"

Cadifor looked over the women. "Most of them. Some are guests."

After some quiet talking, an ancient woman stood from the small seated group. A young woman appeared from nowhere and followed her as the old woman walked toward Cullen and Cadifor. Patience and time emanated from her. She had iridescent blue eyes. Cullen felt as though she knew his mind the instant she made eye contact with him. Her long silver white hair was intricately braided down her back, and simple tan linen dress hung to her ankles. Across her shoulder and cinched at one side of her hip with a silver knot broach was a sash of green, blue, tan, and black tartan.

She smiled at Cadifor and Cullen in a grandmotherly way. "I was told you wished to see me. Am I to be introduced to the striking young man who has the women so enamored?"

Cadifor nodded respectfully, and Cullen imitated the gesture. "This," Cadifor said, "is Cullen Arnauk. We spoke of him."

"Ah, the one who has stolen away Brinah's granddaughter. Perhaps then she will not be completely lost to us," Nora said with a sparkle in her eye.

"Cullen," Cadifor continued, "this is Nora Mong Senach."

Cullen considered what she had said. "Then I can assume that what I've heard about the Circle having eyes and ears everywhere is true?"

Nora's stare seemed to bore through him, but she didn't answer his question.

Cullen wondered if she was reading his mind. "How do you know of me and Aislinn?"

"Brinah has joined the ancients now. Her knowledge has been added to those of us who know how to find her. I believe Aislinn possesses talents that lie there as well."

Cullen knew immediately that this was going to be one of those conversations that involved a lot of nothing being said. He readied his brain for innuendo overload. "I was given a message for you."

"And where did your message come from?"

"Aislinn dreamed it," he said reluctantly. He didn't like the way she suggested that the Circle may have access to Aislinn through him somehow. He assumed through the new alliance that seemed to be forming.

"You don't trust me," she said as she stared at him. "There is nothing you could tell me she is capable of that would surprise me or make her important enough for us to attempt to take her from you. All our people have the ability to choose the life they wish. She has already made her choice. What is your message to me?"

With her answer to his unspoken concerns Cullen was certain that the woman was prodding around his mind. Even so, he breathed a bit easier, with her reassurance. He didn't know if Aislinn would want to take advantage of the ability to learn about the druids now. Even if they didn't try to take her from him, he was faced with the sudden realization that she may want to go. Cullen growled. He hated uncertainty. "Aislinn was told, in a vision, to find Nora Senach and tell her that they were using bone dust of a dire wolf.

She figured that you would know what the message meant."

Nora's eyes took on a weary sadness that was almost palpable. "Yes, I think I do know. It is a shame that Rafe brought our peoples back together in this way. I would have preferred a less destructive reunion. Ah, but the fates do as they please. What do *you* think that means Lord Arnauk? I believe you've been puzzling over it since you were told to tell me."

Cullen cleared his throat and looked at Cadifor, who nodded his unspoken permission to speak freely. "Knowing Jenna, she'd have no use for werecats. She'd also have no desire to make anything stronger than her. She wants to take up where her father left off, in her own warped way. She has the books and Rafe's notes and has kidnapped a group of people capable of making use of them, and she's doing something with dire wolves. I'd say she's looking for a way to increase her own power." He looked at Cadifor who was already coming round to the conclusion that Cullen reasoned out and was starting to take on that pissed off expression again. "My guess is she's trying to get them to make her into something more physically powerful than she is. Then she'd be able to hold her position against anyone in the pack. Question is if she will stop there."

Cadifor growled. "An entire Tairneach pack of what? Dire lycans?"

"That's what Aislinn suggested," Cullen said.

Cadifor paced away and then back again, looking over at Nora. "A way to stop this?"

"That depends on how far she has gotten. The men and women missing are more than capable of doing what is suggested. Traditionally it takes time and patience to create a were. However, Rafe seems to have found a way to shorten the process."

Cullen growled. "He wanted the stone circle for that. So does that mean Jenna's invading now?"

Nora considered for a moment. "He used the ley lines to turn himself. Imbuing yourself with great power is a dangerous process. With the ley lines Rafe's process could be made less painful or he could make himself stronger, but as long as Jenna is using someone else to turn her it's not necessary. I don't believe the men and women who have been taken to help her will volunteer information. However, if she asks about the ley lines they won't lie to her. It would make it easier and safer to do. It also depends on what exactly she wants and how well they are able to adjust the compound creation to work from bone dust instead of blood. That makes matters more complex and increases the risk. She has collected the correct people to accomplish it."

Cullen turned to Cadifor. "You keep Jenna here. I'll take my men to the Tairneach manor and get the muin books before she finishes whatever she's doing."

"No," Cadifor growled. "I told you. Nothing that involves the Pack Council. The laws are the only things that keep our power here. Jenna has not technically done anything wrong that we can prove. Kidnapping and theft aren't strong enough reasons for the Pack Council to become directly involved. All we have is innuendo and guess work based on visions and druids. Imagine the justification given to the alphas and how they'll take it if the Tairneach clan is disbanded and handed over to the Arnauk because we thought Jenna Tairneach *might* be doing something that

- 483 -

may result in her attacking someone else," Cadifor ranted.

Nora shook her head. "My friend, if you wait for her to do what you think is happening; there will be death instead of explanation. What's worse is that her actions will have sparked imaginations with ideas that have long since been buried so deep no one considers them possible. There truly is nothing more dangerous than a mind open to infinite possibility, when mingled with untempered ambition."

Cullen rolled his eyes and walked away from them. His concern was with the immediate threat posed to his pack if Jenna turned the Tairneach into horror movie lycans and released them on his territory. "I'm not just going to sit and wait for her to hang herself. Jenna's not stupid enough to go without a plan. If we keep waiting, then the Arnauk will be destroyed and that will be the Pack Council's justification for involvement. Don't ask me to allow that Cadifor. You know I won't. She made veiled threats already. The only reason she worked with me to kill Rafe was because it was to her advantage. Originally, she believed Rafe would be able to set her up to take me out. She doesn't just want to be Tairneach alpha. She's out to prove that she deserves to be. For whatever reason, she's targeted me and my pack as her means to that end."

Cadifor growled. He agreed with Cullen, but there would be no convincing the Council of this.

"Perhaps," Nora suggested. "The solution is to plan for the worst."

Cullen glared at her. "I'll not run and hide either druid. Brinah tried that one already."

Nora smiled at him. "I'm too old and have known too many lycans to think that you would be willing to hide anywhere. No. I'm suggesting that the Arnauk prepare for war if you believe one is coming."

Cullen looked back to Cadifor and then shook his head. "The only way to prepare for an army of lycans who were already my equal and may now be double or triple in strength would be to double or triple my numbers. I can't import reinforcements from other packs without Pack Council approval." He snarled at Cadifor.

Cadifor's eyes lit up like fire, and he began laughing.

Cullen growled at him. "I don't get the joke."

"Don't be so single minded my friend," Cadifor said with a wicked grin. "No you can't bring in reinforcements without Council approval. And you'll never get approval for war footing on the grounds that we have. However, you can invite other packs to a mating ceremony. Considering you're about to mate to a druid, and we are encouraging diplomatic relations, perhaps we can discreetly increase your number. We import people to stay on the reservation in anticipation of the ceremony. I don't think Jenna would be fool enough to attack if she knows what we've don't, but we don't have to invite the Tairneach. Then, when she chooses her moment or if we provoke one, you'll have the men you need available."

Cullen considered the plan. "Do you truly believe we could triple my pack number without her finding out?"

Nora placed a hand on Cullen's arm. "There are ways of keeping people from finding things out."

"I don't think Aislinn will like this," he said.

- 485 -

Cadifor started laughing again. "You truly are gone over that woman. I never thought I'd see the day." He ran his hand through his hair and grinned. "This is going to be interesting. I can't wait to taste her." Cadifor smiled wider when Cullen growled possessively.

"I think you have enough females to taste around here."

"All right, I'll behave. But for now, you and I need to revise your guest list." Cadifor looked to Nora. "Is there a secret you need to teach us in order to prevent Jenna from finding out what we're doing?"

Nora chuckled at him, making her whole face wrinkle. She didn't appear to do anything; still a man with striking blue eyes and an overly efficient look about him appeared from nowhere. He bowed to Nora and then looked to Cullen and Cadifor.

"This," Nora said, "is Malik. He'll make sure that the messages and phone calls you make only reach the people who you wish." Malik nodded to Nora.

Cadifor considered the appearance they were trying to give. "Would it be appropriate to invite Senach to the mating? The female is your bloodline."

Nora smiled again. "I'll provide you with a list of those who might be appropriate." She grinned at the unhappy look on Cullen's face, but he wasn't arguing. "I'll make sure that they will all be people who can either be of use to Aislinn or will be helpful in the fight."

Cullen growled. "I thought druids didn't fight."

"We don't start fights. However, long ago we arranged to be capable of defending ourselves. You are all proof of that."

* * * *

Jenna skipped up the steps to the front door of her home early that morning without a single sign of the fact that she had no sleep. The door opened for her, and her heels clicked on the marble, echoing down the hallway as she headed for the basement.

Maon came down the main stairwell, half dressed, rubbing sleep out of his eyes. He'd left standing orders to notify him the instant Jenna arrived. Descending the stairs, he followed her to the basement.

Jenna spared him a smoldering look. If he had done as well as he said then she would give him his reward in the middle of the great room. A guard opened the door to the basement for her and she virtually danced down the basement steps with a gleam in her eyes.

Three men sat on the floor in various places about the basement. Two of them were in chains. Jenna looked at Maon in confusion. "I thought you said that it was ready. What is this?"

Maon nodded. "It is ready. It took several volunteers to get it right. The first attempt," Maon pointed to a boy, cowering in the corner in several layers of chains. "He didn't exactly volunteer. It worked, but at the sacrifice of intellect. I didn't think you'd want that. So I put them back to work. They made some adjustments and Raol tried the next batch. You promise a man that he'll gain strength better than any current alpha, and he'll volunteer for anything. Raol was better. Even so, his coordination wasn't what it should be and he's not happy about that. It took six men to get him down here." Maon signaled the third man, who was waiting for his turn. "Devon, however, is still fine, so far."

Devon approached them and bowed his head to Jenna and Maon. "Mistress," he said shakily.

"What's wrong? What do you mean so far," Jenna asked without taking her eyes off Devon.

"It was exceedingly painful. He writhed for hours. The change itself is painful enough to cause screaming and a necessary recovery time after it's done. He's still recovering. The druids claim that it's a flaw they have no solution for. There's a price for what we're asking them to do."

"Rafe managed a muin polar--bear--lion thing without recovery time," Jenna snarled. "I want to see," she demanded.

Devon swallowed. He didn't want to go through that again. The pain was almost enough to cause him to never wish to change to any lycan form again.

"Now," Jenna demanded.

Maon gave him a look that reinforced Jenna's command, and Devon stepped back from the two of them. As he began to change, the cracking of bones was audible and his screams filled the room. The boy in the corner of the room stood up on his hands and knees and followed Devon's lead like an agitated pet dog following its master. The two men howled in agony as their bodies rearranged. The sickening sounds of cracking bodies echoed up the stairs, and people on the floor above them stared at each other in horror, listening to the results of their mighty alpha's experiment.

The change took far longer than any change Jenna had ever witnessed. Even children on their first attempt could manage better. The men writhed on the floor. Tears gathered in the corners of their eyes, and when they finally completed the shift they lay whimpering on the cold wooden panels of the floor trembling.

Jenna smiled at the result. Although the process sickened her, the end product was perfect. The boy in the corner turned into a wolf three times larger, both in height and width, than any lycan she had ever seen.

He snarled and growled when she approached, and Maon held her back. "There's a reason he's chained. Though, he does seem to do as Devon tells him. There must be some kind of primal connection."

Devon propped himself against the wall, as Jenna approached. He was in his hybrid form, having found it less painful than shifting all the way to his wolf. Even sitting against the wall, Devon was still shoulder high on Jenna. If he stood she would only come to his chest. His build was stockier than a standard lycan and he was more barrel—chested, with virtually no neck. Panting, Devon fought off sharp pains that continued to shoot through him. He was definitely larger, stronger, and more formidable than any lycan she had ever seen. She stared into his eyes with excitement.

Jenna ran a hand across his check and then leaned in and kissed his muzzle. "You're perfect," she said softly, staring into his swirling amber eyes. She stood up and turned to Maon. "Take me to the druids."

Upstairs, in the room where the druids were being held the air was permeated with a smell of burning flesh. Jenna nearly gagged as she entered the room. Sneering, Jenna put her hand over her nose and mouth. Jacob and the others were seated in chairs, hunched over in exhaustion. Maon had ordered them to make as much of the stuff as they could and they had not been allowed to sleep or stop all night. They were so tired that Jenna and Maon's entrance didn't encourage them to budge even at risk of another beating.

"Ah," Jenna sighed sympathetically. She was too happy about the fact that she was so close to be angry right now. "It seems that my mad scientists need a nap. The first one to tell me how Rafe was able to manage his transformation without being in all the pain that the poor men in the basement have endured, gets to go to bed."

The druids looked at each other. They were truly beyond caring. Jacob sat back in his chair and called over to the woman on the far side of the room, "Cerdwyn." She was in worse shape than the men. She was older and hadn't adjusted to their situation as well.

Cerdwyn looked up and Jenna could see the tear stains on her face. "Tell her, Cerdwyn. She'll let you go to bed." The resignation in his voice and the look on the woman's face almost plucked at what was left of Jenna's conscience.

Cerdwyn started to protest, but Jacob shot her a hard look and she gave in. "That's why Rafe needed the ley lines. The process of instilling a being with that much power is contrary to laws of balance that nature works on. It either requires time and patience, which you have told us to ignore or more power. Rafe drew on the power that occurs at the site on the Arnauk reservation to compensate for the natural inclination of fates to force the receiver of the power to endure an equally powerful back lash."

Jenna smiled, content with that answer. "Maon, make sure the druid gets something to eat and some sleep." He nodded. "Actually let them all have a short break for not giving me a hard time with getting an answer." She had expected at least some argument, so she was feeling generous.

Jenna walked out of the room with Maon on her heels. "Any other orders," he asked.

She stood a moment looking off into nothing. Maon could almost see the wheels turning in her mind. "Yes, gather a group of volunteers. Make sure they know what they are in for. Introduce them to Devon and explain the benefits. Anyone who wishes to undergo the change is to be provided the ability to do so." Jenna refocused on him. "Afterward, report to my room. I believe I promised you a reward for your efforts last night." A sultry smiled turned the corners of Jenna's mouth, before she turned down the hall toward her room, making sure to swing her hips enticingly for Maon as she went.

* * * *

Sarah tried to talk Keith into sticking around for the conversation with Aislinn. Cullen left it to Sarah to explain to Aislinn what was going to happen at the mating ceremony, tell her why he was going to be longer getting back then he originally thought, and explain to her why the mating ceremony was about to turn into a trap and likely a blood bath.

Keith flat out refused to take part. "Sorry Sarah, but if I'm supposed to find out what's going on at Tairneach manor and get back to Cullen then I'd better get on it. Besides, it sounds like a woman thing anyway."

Sarah glared at him. "Fine. Could you at least have someone send her in here?"

Keith threw her one of his patented Impish grins and backed out the door of her office as if she was going to attack him the minute his back was turned.

He was about to send an omega to locate Aislinn, but found her watching TV in the great room with Rissa and some of the others. Keith stood in the doorway and watching for a minute. He never would have guessed when he first met Aislinn that things would turn out like this. He thought back to the gutsy bartender who woke him up in the middle of the night to come pick up Cullen at that shithole bar.

"Aislinn," Keith called into the room.

Looking up from the show with a handful of popcorn, she ruefully glanced back at the screen once before giving him her full attention. "Uh huh?"

"Sarah needs to talk to you."

Aislinn gave the television one last disappointed look. "I don't think I've managed to catch the end of a single show since I got here," she complained, as she jumped the back of the couch and walked toward the door. One of the guys sitting on the floor took her seat and started making a pass at Rissa as Aislinn left.

She walked down the hall to Sarah's office and tapped on the open door as she walked in. "Keith said you wanted me?"

"Yeah, close the door."

Aislinn raised her eyebrows. "Problem?"

"No. Not exactly. Except that Cullen's an ass and gives me too much of his dirty work sometimes," she groused.

"And you wondered why I don't want your job," Aislinn chuckled.

Sarah glared at her. "Keep that thought. First, he had trouble at his meeting and he won't be back today. In fact he's not sure how long exactly he's going to be. He said to tell you that he'd call when he's able."

Aislinn's face instantly fell. "What happened? Am I allowed to know?"

"Jenna. Apparently the message about the dire wolf dust means exactly what you were afraid it means." Sarah sighed and looked at her sympathetically. "This is the part where you're going to be very happy your mating happened the way it did. The short version is that due to the threat that Jenna poses we need reinforcements, unfortunately interpack law says that we don't have grounds. Unless Jenna does something more blatant we're screwed. But Cullen and Cadifor have come up with a plan to invite extra lycans to your mating ceremony so that we have an excuse to have more people on hand for the possibility of the attack. Keith has been sent to see if it can be determined when the attack will come so we know when to plan the ceremony to happen." Sarah watched Aislinn's face fall.

"I can't believe he'd do that and then have you tell me. Why wouldn't he explain this himself?" Aislinn was pissed.

"I'm sorry Aislinn. I know that it seems insensitive. But unfortunately this is one of those things that being associated with the alpha results in. He's trying to protect the pack. He'll do whatever he has to in order to make us safe. In this case it means sacrificing the intimacy of his mating ceremony. I know we keep saying that everything the alpha does affects the pack and is watched by the pack. The best you can do is appreciate the time you get alone with him. But things like the mating ceremony are always going to end up being turned into political something."

Aislinn shook her head. "Okay. Logically I can see what you're saying. And if I'm told that it really is a choice between this mating ceremony and the safety of the pack then of course I'll do what I have to do. But Sarah," she couldn't even finish the sentence. She felt like she was going to throw up. "How many more people are we talking about? I mean I'm going to have to do what in front of them?"

Sarah tried to think of the best way to explain it all. She gave Aislinn a lot of credit. Technically speaking it hadn't been all that long since Aislinn had been brought into their world. There weren't many people who could make the kind of adjustments that she had made. "Well, you've already done most of it. I guess what you really need to know is that what makes it a ceremony and not just the two of you having sex is the fact that everyone will be watching, some people may participate, and at the end the whole of the pack is to be given access to the two of you."

"See," Aislinn said angrily. "I hate the way you all know exactly how to not say the most important part. You're going to have to tell me what you mean by that."

"Fine. Usually, starting with the more important members of the pack an going through to the lesser members people approach the two of you, after he's come inside you and smell and or taste the two of you together. They acknowledge that you've mated and you're a pair. You're scents as one so to speak. That will go on for the rest of the evening. You have sex then people get to 'acknowledge' the alpha pair. Repeatedly. If the two of you separate for any reason that doesn't stop that part of the ceremony. You become pack property. Actually, any member of the pack at any time can attempt to show you respect in that way. Even after the ceremony. It doesn't usually happen because most of the pack knows what most everyone else smells like. But you are one great big curiosity and I wouldn't be surprised if that particular aspect of pack life were exploited."

Aislinn sat silently. She knew about all the open sex. She'd seen it. Every day she was here she'd seen something. "So when Rissa told me a while back that if Cullen had ever come inside any of the others then she'd rub it in people's faces, Rissa really meant…"

Saran nodded. The room was quiet for a long time before Aislinn spoke again. "So what am I supposed to do? How should I behave?"

"Cullen's the only one allowed to do anything non-oral to you. But if all they want to do involves noses or mouths then you let them. I would suggest that you attempt to enjoy it, but I'm guessing that might be tough for you."

"I'll see if I can wrap my brain around it before it happens. I need to figure out how to be the alpha's mate right?" Aislinn sat there thinking about how much she loved him. She took a deep breath. "He's worth it. I'll survive."

Sarah smiled at her. "Give it a few years and you won't know why it ever bothered you."

* * * *

Cadifor's Harley pulled in next to Cullen's SUV. Makeda got off the back of the bike and handed her helmet to Cadifor as she ran her hands through her hair. Cullen waited for them to get their stuff from the bike and led the way to the elevator.

Cullen had spent the trip feeling his sense of Aislinn growing stronger in his mind mile by mile. As night fell he could tell she had gone to sleep and he wished that he was in bed with her. He was tempted to try and call out to her and wake her up the minute he knew he was close enough to speak with her. But he managed to restrain himself and let her sleep.

He was only a day late getting back. But he hadn't managed to call and talk to her. Things had gotten too complex. Nora's list that she'd given Malik of druids to invite had been problematic. She didn't want to explain what any of them were capable of. He was going to have to just ask the pack to deal with it. The only good point being that Aislinn should be a walk in the park for the Arnauk after having to deal with the entire muin Senach Circle. Either that or they were going to have problems with the fact that Cullen was mating himself to the druids. He growled even thinking about it.

"Hey," Cadifor said. "I thought you'd be happy getting back here."

"We'll see if Aislinn's willing to speak to me. Then I'll determine whether I'm happy to be back or not." Cullen inserted his key in the elevator panel and hit the button for the beta's floor. He wasn't going to put Cadifor and Makeda on the main floor.

"Ooo," Makeda cooed. Her African accent coming through even in just that simple sound. "Look an elevator," she teased Cadifor. It was all stairs at his place.

"Get over it. I'm just not interested in that particular piece of technology. Stairs are better for you and more reliable." He pulled her against him and the two of them kissed roughly.

Cullen rubbed his face. It had been a long couple days. He was the only one in the pack to have ever actually met Cadifor. He figured that Keith and Sarah were in for a shock. The man was an imposing, dominating figure. When that was the impression he chose to give. But put him in a friendly situation and he wasn't any different from Cullen. "I'll have someone bring you keys to the elevator. You can't get off on pack floors without one. It keeps the guests from getting up here." Cullen led the way to the guest rooms on the floor. He kicked loudly at Keith's door as he passed it.

"What about the stairs?" Cadifor asked and Makeda made an annoyed click with her tongue.

Cullen pointed. "That way. But you need keys for those doors too."

"Don't you find it a pain to live so close to the human population?" Cadifor said with disgust.

"When we're sick of it there's the reservation. But mostly it's more convenient. Honestly it's easier to hide in plain sight. We did the little town in the middle of nowhere thing for a while. But scaring off the random tourist was too much of a pain. You never know what they get pictures of. There isn't a human in this town who looks twice at this place. I like it that way." Cadifor could see some of his point.

Cullen opened a door and ushered the two of them inside. Keith appeared groggily at his side. "What the hell? You get to deal with Jay. She pissed and pregnant. Not a good combo. I have half a mind to send you back to my bed and I'll go bunk with Ais for tonight."

"Think again," Cullen said in a far more serious tone than he intended.

Keith threw his hands in the air to say that he was just kidding and then his eyes fell on Cadifor and Makeda. Especially Makeda. He bowed his head to both of them but his eyes never left her. She smiled back at him considering.

Cullen had to laugh. The man was impossible. "Keith is my second." He said to Cadifor and Makeda. "I tend to trust him. Though at times I'm not sure why. You can tell him anything you'd tell me. He probably knows more than I do at any random point in time." Cadifor nodded and then turned to check out the rest of the room. Cullen looked at Keith who was still making eyes at Makeda. "Keith, this is Makeda. And the man she's with is Cadifor."

Keith's eye just about fell out of his head. He looked at Cullen and Makeda laughed. "I never do grow tired of the looks on men's faces when they hear your name," she said as she turned to go after her lover. "I may keep you around for that entertainment factor alone." She kissed him on the cheek.

Cadifor patted her on the ass and headed for the bathroom. Cullen pulled Keith along with him as he left the room. "Get a grip. Make sure they get keys in the morning. They're gonna be around until after the ceremony."

Keith stared at Cullen. "When you said that some important people would be around for the mating you didn't say Pack Council."

"He's the only one. Don't be so dramatic." Cullen stopped at Keith's room and stepped inside. "Jay?"

"What in the name of the Gods do you want Cullen? Can't you ever leave him be for just one night?"

"I'm sorry Jay. How you feeling," he asked.

"Pregnant," she complained.

Cullen smiled. "I'm done with him. Don't be too mean to him."

"Fine. But make him bring me some strawberry ice cream before he comes back in here," she said and pulled the blankets around her shoulders.

Cullen looked over at Keith. "You heard the woman," he said as he patted Keith on the shoulder and headed for his own room.

Aislinn was in the middle of a nice normal nightmare involving the mating ceremony and her having to fight her way through a crowd of men that Cullen didn't care were touching her. Cullen undressed and pulled the blanket's back to snuggle in behind her.

"Shh," he whispered into her ear. He knew she was having a bad dream. He pulled her against his body. When she started to struggle he decided to wake her up. "Aislinn," he said gently. *Aislinn.*

As the dream faded out and she began to refocus she felt him in her mind and then against her body. She smiled and settled in against him. "What time is it," she asked sleepily.

"Near three I think," he said softly, waiting for her to be pissed at him. But she didn't feel pissed.

"Should I be," she asked to his unspoken thoughts.

"I had hoped not. This kind of thing's going to be more regular than you might think or like. I suppose I'm a bit nervous about how you're going to react to normal pack life." He let his hands begin to roam over her body as he talked. He had missed her.

She kept her eyes closed and just felt his caresses on her skin. "Promise me that you'll always find time to come to bed with me and I'll promise you that I'll manage to find a way to deal with the alpha part of you."

He leaned down and kissed her neck, nibbling at it a bit before answering. "I promise. How did you get so understanding? Sarah talk you into it?"

"I had a couple days to dwell. If you had been here for the stuff Sarah told me about I probably wouldn't have been this nice. But I'm tired. And you currently owe me two nights of pleasant dreams." She wiggled her butt against his groin. "Get to work."

Cullen felt his growing erection even through his exhaustion. He pushed it against her, feeling himself slide between her thighs. "Are you sure you don't want to save it for the mating ceremony?" he suggested with a grin.

She growled at him. "Do you want to be sleeping on your couch?"

Cullen pulled her over and rolled her onto his chest.

"Hey," she complained. "I was comfortable." She smiled down at him as she straddled him. She wiggled a little in just the right way and she felt his hard cock slide into her. She closed her eyes and her head fell back against her shoulders as she moaned softly.

He watched her. "Tá tú hálainn. Tá grá agam duit."

She rocked against him and looked down at him. She felt him inside her. In her mind and in her body. "Tá grá agam duit. Cullen." She leaned down so that she could kiss him.

Cullen's hands were in her hair. He ravaged her lips, sucking on one and then the other. Pressing his tongue into her mouth. He loved the taste of her. All the while she rocked slowly against him. The pace insistent as he moved inside her. When he finally allowed their lips to part she lay against his chest, listening to his heart beat and rocking against him.

Cullen wrapped his arms around her. He felt her cunt gently squeezing against him. The soft slow movements were more torturous than any of the times he had bent her over and fucked her so hard she couldn't stand up. They moved together slowly just holding each other until they felt the build-up begin. It was as if their orgasms were being fed by each other as they gripped each other tightly and moaned their release. Aislinn didn't manage to make it off of him. She lay her down on his chest and started purring softly. Cullen's heart jumped a little as she began to purr and he hugged her closer, listening to her as he fell asleep.

* * * *

Aislinn awoke in what had quickly become her favorite position. Cullen was behind her with his arms wrapped tightly around her, his morning erection nudging hopefully at her backside, and his face buried in her hair. She sighed happily. He was already awake. In all the mornings they had together so far he had always been awake first. He hugged her and she wiggled against him. He growled into her hair.

"No time this morning," he said as he threw the blankets off and moved to get out of bed.

"Oh no," she argued playfully. "You started it." She followed him out of bed and virtually tackled him. He let her pin him up against the wall and she nuzzled her face against his chest as she pressed the rest of her naked body up against him.

Cullen grabbed a fistful of hair and brought it to his nose. Sometimes he felt like he needed her to breathe when they got like this. "Mmm, hálainn, don't tease. I have to deal with things this morning. Cadifor is here. And you my love need to play hostess to Makeda.

She's an important woman and currently Cadifor's lover. All by itself that means a great deal."

"Fine," she pouted, giving his cock one final stroke with a feathery touch as she walked away from him.

That earned her a growl which had her chuckling. "I missed you too," he said a bit frustrated and went back to getting dressed. "Get dressed. I should have woken you up over an hour ago."

"Why didn't you," she asked as she pulled her shirt on. Cullen watched her black bra disappear beneath the red sweater. Aislinn smiled at him. "You gonna make it through the morning," she teased.

He growled at her again. "You were purring. And yes I'll be fine."

After some hey headed out of the penthouse. "So what's on the agenda," Aislinn asked as they walked down the hall toward his office.

"I have to find Keith. He never managed to get the info that I needed. I gotta get an update. I'll introduce you to our guests and you can help Sarah by dealing with Makeda while Sarah finishes the arrangements I asked her to take care of. And I have some things to wrap up with Cadifor. Then we get to start waiting." He closed his office door behind her and went to his desk for his phone. Cullen dialed and smiled at her as he waited for Keith to answer.

Aislinn waited patiently. They just stood there staring into each other's eyes longingly while he waited for Keith to pick up the phone. Cullen couldn't remember what life had felt like before Aislinn. As he stared at her and dwelled on how much he loved her she smiled back with a knowing glint in her eyes. Cullen had lost track of the rings.

This is why I'll deal with the rest of the crap, she thought to herself as she felt his obsessive thoughts about her. She closed her eyes and let herself drift in their bond for a moment. Cullen's annoyance and concern brought her back to reality rather harshly. Aislinn looked at him questioningly.

Cullen put the phone down. "I don't remember the last time that fool didn't answer on the first ring."

"Maybe something's wrong. That seems to be the theme of late," she suggested and Cullen growled. Then Aislinn smiled widely. "Or Jaylyn could be having the babies."

Cullen nodded. "That's entirely possible. It seems like she's been pregnant forever." He headed out of the office and Aislinn had to jump to follow him. He stopped at Sarah's office and there was no one there. On the way back through the great room Cullen looked around for the usual group and didn't see anyone. The two of them got in the elevator and headed for the beta floor.

Getting out of the elevator answered the mystery. Aislinn had to be right. The floor was far more active than usual. The beta common room was packed with excited people and there was an unusually large number of omegas walking back and forth from the living quarters.

Cullen and Aislinn headed down the hall toward Keith's room. Aislinn grabbed Cullen's arm. "Do you really think they need more people in there?"

Cullen looked over at her. He stopped momentarily and smiled at her.

"Don't start," she said, blocking his hopeful thoughts about her being pregnant out of her head.

Cullen grinned at her annoyance. "I'm just going to check in and then we're going to go deal with Cadifor and Makeda. I don't intend to stand around and watch. Jay would probably kill me."

Aislinn followed him down the hall. "Are all male lycans this obsessive about getting their women pregnant," she said softly to him.

"Like I said before, that's what mating's for," he answered as he poked his head into the doorway of the front room. Keith's room was set up similarly to his own, just smaller. There was a sitting room off the hallway. Sarah was holding Keith back from the bedroom door. Cullen smiled. He nodded at Sarah who gave him a frustrated eye roll.

Cullen ducked back out into the hall with a huge grin. "Yeah, she's having the pups," he said. "Come on. I put Cadifor and Makeda down the hall."

"Pups," Aislinn said contemplatively.

Cullen looked over at her concerned face and started laughing. "Or babies, whatever you want to call them." He grabbed her hand and kissed it as they walked.

"Sure, babies would probably be a better term considering I'm a cat and you're a dog. What exactly do you think we'll have?"

Cullen shrugged. "Doesn't matter as long as they're yours and mine." He looked so pleased by the idea that Aislinn couldn't help but smile back at him.

Cullen knocked on Cadifor's door. It opened almost immediately. Makeda stepped back from the door and waved them both in. "This must be the woman you turned me down for," she said as she smiled at Aislinn and her eyes roamed over Aislinn's body. "I don't feel so offended now."

Aislinn looked over at Cullen questioningly. Aislinn didn't think she had ever seen such a beautiful woman as the one standing there and undressing her with her eyes.

"Aislinn this is Makeda," he said as if that was an excellent explanation.

Makeda's eyes never left Aislinn. "Cadifor is still in the bathroom. What's all the commotion?"

"Keith's mate is having a litter. It's been expected for some time now. There's a lot of excitement. I have to apologize. I put you both up here because it's usually more calm on this floor. The excitement is normally on the main common floor."

Makeda's smile sparkled at him, eliciting a growl from Aislinn. "No apologies. A litter is a blessing. I'd endure a great deal more noise and commotion for that reason." She looked at Aislinn again. "I'll not touch him without permission," she smiled. Then walked up to Aislinn and ran a hand down her arm. "I'll not make such promises about you, however." She grinned deviously over her shoulder at Cullen.

Cadifor came out of the bathroom as he dried off. Cullen watched Aislinn's eyes shift from Makeda to the naked blonde. Cadifor had scars all over his body from centuries of fighting. Aislinn looked over the unusually pale man.

"Careful," Makeda said in fake confidentiality. "You'll give Cadifor ideas if he feels your eyes caress him so freely."

"Keda," Cadifor said sharply. "I told you not to cause trouble."

"And you know I take no orders from you," she replied unconcerned as she walked across the room and ran a hand over Cadifor's stomach, dangerously close to his cock before going over to lounge on the bed. She looked over the people in the room with pleasure. "This would be a fun group. I have no doubt."

Cadifor didn't seem at all phased by either the fact that he was naked in front of Aislinn or that Makeda was being so sexually aggressive. Aislinn looked over at Cullen, who didn't seem affected by the situation either. *So what would you do if I took her up on her offer,* Aislinn thought at Cullen.

He looked over at her with raised eyebrows, amused at her unsure tone. *I didn't know you were interested in that kind of thing,* he responded trying to not look like he was having a conversation.

Cadifor looked from one of them to the other and then raised his eyebrows at Cullen. "If Keith's busy then I'll assume it's just you and I." He started pulling his clothes on.

"Yeah, Aislinn's going to show Makeda around. You and I will finish getting a hold of the people we need to talk with. I'm assuming that Malik is downstairs by now. They were all supposed to arrive by this morning. But with Jaylyn going into labor I haven't been able to get any of the normal people in one spot to get the information. It's still early."

Cadifor smiled. "I always did like the fact that your pack is less rank and order and more family."

Cullen didn't know how to respond to the compliment. Cadifor looked Aislinn over briefly. "So this is the one with the visions. Pretty," he said.

Aislinn nodded respectfully to Cadifor. Cullen stood patiently as his friend approached Aislinn and walked around her looking her over as if she were livestock at a fair. He leaned into her and smelled her hair deeply. Cullen took a deep breath, but dealt with it. He knew he'd have to cope with a lot of males checking Aislinn out soon enough.

Cadifor's eyes shifted from the icy amber to a golden glow and he stepped away from Aislinn as if he'd been bitten. He looked over at Cullen. "I see," he said and Cullen nodded in return. "We'd better get going," Cadifor said. "But I have to admit, I won't argue if Makeda talks her into some play."

Cullen and Cadifor went to the door and headed out. Aislinn caught a look from Cullen as they left. He was leaving it up to her. When Aislinn looked back over at Makeda the woman was smiling broadly.

"You're surprised," Makeda said to her. "By what?"

"Sorry," Aislinn sighed. "I'm still relatively new around here. I seem to run into something I find surprising on a daily basis. I was raised human. I've only been around here a little over a month. It's been an adjustment to say the least."

Makeda smiled at her wickedly. "Well, I've been around for a long time. And," she got up from the bed and walked over to Aislinn. "I'd be more than happy to help you adjust."

"Why don't we start with that tour I was told to give you," Aislinn said.

Makeda shrugged. "Whatever you like. I tend to find people much more interesting than buildings. But anything's better than sitting in this room all day."

* * * *

By noon Cullen, Sarah, and Cadifor with the help of Malik were entrenched in compiling a list of confirmations of lycans that would be joining the Arnauk on the reservation until after the mating ceremony. A group of Senach had arrived and were being more a little secretive as they sat in confidential groups in different areas of the great room, library, and any other gathering place they could get to. A meeting had been held with the elders, who were in awe of the fact that Cadifor was actually in the Madadh-Allaidh Saobhaidh. A general announcement was made about what the druids were doing there and why. The pack was told that Cullen and Aislinn would be mated and that the druids were being brought in as well as other lycans from outside packs as a diplomatic message for the future relations of the Circle and the Pack Council.

Cullen had complained about not giving the pack the truth. But Malik and Cadifor had been adamant that it was a need to know basis. This way if word did leak to Jenna she would only get the impression that she was being left out of a party. Not that they were preparing for war.

When Keith finally arrived he looked haggard but happy. "Two girls," he announced and there was applause. He got a lot of pats on the back and jokes about sympathy for the new father of two girls.

Cullen stepped up to Keith and shook his hand, then pulled his best friend to him and hugged him hard. "Thanks," he said.

Keith laughed. "No problem. What for?"

"Another reminder as to why I bother with the rest of this bullshit," he said and indicated the reports on his desk that the group had been working on.

Malik watched with pleased interest as the alpha interacted with his men. He knew that Nora would be happy to know that not all alpha lycans were war mongers. The Circle had been concerned about the forced re-involvement with the lycan population. But

Malik was coming to the conclusion that it might not be as detrimental as they were thinking.

Malik continued to help with phone calls and by having very specific messengers relay information to alphas that Cadifor wanted involved. Their intent was to make it into a diplomatic meeting just like they said it was. With the correct alphas and a small group of betas from the various trustworthy packs in the area, in combination with the druids it would be much more difficult for Jenna to win this fight. They were still concerned though that they didn't know exactly what they were up against. Unfortunately Malik had no connections inside any lycan packs. The druids had kept their distance from the lycans. It was one thing to hide amongst a human population. But lycans knew their own and that made observation of inner pack workings impossible for the Circle.

Malik was more than happy to help Keith however, and the two of them were more able to get information out of Keith's contacts in the Tairneach. Between the two of them it was much easier trying to ferret out what exactly Jenna was up to and none of the word he managed to get was good.

* * * *

It seemed that everywhere Aislinn looked there were strange faces. As much as she wanted to speak with the druids that were arriving she found that they were no easier to talk with than the lycans had been in the beginning. The druids kept to themselves and managed to make everyone uneasy since it seemed that they were watching everything.

Makeda was a great deal more helpful than Aislinn had ever dreamed and she started to wonder who was giving the tour to whom. Makeda appeared to be an expert on lycan and druid behavior. Aislinn would lead her into an area of the den and Makeda would study the lycans about the room then point out to Aislinn appropriate and inappropriate things that were going on. Then she'd watch the druids for a while and tell Aislinn what had their attention and why. Aislinn loved the fact that Makeda was frank, honest, open and actually seemed to be enjoying explaining pack behavior to Aislinn. In that one morning Makeda managed to cover everything from the way Cadifor and Cullen had behaved in the bedroom to why the different ranked lycans were behaving in different ways toward the new arrivals, lycan and druid.

"I don't get it," Aislinn said after a while. "I don't understand why you have no problem telling me all this and no one else seems to think I can handle it."

Makeda shrugged. "I have nothing to gain or lose by it. The rest of the pack is concerned that they may say or do something wrong. It doesn't matter if the consequence is that you'd misunderstand and become upset or do something that may upset the alpha. You're real problem is that Cullen Arnauk is a strong leader and his pack cares for him. They're trying to not scare you away and they don't know what will do it. I on the other hand have no concern for his feelings or truly for yours. Mostly I'm fascinated by your reactions to all of it and the fact that you could be here for even a month and still be in the dark." She grinned in amusement. "There's something very sexy about your naivety."

"You always turn things into sex." Aislinn raised her eyebrows at Makeda. She was growing to like the woman quite a bit.

"After you've lived as long as I you find that the only true pleasure in life is pleasure. If you do it right then it's better than any drug or food or thing you could own," she stepped up to Aislinn. "It combines control, risk, domination, submission. Can you think of a single thing right now better than what it feels like when you come?"

Aislinn's breath caught in her throat. Makeda's eyes sparkled. "See," she said huskily. "I grew bored with other pursuits a long time ago. I have more than enough money to buy anything else. But there's nothing quite as exciting as a new conquest," she grinned at Aislinn. "Especially if she puts up a fight."

"Fight," Aislinn said shakily, grabbing onto the last thing Makeda said. Regretting having asked the sex question. "How about some sparing. I'm told I'm not too bad and that I'm supposed to 'establish my rank' around here some time soon. There's a gym in the basement. I really can't think of anything else to show you up here."

Makeda smiled. "All right. Though I may not be comparable to the others around here." She knew that Aislinn didn't really know who she was dealing with. There wasn't a woman who knew her that would have suggested such a thing. But it had been a long time since she had been treated like everyone else and she liked it.

* * * *

Jenna sat at her father's large mahogany desk. She wasn't sure what he had always done while he was here but she had never seen him sitting at the desk and not hard at work on something. She fingered the large ruby ring around her neck in frustration.

Maon was having a very difficult time finding out when Cullen's mating was to take place. She was starting to wonder if he was hiding the date on purpose. Maybe he knew her intent. She just thought it would be fitting for her to destroy him during his mating with the bitch who had ruined her first set of plans. Jenna was firmly convinced that if Aislinn hadn't come into the picture then Rafe never would have appeared, Cullen would have just sucked it up and mated with her, and Brennus would still be alive.

Seeing Rafe's death had been healing. But seeing Aislinn destroyed would finish it. Maon knocked on the door and then walked in. He was getting less and less formal with her. Jenna knew full well that none of the pack was taking her seriously and if she was going to keep control she was going to have to act soon. She was also more than aware of the fact that Maon thought her best bet would be to let him mate with her and give over the alpha position to him. He was a definite contender for the position anyway.

"Do you have the list of volunteers," she asked.

Maon handed her a paper with a couple dozen names on it. There weren't as many as she would have liked. She took a pen to it and crossed a couple off. She was no fool. There were some men in this pack who didn't need any more power than they already had. Maon noted the men who were crossed off and smiled. She was definitely a thinker.

"You're not on the list," she cooed at him. "I have to ask why?"

"I'd prefer to wait until we're standing in the stone circle. Though I don't fear pain. I'd rather the alternative that exists." Maon watched her eyes. He was judging her reaction. He was coming to the point where he was growing tired of her games and he was considering just taking her and putting her in her place.

She let an amused grin play about her lips. She needed to make the entire pack stronger. But not stronger than she would be. If Maon was turned in the stone circle then he'd be stronger than her, since he was starting out stronger. That might put a dent in her plan if he chose to be difficult. She still needed him. "If there were anyone I would trust that much it would be you," she cooed at him.

He smiled. He wasn't stupid enough to think that was a promise. "They don't know that there is an alternative to what they've been shown?"

"As you said. We showed them Devon. They know about what it will do. But they're all willing to endure the pain for the end result. I will warn you that there are a significant number of our own who don't like this. They're saying that Rafe fucked you up and this is proof that you've gone mad." He was blatant. He liked the idea of power as much as the rest. But he knew this would start a war with the Arnauk. There was no guarantee that the Tairneach would survive that. He was concerned that Jenna would destroy the pack before he could his hands on it. The only thing holding him to his current path was the fact that he wanted to mate with her so badly and he wanted her to be willing.

Jenna glared at him. "What right do they have?"

"Anyone can say as he likes. You're behavior is questionable. You're not above pack opinion. You haven't earned their respect yet. You were on your way. The way you helped to deal with Rafe certainly had them all looking at you differently. But most of them have been content to be allies with the Arnauk for centuries. Brennus arranged that. They respected him and his decisions. Starting a war with the Arnauk for no apparent reason has some of them concerned."

"Anything else," she asked angrily.

"We've managed some word on what's going on with Arnauk's mating. I told Terrick that if he gets us what we need to know then I'll give him access to the ultimate steroid. I promised him that he'd be stronger and faster than Cullen when it was done. He's suddenly become more helpful. Though it's still reluctant. When he asked for more details about what I meant I told him he'd find out if I got what I needed. So he told me what was going on at the Madadh-Allaidh Saobhaidh. He's only giving out information that we probably would manage to get in the long run. But at least we're getting reports of something. Apparently the Pack Council is turning the Arnauk mating into a circus. They've arranged for druids and others to be present due to the fact that the woman he's taking is one of them and the Council is setting up ties to the Circle." Maon watched her begin to seethe.

"How is it that the little galla seems to have come out of nowhere and gained more power in her short existence than I've been capable of gaining in a lifetime? She's not even lycan!" Jenna's eyes were on fire. She couldn't believe that Aislinn had not only managed to get Cullen Arnauk, but now the Pack Council. Jenna stood up and began pacing back and forth across the office. Her voice took on a deadly calm. "I want her dead. That's it. So when is the mating?"

"That is still being determined. But soon. They're already bringing people to the reservation. I know your intent is to disrupt the mating. But with the number of people who will be present that's looking more difficult. Wouldn't it be better to go in and make use of the stones when there isn't an entire army there?"

Jenna glared at him. "What kind of show of power would that be?"

* * * *

Keith and Malik walked into Cullen's office with smirks on their faces. Without a word Keith walked over to the nearest chair and plopped down then propped his feet on the edge of Cullen's desk, right on top of some papers Sarah had been writing on. Sarah looked as though she might rip his head off.

Cadifor shook his head. Keith and his blatant lack of concern for superiors was interesting. Cadifor gave him credit for appearing to know when to turn it on and off, but this wasn't one of those occasions.

Keith looked around at all the glaring people. Malik at least had the courtesy to wipe the smirk off his face. "Okay okay, I give in I'll tell. Guess why I can't find out when Jenna intends to attack." There were more glares. "All right I'll give you a hint."

"Keith," Cullen growled. "Enough."

Cadifor smirked this time. At Cullen's tone the look on Keith's face immediately vanished and he sat up in the chair. Sarah brushed the paperwork off and gave him the kind of amused look a big sister gets on her face when little brother is getting yelled at by dad.

"Sorry," Keith said. "I just find it amusing. From what I just found out it seems that the reason I haven't been able to track down when she intends to come over the border is because she's trying to find out when the mating ceremony is. I think her plan is to hit the ceremony. Turn about being fair play so to speak.

She's pissed that you and her got interrupted so she's looking for revenge. Actually when I stopped and thought about it I wondered why we hadn't come up with it in the first place."

Cullen sat back in his chair. "I wish I knew how to stop this. It's pointless. I had really hoped, after Rafe was dealt with, that Jenna had gotten a grip and would back off."

Keith shrugged. "Jenna's too much like her mother. In any case the rest of what I found out is that she's already started turning people. She's got a number of families in the pack looking to find shelter somewhere. I thought I'd ask you before I suggested we could offer asylum."

Cullen nodded. "We have too many ties with the Tairneach. Do we know how many of ours mated into their pack over the years?" Cullen looked at Sarah.

"I could find out. Do you really want to know," she asked.

"No. It was just a thought. Anyway. Yeah, offer asylum. But on the off chance that it's a trick keep them separate from our own for now. Anything else?"

Keith grinned again. "The best part. She knows we're importing people for the mating. But it seems that she intends to go ahead with the attack anyway. So she's either mad or stupid. At least that's what the Tairneach are saying. So, pick a good day for a fight. I'll leak the info. We'll be set."

Cadifor sat grumbling. "How did Brennus manage her?"

Malik cleared his throat. "I hate to point this out, but considering the information we were able to retrieve from the Tairneach and all the precautions I took with the information that left here with messengers and over the phones, I think it can be assumed that the Tairneach are getting their information from inside your pack."

Cullen growled. "That's why the elder were fed the story they were given. Keith, find out who. After all the caoch with Rafe I thought we had it taken care of."

Sarah looked at Cullen sympathetically. If there was one thing that could piss Cullen off this was it. He'd had too many issues with loyalty lately. "Cullen, there's a chance that the information wasn't leaked to cause trouble. You didn't tell anyone not to speak to the Tairneach about it. There are a lot of shared families, like you said. I could have just gotten out."

"That's what Keith is going to find out," Cullen said with emphasis.

* * * *

Aislinn and Makeda walked into the gym. They had managed to get and omega to produce sweatpants and t-shirts for them to wear. The two women walked around looking over the weights and other gym equipment. They decided they weren't interested in that kind of work out. They found their way to the big open area that was used for drills and sparring matches. There were blue mats lining the floors and walls. In one section of the room there was a virtual obstacle course of bars to climb on and over, making a fight more difficult. In another section there were ropes to climb and a simulated rock wall. But it was mostly open space with padding.

Makeda sat down and took her shoes and socks off. The t-shirt and sweatpants would adjust if she chose to shift but the shoes would be a problem. Aislinn followed her lead. Makeda was smiling widely as she watched Aislinn. "Ready?"

Aislinn nodded. The two of them paced around each other. Aislinn thought back to some self defense classes she had taken. "Do you want to practice anything in particular?" She wasn't exactly sure what she had intended now that they were in the middle of it.

Makeda's eyes suddenly turned golden. "How about a game of dog and cat," she growled through her accent as her body took on her hybrid form.

Aislinn stepped back and watched as the dark woman took on a form that was wolven but a great deal more lithe than the lycans she had met to date. Makeda's form was lanky but graceful. Her ears were much longer and higher on her head than the others and her muzzle was more narrow and longer. As Makeda finished her shift Aislinn realized that she looked a bit like Anubis in sweatpants and a t-shirt.

As Aislinn completed the thought Makeda jumped at her. Aislinn was rolled onto her back. *I thought you said that you weren't that bad at this. I'm not really trying here.*

"Sorry. I was staring and not paying attention at the same time. Gimme a chance."

Makeda got up off of her and crouched for another lunge attack. Aislinn started her shift and this time it was Makeda's turn to be fascinated. Makeda stared as Aislinn's face took on an indescript cat-like appearance, but retained most of the human features as well. Her eyes shifted to molten amber with blue flecks that gave them an almost iridescent green hue at times. Her arms were covered in spots and Makeda could see the spots dip into the front of her t-shirt.

Aislinn was quite proud of herself that she had managed to shift to her hybrid form with no trouble.

Makeda was not as easily knocked down as Aislinn had been however. Makeda stepped aside easily when Aislinn jumped at her. *And so it begins,* she said, her accent clear even in Aislinn's mind.

Neither woman paid attention to the audience they had attracted. A majority of the pack had never seen Aislinn shift and was curious about that alone. When word spread that Makeda was involved as well, there was an additional group that made their way down to the gym to see if the rumors about the ancient lycan were true.

* * * *

Cullen felt Aislinn shift. He knew she wasn't upset or in trouble. But it concerned him that she would be in a situation that cause her to change forms. He was trying to get a sense of what was happening to her but she was wrapped up in whatever it was and was concentrating enough that she wasn't open to a conversation.

"Cullen?"

He looked up at Cadifor's voice. "Sorry. What?"

Cadifor sighed. "Maybe it's time for a break. We've been at this all day. We missed lunch. How about an early dinner. I think we're mostly set anyway."

Cullen nodded and all the others in the room were looking hopeful at the suggestion. "I think I need to find Aislinn anyway." They saw Cullen's vision fog over again before he looked around the room. "Why don't we all meet in the Taigh-O\sda in half an hour."

There was an easy consensus and the group dispersed. Cadifor got up to go with Cullen. "Last I saw Makeda she had her eyes set on your woman. I believe I'll be most likely to find her still with Aislinn."

Cullen briefly wondered if Makeda was the reason for Aislinn's shift.

It didn't take long for Cullen and Cadifor to find out that Aislinn and Makeda were in the gym. Cullen and Cadifor got into the elevator and headed down.

Cadifor looked at Cullen with amused confusion. "Why do you look so concerned."

Cullen shrugged. "I don't know exactly."

"Truth. You've already mated the woman," Cadifor said knowingly and shaking his head. "What are you getting that's distracted you?"

Cullen looked at his friend. "I don't know why I thought it would be easy to hide something that was only in my own head."

Cadifor laughed. "Don't sound so insulted. I've been around a long time. I've know the bond twice over in different ways. Not every man will see it. But don't take me for a fool."

"Sorry. She shifted for some reason. She was having trouble with it. Until now apparently. But I can't get why she would do it. It's not like her. And she's in the gym?" Cullen looked at Cadifor. "It just doesn't make sense." Cullen sounded despondent.

"You're still dwelling on the possibility of a traitor in your pack. That's another thing I've endured. It's not so unusual, Cullen." Cadifor's voice took on a deadly serious note. "What makes you think you're so different from every other alpha that you'd command complete, unwavering loyalty from every man within your pack? You're only alpha until someone else beats you down." The elevator doors slid open. "That kind of incentive is not meant to breed loyalty."

Cullen walked into the hall. Cadifor was right. "It's the first I've had to deal with it here," he said flatly.

The men could hear cheering and commotion coming from down the hall. They looked at each other uncertainly and continued toward the gym. The crowd was so wrapped up in the show that they didn't notice the alphas' approach. Cullen growled and the people in the door moved so that he could get into the gym.

Aislinn and Makeda had found that they were more on equal footing than either of them had thought they would be. No sooner than one would pin the other then the first would be thrown. They had each gotten in some good hits that had resulted in torn clothes and some blood. But it was mostly superficial.

Aislinn had led Makeda over to the obstacles, hoping that Makeda wouldn't be as good at climbing as she was. Makeda was faster than Aislinn though and as Aislinn took to one of the higher bars in a leap that impressed Cullen and Cadifor both, Makeda grabbed at her leg. Makeda through Aislinn off balance just enough to keep her from making the higher bar. But she didn't have enough of a grip to get her down and only managed to come away with what was left of Aislinn's sweatpants.

Aislinn turned and a jungle cat growl warned Makeda back. But that wasn't nearly impressive enough to stop Makeda. Aislinn watched the lycan pace until Makeda came just within reach. Then she launched herself at Makeda, swinging off the bar in an acrobatic fashion that would have impressed an Olympic judge. She managed to get a hold of

Makeda's shoulders and the two of them hit the ground wrestling for the pin as the rolled across the matt.

The crowd cheered with each impressive move and bets were being made as to who would win. Cullen and Cadifor watched in amused silence. There was something more than a little erotic about watching the two beautiful women wrestle.

"How long should we let this continue," Cadifor asked through a wide grin, his eyes never leaving the women.

Cullen shrugged. He was suddenly feeling a great deal better. "I see no reason to stop them now. I'm curious who'll win. I wouldn't have thought she'd stand a chance against Makeda."

"Women often are full of surprises."

Makeda was on top of Aislinn when they rolled to a stop. Aislinn growled menacingly at her and tried to overpower her. But Makeda had won this time. She was straddling Aislinn at the waist and holding her wrists to the matt. Makeda's eyes gleamed as she stared down at Aislinn. Finally Aislinn stopped struggling. Makeda leaned down and ran her nose over Aislinn's sweat covered neck. Her tongue snaked out to taste Aislinn. Much to Cullen's amusement Aislinn was finding the caress exceedingly pleasurable.

The crowd could tell that the fight was over. Most of them began to disperse. Makeda's tongue traveled the line of Aislinn's jaw and Makeda caught the scent of Aislinn's arousal over the smell of sweat and gym mats.

Cullen smiled widely. He was tempted to let it continue. But he had promised to meet the others for lunch. And if she was going to play with Makeda Cullen knew that Aislinn would prefer privacy. She'd be upset if he let it continue with an audience. Cadifor gave an annoyed growl as Cullen headed for the women.

He looked back at his friend. "Not here," Cullen said. Cadifor rolled his eyes but backed off.

Cullen knelt next to the women. "If you're both finished. We came to take you to dinner."

Aislinn jumped as though she had been caught doing something wrong and blushed furiously as she looked up at Cullen.

Makeda sat back, releasing Aislinn's hands but not getting off of her and changed back to her human form. "You're no fun Cullen. It took me all morning and afternoon to get her to give in."

Aislinn pushed Makeda off of her and Makeda landed on her butt next to her on the floor. Her heart was racing. Aislinn looked from Makeda to Cullen as though she expected to be in trouble.

Cullen started to laugh. He could feel Aislinn's upset, embarrassment, and confusion. He put his hand under her chin and made her look into his eyes. *I'll not hold women against you. Especially if I get to watch.* His smile broadened. *I know your heart is mine. Calm down. Let's go to dinner.* He leaned in and kissed her, biting at her bottom lip before pulling away from her again and standing up.

"The both of you should go get cleaned up. You've got ten minutes. If you're not back from the showers by then we'll come after you," Cullen said. "Not that I think any of us would mind that, but there are a number of people waiting at the Taigh-Osda for us."

Chapter 23

Expecting is the greatest impediment to living. In anticipation of tomorrow, it loses today.
-Lucius Annaeus Seneca

Cullen decided that the less time Jenna had the better. Cadifor called in quite a few favors, but it looked as though they were going to pull it off. The group ate dinner, finished their phone calls, and the mating was set for the next day at sunset. Cullen sent as many lycans ahead to the reservation that evening as could be managed. The rest would follow the next day.

There was some argument as to whether Keith would be joining them. He refused to allow Jaylyn to leave the Madadh-Allaidh Saobhaidh, and he didn't want to leave her with just omegas to look after her. In the end she insisted that he go and leave her in peace for the night. She had her hands full with Eiros and Eira. Even so, Keith decided to remain behind with Jaylyn for as long as possible. Mostly he held her gently while she slept.

Eerie quiet permeated the den that night. Cullen, Cadifor, Aislinn, and Makeda sat with bottles and glasses in hand in the main room of the penthouse. Cullen and Cadifor laughed and told stories about situations they were in that had been worse than this. All the while, Makeda watched Aislinn hopefully and refilled her glass as it emptied.

When Aislinn stood shakily and walked away from the men Makeda followed her. "Are you all right?"

Aislinn ran her hand over her stomach and looked over at Cullen shaking her head. "I'm nervous. Uncertain. Have you ever done this before?"

"Mating? Yes. Once." A haunted look overtook Makeda for a moment. "A very long time ago. He's been lost to me for over a century now. No pity," Makeda said with a strange strength when Aislinn's features glazed with sympathy. "I choose to believe that what time we had was worth an eternity alone, if only for the memories we made."

Aislinn sighed, moving back to the original topic. "I don't like not knowing what to expect. And I especially don't like having to do a public performance."

"Why? What difference does it make if others watch? Will you behave differently? Do you think you might do something wrong?" Makeda was obviously amused.

Alcohol spun the room gently around Aislinn. "I don't know. I'm just not ready for this."

Makeda stepped closer to her, and Aislinn laid her head on Makeda's shoulder. "You're ready. You're stronger than you think," she said and started stroking Aislinn's hair.

Aislinn looked up. Makeda's hand traveled down her back, sending shivers along Aislinn's spine. Aislinn could hear Cadifor and Cullen laughing in the background. The small distraction did little to quell the building excitement. Between the wine and Makeda, she felt like she was on fire.

Smiling at the look in Aislinn's eyes, Makeda leaned closer. "How drunk are you?"

"Not as drunk as I should be for what I'm thinking, but drunk enough for it to look like an excellent excuse," she said softly.

Makeda's eyes sparkled as she placed a hand on Aislinn's cheek and kissed her. Aislinn responded much more eagerly than Makeda expected. Aislinn caressed Makeda's cheek and her hand slid back into Makeda's hair as her lips parted and Makeda's tongue stroked her lips asking for entrance.

Cullen and Cadifor were so engrossed in their conversation that they missed it at first. Arousal flowing through Cullen's mind, suddenly caught his attention. It was strange to feel Aislinn excited and not be part of the reason. Cullen looked over at the two women standing near the fireplace. Sitting farther back in his chair, he nodded in their direction.

Cadifor followed Cullen's gaze. He chuckled and shook his head. "Leave it to Makeda. I've never able to tell her no. Seems like Aislinn's having trouble with that as well. You gonna stop it this time?"

Cullen shook his head. "As long as she's okay with it, I don't see a reason to stop it." He leaned forward as Makeda's hands began to work their way beneath Aislinn's shirt.

Aislinn's skin was burning up. When Makeda's fingers pressed the flesh along her waist, pulling Aislinn closer, she let a soft moan escape into Makeda's mouth. They stopped kissing and gazed into each other's eyes. Molten amber met glowing gold and the two of them smiled. Aislinn bit playfully at Makeda's lips, then stepped back and pulled her shirt off. She dropped it on the floor, and much to everyone's surprise, she took Makeda by the hand and headed for the bedroom.

A sense of incredible disappointment stopped her as she reached the doorway. She turned to Cullen, who was watching them head for the bedroom with a frustrated look on his face. She glanced questioningly at Makeda, and the two of them started laughing. "Well come on then," she said to Cullen. Then she looked at Makeda and doubt seeped into her features.

Easily reading Aislinn's concern, Makeda reassured her. "So there aren't any ground rules," she said, as the two men eagerly approached. "Cullen keeps himself to you. And Cadifor can wait until he's invited. I've got not claims to him. He can do as he likes." She gave him a warning gaze. "But I suggest he stick to known territory for now."

Cadifor laughed and threw his hands up. "If I'm not wanted," he started.

Feeling Aislinn's uncertainty, Cullen nearly suggested that he and Cadifor could go downstairs for a while. Aislinn shook her head at the unspoken thought. "I'd rather someone show me what's going to happen tomorrow." Cullen knew she didn't necessarily like the idea, still she would rather know exactly what she was in for.

"I think we can handle that," he answered.

Nodding resolutely, Aislinn turned and walked into the bedroom, pulling Makeda happily along behind her. Cullen and Cadifor stood back while the women undressed each other, kissing again. Makeda did her best to remind Aislinn why she originally thought this was a good idea.

Aislinn pulled Makeda's shirt over her head and kissed the bare skin on her shoulders as Makeda unhooked Aislinn's bra. Slowly, in between caresses, the rest of the women's clothing found its way to the floor. Aislinn's lips traveled down Makeda's collar bone and then to her breast. When she reached Makeda's hard nipple she ran her tongue around the bud before drawing it into her mouth to suck and bite it, causing hungry growls to bleed from Makeda's lips.

The scent of arousal emanated through the room. Makeda pulled Aislinn down onto the bed, sparing a wicked glance at the men, as she straddled Aislinn's waist and pinned her down. Not that Aislinn was putting up a struggle. Makeda stroked the flesh around Aislinn's breasts, working her way in gentle touches to her nipples. She pinched the hard knots viciously, as she leaned in to capture Aislinn's moan with her mouth.

The kissing and touching took a sudden needy turn. Aislinn rolled Makeda to her back and knelt above Makeda's head. Leaning down she bit playfully at Makeda's thighs. Makeda pulled on Aislinn's hips, as Aislinn pressed her legs apart, taking in Makeda's musky arousal. Makeda's spicy hot scent seeped into Aislinn's senses as she leaned in to taste Makeda.

Wanton growling filled the room as Makeda pulled Aislinn's sex to her mouth. Tongues danced in wet folds. Aislinn pressed a finger, and then two, into Makeda's open slit. Growling escaladed, as they took turns sucking on each other's clits.

Cullen and Cadifor didn't know how long to hold back. They stood there watching and tentatively stroking themselves, while the women licked and sucked each other. Cadifor was the one who gave in first, mostly because he was less concerned for Aislinn's reluctance than the others were. He knelt on the bed between Makeda's legs.

The movement drew Aislinn's attention, and she looked up to see Cadifor's strange, foggy golden eyes staring down at her. His rock hard member was in his hand while he stroked Aislinn's hair. Cullen stood by, considering what he would do if Aislinn changed her mind. Aislinn sat up a bit, seeing Cadifor move closer. He watched Aislinn with amusement, as she stared down at his cock, pushing into Makeda. Aislinn felt a rumbling vibration against her clit, as Makeda growled her pleasure at the intrusion of Cadifor's cock. Aislinn closed her eyes and felt the delicious sensation surge through her.

Cadifor growled as he moved in Makeda, then he leaned down and whispered into Aislinn's ear. "You don't have to stop. She loves it when someone licks her clit."

Aislinn stared down at the man's huge cock sliding slowly in and out of Makeda's pussy. It had to be one of the most erotic things she had ever seen. She leaned back down and let her tongue stroke Makeda's clit. There was no real way to go about it without taking in Cadifor's scent or brushing the base of his cock as her fucked her. The taste of Makeda's sex mingled with Cadifor and Aislinn found that it was much more pleasant than she originally thought it would be.

Having established that he wouldn't have to come to Aislinn's rescue, Cullen found himself the only one left out. He stepped up to the edge of the bed where Aislinn was kneeling and felt Makeda's tongue snake up to taste the pre-cum on his cock. Her tongue dragged along his length as he pushed into Aislinn. Cullen couldn't help the moan of pleasure that escaped as he filled her.

The scent of sex flooded the room as the men thrust into the women. Overwhelmed, Aislinn took in the taste, the smell and the feel of the entire situation. It was nothing like she thought it would be. She was the first one to give into the building pleasure. She felt it building deep in her stomach. Between the assault on her senses from watching Cadifor pound into Makeda as she tasted it and feeling Makeda's tongue lap at her clit as Cullen thrust into, her she couldn't hold back. Cullen growled as he felt Aislinn's body tense in his hands, and her orgasm surge through his mind.

Aislinn cried out, and Cullen held her trembling body up to keep her from collapsing on top of Makeda. He pulled her up so that her back was against his chest as he continued to pound up into her. Makeda pushed a growling Cadifor back so that she could turn around and give him a better angle. Cadifor grabbed a hold of her hips roughly when she stood on her hands and knees in front of him. He plunged in again and began driving into her harder than before.

Makeda growled and moved forward so that she could get to Aislinn. There was a brief struggle between as Cadifor tried to pull her back to himself for better leverage, and she tried to move forward to play with Aislinn as he fucked her. Makeda won the contest of wills and Cadifor gave in, moving forward on the bed.

Aislinn moaned and wiggled as Makeda leaned down and tongued her clit again. Wave after wave of pleasure washed over Aislinn, and she held onto the arm which Cullen had wrapped around her chest, supporting her. Makeda reached up and began stroking the base of Cullen's cock with one hand as he thrust into Aislinn. The growling and moaning got louder and louder as the four of them moved closer to their climaxes.

Out of control, Cullen started to shift, his wolf surging forward. Somewhere in the haze of sex rushing through her, Aislinn heard him in her mind. She only barely registered what he was saying to her. *This is what will happen tomorrow night,* he growled.

Aislinn could feel him swelling inside her. His thrusts became more manic. Aislinn had long since lost the ability to do anything beyond moan incoherently through the pleasure onslaught. She felt his claws dig into her body and then his mouth on her shoulder. Cullen bit down on her when he started to come. Blood rushed into his mouth as Aislinn cried out and came again. Her body jerked in his arms. Makeda rolled away from Cadifor, and he pulled out of her jerking madly on his cock before spraying cum across her stomach. Makeda moaned happily and ran a finger through the mess he made before putting it in her mouth.

Cadifor grinned at Makeda then looked hungrily at the other couple. Cullen and Aislinn were still trembling and clinging to one another. From the look of things Cadifor guessed that he and Makeda were done here for the night. He crawled across the bed, shifting into a large snow white wolf. Aislinn looked at the beautiful animal as it approached her. Cullen was licking at the wound he created on her shoulder and was ignoring Cadifor. He sniffed at Aislinn's sex. Cullen was still inside her and would be for some time yet, but Cadifor didn't seem to care. His tongue snaked out, and he ran it along the join between the two, tasting the mixed scents. A rumble of approval issued from his chest, and then he turned and jumped down from the bed.

Makeda watched the two of them collapse on the bed, Cullen wrapping himself possessively around Aislinn. He was already trying to coax her into round two, and Aislinn wasn't putting up much of a fight against it. They gave the obvious impression that the other couple wasn't invited to the next session of fun though.

For a short time, Makeda watched as Cullen, in his hybrid form, pulled Aislinn to her knees again. She was this tiny little thing beneath the large dark lycan, but she was certainly holding her own against him. Makeda smiled and went to join Cadifor, making a mental note to coax Aislinn into another couples night before they left. Cadifor grabbed her roughly and pulled her to the floor with him, Makeda laughing and letting him have his way.

"Again?" He growled into her ear, and she grinned.

"Let's leave them alone," she said, pushed him off of her and grabbed her clothes up off of the floor, while he chased her around the room.

* * * *

The only calm part of the day was the drive to the reservation. Cadifor left his motorcycle at the den in favor of riding in the SUV with Cullen and Aislinn. At first, Aislinn refused to look at the couple in the back seat, and Tension radiated from her. She was nervous about interacting with Cadifor and Makeda after what happened the night before. But when it became clear that she was the only one concerned about it, she quickly reverted back to herself. It amused Cullen to see that she almost instantly began flirting with Makeda when she calmed down.

Upon arrival at the reservation, everyone showered and changed. Cullen and Cadifor were both barefoot, wearing black suit pants and black button up shirts as well as black suit jackets. They were definitely more dressed up than they usual, but the shirts weren't tucked in or completely buttoned up. They gave Aislinn the impression of groomsmen at a human wedding, at the end of the reception after they'd all eaten and drank too much and made themselves comfortable for the night. The only difference was that they weren't drunk or disheveled, just not completely put together. Aislinn found it to be an incredibly sexy look.

Cullen pulled her against his chest and kissed her deeply. "Don't get too used to it. I don't like dress clothes, and clothes never last long at ceremonies like this anyway." He smiled at her. "This is for greeting the guests."

Makeda pushed Cullen away from Aislinn. "He has something else especially for you, but that will come later." Her eyes sparkled. Turning, she began shooing Cullen and Cadifor toward the door. "Go. You both have jobs to do. We'll be down shortly."

"I just have one thing to get," Cullen said and walked over to the bag of clothing he'd brought in from the car.

As if on cue, there was a knock on the door, it opened, and Sarah and Drake walked in. Drake was dressed exactly like Cullen and Cadifor. Sarah wore a black silky black dress which clung perfectly to her curves. A small clip held her hair up and a few loose curls hung around her face. She carried a duffle bag over one shoulder, and she walked into the room with a serious determined look on her face. Sarah always seemed to be on a mission. Drake stood, watching her with adoration in his eyes and his hands in his pockets as she began to pull things out of the bag. Cullen walked over to Sarah and left a small black box with her. Then he looked up and smiled at Aislinn.

Makeda shooed the men out the door impatiently, before joining Sarah in looking over the things in the bag. Curiosity pulled Aislinn up behind them, and she tried to peek around them. "What are the two of you up to?"

"We're getting you ready for the ceremony," Sarah said, smiling over her shoulder at Aislinn.

"I thought I was supposed to be naked and on display," Aislinn said wryly. What she'd seen of Jenna's mating involved nearly everyone being naked. She scowled as she remembered watching Cullen get a blow job from Jenna.

Sarah turned around, raised her eyebrows and crossed her arms. "That's fine too. If you just want to get undressed now and walk around like that all night I won't stop you. No one around here will think anything of it. You're the one I thought was modest."

Makeda chuckled at that and gave Aislinn a knowing look. "She's not so modest when given the correct motivation," Makeda said, and stroked Aislinn's arm as she went over to her own bag to pull out a beautiful black lace dress covered in delicate flowers woven on with golden threads. It was nearly see through. Upon a short inspection of the beautiful garment Makeda began shedding clothes.

Aislinn looked at Sarah with embarrassment, and Sarah laughed. "Why wasn't I invited?"

Makeda smiled over her shoulder at Sarah. "We've time now," she suggested in a teasing tone. "Especially if Aislinn doesn't want to dress for the evening. I tell you what," her eyes brightened and a golden swirl showed in their depths, "I'll not-dress with you." She tossed the dress on the bed as if it were a rag and stood there proudly naked in front of the other two women.

Aislinn's face fell instantly. "All right I'll be cooperative," she pouted and began examining the things Sarah unloaded from the bag. "You didn't tell me about this."

Sarah started to grumble. "You spend too much time worrying about the small details. You can't expect me to be able to educate you on all the things that people start learning as children. I'm not that good. I never remember everything that we do different from humans. Besides. This is relatively similar to a normal wedding. You, the bride or whatever, has to dress for the party. I told you about the parts that I thought you were concerned with."

"Sorry," Aislinn said. "I don't mean to be a pain. I'm just nervous."

Scowling at Sarah, Makeda came up behind Aislinn, setting a hand on Aislinn's shoulder reassuringly. "It's your mating ceremony. It's your prerogative to be a pain."

Sarah smiled again. "Come on. It won't be as bad as you think. I have to admit; when Cullen first started things with you I truly didn't think it was a good idea. There you were, this headstrong non-lycan with weird connections to problems. But, you are a good match for him. It's obvious when anyone looks at you. Just think about him and don't worry about who's watching. You'll be fine."

Aislinn took a deep breath. "All right. What do you need me to wear?"

Sarah went back to pulling things out of the bag, and Makeda went over to the bed to retrieve her own dress. Sarah produced a long black silk dress. It was incredibly simple. The front was a halter that would leave Aislinn's back completely bare. It dipped low enough in the back that Aislinn was afraid it might not manage to cover her butt completely. The dress would fall all the way to the floor and pool just a bit at Aislinn's feet. She began to undress so that she could pull the dress on.

"Don't go so fast. First your hair and make-up," Sarah said and ushered her over to the edge of the bed. Sarah and Makeda each grabbed makeup and hairbrush respectively, causing Aislinn to grumble a bit more as the women proceeded to fuss over her.

"This is ridiculous. I don't wear makeup like this," she groused. "He's just going to mess it up anyway."

"You said you were going to cooperate," Sarah warned.

Aislinn growled in response, and the other two women laughed. After some time, they were satisfied with her face and her hair. Aislinn managed to convince them to leave it down. "It's either a pony tail or long. My hair won't stay up in twists or whatever else you want to do to it."

They let her win that one. Aislinn allowed a curling iron, but ultimately her hair lay in long brown waves down her back. When they stepped back and gave her a satisfied look, Aislinn got up and went after the dress again.

"Don't put it on yet." Sarah held up the box that Cullen gave her before he had left. "Cullen picked these out for you," she smiled. "Let's see if he has any taste," she added as she held out the black velvet box.

Aislinn's stomach fluttered a bit. He'd never given her a present before. She wished he had given it to her himself instead of leaving it with Sarah. She opened the lid on the black box to see a great deal of white gold and diamonds.

"They're beautiful," Aislinn said in awe, breathing again.

Sarah made Aislinn put the box down so that she could help her put the jewelry on. There were quite a few pieces. They were all made of heavy, loose fitting, white gold rope chains that had diamonds dangling from different lengths of smaller delicate chains. It looked almost as if it was raining diamonds from the heavy chain. There was one for her ankle, one to wear around her waist, and one for around her neck. There were barrettes for her hair as well. That resulted in a great deal more fussing. They were all fitted loosely enough that they wouldn't be broken when Aislinn shifted into her hybrid form.

"It's considered bad luck," Sarah explained. "Not to mention it would really suck to mess this set up." She held up her skirt so that Aislinn could see the golden chain around her ankle. It was simple and very pretty. "Drake bought this one for me when we were mated. He didn't quite have the resources that Cullen does though."

Aislinn looked at herself in the mirror. The effect was stunning. Light danced off the diamonds, sending white dots of refracted light around the room. Her heart was beating a mile a minute. Both Sarah and

Makeda could see her nerves failing her again. The jewelry scared her. *I'm not really in his league,* she thought. *I can be dressed up. But this isn't me.* Aislinn felt a strange calm from the back of her mind reassuring her.

Cullen, she asked him. *Are you sure you want me? I mean. This is so much.*

Cullen was talking to a small group of men he had just been introduced to. Taking a sip from his drink, he tried to send Aislinn as much reassurance as he could. *Calm down. It's a little late for you to change your mind. That conversation should have taken place before the last time we were here.*

Aislinn could feel how amused he was that she was this nervous. *Cullen,* she started, but didn't even know what she was thinking.

He answered something that someone asked him, but it wasn't quite the right answer. He cleared his throat and took another drink out of his cup, looking around the room so he wouldn't have to participate in the conversation he should be having. *My love, I want you more than I could ever say in words. And I hope you want me. You don't have to come down here. I know I'm asking a lot of you in this and I didn't even really discuss the situation with you. It's up to you.* Cullen's worry shifted at that point from the possibility of Jenna's attack to the reality that Aislinn was just nervous enough to bolt.

Aislinn could feel his entire train of thought shift from Jenna and how the woman dominated his mind for days now to being scared to death that she was going to leave him, that he pushed too much on her in too little time, and that she didn't want him enough to be capable of putting up with his life. *I'm not going anywhere. I love you too much for that*, she told him. Still she could tell that her reassurance didn't help his new upset. He wasn't sure he believed her. Aislinn decided that she needed to hurry.

Makeda and Sarah could see the vague distance in her eyes and knew she was having a private conversation. From the look on her face, it was serious enough to leave her be until it was over.

Suddenly Aislinn's vision seemed to clear, and a new resolve over-took her features. "Are we almost done?"

"Yeah," Sarah said. "Are you okay?"

Aislinn took a deep breath. "No. But I will be. I want to go down and see Cullen. You guys don't do that bride before the wedding bullshit do you?"

"No," Sarah said, concern by the new tone in Aislinn's.

"So then I can put the dress on now?"

"Yeah."

Sarah and Makeda exchanged concerned glances, but helped her put the dress on over her hair and jewelry so that it wouldn't be caught. The black silk clung to her hips and breasts and any other body part that curved. Aislinn looked herself over in the mirror. The halter dipped low between her breasts in front and just grazed the sides. The skirt clung to her hips and legs and flared past her knees to pool on the floor about her feet. She walked away from the mirror a bit, and then turned to look at her back in the mirror. There were a few folds of the dress that sat just above her butt and left her entire back and lower back bare, except for the white gold and diamonds. She had to admit it was impressive.

"It's too bad I'm not better at controlling my shifting," she said softly.

Makeda was confused by that. "What?"

"I've only been able to do it a short time. I'm not very good at it. Cullen likes the stripes and spots. I've seen him just change parts. So I guess I was thinking it's a shame that I couldn't just have the markings, bare back and all. Thing is, I don't really want to do the cat thing yet and it's pretty much an all or nothing process with me."

Makeda grinned. "I didn't know you had stripes. I've only seen parts of you in lighted rooms," she chuckled.

Aislinn couldn't help but smile at that. And the women got another amused look from Sarah.

"I agree. That would definitely add to the affect," Sarah said. "But unfortunately it really is a learning process. I don't think I'm able to just tell you how." She held out one hand and shifted it to a clawed paw then back again. "It's not easy to describe," she said contemplatively.

Aislinn walked over to Sarah and hugged her. Sarah didn't know exactly how to react. When Aislinn let her go she looked at the surprised woman. "I just wanted to say thanks."

Sarah smiled back. "Well, I think we're ready then. Would you like to make an entrance or just appear in the crowd?"

"I'm not the entrance making type."

Makeda shook her head. "Oh but you could be." Makeda was eying Aislinn wantonly. "Too bad," she sighed, "you're not for me tonight." Grinned wickedly, she walked to the door. "We'll go with you. Are you ready?"

Aislinn nodded and reached down to pick up the front of her skirt. The three women walked across the balcony and down the large staircase that descended to the main room. Sarah and Makeda walked just behind and beside Aislinn. There were enough people coming and going on the staircase at that moment that no one in the main room noticed the group as being any different from the rest of the crowd. There were quite a few beautiful women in the cabin that night.

Aislinn looked over the gathered people in the room below them. There were very few people who weren't dressed in black. Even the druids were in suits or gowns. The women who weren't in black were obviously trying to draw attention. There was a red-head in a fire red dress, surrounded by numerous men.

Makeda laughed and pointed to the woman over the rail of the staircase. "I'll not tell you her name, so that when you do meet her you'll be able to say honestly you've not heard of her. That will drive her crazy. Be sure to mention knowing me during the conversation." Makeda's eyes sparkled mischievously. It was strange, but that little joke was enough to make Aislinn feel much better. Perhaps it wasn't as scary out here as she thought it would be.

Cullen and Cadifor were talking with a small group of alphas from outside of Cadifor's territory. Cullen was doing his best to look like he was enjoying himself. The last twenty minutes had been pure misery. He wasn't sure if Aislinn would be joining them or not.

Makeda and Sarah were pleased and impressed to see that even if Aislinn was upset she was managing to look every bit the part of alpha mate. It was an important skill that not everyone could manage, bottling feelings when appropriate for appearances.

Aislinn felt guilty for having upset him so badly. She led the way through the people in the main room. Heads turned as members of the pack recognized them and pointed them out to others who didn't know Aislinn.

Cadifor saw them before Cullen did. When Aislinn's eyes met Cadifor's he bowed his head to her slowly, as if he was mesmerized. Cullen and every other alpha in the group turned to see what or who had earned that great of a compliment from Cadifor.

Cullen thought his heart might stop. Aislinn approached him with cat-like grace, gliding across the floor between people in the crowd. Without hesitation she ran her hands up his chest and over his shoulders, pulled him down to her level and kissed him. Cullen slid his hands over her bare back and held her to himself as he passionately returned the fiery kiss.

Cullen, Aislinn broke the kiss, breathless, and pressed her forehead to his. *Tá brón orm. Tá grá agam duit. I'll do whatever you need me to do. Anything.* She told him emphatically and kissed him again.

The group who had been talking with Cullen watched the pair kiss and exchanged amused grins. Some of the men had women standing with them, but most of them were alone. There was some joking about not being able to wait as Aislinn kissed Cullen. Finally he pushed her away gently, before things got out of hand. Aislinn bit her lip and looked into his eyes. He was all right now. She smiled, having accomplished what she ultimately wanted.

"Tá tú iontach álainn," he said, bowing his head to her. Very few people ever gained that compliment from an alpha, and Cullen could see how she had managed to get it from Cadifor. There wasn't another woman in the room who Cullen believed could outshine Aislinn tonight.

"It's all the diamonds," she said and gave him a hard look that told him he had taken it too far.

"I never get to have any fun," he replied and flashed her a devilish grin. "Besides, no one will even notice the diamonds if you continue to smile like that."

The group Cullen had been talking with started to return to the conversation. They didn't know if Cullen would be rejoining them or not. "A man can only take so much blatant affection," someone said loudly and eliciting more laughter.

Cullen gazed back at the group and then to Aislinn again. "All right. They'll return you to me when it's time. For now you're supposed to be mingling with the rest." He ran a finger along her jaw and his thumb over her lip. She kissed it before turning away.

Makeda and Sarah led her off through the crowd to introduce her to leaders from other packs she would have to know. Cullen watched her disappear into the crowd before he returned to the conversation, a little out of place. The next few hours turned into a political chess game, and Aislinn was grateful that Makeda and Sarah were close at hand to help her with it all.

Cullen's eyes traveled the room. Most of the people here had no idea how much danger would be coming that evening. Cullen wasn't sure whether he should hope for Jenna to get a grip and leave them be, or if he should hope she would just attack and be done with it. The worst case scenario would be for her to decide to come to her senses enough to not attack tonight, but plan for a different night instead. Cadifor reassured Cullen that if the attack didn't come, then they would use the night as it was set up, a diplomatic meeting, and worry about the next move later. Mostly Cullen was hoping that Jenna wasn't bitch enough to use the beginning of the ceremony itself as her cue to attack, knowing full well that it was the most likely scenario.

Cullen and Cadifor were standing to the side of the crowd, in one of the rare moments that they weren't surrounded by a bunch of people. "The part that bothers me the most," he said quietly, "is that there are so many strange faces here, Jenna could have her men in the middle of this room, and there's no guarantee I'd notice."

Cadifor clapped his friend on the shoulder. "Stop worrying," he said quietly. "We're as prepared as we can get. The alphas are aware of the situation. They'll keep tabs on their own. Yours are still wary from the last time. We're ready for this. Enjoy the moment. When have you ever seen this many alphas in a room getting along? And druids as well," he said, as excitement tinged his voice. "Our time is changing before your eyes Cullen. This is perhaps the most exciting party I've attended in centuries. I, for one, am thinking that this may need to become a regular thing."

Cullen had to admit that Cadifor was right on that count. He looked around. The place was nearly a United Nations convention due to the different groups that Cadifor had invited. Some of them had even flown in from different Council member's territories in order to meet the druids. Cullen knew that any number of the alphas who came had come *only* to meet the druids and because of the need to understand the newest danger in their world. Still, the men and women were all mingling and there had been no angry outbreaks or threats. Cadifor made it amply clear when the invitations went out that this was to be a friendly evening, and he would personally deal with anyone who made his friend's mating ceremony into a brawling match, outside of the possible attack that is. They all appeared to be staying true to their word.

Evening steadily approached, and people began to discard clothing. The smart ones had already left shoes and extraneous items in their cars, so that they'd be able to find their things come morning. Others were delivering things to their cars, in anticipation of what was to come.

Malik approached Cullen and Cadifor, "I was briefed on how the evening should go, but there are a number of others who wish to know if they are permitted to make use of the stone circle before your ceremony begins."

Cullen looked at Malik with concern. "What do they want to do?"

"Bless the event." Malik's gaze was unwavering. "It's one of our traditions, and I must admit that none of them had thought they would feel inclined to do it. However, after having observed you all night long they feel as though they wish to participate. Consider it a gift, and an act of good will for our joint future."

Cullen spared Cadifor a questioningly glance. He nodded. "This is supposed to be a joining of the druids with the lycans." He smiled at Cullen's flat affect, knowing Cullen didn't like that his mating to Aislinn had taken such a dramatic political turn.

"Is anything required of me or Aislinn," he asked.

"No. However, you may wish to be present. It should be beautiful to watch." Malik bowed in thanks and disappeared to tell the others that he had received permission.

Cadifor sent a couple omegas to tell the alphas that the druids were going to demonstrate a ceremony for them if they wished to be present. Cullen and Cadifor didn't have any trouble finding their women. They just followed the trail of moon-eyed young males.

Chapter 24

Behold a worthy sight, to which the God, turning his attention to his own work, may direct his gaze. Behold an equal thing, worthy of a God, a brave man matched in conflict with evil fortune.
-Lucius Annaeus Seneca

Maon's mind churned miserably with concern and distaste for the situation he was in. Jenna worked her way through the woods. He followed close behind, debating whether she was worth the amount of trouble she caused. *Sure she's beautiful*, he told himself. He used to think she was brilliant, not to mention his wolf wanted her in a way that drove him mad. *Even so, this is insane,* he argued with himself.

The men who took advantage of Jenna's offer to become dire wolves shifted to hybrid form before they left the manor. *Jenna wouldn't want too many others to see the pain and hear the screams*, he thought with distaste. *Still, they are impressive.* The dires slunk through the shadows ahead of them, barely managing to remain unseen due to their size.

In the end, Jenna had approved twenty four for her special project. Nineteen men and five women took advantage of the opportunity to make themselves into what Jenna was calling the future of the alpha. *And not one has questioned why Jenna has yet to take the form herself. Perhaps the Tairneach aren't as intelligent as I have always believed.* Maon couldn't decide if he was angry at the pack for not being smart enough to see through the woman, or if he was angry at himself for not being able to resist her.

Maon adjusted the bag on his back which contained the bottles of mixtures that the druids needed. He listened to the carefully wrapped glass clink together in the pack on his back as they slunk through the woods toward the Arnauk cabin. He wondered how many alphas were there, how many druids were there and if they had any idea what was coming. Maon was fairly certain that no number of alphas was going to be capable of competing with the twenty-four dires he was leading in. His concern was with the fact that they were about to disrupt an event that appeared to be being sponsored by the Pack Council.

When Maon voiced his concern with going against the Council Jenna cooed at him and stroked his chest the way that always managed to make anything she said sound more reasonable. "So kill Cadifor and take his place on the Council," she'd said. "After what Rafe did the Council is ignorant to want to bring druids into their trust. You'll be saving the Pack Council from a monumental mistake if we manage to break this up. They'll thank you."

Maon growled. In hindsight he wasn't sure it sounded as good as it had in the office. *It's a little late for rethinking it all now*, he chastised himself.

Cullen planned the mating for nightfall. Darkness already enveloped the woods that covered the Arnauk reservation, even though the sun was yet to set completely. The Tairneach were nearing their goal. If Cullen took his time with the mating, they would have ample opportunity to interrupt the ceremony, kill Aislinn and use the stone circle to turn himself and Jenna into the much improved version of the twenty-four lycans who were making it all possible. The rest of the pack was trailing behind with the druids who would perform the ritual.

Maon watched Jenna move around another bush. They were getting close enough that people needed to start watching for stray couples playing in the woods before the ceremony. This was it. There wouldn't be another chance. If Jenna didn't succeed, the pack would replace her one way or another. If Maon wanted Jenna and the pack, this was going to have to work. He kept going over the situation in his head. They had the strength to counter the Arnauk numbers. *This should work*, he growled in frustration. *Something just doesn't feel right.*

* * * *

Malik examined the gathered lycans with the eye of a scientist. A rare smile barely touched his lips. *They don't trust us yet. This should help to put their minds at ease*, he thought. He was pleased that the others decided to bless the mating, if only to show the people here that Rafe was an exception and not the rule to their kind.

Malik noted with pleasure that Cullen and Aislinn choose to attend the blessing, and he motioned to them. "It's not necessary. So please feel no obligation. As the couple to be joined, even if it isn't the way we would conduct the ceremony," he added, clearing his throat, "you could stand in the center." Malik indicated the stone slab at the middle of the circle.

Spying Cadifor nearby, Cullen waited for direction expectantly. "Trust them," Cadifor said. "That's the only way this alliance is going to go anywhere."

Cullen took Aislinn's hand in his and lifted it to his lips, before leading her toward the stone circle. Aislinn briefly hesitated. She cleared her mind and prayed that the circle wouldn't act the same way it did the last time she was here. She could just imagine what Cullen would do if she disappeared again.

As Cullen and Aislinn approached the entire circle seemed to surge with palpable energy. Any lycan standing nearby could feel it. A druid stood in front of each of the stones and they watched each other expectantly as they waited for the couple to step onto the slab. Aislinn was just relieved that nothing traumatic happened when she passed the perimeter of the Circle.

Malik ceremoniously stepped toward them. He stared into Aislinn's eyes. She seemed so innocent as she stared back at him. *She doesn't even realize how attuned to her this place is*, Malik mused. "I believe you may be favored by the Fates."

Aislinn assumed it was part of the blessing. "Should I thank you?"

Malik's eyes beamed with curiosity. "I wonder what the day will be like, when you truly come to understand," he replied cryptically. Noting the uncertain, unhappy shifting in Cullen's stance Malik decided that this was his cue to return to his place. *The Fates will bring her to understand, if and when they chose to. Tonight is not the time for lessons of that kind*, he decided.

There didn't seem to be any kind of signal. In unison, the druids began singing. Haunting voices carried over the crowd and everyone stopped to listen. Gaelic words in harmonic tones echoed through the woods. "Móran làithean dhuit is sìth, Le d'mhaitheas is le d'nì bhi fàs."

The sweet words enchanted the listeners. They all felt like they knew the song from somewhere, but they couldn't quite place it. On the third chorus of the beautiful melody, the druids who were outside of the stone circle began to sing as well, and the whole of the wood seemed to sway with the captivating song. Suddenly lights began to flicker about the stone circle.

Blinking to clear her vision, Aislinn glanced around to see if anyone else had noticed. The mesmerizing song made her feel a bit sleepy as she listened. It was as though she wanted to close her eyes and get lost in voices and harmony. Then the strange lights flickered again. Then again.

The druids raised their voices, and the lights flickered longer and longer until finally the clearing was filled with fluttering faeries. They flitted from stone to stone as though they were curious where they were. Slowly they all gathered within the circle. The beautiful creatures fluttered and hovered like humming birds. They were all different sizes, but none larger than a rosebud. Glowed like starlight, they left sparkling trails as they danced about the clearing and the stones. There was no counting them or seeing exactly what they looked like. As the song progressed, some hovered just long enough to see a body with wings, before the beautiful ball of light would flit off in a different direction.

Enchanted couldn't even begin to describe how Aislinn felt. She had never seen anything so beautiful in her life. Seeing one of the faeries fly closer, she held up her hand with her palm up to see if the little light would come to her. It darted and danced about her head and she thought she could almost hear it whispering to her.

As the singing slowed and quieted, the lights began to flicker again until they vanished with the end of the song. The lycans stood still and enraptured by what they saw. No one knew if they should applaud or thank the druids. Malik and the others exchanged pleased glances, and each of them in turn approached Cullen and Aislinn, kissed Aislinn on the cheek and wished her long life, children, and happiness.

Malik was the last of them. "I've never seen so many of them come to our song," he said. "You must have a fair number of gentry living here. It shows your care for this place and each other."

Aislinn smiled at him, curiosity evident in her eyes. "I don't understand. They live here?"

"They live everywhere," Malik replied, having to hold himself back from a more detailed explanation. "But prefer places like this. They came to listen to the song. They don't always." Malik kissed Aislinn's cheek and bowed to her the way the lycans had been doing. Then he walked away as the others had done.

* * * *

The Tairneach thought they were imagining it at first. They could hear singing echoing though the woods. It was beautiful, almost like a church choir in a cathedral, and a number of them stopped to listen without realizing it. Jenna thought she was losing her mind when the lights started to dance about the woods. They were too far off to make out, but there were definitely lights.

Maon caught up with her. "Does that look like someone with a flashlight," he whispered and pulled her back behind a tree.

Jenna shook her head. "Don't be a fool. Why would any of the people here tonight need a flashlight," she growled as she stared into the trees ahead, looking

- 552 -

for someone with a light, just the same. She couldn't think of any other reason there would be lights.

Between the singing and the lights, the woods were taking on an eerie appearance. The Tairneach suddenly had the strong feeling that they were being watched and were not welcome.

* * * *

Cullen spared a fleeting look for all the pleased lycans around them and grabbed Aislinn around the waist, pulling her against himself. He breathed her in and growled as he stared intensely into her eyes.

Something about the way he was looking at her made her blush. "It's time isn't it?"

"Well, we're all here," he said. Then he leaned in and nuzzled her face. Aislinn giggled and kissed him.

With the little display, growling and howling signaled the audience approval at the beginning of the ceremony. The moon shone brilliantly through the green leaf canopy, and people still felt the enchantment that the song and the faeries caused. Affectionate cuddling broke out all around the clearing. They would wait for Cullen and Aislinn to begin before they went any farther, but people were pairing off in anticipation. Some of them howled eagerly, encouraging Cullen to get going.

Aislinn broke their kiss, noticing all the eyes focused on them. Cullen could feel her shell of confidence starting to crack. He put his hand on her cheek and drew her eyes back to his. "Look at me, not them."

Aislinn could see in his eyes how much he loved and wanted her. Holding her gaze, he kissed her again. His hands found the catch at the back of her neck to release the halter top on her dress. He couldn't help the heated growl that issued from his chest as the top of the halter fell away, exposing Aislinn's breasts.

Aislinn forced herself to watch Cullen and ignore the growling calls from beyond the stones, as his arms slid around her waist and he pulled her in for another kiss.

Lips peppered feverish kisses along her jaw and down her neck. He nibbled at her collar and she groaned with the little pricks of pain as his teeth scraped skin. She twined her fingers into his hair as he kissed down her chest and her breast to draw one nipple into his mouth. His hands on her back supported her as she arched toward him. Aislinn's needy moan heralded that she was finally relaxing.

"Take my clothes off," he ordered impatiently.

Aislinn's eyes swirled with amber. She began pulling at the buttons on his shirt, laughing and struggling to push him away so that she could get to the rest of his buttons. Cullen growled in annoyance with her overly delicate touch and ripped the front of the shirt apart, tearing the last couple buttons off. Aislinn pushed the shirt and jacket over his shoulders, wrapped her arms around him, pressed her naked breasts against his chest and kissed him.

Cullen slid his hands down her body and over her hips to push dress off, leaving Aislinn standing in only a black thong and the jewelry he gave her. The diamonds sparkled magically in the night around them. Cullen stepped away from her and let the crowd get a look at the woman who belonged to him and howled loudly into the night. The possessive declaration was echoed by the others as they watched him drop his pants to the ground and approach Aislinn again.

With a vicious yank he ripped the thong off of her body. Cullen paced around her, trailing a hand along her hip, and she watched him walk purposefully behind her. The proof of his intent stood hard in front of him. His eyes were molten, swirling amber. Cullen reached out and drew a suddenly clawed hand down her back. As he stepped up to her, the men and women in the clearing began shedding their own clothing.

Aislinn felt his hard cock jab her lower back when he pulled her against him. His hands reaching around her body to maul her breasts, while lips burned kisses and bites along her shoulder. If anyone present noticed the evident bite mark already there, no one dared question it.

* * * *

Jenna heard the howling and looked around at her bewildered men. The charge was nearly stopped by the singing and strange lights. "It had to have been the druids," she said loudly, trying to re-instill confidence in her men. "Regroup and start the attack. The mating has begun," she growled.

* * * *

Without warning, Aislinn felt energy surge from the circle. "No. Not now," she cried angrily.

Frightened confusion stopped Cullen. He hoped she wasn't telling him 'no'. When she dropped to her knees and put her hands to her head, he knew that it had nothing to do with him. He felt her mind drift and watched her try to fight it. Uncertainty forced the smiles from the faces of the watching lycans.

Finally, realizing that she couldn't fight it, Aislinn gave in. The Fates wanted to tell her something now, and she wasn't going to get out of it. As she relaxed into the vision, it felt as if she was flying haphazardly up and out of her body, above the stone circle. She looked down briefly to see Cullen kneeling next to her and trying to bring her back to him. She could hear his voice in her mind, but the Fates weren't letting her respond to it this time. Suddenly, she was torn away from the stones and through the trees. She didn't have to go far. She felt as though she was being yanked from one lycan to another. The beasts that she was seeing were more frightening than she could have imagined. One after another. Aislinn's heart was caught in her throat. Then she landed in front of Jenna. Aislinn stared at the angry woman, trying to discern what she was supposed to understand. Jenna was fiddling with a ruby ring on a chain about her neck.

She only stood there a moment before being snapped back to herself. Her eyes opened to see Cullen's concerned face. "She has some kind of ring," Aislinn said. The image blazed fresh in her mind. It was important for some reason."

Cullen nodded. He didn't understand what that had to do with anything. "It was her father's. Brennus wore it 'til the day he died. Are you all right?"

Aislinn nodded. "They're just north of here. In the trees. They're huge." Cullen looked into her frightened eyes. "And there are so many," she whispered.

Cullen stood up and eyed the surrounding alphas with intent. Each watched with uneasy anticipation. Anyone less than alpha didn't have any idea what was going on, but the alphas saw it on his face before Cullen even called out the warning. "We're under attack. They come from the north," he said, in a low deadly growl. Then he shifted to his hybrid form and howled the warning to the rest of the Arnauk. The other alphas joined their voices with his and the entire reservation reverberated with the sound.

* * * *

There was no misinterpreting the howling. It was obvious that the Tairneach were spotted. Jenna's mind worked quickly to assess the situation. *We're not as close as I wanted, but we can still make the circle.* Her men were all uneasy and disorganized. The strange singing and then the lights had more of an effect on the Tairneach than Jenna was willing to concede.

"Muin! They know we're here. Attack," she screamed into the wood, before shifting and howling her advance. The Tairneach charged through the trees toward the cabin, the stone circle, and the packs gathered for the celebration.

* * * *

Mack and Celia were inside the cabin squabbling. Celia was self-conscious. She had started gaining weight and didn't want to go out to the main gathering. The doctor said there were at least three, and she was already picturing herself as a whale. Mack was ecstatic, but no matter how many times he told her that she was pregnant, not fat, it didn't seem to sink in. Mack was in the process of telling her that they owed it to Aislinn to be present for this, when the unsettling howl from outside stopped everyone still inside the cabin cold.

"Muin! Can't we have just one ceremony go normally around here," Celia swore angrily. She started to shift and Mack grabbed her by the arm.

"You're not going out there," he growled at her as he shifted.

Technically we're not mated yet. Even if we were I wouldn't let you tell me what to do.

- 557 -

Technically we are mated, but more than that you're pregnant. I'm not going to lose you again, he said to her with a tone that had her pausing. *Not like this.*

She sighed, giving in against her nature. *Don't get hurt.* Celia let her hybrid form slide off of her, leaned in and kissed him on the muzzle.

Having established that Celia would stay safe in the cabin, Mack jumped and bolted out the door, leaving Celia to direct the confused visitors inside the cabin and let everyone know what the howling meant and why the Arnauk all shifted and charged out of the cabin without warning.

A short period of uncertainty and outrage caused some havoc, while the strangers who weren't warned computed the situation. They couldn't believe that any pack would have the audacity to interrupt a mating ceremony, let alone a ceremony that sanctioned by the Pack Council. As rage filtered through the lycans in the cabin another wave of hybrids charged out to join the fight.

* * * *

Aislinn stood to shift and go with Cullen, but Malik's voice stopped them. He sounded strangely strong over all the howling and commotion. "She'll be of more help here," he said simply.

Cullen growled. While he didn't want to leave her behind, he didn't really want her anywhere near the dires or what was about to happen. He considered Malik's comment and decided that it was excellent excuse. *Stay,* he ordered and started to turn toward the woods.

"Don't you dare pull that bullshit on me," she growled right back. "You're my mate not my father."

Cullen growled back angrily at her. He could see Cadifor and Makeda charging into the woods with others. His place was in the front of the charge. He already missed that.

Malik reached out and placed a hand on Aislinn's arm. "If you help us, fewer men will die."

Aislinn turned indecisively to Cullen, then back to Malik and she nodded. The instant he thought he could trust her to not follow, Cullen bolted for the woods. Aislinn was amazed at how fast he moved. As he entered the tree line, a terrible fear twisted in the pit of her stomach and a tear dropped from her eye for no reason that she knew of. She was terrified.

"So," she turned to Malik, "what can I do to help?"

"You'll know when it's time."

Aislinn's eyes opened wide in anger. "You did not just say that. I let him run into that alone and you're going to go all druid on me?"

Malik couldn't hide the grin on his face when she said that. He swallowed to stop himself from laughing at her. It was an odd feeling to have in the middle of the situation they were in. "He's far from alone in that fight. I can't tell you what to do because I don't know what to do. You are a strange one Aislinn. You've learned to give in to the Fates enough that you can bring messages back from premonitions. That isn't an easy feat. Yet, you haven't learned to extend the faith beyond those situations. Usually a druid learns to trust the Fates in all ways before he has enough strength to surrender his will in a situation as uncontrollable as a premonition. You really are quite intriguing."

Aislinn was speechless. "This isn't the time or place for lessons. If you don't know what I can do to help, then why did you stop me from leaving with Cullen? I can definitely help him."

"I felt that you would be of more help here," he said. "That's all."

"Fine," she growled, wondering if she could catch Cullen if she followed. "What are you going to do?"

"Protect the circle," he said.

"They're not here yet."

"They will be."

* * * *

Screaming and growling drove Cullen through the trees. The smell blood assaulted his senses and warned him that he was nearing the perimeter of the fight. When he burst through the trees and caught sight of the actual battle, rage seared though him. A thing that could only be described as a monster, surrounded by eight or more lycans, tore them apart, and tossed them into trees as if the lycans were pups. The dire wolf was head and shoulders taller than the largest of the lycans surrounding him and twice as wide. Lycans clawed at his back and face and ripped chunks of flesh away, with no effect. He didn't seem to have a neck beneath all the muscle. That made it difficult for the lycans to take his throat out.

As the shock wore off, Cullen charged in with the rest to take his turn. The lycans instinctively attacked as a team. Cullen growled in rage as one of his men was thrown bodily into a tree. Even in the chaos a sickening crack could be heard and, the man didn't stand back up. Cullen charged again as the beast turned to claw at another lycan. Cullen managed to knock the dire to the ground, and instantly the other lycans swarmed it. The amount of damage that had to be done in order to kill the dire lycan was frightening.

They all stood over the monster on the ground breathing hard and waiting to see that it didn't stand back up. Somewhere in the woods Cullen could hear gunshots. That meant the lycans who had been in the cabin were involved, if someone was using real weapons. Cullen turned toward the nearest sound of hand to hand fighting and darted through the trees toward the next target.

One at a time, he told himself in frustration.

* * * *

Mack caught up to Keith as they charged north through the woods. When they came across the gigantic wolf-beast Keith couldn't help himself. *Which one of the human Hollywood makeup artists came up with this one?* He followed his comment with the closest thing to a snicker that his hybrid form could manage through a muzzle.

Mack growled his annoyance at Keith's attempt to be humorous. *Not funny,* he growled back. Together the two of them joined the group which was already futilely swarming the monstrous lycan. Bloody, broken bodies littered the ground around the thing's feet. Keith vaulted over one of the bodies, straight at the dire's head. Mack's lunge was aimed at the thing's chest. Keith hit it first and Mack's weight added to the tackle, knocking it backward into a tree. Keith's claws raked at its head, and Mack's jaws crunched down on its arm.

The dire roared in pain as Keith managed to take out an eye. The others were going after its legs and stomach. The dire flailed for anything and managed to get its claw's on Mack. Keith was thrown to the ground, as the half blinded dire lycan lifted Mack in its massive claws to bite down on Mack's shoulder.

Blood gushed from the wound while Mack screamed in pain.

Keith tried to stand, but found his leg wouldn't hold him. Forcing himself up, he tired to go to Mack's aid, as the dire lycan ripped at Mack's stomach with one viscous claw. The other lycans managed to get its arms and the dire dropped Mack's bleeding form to the ground. Keith grabbed his friend by the arm and pulled him back from the frenzy, just as the other lycans brought the dire to the ground.

Mack coughed up blood and read bubbled from his nose as he lie on the ground. He closed his eyes as Keith begged him to hang on for just a little longer. *We only need to get back to the cabin. Mack!*

* * * *

Cullen burst into a small clearing in the woods where one monster was fighting off six or more lycans. In his peripheral vision he caught sight of a group of Tairneach sneaking around the fight, working their way toward the standing stones. Cullen started toward the strange group when Maon appeared in front of him. He hadn't changed yet.

Cullen knew Jenna's favorite lackey well. *Maon,* Cullen said. *Jenna must be somewhere nearby. She never let's your leash out too far.*

Maon growled, but continued to smile. He nodded toward the fight with the dire lycan, taking place nearby. "You gonna let your men die so you can banter with me Arnauk?"

Cullen's head snapped around. The dire had two men pinned under its gigantic paws and the others couldn't get in close enough to do anything about it. Without another glance at Maon, Cullen charged the dire lycan, barreling hard enough into its side for one of the men to crawl free. Still the wounded wasn't getting back up to join the fight.

Cullen's teeth tore into the dire lycan's side, causing the beast to roar angrily and swipe at Cullen with a blow hard enough to crack a rib or two, as claws slashed a gash in his side. Cullen ignored the pain and charged back into the fray. One of the lycans who had been thrown from the fight panicked and ran off into the woods. Cullen watched the man flee, regretting the loss of number, but understanding the feeling as he watched the monster's jaws shred the lycan he was holding down. The man screamed in pain as his arm was ripped from his body and thrown into the bushes, leaving a trail of blood behind. Cullen howled his fury, jumped onto the creature's back, and with all his strength grabbed hold of the dire's head. Cullen threw himself bodily to the ground, using his weight and strength to try and break its neck. For a brief instant, Cullen felt the world flash, as the beast swiped at his head and only barely missed his eyes, leaving a gash along his forehead and cheek. Then came the cracking of bones, and the beast crumbled to the ground. Cullen knelt bleeding, chest heaving as the others ripped into the limp body to finish the dire off. The massacre continued long after the body stopped twitching.

* * * *

Jenna sauntered into the clearing entirely pleased with herself. The Arnauk and their guests were all in the process of dealing with her new army. There were only two people standing in the circle. It was as if someone had given her a present. Maon could deal with the druid. She planned to kill Aislinn personally. The idea sent pleasant chills through her body.

Maon led the druids and their guards into the stone circle behind Jenna. He took the bag of supplies off of his back and set it down. So far the plan was going as it should. Still, he felt as though something was going to go wrong.

Aislinn turned to Malik. "Do you know what I'm supposed to do yet," she growled, as they watched Jenna's troops walk into the clearing. Aislinn guessed that Maon was at least a beta. She had never seen him fight, but she knew that Jenna was rarely without him. She also figured that the others had to be decent rank as well, just in case Jenna found a fight at the circle. It certainly appeared as though the circle was their goal. *Why else bring druids along?*

Malik didn't answer her. He seemed to be waiting for something.

Aislinn was getting pissed. "I guess I don't make a very good druid," she spat. "I don't like waiting well enough."

Jenna tilted her pretty blonde head and smiled at Aislinn. "Maon," she cooed. "Kill the little man."

Instantly, Maon dropped his clothes to the ground, shifted, and attacked Malik. Jenna stood there watching Aislinn with a wicked grin on her face. "I dare you," she taunted.

Aislinn glared defiantly at Jenna and shifted into her hybrid form as Malik backed away from Maon into a stone. Fear filled his wide eyes as he stared at the oncoming lycan. Malik found that he couldn't think straight. He thought he was prepared for this. His brain searched desperately for the words that would save him and started to speak in Gaelic. He hesitated as some of the words seemed to blend in his mind.

Maon single-mindedly charged the confused druid and missed Aislinn's attack. She hit Maon hard in the side. He never expected her to actually attack him. He soon discovered that she wasn't as incompetent as Terrick made her sound. Her claws bit into his flesh, and Maon growled angrily, turning his attention from the apparently harmless druid to Aislinn. Jenna motioned for the other guards to grab Malik. While Aislinn was busy with Maon, Jenna made the druids begin setting up the circle for the transformation.

One of the lycans grabbed Malik and stuffed some waded cloth in his mouth to keep him from saying anything that could impede their progress. Malik frantically scanned the woods and clearing for other druids, only to find that they all had gone into the woods to aid the wounded. He couldn't remember ever feeling this trapped and helpless. He watched as Aislinn fought with Maon. She was doing well. Maon bled and growled at her wickedly. He limped on one leg as crimson seeped from a gash on his hindquarter. Aislinn had taken a few hits, but she didn't look nearly as bad as he did.

"Enough," Jenna shouted. "Kill the druid if she doesn't submit."

Aislinn turned to see what Jenna was doing and Maon took advantage of her shifted attention. He knocked her roughly into a nearby stone, and her head cracked against it with a disgusting thud. Aislinn felt a wave a nausea as the stone circle spun around her, and the world went black.

Pleased, Jenna stepped up to Aislinn's limp form. She scrutinized the cat with jealousy. Cullen had given Jenna a simple gold anklet for their mating. It was nice, but nothing like the jewelry that adorned

Aislinn's unconscious form. Jenna had a strong urge to scar her pretty little face.

"Mistress," someone called, and Jenna turned from her musing to see what the voice wanted. "We're ready for you."

Jenna accepted the fact that she could have company any moment and this could suddenly get harder. "Get her body out of the circle. I'll deal with her after this is done."

One of the Tairneach came over and dragged Aislinn roughly out of the circle. Maon limped to join Jenna on the slab in the middle of the stone circle, as Jenna stripped out of her clothes, and Maon shifted down to his human form. With a nod from Jenna, the druids began drawing symbols across her chest with blue woad. They spoke softly as they drew each symbol, and all around them energy began to crackle in the air.

* * * *

Drake felt Sarah fading. She lie on the ground nearby, blood poured from her nose and one ear. Her leg was bend at an odd angle and she didn't look like she was breathing. Drake roared his anger and charged the dire lycan. He didn't know if he wanted to die or kill it. One way or the other this fight wasn't over.

The monster accumulated quite the body count. Dead and dying lycans lie scattered about the clearing. Drake and two other Arnauk were the only ones left fighting the beast. As Drake jumped at the dire, it grabbed him out of the air. Pulling Drake to its open maw, the dire bit down on his throat. Drake screamed and coughed blood as the other lycans tried futilely to free their friend. The beast seemed to be indestructible.

Out of nowhere, the lycans heard someone speaking Gaelic. The voice wasn't making any sense. The words didn't seem to go together correctly. Suddenly, the tree next to them began to move, and vines slithered like snakes out of the woods. The strange green plants twisted around the monster's legs. The two Arnauk tripped back away from the nightmarish scene. The tree appeared to come to life, and the vines lifted the struggling dire up into the branches. It dropped Drake to the ground slashed manically at the vines, trying to free itself. The dire made short work of the plants and was nearly through the mass of vines when the tree shoved a number of branches through the it's contorted body, impaling it. Then the tree went still, blood dripping from the branches.

Three druids walked out of the wood from behind the tree. They looked tired and pale. One of them vomited at the sight of the body in the tree branches. The other two began walking amongst the bleeding lycans on the ground.

* * * *

A number of omegas tried desperately to keep Celia inside the cabin. She could feel Mack fading from her mind. He had been there for so long that she didn't realize what was happening at first. There was pain and confusion, a torrent of pain and confusion. She tried reaching out him, but he was too far away. Their bond wasn't complete and was never really strong enough for communication out of visual range. Even so, she tried over and over again. Her panic was working up some of the others. Celia wasn't the only one feeling the loss of someone, but she was the only one going crazy over it.

"Celia," Rissa insisted calmly. "What do you think you'll be able to do if we let you out of here?" She was standing in front of the door and there were a couple other omegas at the nearby windows.

Celia paced. Tears welled in her eyes. "I don't know," she cried and fell to her knees on the floor. "I don't know Rissa. But something."

Rissa came over to Celia, sat on the floor next to her, and wrapped her arms around her. "It won't help if you get yourself or the babies hurt," she said softly. Rissa rocked back and forth as Celia cried in her arms.

* * * *

Cullen felt it the minute Aislinn shifted. He knew that she was in the middle of a fight. Fear coursed through him, and he prayed that it wasn't with one of the dires. *I shouldn't have left her alone,* he cursed himself, as the lycan he was fighting collapsed, his windpipe crushed in Cullen's jaws. Shoving the man aside, Cullen darted into the trees, following his senses toward Aislinn. His head-long rush brought him to a clearing where another dire was destroying a small group of lycans.

Cullen recognized the group as one of the packs from Cadifor's territory. They were losing ground fast. The dire already had several of them down and was working on disemboweling one he held up by the neck. Cullen forced himself to go to their aide. His wolf was howling at him to go to Aislinn, but he couldn't just pass the men up. Aislinn didn't seem to need him yet, these men obviously did.

Snarling viciously, Cullen joined the fray. He hurtled toward the dire and pummeled into the back of its knees with all of his weight. The monster's legs collapsed and he fell back onto Cullen, dropping the mauled lycan from his claws. Someone pulled the lifeless lycan out of the way, as the dire scrambled to get back to his feet. Cullen bit down hard on the creature's hamstring and yanked his head back, stripping muscle from bone. The dire howled in pain, and the rest of the lycans surrounding them descended on the crippled beast.

Seconds felt like hours, while Cullen helped them kill the dire. Suddenly he felt pain in the back of his mind, and Aislinn's voice went silent. She was still there and still strong, but she wasn't conscious. When he felt his sense of her fog over he raced to the stone circle, cursing himself for being distracted by anything.

* * * *

Jenna felt power surging through her. With each line that the druids drew on her body, she tingled a bit more. A strange euphoria flowed through her body.

Nearly incapacitated from blood loss, Maon knelt in the middle of the circle. The woad burned where it touched bloody gashes in his flesh. *If this works I'm gonna flay that bitch*, he thought. He couldn't stand the idea that such a little thing from another pack had so thoroughly beaten him in front of Jenna. *Maybe Jenna's right to be so jealous of her*, he begrudgingly conceded. *Nothing worse than admiring something you hate.*

The druids spoke quietly, their words ominous, senseless contortions of the language. Jacob handed Jenna a jar containing a yellowish foul smelling mixture and she gagged as she drank it down. Another jar of the same stuff was placed in Maon's trembling hands, and the druid helped him tip it to his mouth.

Malik eyed Jacob, and the man shook his head. Terror paled his face as he continued to speak the powerful words softly. Jenna unexpectedly felt an orgasmic surge of pain and her body began to rearrange itself. She fell to her knees and laughed manically, believing she already won. Maon was not enjoying the sensations as much as Jenna. He was light headed and feared that he may pass out. Will power and the belief that Jenna would think kept him standing.

Cullen exploded through the trees into the clearing. His mind reeled indecisively, when the scene began to solidify in front of him. He saw Malik and considered freeing him. There was Jenna and Maon, but Cullen was wary of entering the circle. When he saw Aislinn on the ground, his mind was made up for him. The Tairneach who had dragged her from the circle stood over her collapsed form menacingly. Cullen shredded him instantly without thinking about it. The fool shouldn't have stood in his way. Cullen knelt next to Aislinn and pulled her into his arms gently.

He stroked her hair off her face. *Aislinn, baby, please,* he begged. It was a strange sight to see the large lycan being so gentle with her. Cullen's heart skipped, when her eyes fluttered open, and she looked up at him. Tears glazed his eyes. *You're all right.* He pulled her to his chest and held her tightly. *You scared me,* he growled at her. Aislinn couldn't help but smile, even though her head was splitting. She nuzzled her face into his chest, not realizing that the fight wasn't over yet.

A wicked howl like nothing Cullen had ever heard drew his attention back to the circle. The change was complete. Jacob retreated toward Malik, hoping that there were enough other things going on that he wouldn't be noticed.

Cullen reluctantly released Aislinn and stood up, stepping between her and the howling dires in the center of the stones. Cullen glared in disgust at what Jenna had done to herself. She was definitely formidable enough to keep her seat as alpha now.

Aislinn scrambled to her feet, staring wide eyed at the two lycans who were menacing them. Maon was still a bit light headed, but the change healed a great deal of the damage Aislinn had done.

Are you frightened of me now, Jenna asked.

No, Cullen growled. *I wonder what Brennus would think of you now?*

"Brennus," Aislinn said, as her mind wrapped around something.

Fury blazed in Jenna's eyes at the mention of her father. A low threatening growl emanated from deep in her chest and without warning she rushed at Cullen. There was no time for thought. Aislinn came out of nowhere and ran into the stone circle. She didn't know if it would work, but she figured that it was worth trying. She focused her mind on Brennus Tairneach. As she stepped beyond the stones, the ruby ring around Jenna's neck flashed blinding red, and suddenly Aislinn and Jenna were gone.

Cullen felt his sense of Aislinn fog over, and he roared in anger. She trapped herself somewhere with a dire lycan. *Aislinn,* his mind screamed futilely. In that instant Maon attacked him, and his attention was forced back to the circle. Cullen rolled away from the monstrous lycan and howled for reinforcements. He managed to dodge the brute again, at the same time he heard a response to his call, but it was far off. Cullen was no fool. He knew that he couldn't take on Maon as a dire alone. He thought back to fighting Rafe, and really didn't want to go through that again. In the end, Brinah's sacrifice won that match.

Jacob watched Cullen dodging artfully out of the way of the giant lycan he had just created. He stood next to Malik and tried to be sly about reaching up and pulling the wad of cloth out of his mouth.

The Tairneachs for the most part seemed unconcerned with the druids now. "Where the hell is Jenna," the blonde Tairneach next to Malik swore.

"As if I should know. Muin." The other Tairneach searched the tree line as if Jenna would come walking out at any second. "Arnauk has reinforcements coming," he added with uncertainty.

The blonde nodded, "I think Maon has Arnauk under control. Get the others and brace for whatever's coming. Jenna will skin us if we lose ground at this point." More howling spurred the two lycans to action, leaving Malik, Jacob and the other druids to their own devices

Jacob untied Malik the minute that the lycans were distracted. By then, the other three druids had worked their way over to Malik as well. "Strength in numbers," Jacob said. Concerned nods answered his comment. There was a quiet conversation as more lycans burst into the clearing around the stones. The Tairneach, already in position, met the attack head on. As the lycans brawled, the druids silently spread out. They hid unobtrusively around the stone circle and began to speak quietly in unison.

Cullen was running out of steam fast. When he noticed that his call for help was being intercepted, he wasn't sure that he was going to be able to keep avoiding Maon long enough for it to do him any good. Cullen leaped out of the way of the huge lycan and ran head-long into one of the standing stones. Falling to the ground, he knocked over a glass jar at the base of the stone. Before he could stand, Maon was coming at him again. Cullen picked up the jar and threw it at the lycan's head. It shattered against his face and Maon roared in pain as glass shards sliced into his muzzle.

Cullen rolled under another grab, desperately trying to think of something. Maon was bigger than the others Cullen fought. He obviously lost speed in the transformation, but if he got his hands on Cullen it would be all over.

The druids continued speaking quietly. Their voices carried through the area as if the sound was coming from everywhere. It drew the attention of several lycans, however they had their hands full with actual fighting and didn't have time to deal with the little men talking quietly to themselves in the background.

Cullen dodged again, but this time Maon got a hold of his foot. With one yank he whipped Cullen back and threw him against one of the stones. Cullen slammed into the stone with a solid crack and he wondered if his back was broken. He crumbled to the ground at the foot of the stone, the wind knocked out of him, and felt a glass jar beneath him break and slice into his side. Maon reached to grab hold of Cullen again. Cullen took a huge chunk of glass with him as Maon held him by the neck and slammed Cullen against the stone with one hand. Cullen felt the air forced out of his lungs and nearly forgot the glass in his fist, as black spots dotted his vision.

Cullen felt Maon's grip on his neck tighten and his windpipe begin to crush under the pressure. He struggled against the ungodly strength of the dire lycan. Remembering the glass he slashed at Maon's wrist and arm with the chunk of glass, trying to get Maon to release his hold. Cullen couldn't breathe. The entire circle was spinning around him Maon's disgusting muzzle was in his face, and the man was growling savagely at Cullen as the world went black.

* * * *

Aislinn scanned the area cautiously. She didn't really know what she had done. Eerily still silence enveloped the circle. A vague sense that the battle raged on nearby whispered in the back of her mind. Here there was only power and the stones. A ghostly Brennus Tairneach stood statuesque on the slab at the center of the circle. Apparently dazed, he stared at Aislinn suspiciously. Then his eyes fell on his daughter.

Confusion blurred Jenna's thoughts. She didn't know where everyone went or why it was suddenly so quiet. *Just kill the bitch,* her brain screamed in single-minded determination. *Figure out what the muin happened later.* Jenna jumped to her feet and turned, searching for Aislinn. A combination of cold fear and uncertain joy brought Jenna to a standstill, as she came face to face with her dead father. Jenna immediately shifted to her human form. The look on her face was that of child caught doing something wrong. "Daddy," she whimpered; then turned on Aislinn with tears in her eyes. "Is this some kind of trick?"

"No," Aislinn answered softly. She didn't know what to expect, but obviously this was doing something. "Brennus Tairneach is dead. I brought you to him."

Jenna's eyes widened. "Am I dead?"

"No," Aislinn said, cautiously. "You're wasting time."

Jenna looked back to her father. Anger contorted the features of his face. "What have you done to my pack, Jenna?"

There were more tears. "I'm making them stronger," she said defiantly.

"By turning them against the Pack Council," deadly wrath bled from his voice. Aislinn found herself stepping back. She didn't know how Jenna could stand up to that.

"No. By making them-"

"Freaks," Brennus finished. "I see all of it Jenna. I know you now."

Jenna sobbed. "I want you to be proud of me Daddy."

"And when did I ever give you the impression that this is the way to go about that?"

Jenna shook her head. "I'll show you. I can be the alpha."

"No, Jenna. You were never meant to be the alpha. That doesn't matter. It never did." Sadness softened his voice. "I love you, Jenna. You'll always have my love. But you're wrong, and you're destroying everything."

"No Daddy. It'll work. You'll see," she pleaded.

Brennus stared at her. "You want to make me proud?"

"Yes Daddy. Please."

"Then fix this," he demanded.

Steadily increasing pain pounded in Aislinn's skull. She didn't know where it was coming from, but she was too involved with watching Brennus and Jenna to think about it now. She pitied Jenna. Aislinn didn't understand how the girl got so warped. Brennus sounded somewhat intelligent from this angle. She blinked through the throbbing pain.

"How Daddy? How do you want me to fix it?" Jenna tried to touch him, but her hand went through the ghostly figure.

"Put things back the way they were."

Jenna's eyes widened. "I'll look like a fool. I'll not be able to keep our bloodline leading the pack. They'll never follow me," she pleaded desperately.

"That doesn't matter. Bring the peace back Jenna. That will make me proud of you."

Aislinn couldn't take it any longer. She staggered back from the stone she was leaning against and everything flashed back into motion, along with the realization that Cullen was in danger.

Jenna turned on Aislinn when Brennus disappeared. "Bring him back," she screamed and ran to Aislinn, only to be shoved away.

Even after seeing the woman as a sobbing child, Aislinn couldn't bring herself to comfort her. Violently grabbing Jenna by the arm, Aislinn made her look at Maon. "Make him stop," Aislinn ordered in a desperate voice. "Make him stop now Jenna. Brennus said to make it stop."

At first Jenna's face was confused and defiant, until the mention of Brennus' name. Reluctantly, she pulled away from Aislinn and went to Maon. Cullen's eyes rolled back in his head and Aislinn felt the pain quiet. "No," she whispered, her body trembling in disbelief.

Jenna seized Maon's wrist and yanked him away from Cullen. "It's done Maon. Make them stop," she said weakly.

Maon growled at her. *Pathetic bitch. We're winning and you're giving up now?*

"Just make it stop Maon," she begged.

Maon wrenched Jenna around by the hair, and leaned down to meet her eye to eye. *I've had enough of your incompetence. First we're going to finish this fight. Then I'm going to take you back to the manor, and we'll decide how I'm going to deal with you.* He threw Jenna to the ground and started toward Aislinn. *You may be able to cow Jenna, druis, but let's see how you handle me.*

Aislinn knelt over Cullen with tears in her eyes. "This isn't happening." Her head ached with each word Maon forced into it. "Rach-air-muin," she screamed at him through the tears. Aislinn could barely think. "I'm dreaming. This isn't real," she sobbed as she held Cullen in her arms, rocking back and forth. "Cullen please. You can't do this." Aislinn closed her eyes and reached into his mind, but she couldn't feel him at all.

As Maon came up behind Aislinn, Malik stepped in his way. Quiet nonsense Gaelic poured from his lips Malik, and determination masked his face.

Maon laughed, guttural and menacing. *Out of my way little man. I may need you yet. Don't make me kill you.*

Malik almost faltered, as the words rushed through his head. He fought to keep his concentration. Out of nowhere, Jacob appeared behind Maon, and with fear in their eyes the two men knelt, touching their hands to the ground.

Maon watched them with amused confusion for a moment. *Do you think bowing before me will earn you something?*

Malik and Jacob stopped speaking, and the ground beneath Maon's feet began to crumble. Before Maon could react the earth opened up, and he fell. The sound of his screaming was cut off, as the ground closed up again, and appeared as if nothing had happened. He was gone.

Jacob stared at the spot where Maon had been swallowed by the earth. "D'anam don diabhal," he said softly.

Stunned, Jenna gaped at the druids, until she realized that there were three of them standing around her. She shook her head, fear gripped her stomach, and she envisioned herself being swallowed up as Maon had been. "No," she said desperately to the men she had been torturing for days. "I'll stop it. I can fix it. I swear." Jenna howled into the night, and the confused Tairneach began to stand down. The druids remained encircling Jenna, holding her there by threat alone.

Malik and Jacob knelt next to Aislinn. "He's still here Aislinn."

She turned on them, sobbing. "What? In spirit? I need him here," she cried, and she pressed her hand to his chest. Aislinn felt the power of the circle surge through her again, a cooling sensation tingled through her body, taking away her pain, and suddenly Cullen gasped for air.

Malik put his hand on her shoulder, as she watched Cullen in shock. "I told you. His soul had not yet moved on."

Then Malik pulled a vial from his pocket, uncorked it and poured the liquid into Cullen's mouth. He choked on some, but swallowed most of it. Aislinn helped him to sit up. He was staring around bewildered and trying to catch his breath. Aislinn buried her head against his chest. She couldn't stop the tears. Putting his arms around her, Cullen looked questioningly at Malik. The fight seemed to be ending, but he had obviously missed part of it.

* * * *

Celia paced and waited impatiently, as the wounded were carried in one at a time. "Maybe he's just unconscious," she kept saying. Rissa watched her. Celia kept trying to get out when the door was left unattended. Each time, Rissa intercepted her and reminded her why she was inside.

Keith came in the front door carrying Sarah. She was too badly hurt to completely regain consciousness. Still, she would survive. Celia came up to them and looked down at Sarah with fear in her eyes. "She'll be okay Cel. But move, we've got a lot more coming in."

"Have you seen Mack," she asked softly.

"Yeah, he's coming." Keith walked passed Celia with Sarah and headed for the elevator in the back of the main room. He wasn't about to use the stairs tonight.

Despondent, Celia turned around to continue watching the door and almost started crying. Mack was helping Drake to limp into the room. Celia rushed over to them and grabbed Mack around the neck, hugging and kissing him.

"Hey," Drake yelled when Celia nearly pulled them over. "Save it for after I get put down," he growled.

Celia reluctantly let them go, following them over to the couch where Mack helped Drake to sit down. Then he called some omegas over to take Drake the rest of the way upstairs.

When he looked back to Celia, she had tears in her eyes. "Our bond is broken," she said unhappily. She didn't even want to imagine what had happened that would have been bad enough to break their connection.

Mack took her hand and pulled it to his lips. "We never completed it in the first place. We'll put it back. And we'll do it right this time," he said.

She smiled at him through the tears and wrapped her arms around him again.

"Careful," he said, wincing as she squeezed some soft spots. "I'm still tender."

* * * *

Jenna and the rest of the Tairneach were rounded up. Cadifor decided that the Pack Council would have to be formally informed, and then they would decide what to do with Jenna and the rest of the Tairneach. He wasn't sure if the pack would be disbanded and the territory redistributed or if the Tairneach would be trusted to resolve the issue within their own structure. The Council would have to discuss it.

By the time the druids finished assessing the wounded and mostly dead lycans the body count was reduced to five. As much as they hated to lose anyone, five was a great deal more acceptable than what it could have been. The Tairneach weren't so lucky. The dires who were killed had been ripped apart. There was no salvaging that kind of death. There were limits to what could be healed in a body.

Cullen spent most of the rest of the evening thanking people for helping them and making sure everyone who needed anything had it. Aislinn refused to leave his side, no matter how many times he suggested she go upstairs and get some sleep. The most she did was summon an omega to bring her some clothes to put on and to take her jewelry up to their bedroom. Cullen watched her carefully remove the diamond covered chains. He had to admit that no matter how beautiful she was with them on, she was more beautiful just standing there naked.

"I heard that," she said softly and smiled at him over her shoulder.

Keith walked up to them and watched them stare at each other a moment, before he started laughing. "So are you two ever going to get mated? I mean this is getting ridiculous."

Cullen kicked at Keith's bad leg for the comment. Keith, for his part, dodged the half-hearted attack gracefully. "I'm just saying that I need to know what to tell all these guests in the morning when they start asking what's going on," he grinned widely.

Cullen shook his head. "We need recovery time."

"Again," Keith added emphatically, and Cullen kicked at him again.

"We have five deaths and a bunch of injured people. Tell them all we reconvene in a month's time. That should give us all a chance to regroup."

Keith shrugged. "Are you sure you want to drag this out for an entire month?"

"Yeah, it should have been planned that way anyhow. We rushed things for any number of reasons. All of those seem to have been dealt with. Though, at this point I'm not counting on anything," he growled. Aislinn scoffed in agreement. "Just tell them all that everyone who is here now is welcome back in a month."

Keith nodded and took off to spread the information, leaving Cullen to finish dealing with the rest of the people he needed to personally see to that evening. It was nearly morning by the time they managed to go up to their room. Aislinn followed Cullen into the shower and then into their bed. They were so exhausted that they were asleep instantaneously.

Chapter 25

Avoid the evil, and it will avoid thee.
-Gaelic Proverb

The pack at large slept significantly later than they normally would have. There was almost no one interested in breakfast. Cullen actually opened his eyes at roughly the same time his alarm ordinarily would have rang, but he growled, wrapped Aislinn more tightly in his arms, and went back to sleep, listening to her purr and breathing her scent.

Around noon a few of the omegas knocked on the main door to the alpha's room. If the bedroom door hadn't been left slightly open on the sitting room, Cullen and Aislinn probably wouldn't have heard the knock. An annoyed growl from inside almost sent the omegas away, before Aislinn called, "come in."

Cullen grinned without opening his eyes. He liked the fact that she was getting confident enough to speak up as if this was her room as well as his.

Aislinn sat up, holding the blanket over herself to see who it was. Cullen growled and tried to pull her back down in the bed. "Whoever it is, it can't be good. You should have let me scare them away."

Aislinn sighed. "But there are so many people here. We should be downstairs already."

Cullen popped one eye open. "That's my line." He rolled onto his back and looked at her. "What has Makeda been telling you?"

"What makes you think it was Makeda?" Aislinn grinned and wrapped the blanket around her, as she got up and walked toward the door. He watched in amazement.   She had come a long way in so short a time.

When Aislinn poked her head out the bedroom, three omegas were in the process of bringing food into the sitting room. "What's this," she asked as she approached them.

The man barking all the orders looked distressed when he saw her standing there. "You don't have to get up, Mistress. We'll bring it in to you. Keith sent up breakfast or lunch. There's a little of both."

"Thank you," she said, smiling gratefully, and led the way into the bedroom.

Cullen lounged on the bed with his hands behind his head, not caring that he was completely naked, or that there were three people walking in behind Aislinn. He was even more impressed, when Aislinn studiously ignored the looks that the pretty omega, helping with the trays, flashed him.

Aislinn got back into bed and laid down against Cullen's side, putting her head on his shoulder and draping her arm across him, taking the blanket she had wrapped around her with it and covering the parts of Cullen she didn't want the girl to look at.   Cullen grinned and kissed the top of her head. She wasn't really jealous or upset by the situation, just making sure the girl was aware of the fact that he was claimed.

Stomach growling, now that food was in sight, Cullen sat up, forcing Aislinn to sit up with him. She was meticulous about keeping herself covered. Cullen figured that it would be a long time before she got completely over that. There was a small possessive part of his brain that kind of liked the fact that she kept herself for him. The lycan part of his brain, however, was amused and wondered why she thought she needed to cover up. She was beautiful and should appreciate the fact that people enjoyed looking at her. He leaned over and kissed her cheek as the omegas set up the trays. She smiled at him knowingly. She caught the entire thought process and was keeping her comments to herself. He kissed her again.

The omegas smiled at each other and finished putting the trays of food together. There was a lot more food than either Cullen or Aislinn would eat. Aislinn's stomach was bothering her a bit, so she wasn't really hungry, still she smiled gratefully at the omegas and said, "thank you," again as they left. When she got strange but appreciative looks from them, she shook her head.

The door closed, and Aislinn examined her plate. "You know it really isn't right that no one ever seems to be grateful of the omegas. I know the rank thing and all is important, but I feel guilty when I say 'thank you' and get looked at as if I've just given someone a present."

Cullen pulled a piece of bacon off the tray and popped it into his mouth as he settled back into the bed. "You're probably right. 'Thank yous' wouldn't kill anyone. But I have to point out that the Arnauk omegas are generally treated better than most. You were just raised with a different idea about rank. If they want to be more appreciated, then they should work a little harder and get themselves out of the omega role."

Aislinn rolled her eyes at him, as she poked at a waffle covered in strawberries and whipped cream. "So what's on the agenda for today?"

Cullen took in a deep breath and let it out as he thought about that. "Clean up. Why? What are you concerned about?" He could feel she was pushing in a particular direction.

"The books that caused all this trouble are still at Tairneach manor."

He growled. If he had gone after those damn books back when she told him about them in the first place...

She interrupted his thoughts. "Not to mention the original implication was that I was supposed to stop someone else from getting the books away from the Tairneach. I still haven't managed that and we don't know who the someone I'm supposed to intercept is." There was a level of confidence in her tone that made him look at her differently.

He nodded. "All right. When we're done eating, we'll go down to the rooms where we put the Tairneach and get Jenna to tell us where the books are." He pulled her closer, kissed some whipped cream out of the corner of her mouth and licked his lips.

Aislinn giggled at him, and they ended up laying back in the bed and kissing some more. Cullen's hand explored her breasts, pinching at one nipple and then another. The breakfast was about to be knocked to the floor when his cell phone rang. Groaning, Cullen fell back onto his pillow and acted as if it was more effort than he was capable of to answer it.

Aislinn reached over him and picked it up, knowing that he was finding her new sense of initiative amusing. "Yeah," she said into the phone, as she pushed the blanket back, ran her hand teasingly down his stomach and began to toy with Cullen mischievously.

"Aislinn?" Keith's voice was a bit bewildered.

She laughed. "Yeah, what do you need?"

Keith laughed with her. "You two didn't finish the ceremony yet. Since when do you qualify to answer the great and mighty alpha phone," he teased.

"Cute," she said offhand as she lay across Cullen's chest. "I reiterate. What do you need?" Cullen's hands ran over her butt, sliding his fingers between her thighs and probing into more sensitive areas.

"Oh," Keith teased. "You've been taking lessons on how to talk mean to underlings. Cul can be pretty good at that when he wants. You know, the angry insistent tone, short snippy sentences…"

"Keith," Aislinn insisted. Her breath hissed out when Cullen pressed his fingers against her clit and began circling the little bud. Her legs spread involuntarily as he slid a finger inside her, and she accidentally knocked her tray off the bed.

Keith laughed whole-heartedly as he heard the tell-tale hiss of breath and then the crash in the background. "I see. That's pretty much my answer. I just needed to know if and when you two were coming downstairs. But I can tell you're busy."

Aislinn bit her lip and glared at Cullen over her shoulder as he played with her. Cullen chuckled and took the phone from her hand, refusing to quit. "We'll be down in a bit." Keith always asked the same question when he called. Cullen knew the man too well.

"Fine. Do you want anything specific done with the Tairneach in the mean time? They're getting antsy. Jenna's distraught. She keeps asking if she can see her father again. You have any idea what that means?"

Cullen hadn't gotten around to telling the others how Aislinn had dealt with Jenna. "Yeah, I do." His hand slowed in his assault on her body, and she looked at him questioningly. "I don't know if she can do it again. We'll deal with it when we come down. We needed to talk to her anyway. Fortunately, you've given us a bargaining chip. That is unless you can get her to give up the books and notes Rafe left behind without arguing."

"I'll see what I can do. I'm pretty bored at the moment. After all the excitement recently, this sudden down time is disconcerting," Keith said. Cullen heard some knuckles crack on the other end of the line. "I could do with an interrogation," he said, in mock macho mode.

"Don't ruin the fact that she seems willing to call an end to the fighting," Cullen said seriously.

"I'll behave," Keith answered like a kid. "Don't worry. Have fun. Play with Aislinn a bit, and then come down to real life. There are a lot of people waiting down here for you, but they're all being patient and understanding."

Cullen and Keith hung up the phone, and Cullen tossed it across the room. With a wicked grin, he grabbed Aislinn and flipped her onto her back, knocking the other tray onto the floor beside the bed. Aislinn squealed and tried to get away as he grabbed for her hips.

"Not so fast," he growled and caught her before she could get off the bed.

She giggled, as he hiked up her hips, taking a minute to look down at her wet lips before lining himself up and thrusting his ready member into her. Aislinn purred happily and pushed back against him. Cullen took his time. Long slow strokes forced greedy moans from Aislinn. She fisted the sheets on the bed and lifted her hips with each thrust, but he held her hips solidly and tortured her. She wiggled wantonly and he closed his eyes feeling her cunt clamp down on his cock. He brought her to the edge, but wouldn't let her come.

Aislinn began begging. "Cullen please," she said desperately. He growled. He couldn't argue any longer. The fluttering of the walls of her sex against his cock was driving him nuts. Her moaning and begging made it impossible for him to resist. Aislinn whimpered when he pulled out. He flipped her over again, setting her on all fours. Repositioning himself behind her, Cullen gripped her hips hard and began thrusting intense and fast. Aislinn's breasts swung with each thrust. She moaned and writhed beneath Cullen. He listened to her voice raise in tenor. When he felt her tense beneath him, he doubled his strokes. They groaned, and their bodies jerked in unison as he emptied into her.

Aislinn felt the waves of pleasure flood over her and the heat as he came inside her. She let out one last happy groan before collapsing onto the bed in bliss, as Cullen fell onto the bed next to her. "I don't know how I survived without you," she said in a soft serious tone.

Cullen didn't know why what she said reached into him like it did. Maybe it was the way she said it or the way she felt in the back of his mind when she said it. He wrapped her in his arms and held her tightly, as they lay cockeyed on the bed. He kissed her shoulder and nibbled lightly at the scared mark he left there. "I love you too," he said softly in return.

* * * *

They showered quickly, forcing themselves to behave, although Cullen couldn't resist a little extra soap on the areas of her body that he liked best. By the time they got downstairs, pretty much everyone was in the great room talking about what had happened the night before. Sarah was still laid up, so Keith had helped Cadifor deal with the majority of the questions. In the end, Cullen only had to smile, nod, and apologize for having invited everyone to a battle instead of a mating, and play the role of diplomatic host again.

An oddly good mood persisted, even in the face of everything that had happened the night before. Lycans in general didn't mind a good fight as long as they won, and since there were relatively few casualties, thanks to the druids, the losses weren't bringing down the atmosphere. The druids and the lycans mingled and talked. The druids wanted as much information about lycan culture as could be absorbed in an afternoon, and no one begrudged them answers after all the lives they'd saved the night before.

Cadifor smiled widely. The entire affair had gone better than he ever dreamed it could. Cullen stood next to him and watched all the different alphas and the druids talking in friendly tones.

"Nothing unites people like a common enemy," Cullen said flatly. "Will it continue to be this pleasant once the excitement has died down?"

"Don't be so pessimistic," Cadifor scolded. "A good start is better than what we had, however the start may have occurred."

Cullen nodded and scanned the room for Aislinn. He spotted her near the large fireplace at the far end of the room, flirting with Makeda. "Those two have certainly taken to each other," he said with a hint of jealousy. Aislinn looked up from her conversation and met his gaze. He felt her amusement in the back of his mind. She winked at him and blew a kiss, before returning to her conversation with Makeda.

"Makeda tends to have that effect on people. I should know. I must say she has taken to Aislinn more than I would have expected." Cadifor grinned. "They do put on a good show. You'd best keep an eye on that one. Someone's liable to try and grab her from you." Cadifor's eyes never left the two women.

"She's already claimed," Cullen reminded him in low tones.

"So she is," he said, clapping Cullen on the shoulder. "I intend to be here for the actual finish of what you started last night. I'll not miss a chance to taste her when you're willing to share."

Cullen nodded, feeling increasingly more possessive by the minute. A quiet voice eased into his mind. *You've nothing to be concerned about,* Aislinn said to him. *Cadifor smells like wet hound dog.*

Cullen burst out laughing, and Cadifor eyed him with curiosity. "Private joke," Cullen responded to Cadifor's quizzical stare.

After a reasonable amount of time and mingling, the four of them excused themselves from the gathering and left to take care of business. A hall in the west wing had been cleared and transformed into a makeshift prison. Betas stood guard at each door in the hall. Cullen knew that if he walked outside he would find a similar lineup of betas by the windows as well. Since the rooms ended up being used as prisons, the omegas who would have been in this hall were sharing rooms in a different wing. It was incredibly inconvenient to keep the Tairneach, considering the number of extra guests they already housed and the fact that they had to have guards. Unfortunately, the feds didn't show up this time, and there were enough high ranking lycans to watch them. So it worked out, if not well.

Cullen leaned confidentially toward Cadifor. "I just thought of something. Did you call the feds off?"

"What?"

Cullen flashed Aislinn a concerned look, and Aislinn sighed in frustration as she understood what he was implying. He could feel the 'I told you so' emanating from her. Even so, she didn't say it.

"I usually get a call from Stevens when there's any commotion," Cullen explained. "This is the first time in years that I haven't heard from him when there was some kind of uproar. When you consider the reports they received after the last fight here and that the Council was involved, it's just strange that another fight between the same two packs wouldn't draw excessive attention from the government watch dogs."

Cadifor growled under his breath in agreement. "I'll look into it."

As they reached Jenna's door, Keith was coming out. He shook his head. "She's not really in a talking mood. I was nice about it," he said in answer to Cullen's raised eyebrows. Keith's usually mirthful voice was somber. "That's not the same Jenna." He looked at Aislinn. "Whatever happened with you two really hit her hard. She's a real downer at the moment. She won't talk to me at all. She either asks about Aislinn or sits crying." Keith stretched. "Now that you're all here acting nice and concerned I can go back to me. I don't like the serious bit. It just doesn't feel right."

When Cadifor looked at Aislinn questioningly, she shrugged, trying to make the situation seem less dramatic. "Jenna finally really talked to her father. I don't think she expected what she heard."

Cullen snorted. "If Brennus came to his sense and stopped coddling her, then I can only imagine."

Cadifor and the others looked confused. "Brennus is dead," he said harshly.

Just tell them, Cullen said in the back of her mind.

Aislinn took a deep breath. "It seems that one of my talents involves--" She paused while she thought about how to say it, then she decided that blunt was best. "I can call the dead," she said, feeling a tug at her soul, as she remembered the night before. "I took Jenna into the stone circle and called her father's soul to her. I didn't really know if it would work or that I could definitely do it. Lately, there have been enough situations where I had an idea, and it just worked out. So I tried it, and there he was. Brennus Tairneach. Something tells me though there was more to it than just me. Don't ask me to explain, because I really don't have the answers. Sometimes I just understand, without knowing why."

A new light shone in Makeda's eyes. "Talking to the dead can be a very powerful skill. When added to your other apparent talents, woman, one has to wonder exactly how powerful you truly are."

Aislinn shifted uncomfortably as they all stared at her. "You're not the only ones wondering that," she said and turned to knock on Jenna's door. She wanted out of this conversation. There was no answer, so rethinking it wouldn't do any good.

Without waiting for Jenna to respond to the knock, Aislinn opened the door and stepped in. They others decided to wait in the hall, but Cullen left the door open so that he could keep an eye on things. Jenna was sitting on the bed, staring at the window with her knees drawn up to her chest and tear streaks on her cheeks. The red ruby ring in her hands, she was twisting it round and round with a lost look on her face as she stared out the window.

"Jenna," Aislinn said softly.

Jenna turned her head to see if it really was Aislinn. She had been hoping to see her again. She had known that the probability was slim. After everything that had happened, there was the distinct possibility that Aislinn wouldn't be willing to speak with her. "I didn't think you'd come."

Aislinn shrugged. "Keith said that you wanted to talk to me about your father."

Jenna's eyes lit up when she realized there might be a chance that Aislinn would let her talk to him again. Still, Jenna was cautious. If their positions had been reversed there was a very good chance that Jenna would just torment Aislinn with what she wanted and then leave. It was either that, or Aislinn wanted something. Since the mighty Arnauk prided themselves on being the good guys, Jenna figured it was the later. She felt a bit of hope when she realized that she still had one bargaining chip. Keith tried to get the books out of her. Jenna was willing to bet that was what Aislinn was here about as well. After all, she was the druid, not Keith. "Will you take me to him again?"

"Jenna," Aislinn said uncertainly and honestly. "Last night was desperation and a wild guess. I suppose I can try to do it again, but I'm not positive I can."

Jenna assumed that Aislinn was messing with her. She wasn't inclined to trust Aislinn in anything. "So what do I have to do? I mean I stopped the attack.

There's no way the Council will let me keep the alpha position in the Tairneach." Her voice lowered. "I suppose my father didn't want that anyway." Jenna's voice cracked, and tears overflowed her red eyes. "I have something I need to ask him. Can't you just pity me and take me to talk to him? Or maybe one of the other druids can do it if you won't."

The annoyed superior tone Jenna used was making it hard for Aislinn to feel bad for her. The woman's actions had nearly killed Cullen, and now she wanted favors. *Remember,* Aislinn thought, *get the books. Hate her later.* "I told you that I'll try," she said the kind of calm voice that a person uses with a whining child. "I don't know what the others are capable of. If I can't manage, we can look into whether or not the others can. Jenna, I'm curious why you think you can ask for anything in your position. How many people did you intend to kill in your little quest for godhood?"

Jenna flinched. *You for one,* she thought angrily. "Look. I know that I'm in trouble here. I also know that I could have made things much worse for you last night and didn't. What's the chance that you as the supposed good guy will meet me half way?"

Aislinn shook her head. "I'm not real inclined to be overly helpful to you. I happen to think that the fact you being in this room instead of strung up somewhere is half way." Somewhere in the hall, back to his usual self, Keith chuckled.

"Fine. You know what? I'm tired and don't really want to play mental chess right now," Jenna sneered. "How about you take me to talk to my father again, and I'll tell you where the books are?"

Aislinn smiled. She was glad to be done playing games with Jenna anyway. "No. How about you tell me where the books *and* the notes *and* anything else that might hint at the fact that a druid ever existed in or near the manor is, we go get them to make sure you're not lying, and then I'll take you to talk to your father?"

"Damn," Keith said a little too loud. "She's tough." Cullen half-heartedly glared at Keith to be quiet. He was pleased that she was doing so well. He hadn't been entirely sure this was a good idea.

Jenna shifted her attention toward the door and smirked at the men standing there through tears. "Fine, whatever," she said. "You're the good guys right? I'm supposed to trust you. Most of the notes and papers are locked in my father's desk in his bedroom. The books and all the information the druids used is in a workroom in the basement, on a table, out in the open," Jenna said with a note of sarcasm.

Keith snorted. "So you're saying that if we had raided the place, we would have found it all no fuss no muss."

A real glare from Cullen stopped Keith's commentary.

"Something like that," Jenna replied to the voice in the hallway.

Cullen stepped through the doorway. "Aislinn, we're done here for now," he said, obviously wanting her to leave with him. "Given that we find everything, we'll see about granting your request, Jenna. I suggest that you remain cooperative until then."

"What else am I going to do," she sneered.

Aislinn joined the others in the hallway and Jenna's door was closed and locked. "You know if she shifts that door won't do any good right?"

Keith harrumphed. "You think we should leave it open for her? Though that might save the cost of replacing the door, should she decide to break out."

Cadifor growled. "For now let's leave the door and place some more guards now that the prisoners have had a good night's sleep and time to consider escape."

"I'm already there," Cullen said. He signaled one of the betas and gave a short set of instructions for pulling stun guns out of the armory in the basement and tripling the guard.

When Cullen turned back to his friends, Cadifor had a thoughtful gleam in his eyes. "I suppose you're going to have to tend to pack matters?"

"I would have thought that a given," Cullen replied.

"Oh sure," Keith taunted, "I do all the work while you sleep in. That's really important business to deal with."

Makeda laughed, "I'm surprised you didn't stick your tongue out at the end of that statement."

Grinning, Keith couldn't resist the opening. "Like this," he said, and added some stomping feet to the pseudo-tantrum. His little display was received with a group eye roll.

"Okay," Cadifor said with authority. "That's enough. How do put up with this all the time?"

Cullen shrugged. "I got used to it a long time ago. Besides, everyone needs a comic relief side kick."

"Side kick," Keith pouted.

The sincerity in his tone had everyone snickering.

A deliberate cough from Cadifor ended the laughter. "Seriously, Makeda and I will deal with the Tairneach issue. You have enough going on here."

"Normally I would argue," Cullen said as Aislinn sidled up beside him and slipped a hand into his. "But I think I'll let you have this one."

Makeda winked at Aislinn. "Consider it a gift for your mating. Besides, Cadifor has been playing the sedate politician too long now. You should have seen his face during that battle. It'll do him some good to be off the phone and moving around."

Cadifor scoffed at the comment, but didn't argue the point.

"Then tomorrow," Cullen replied, "we're heading back to Madadh-Allaidh Saobhaidh."

* * * *

The month passed quickly. Cullen couldn't believe how much he missed the standard, nobody's life's at stake, everyday paperwork that he dealt with before all the bullshit started. A pleased smile on his face, he sat at his desk in his office on the13th floor and opened another bill. Sure he could have had an accountant or someone take care if this stuff, but then what would he do all day?

Momentarily he was tempted to get involved with the mess Cadifor was trying to resolve. Unfortunately, when he had arrived at the Tairneach manor to collect the books and notes, the feds had already been there. For the last couple weeks, he had been dealing with phone calls and private meetings. He tried to talk to Cullen about it at one point, but Cullen had stopped him. He didn't want to know about it unless he had to be involved in it. Cadifor laughed at him and moved on. He figured that Cullen had earned a reprieve for a while.

Even Sarah was in a good mood. With Aislinn around to take some of the load off, she'd been spending more time with Drake. That was always good for her mood. Cullen took some of Keith's workload. He still had Keith dealing with the internal morale issues Terrick caused, but for the most part he left Keith to help Jaylyn with the new babies. Thinking about that had him chuckling. Jay called that morning and asked Cullen to *please* find Keith something to get him out of their room and away from her for a little while. Apparently he was trying to be helpful with the babies, and he was driving her nuts.

In between diaper changes, Keith managed to track the last leak within the pack back to Terrick. That was no surprise. The problem ended up being that there wasn't anything solid to get Terrick with. He had been talking with the Tairneach, but he hadn't leaked anything that he had been *told* not to say. So they were keeping an eye on him, and he was removed from the elder council, but he was still around and still causing problems. Oddly enough Cullen found that he didn't care. Dealing with Terrick was better than dealing with the other caoch that had been dominating his life lately. Besides Terrick had never been a loyalist or a good friend. If there was anyone in the pack who Cullen could have expected to stab him in the back, it was Terrick.

After it was established that there would be no fighting, Makeda stayed around the Madadh-Allaidh Saobhaidh to spend time with Aislinn while Cadifor took care of the Feds and the Pack Council. That first week had been something else. Makeda's influence on Aislinn was interesting. Aislinn couldn't behave more like an alpha's mate than she did under Makeda's diligent tutelage. For all of Makeda's effort with helping Aislinn she was repaid in her favorite way.

Cullen had never figured Aislinn for being that enthusiastic with a woman, but she was always surprising him with something.

Cullen finished with the bills for the casino and hotel. Liam was possessive of the bills for the Taigh-O\sda, so Cullen didn't get to take care of those. But he took a moment to look over the last of the arrangements for the mating ceremony. It was set. All the guests outside of the pack had received actual invitations. Nora was invited. There would be fewer druids present, but enough to make a showing for the groups of lycans who were only attending the mating to meet the druids. The guest list actually got larger after word spread about the first mating attempt and all the things that happened.

At first, Cullen tried to talk Cadifor out of doing the diplomatic thing, and make it a nice small mating ceremony. Aislinn was the one who said she wanted the druids there, and Keith pointed out that Cullen had already told everyone that they would reconvene in a month. They were stuck with the big party. Sarah went to extra lengths this time. There seemed to be more of everything. Liam came to Cullen's office complaining about the food she wanted, twice. The kitchen at the reservation apparently wasn't sufficient for his people to make it all out there in the quantities Sarah wanted, and Liam refused to bring it all in cold and heat it up there. Cullen finally conceded to buying some additional kitchen equipment for the cabin. He told Sarah that she was getting out of hand, but she smiled at him and told him that after all the trouble the first time, they owed it to everyone to make this a night to remember.

Aislinn helped Sarah make most of the arrangements this time, and she seemed okay if not pleased with all the fuss. Every time Cullen began to sound annoyed with the way things were turning out, Aislinn reminded him that he had said the two of them wouldn't get a chance to do anything in a small way. With Makeda around doting on Aislinn, and Sarah pretty much using Aislinn as her right hand the rest of the pack stopped questioning Aislinn's rank and motivation. It was as if she had been part of the pack all along. She decided to put off exploring her druid half until after the mating was finished. She wanted to make sure she was accepted by the lycans before expounding on anything that would make her more distinct than she already was. The only druidic thing she did was take a couple trips out to the reservation to speak with Brinah.

Cullen put the last of the papers aside and pushed back from his desk. He felt a bit disappointed that there were no phone calls today to interrupt his nice normal morning with more normal hassles. It would be a while before any of the standard day stuff would bother him again. He got up and left his office. It was time for lunch, and he wanted to eat with Aislinn. That meant tracking her down, though.

Ringing from his pocket drew Cullen's attention. He pulled the phone out of his pocket and read the caller ID, smiling when he saw Cadifor's name. "Yeah," he said into the receiver.

"Hey, is Aislinn still willing to take Jenna out to talk to Brennus?"

Cullen stopped in the middle of the hall. That wasn't what he had been expecting. The last thing he wanted to do two days before the mating ceremony was revisit the last time. "I take it that you finally got the books back?"

"For the most part. We got the books back, but the suspicion is that the Feds already took what they wanted out of them. This isn't over. The only reason I asked about the Jenna thing is because when we turned the books over to the Circle they seemed to think there's something missing. The Feds insist they don't have it. I'm leaning toward believing them, if only because they would have just copied the information and given us the original back. The Tairneach are the only ones who could have it, if it's still out there."

Cullen growled unhappily.

"You're too overprotective of her," Cadifor said in annoyance. "Jenna isn't going to tell us anything until Aislinn takes her to Brennus. I guarantee that she's been sitting on this card since the beginning, in case we went back on the arrangement."

"Fine," Cullen agreed. "I'll talk to her about it. You'll need to arrange to have Jenna at the reservation tomorrow, so we can get this out of the way and over with before the mating. I'm not going to have any more ceremonies. This is it."

Cadifor laughed. "All right. I'll see you there tomorrow round noon."

"We'll be there. Make sure you have enough guards to deal with Jenna in case she decides to go dire and try to kill people again."

"No problem. I don't think that will happen, but I'll have the men to deal with her if it does." There was silence for a minute. "Are we sure that Aislinn's going to be able to do this?"

"Yeah, remember Peter?" Cullen sighed.

"No. Who's Peter?"

"Was," Cullen said sadly. "Peter was the only one of my guys that Rafe had gotten to who tried to tell me what was going on. Rafe tortured and killed his mate. When we all got back and things settled down Peter asked Aislinn to help him talk to Zoe. We thought it would help him. He had been so depressed since Zoe died. We went out to the reservation and Aislinn managed to bring Zoe. Shortly after that Peter killed himself."

"Caoch," Cadifor said softly. "Well, it's not that surprising. Too bad for the loss of a good man."

Cullen let the air out of his lungs in a long slow breath. He had been in such a good mood. "Yeah." He paused. "Anyway, make sure Jenna brings that ring. I suppose it should be expected, but just make sure she has it. Aislinn finds it easier to do if there's something that was important to the soul she's trying to contact."

"Consider it done. I'll see you tomorrow."

* * * *

Aislinn sat in the infirmary of the sub-basement, down the hall from the gym. She hadn't been feeling well all month, and she was pretty sure she knew why. Rhona came into the room smiling at her. Aislinn nodded back. She had figured. She sat there trying to decide how she felt about the situation. It wasn't like the entire pack didn't know they were already mated at this point. They were all playing along with the pretense that Cullen and Aislinn still needed the ceremony. It had really come to the point where it was entirely for appearances. Most everyone was grinning and laughing about it when they thought no one was listening.

The one time she had walked into the great room while Terrick was trying to turn the fact that they had jumped mating protocol into an issue, she had heard several of the others telling him to can it. Aislinn even talked to Sarah about canceling the whole ceremony thing. Sarah said it was more a matter of pack unity than whether or not it needed to be done. To some extent, it was their penance for having gone about things on their own.

Rhona stood there intrigued by the wheels turning behind Aislinn's blue eyes. "This is a good thing," she said, as if she was trying to convince Aislinn.

Aislinn snapped into the moment. "I know. Cullen's going to be thrilled." *He put so much effort into to it after all,* she thought with some annoyance. Then suddenly another thought occurred to her. "How many," she asked, already wincing.

Rhona smiled again. She had Aislinn lean back, and she pressed on her still relatively flat stomach. Then she pulled out a strange looking box with a speaker and a cord leading to a probe. Rhona squirted some cold clear gel Aislinn's stomach and pressed the probe around. After a moment of searching she stopped on one heartbeat, before moving to another spot on the other side of Aislinn's stomach. "As far as I can tell only two."

At first Aislinn was relieved. Everyone kept calling pregnancies around here liters and that implied something like six puppies. Two sounded great compared to the alternative. Then the statement sunk in. "What do you mean 'as far as you can tell'?"

"Well it's an imperfect science. There might be more than two. Currently it looks like there are only the two. I'm only hearing two heartbeats."

Aislinn felt a kind of pleased feeling come over her all of a sudden. "Those were heartbeats?"

Rhona nodded, her eyes sparkling. This was really the best part of her job. She loved delivering babies. "Do you want to hear it again?"

"Yeah," Aislinn answered in awe.

Rhona ran the instrument over her stomach again. Aislinn felt her own heart flutter a bit when Rhona found the heartbeats again. "There's one," she said, pausing for a minute, so Aislinn could listen. She moved the probe around Aislinn's stomach. "There's the other one."

A small smile played on Aislinn's lips. "I suppose we should really get through the mating ceremony then," she said, with a guilty look.

Rhona laughed. "Yeah, that might be good." She shook her head. "If you come back tomorrow I might have the ultrasound fixed. Sorry, it's on the fritz at the moment. I'm getting it looked at sometime this afternoon."

"It's only been a month. What are you going to look at?"

Rhona turned to Aislinn, only just realizing that Aislinn might not be familiar with how lycan pregnancies go. "Um, well they'll be born in about half the time of a normal human pregnancy. So if you take nine months and turn that into four and a half, then you're looking at being closer to three months along human-wise right now."

Aislinn was staring a bit wide-eyed. "Is there anything else I need to know about this?"

"Not that I can think of right now. Make sure to start eating more. I know you've been feeling sick, but

I don't want you losing any more weight. If you have any more questions I'll be happy to answer them."

Still in shock, Aislinn nodded at the first comment and then shook her head at the second, as it only vaguely made sense to her.

"All right then. You're all done for now. Go get some lunch." Rhona smiled at her. Aislinn wasn't the first woman to leave the infirmary stunned, after having been told she was pregnant. Rhona was pretty sure, based on the smile she got when Aislinn heard the heartbeats, that she would come around relatively quickly. Then she started chuckling to herself as she imagined Cullen a father.

* * * *

Aislinn was stepping out of the elevator on the thirteenth floor as Cullen was stepping in. They both gave each other a long suffering look. Neither knew what the other's problem was, but they were both relatively unhappy at the moment. Aislinn was annoyed with that because if she hadn't been so concerned about what was happening to her, she would have known what was bothering Cullen.

"Lunch," he asked.

"Yeah," she said, forcing a smile. "I was going to suggest the same thing."

Cullen backed her into the elevator and hit the button for the lobby and the Taigh-O\sda. Aislinn sighed heavily. She had recently been thinking that she was eating too much rich food since she had access to the town's best steak house on a nightly basis. Now, she figured that it didn't matter. At least not for another three months. She suddenly put her hand on her stomach as she thought about that. *I'm going to be a mother in three months?* She was careful to keep that thought to herself.

Cullen stared at her and wondered opening what was going through her mind that made her look so distressed. "Aislinn?"

She snapped her head up and dropped her hand from her stomach. "Yeah?"

He stared into her eyes. "Are you all right?"

"Yeah," she said, unconvincingly.

"Okay. I don't believe you. But okay." He was annoyed. "Well, I'm upset because Cadifor wants you to take Jenna out to the circle and let her talk to Brennus. See how easy that was?"

"What," she scowled, as if she didn't know what he was getting at.

"Me telling you what the problem was. But you could have found that out from me without me saying it out loud," he said, sarcasm leaking though his voice.

"Cullen," she said, emphatically. "I'm okay. I am. I just need to think about this a minute. Then I'll tell you. I just need to think first."

Cullen looked deep into her eyes. She could feel him probing her head for reassurance. "All right," he said with genuine concern.

She put her hands on either side of his face and pulled him down for a kiss. "I love you."

Cullen melted a little. He couldn't be upset with her when she said that. They walked through the lobby and into the restaurant, hand in hand. A pretty omega held the door open for Cullen and Aislinn, as they walked in. Cullen and Aislinn took their usual booth without waiting for the hostess and were immediately given menus that they didn't look at. They placed their orders and sat there staring at each other in silence, waiting for the other to start the conversation.

Finally, Aislinn cleared her throat. She knew he would be thrilled about it. She didn't know why she was having such a hard time saying it. "So when do I deal with Jenna?"

"We're meeting Cadifor tomorrow noon. I wanted to deal with it before the mating ceremony. You still want to have the mating ceremony right?" He guessed at what was upsetting her. "If it's bothering you that much--"

"No, Cullen." She wasn't going to be able to keep it to herself. She wasn't going to be able to think. He could feel her upset and her blocking, and he wasn't going to let it go. "The ceremony's fine. I wouldn't do that to you after all the setup and time. Besides I'm getting used to the idea." She took a deep breath. He was staring at her with more and more concern. The waitress came back, smiling sweetly at them. Everyone seemed to be smiling sweetly at them. It was driving her nuts. *Maybe it's the hormones.* Aislinn watched the girl retreat from the table to go check on their order. "Cullen I'm pregnant," she blurted out, as soon as the girl disappeared into the kitchen.

A goofy grin started in the corners of his mouth. "You're pregnant? That's what's got you worked up?"

Aislinn didn't say anything, but she dropped the block she'd erected in her head. Cullen felt uncertainty flood his mind. Most of her fear came from understanding human pregnancy and human babies, but the idea of having lycan babies, a litter of lycan babies, was terrifying her. Although she had gotten used to the fact that she had a learning curve in the pack environment, she didn't feel like a baby was something a learning curve was allowable with.

Cullen stood up and moved around the table to her side of the booth. Aislinn could feel his happiness through their bond, and it was helping a little. He put his arm around her and pulled her into his arms, kissing her forehead and holding her. "You will be an incredible mother," he said though his smile. He didn't know what else to say. He couldn't believe she was pregnant. Already.

Aislinn started to wonder if he was going to get up out of the booth and start dancing. It was hard to be scared and uncertain with that much happiness pouring into her mind from outside. She rolled her eyes at him, when she looked up and saw the goofball grin on his face had gotten impossibly wider. His eyes were shining, and he was nearly laughing. "I'm glad you're so happy," she said trying to keep herself from smiling and then finally giving in.

Cullen suddenly frowned. "I don't want you around Jenna."

"It'll be fine," Aislinn said. "See? Now you're going to get more overprotective than you already are."

Cullen growled.

"Don't do that," she snapped. "I can still do what I'm supposed to do for now. No one can even tell yet. Though in a week or so, it'll be pretty obvious," she said, mostly to herself. "If there was anyone left who doubted that we'd already mated, they'll all have those concerns put to rest now."

Her sarcasm bit into him, but he wasn't giving on this. "Jenna's dangerous. If she decides she's no longer cooperative for any reason while you're alone with her then you're dead."

"Cullen, I don't see that as being as likely as you do. Brennus appears to be able to control her fairly well."

"I don't care. We'll get the rest of the caoch that's missing some other way." Cullen pulled out his cell phone and started paging through the numbers for Cadifor's name so that he could call and cancel.

Aislinn grabbed the phone out of his hand. His eyes flashed dangerously at her. "You wouldn't dare," she smiled sarcastically.

The waitress appeared with their food and was instantly frightened by the deadly staring match that was taking place. "Aislinn," Cullen growled. "Give it back."

"Or what?" Aislinn looked over at the concerned waitress. "It's okay. Just leave the food," she said sweetly to the girl.

The plates were dumped hurriedly on the table, and the pretty waitress instantly disappeared. Aislinn watched her go. "Now see what you did? You scared her."

Cullen looked like he might explode.

She sighed. "Please stop it. What do you mean 'missing caoch'?"

"We're not going to do this. It isn't a debate. I won't have you in that kind of danger regardless of the situation. Now give me my phone back before this table ends up on the other side of the restaurant."

"Liam would kill you," Aislinn answered. But she put the phone down in front of him. She really didn't want to make him this angry. She knew she wouldn't get anywhere with the situation if he was so pissed he wouldn't listen to reason. "Cullen. I need you to try and understand that this is stupidly scary for me. I know you don't really get why. But it is. It's important that you let me do what would be normal so that I can pretend in my head that this isn't as big a deal as it is. Please."

Cullen took the phone and stared at her indecisively. He growled some more. He could feel how upset she was and how much she needed things to stay normal, but his instincts told him to protect her. Putting her in a situation where he couldn't get to her if he needed to and with someone as dangerous as Jenna was just stupid. "Aislinn," he started.

"Please, Cullen."

She heard a crunch and a strangled beep as the cell phone in his hand crunched. Cullen looked down at the phone. He was upset enough that he'd actually crushed the damn phone in his hand. He put it back down on the table to prevent himself from throwing it across the room. "All right, how about a compromise? We'll go and see what kind of mood Jenna's in. You let me talk with her first and get a feel for how dangerous she is at the moment and then I'll decide if I want to let you be this stupid."

Aislinn glared at him. "I want to know why it's so different now that I'm pregnant. When I took her to Brennus a month ago it was just as dangerous as it is now. I still would have ended up dead. If I weren't pregnant now and took her to see Brennus I'd still be in danger. It's not like this makes me incapable of something I was previously able to do. In essence the situation really hasn't changed in any way other than an extra couple of lives are involved. And no one will know that other than you and me."

Cullen fumed some more. He couldn't argue with that. "I told you. Let me talk to Jenna first."

"Fine. I'll compromise. But don't think I won't argue with you if you decide in a way I don't agree with tomorrow."

"Fine," he said back, just as snottily.

The two of them sat there eating in silence. Aislinn hated that he was so angry. She sighed. "Cullen?"

"What now?"

She looked into his eyes and gave him a half-hearted smile. "I'm pregnant," she said again trying to sound happy.

Cullen couldn't help the pleasure that her saying that gave him. He smiled back, knowing she was trying to help.

* * * *

Cullen recruited a number of betas to go with them. Keith, Sarah, Drake, Mack, and Makeda all sat and chatted in the great room of the cabin, as they waited for Cadifor to show up. There were omegas rushing around with decorations and trays, getting everything ready for the mating ceremony the next day.

"I'm telling you this is a bad idea," Keith said. "Luck just hasn't been with Cul making this official. I say we cage Jenna until after it's over. I don't care what she's hiding that's so important."

"Or," Mack suggested, "alternatively, we could all take turns beating it out of her instead of giving the bitch what she wants."

Drake smiled and nodded. "I'll go with that."

Keith shook his head. "That'd probably be harder to do than you think now that she's a dire bitch." He grinned. "But she was a dire bitch before she went through the trouble of making it physical as well as mental."

There were some eye rolls as they listened to Keith's little crack. Sarah watched Cullen and Aislinn reemerge from the room they had gone into so they could argue in private. "You were really reaching for that one Keith," she said, wondering who had won the argument. From the look on Cullen's face, it seemed that Aislinn was the winner. Something was going on with those two.

Cadifor walked through the front doors. There were a number of large lycans surrounding Jenna, who was cuffed and being marched in between them. Jenna looked like hell. She was wearing a plain gray sweat suit and sneakers. She didn't have on any makeup, and her blonde hair was pulled back into a messy ponytail. She didn't look like the same person.

Keith couldn't help himself. "Prison's not been nice to Jenna," he chuckled.

Makeda got up and walked across the room. Her hips swung with more emphasis than usual. She stepped up to Cadifor and slid her arms around him. "You've been missed," she said, in her deep sexy accent. Then she leaned in and kissed him. Most everyone ignored the display. Jenna sneered.

Cadifor smiled at Makeda. She released him and walked back to the others, returning to her seat as if nothing happened. "Well," Cadifor said. "Are we ready to do this?"

"Yes," Aislinn said with emphasis as she walked past Cullen, headed straight for the group holding Jenna.

Cullen growled sharply, and everyone looked at him, except Aislinn. Everyone headed out the doors of the cabin and down the trail to the stones uncertainly. Cullen was fire and brimstone incarnate as they reached the standing stones. He walked up to Jenna purposefully. "If anything happens to her," he said in a low deadly tone, "I won't need help ripping you apart."

Jenna could see the truth in it. She nodded in compliance before the defiant look came back into her eyes.

Cullen stared into her face, reading her for a moment before he looked back to Aislinn. "Five minutes," he insisted.

Aislinn smiled at him and nodded the same way Jenna had.

Stop challenging me for the sake of it, Aislinn. I don't want to make an example of you, but that doesn't mean I won't.

I'd like to see you try, Aislinn glared back.

Jenna laughed. "Trouble in paradise?" This was the most entertaining thing she'd seen in months. "It was almost worth the trip, to watch you both growl at each other."

Cullen's head snapped around to see everyone trying not to stare at them and Jenna smiling with amusement. Then he looked back at Aislinn. *You're making a fool out of me.*

This was not how things should be going. She growled to herself. "I'm sorry," she said and stepped up to him with her head bowed. "Five minutes."

How the hell do you get to me so easily, he asked. Then he stroked her face, giving her permission to look up at him again. He half smiled and kissed her forehead. "Get it over with."

Aislinn approached Cadifor. "What exactly is the agreement here?"

"You take her to Brennus, and we get the last of the notes she has hidden at the Tairneach manor. In a way

I suppose it was good. The Feds are missing some pretty key information. But we still don't want it out and about, do we Jenna?"

Jenna smiled. "Of course not."

"Do you have Brennus' ring," Aislinn asked.

Cadifor stepped up to her and pulled on a chain around her neck. The ring came free from under Jenna's shirt. He let it fall back onto her chest. "We'll leave her hands cuffed, I think."

Cullen growled his agreement.

Aislinn looked at Jenna and nodded toward the stones. "Let's go." Jenna was allowed to walk out of the group of guards. Together Jenna and Aislinn stepped passed the stones. Cullen and the others all watched as there was a red flash from the ruby on Brennus' ring and the pair vanished.

Cullen felt the fog take over his mind, and he began to pace impatiently.

* * * *

Relaxing, Aislinn focused on Brennus Tairneach. She felt the energy from the ley lines running through her, and he appeared.

Brennus appeared on the slab in the center of the stone circle. He stared vacantly at first, and then his eyes focused on his daughter. "What is it Jenna?" His voice was gentle, and a tear formed in the corner of the proud alpha's eye.

"Daddy," she said, not really wanting Aislinn to be here, but knowing there was no other way. "I need to know something. Why," she sniffled a bit. "Why did you never think I was good enough? Was there anything I could have done?"

The tear dropped from his eye. "Jenna, you were the one who thought you weren't good enough. You're my daughter. I always did and always will love you. You don't have to be me."

"But you wanted us to always rule the Tairneach," she said, with a cracking voice.

"Jenna, I wanted any number of things. The most important thing was your happiness. I was never able to give you that. I'm sorry."

Jenna tried to reach for him, but her hands were cuffed, and there was nothing there to touch. "Daddy I put it back the way it was. I want you to know that it's the way you left it again," she said. "But I can't do this without you. Please. I'm scared. They're going to keep me in prison forever."

He nodded. "I know." Then he looked at Aislinn. "Let me go," he said.

Jenna glared at Aislinn. "No," she said. "Daddy, don't go."

"I won't sweetheart. I'm going to help you."

Aislinn felt a sharp pain in the back of her head. She looked up at Brennus. His eyes met hers, with a wicked determination.

"What are you doing," she asked in pain. "Brennus?"

Jenna screamed as the image of the alpha vanished. Blood red light flashed from the ruby on the ring. Aislinn's head seared with pain. She fell to her knees, as Jenna began to shift. The cuffs cut into Jenna's wrists. She screamed in pain as the cuffs nearly took her hands off before they shattered. Aislinn stared in fear. After a dazed moment, Jenna turned on her and Aislinn scrambled backward into the clearing.

* * * *

Cullen felt the pain start even through the fog. "What the muin is happening," he growled. "She's in pain."

The others attention was divided between Cullen and the circle. "What can we do," Cadifor asked. "Is there a way to pull her out of there?"

"No," Cullen paced angrily, swearing as he walked into the stone circle and around it.

When Aislinn crawled out from between the stones, all of the others were already on guard and waiting for the worst. Jenna took one look around at the number of lycans there, turned and ran into the woods.

Cadifor immediately changed and started the chase. His group of guards went with him. Cullen ordered Sarah to stay with Aislinn and then led the others after Cadifor. Aislinn remained on the ground holding her head. A bloody tear streamed out of one eye and down her face. She had no idea what had happened.

Cullen was on Cadifor's heels, but they were still losing ground. When they realized that they weren't going to catch Jenna the group pulled up. Cadifor had the fastest of his men continue following and pulled out his cell to call for help with a manhunt. It wasn't until he was looking at his cell that he remembered the damn reservation had no muin service. Cullen's reservation was huge and there was more wild land surrounding it. A lycan could disappear into the mountains relatively easily. He was pissed.

"Cullen," he growled. "How the hell do you call out of this place if you need to?"

"I have a sat-phone in the office."

"Then we need to get back. I have some calls I have to make."

Cullen, Cadifor and the rest of the group went back to the cabin. When they got to the stone circle, Aislinn was sitting with her back against one of the stones. Sarah took one look at the angry men and didn't bother to ask. She knew that they hadn't caught Jenna.

Cullen bent down and picked up Aislinn. She protested weakly at first, but quickly gave in and laid her throbbing head on his shoulder. As soon as they reached the cabin, Cadifor was on the sat-phone and had helicopters on the way. They were going to try to use the gps in the phones that the men following Jenna were carrying.

Cullen took Aislinn upstairs and laid her down on their bed. She smiled at him weakly. "So say it," she said.

"What?" He was still angry.

"Say 'I told you so'. It'll make you feel better."

He looked down at her and smiled finally. "You know I was right. Just remember this next time."

"Can I get some aspirin or something? My head is killing me." She pulled the blanket up around herself and turned onto her side.

Cullen pulled the drawer in the stand next to the bed open. She needed more than an aspirin. He took a vial of the healing drink the druids made out of the drawer. Keith was the one who decided that the alpha and betas should have the stuff readily available. He pulled the cork out of it and held it to her lips. "Drink this," he said, concerned. After she drank the entire vile down he put it aside and wiped the bloody tear off her cheek. If Jenna had really hurt her he would hunt her down personally. "Do you feel like there is anything wrong besides the headache?"

"No. I don't think so. It was weird. One minute everything was fine, and the next minute Brennus said that he'd protect Jenna. Then my head started throbbing, and there was a flash. The next thing I knew Jenna was screaming. Then I fell down, and she turned and came at me. That's when I crawled out of the circle, and you guys took it from there."

Cullen didn't know what to think about it. "I need to talk to Cadifor. Will you be all right until I get back?"

"I'm fine. Just a little tired."

Cullen tucked the blanket in around her, kissed her, and then headed downstairs. Cadifor was in the process of swearing and coming in the front door as Cullen came down the steps to the main room. He growled impatiently, pocketed his phone, and then looked at Cullen. "How's Aislinn?"'

Cullen shook his head. "She's got a terrible headache, but appears fine otherwise. I take it that we're having no luck with Jenna?"

"No," he said angrily. "She's getting away. She's gotten far enough ahead of my men that they're having trouble tracking her. By the time the helicopter gets there, who knows."

"Perfect. You don't know how close I am to canceling things," Cullen growled.

"You can't," Sarah said. "It's all set. What's she going to do at this point? She's alone and running. She won't be back here. She's not that stupid."

Cullen scoffed. "I'm not so sure about that."

Cadifor shrugged. "You'll have the same setup as last time. If she does something, we'll be here, and she won't get away with it. Who knows what you'll have if you put it off. How long are you going to wait before mating that girl?"

Suddenly, Cullen smiled for apparently no reason. *I really can't afford to wait any longer*, he thought. *The litter will be here before it should as it is.* They were all staring at him curiously. "You're right. It'll be fine."

Keith sat forward in his chair staring at Cullen and smiled himself. "What exactly changed your mood so suddenly?"

Cullen shook his head but the dumb smile was stuck at that point. "Nothing. Don't worry about it."

"Well," Sarah said, still staring at Cullen, "I suppose we should all just stay here tonight. Unless you're going to wake Aislinn up and force her into a car ride. Are you sure she's going to be all right for tomorrow? That's the only excuse I would see as reasonable for cancellation."

"Nah," Keith grinned wickedly, "she just has to stand on her hands and knees for a while. Cul could handle doing all the work." Some of the other guys chuckled at that.

Sarah glared at him. "I don't see Aislinn as the type to be happy with allowing anyone to do all the work."

Cullen smiled and nodded at that one. "No, she's not that type. But I hope that the headache won't last that long anyway. It wouldn't be any fun." There were smiles all around at that comment.

The rest of the evening was spent with Cadifor heading out to use the sat-phone, waiting for the others to get back, watching the omegas finish decorating for the next day, and checking on Aislinn. She told Cullen repeatedly to quit waking her up and leave her be.

Chapter 26

Brìgh gach cluiche gu dheireadh.
The essence of a game is at its end.
-Gaelic Proverb

Take two, Aislinn thought, as she walked out of their room and down the stairs to join their guests and friends. Sarah had outdone herself. Aislinn knew that she had helped with the arrangements, but Sarah really deserved the credit. The entire cabin was decorated with twinkle lights and white roses. The food on the buffet was beyond extravagant. There was soft Celtic music being played by a live band, sounding medieval and enchanting.

The guests were all smiling and joking about what they would do if there was another fight. They didn't realize that their hosts considered it a possibility since Jenna was not recovered. Tairneach manor was in the process of being thoroughly ransacked, by order of the Pack Council. In addition, the entire Tairneach pack was rounded up to be questioned about the missing information, but it wasn't looking promising at this point.

Even with those considerations, the night went off without a hitch. They waited until sunset, and the druids performed the blessing again. This time Nora led the song. Even the lycans who had seen it last time were amazed at the sight again. Then it was time.

Aislinn found herself in Cullen's arms, his eyes intent only on her, as he kissed her. His tongue ran over her lips, and she opened her mouth to let him taste her. Hands danced over her skin, undressing. Aislinn pulled at the buttons on his shirt then pushed the shirt and jacket off his shoulders. Aislinn ran her hands across his chest, scraping her fingernails across his nipples. Cullen growled and watched as she knelt in front of him, dragging her nails along his skin as she went.

Cullen watched her, as she opened her mouth and her tongue slipped out to taste the pre-cum on the tip of his cock. He drew in a sharp breath, staring into her swirling amber eyes while she drew his cock into her warm wet mouth. Aislinn sucked gently on the spongy head, drawing him deeper into her mouth. There was growling and howling all around them, as the lycans watched her. Cullen wove his fingers in her hair, encouraging her to go faster. She readily took his direction and began sucking ravenously. Cullen groaned as her tongue circled his cock deftly. As she stared into his eyes, obviously pleased and enjoying putting on the show, he was getting dangerously close to overload.

Cullen pushed her away gently and walked around behind her. Aislinn watched him, her hand trailing along his thigh as he stepped around her. As he knelt behind her, Aislinn felt his cock stroke down her back. He caressed her shoulder with a gentle touch, pushing her hair away from her neck, exposing the scarred bite mark that was already there. He smiled, leaned down and kissed the scar, then began trailing kisses along her neck and up to her ear as he pulled her more tightly against his chest, reaching around in front of her and caressing her breasts.

Aislinn moaned sweetly for him and began purring. He was being too gentle, not that she wasn't enjoying it, but the audience was getting antsy. They were supposed to follow the alpha pair's lead, and Cullen was taking longer than they would have liked to get to the good stuff. One of Cullen's hands ran down her ribcage to pause at her stomach on its way to his ultimate destination. Aislinn laid her back on his shoulder, as he kissed and nibbled her neck. She could feel his erection against her lower back, and his fingers tripped over the diamond chain around her waist when his hand rested shortly on her stomach.

"Tá grá agam duit, Aislinn," he whispered into her ear. "I don't know what I was or how I lived before you."

The intense sound of his voice, coupled with the love she felt pouring into her from him brought a tear to her eye. She turned her face to him and looked into his eyes for a moment. She couldn't say anything. For the first time in her life, Aislinn felt like the world really was perfect. There wasn't anything else she wanted. *People have it wrong*, she realized. *Jobs, degrees, hobbies, vacations, marriages, family, money. None of it is what people think it is. This is what everyone is looking for.*

The sound of desperate lust coming from the surrounding lycans broke the moment between them. Aislinn sighed, blinked the tear out of her eye, and nuzzled against his neck. She put her hand on the back of his where it was stroking her bellybutton with knowledge of the children he had placed there. She pressed gently against his hand, encouraging him to continue its descent.

Cullen looked up at the anxious crowd. The younger unmated lycans were the ones making most of the noise. Cullen's eyes fell on Cadifor. He smiled a sad knowing smile. He had lost a mate a long time ago. He understood exactly what was taking Cullen so long. Makeda stood at his side waiting just as patiently and watching the two with a smile and tears on her face, a little envy in her eyes.

Cadifor glared at the surrounding crowd, eliciting a respectful lull to the cacophony. He stepped up just enough to get some attention and bowed his head toward the alpha pair. Makeda did the same and the rest of the crowd silenced a little, echoing the acknowledgement.

Excited howling rang out from the clearing to the cabin. The gathered druids watched in awe. It was a strangely beautiful ceremony, even if they believed there should be more dignified reverence and less rutting. The moon came out from behind a cloud and lit the clearing brightly as if on cue, and Cullen decided to finish it. They could be sweet and embrace each other later in their room.

Cullen briefly dipped his fingers into her dripping slit. The moment he touched her, she let loose a needy moan that had him incapable of making her wait any longer. Her pussy was on fire and dripping, the lips swollen, ready and hungry for his cock. He pulled his fingers from her and pressed them into his mouth. The taste of her brought his wolf surging to the surface. Cullen growled as his body shifted into his hybrid form. Aislinn felt fur against her back, and the arm around her chest grew in width and strength, as claws on his fingers bit into her breast. She drew in a sharp breath as her cat responded to the change in tempo. Aislinn growled excitedly and pushed his arm away from her chest, as her body shifted.

The crowd roared with approval as Aislinn leaned forward so she was on her hands and knees in front of

Cullen. He looked down at her stripes. *By the Gods, you're beautiful.* The diamonds tangled in her fur as it grew along her body. Cullen grabbed her hips roughly and pulled her back to him, growling as he thrust deep into her.

Aislinn growled as he began fucking her relentlessly. His knot worked deep into her and swelled inside her. *That feels incredible,* she said to him.

His claws drew blood at his finger tips, as he forced himself into her over and over. She moaned through the pleasurable pain, wanting more. Aislinn's breasts shook beneath her as he drove himself into her. The sounds of rutting wolves rose into the night sky around the clearing and woods surrounding the cabin. Aislinn was surprised at how turned on she was by the idea of being watched like this. Cullen completely lost the ability to think beyond the next touch, thrust or moan.

Aislinn felt her body begin to tense under the assault. She lost track of everything else, as the pleasure began to surge through her. Cullen was grateful that she had finally started to come. He didn't think he could last much longer. Leaning over her, he bit down on her shoulder. Aislinn cried out as she felt his teeth cut into her. He released into her as she began to purr breathlessly with the last of her spasms. His body jerked hard and he thrust involuntarily as his cock emptied into her. Cullen released her hips from his grip and wrapped his arms around her chest, pulling Aislinn into his lap as he sat back on his heels. Her body heaved with her breathing as she tried to catch her breath.

It took a few moments for them both to recover from the intensity of the orgasm they shared. Blood dripped from Aislinn's scarred shoulder and the corner of Cullen's mouth. He stroked the fur on her back, tracing the stripes to where they faded into spots down her side. Aislinn giggled a bit when his gentle caress touched the right spot along the side of her ribcage. It was a strange sound coming from a cat. Cullen smiled as much as he could with a muzzle.

The crowd was already milling about. There were quite a few alpha visitors who had met Aislinn, caught her scent, and were dying to find out what she tasted like. Cullen readjusted their position so that he was sitting on his knees and Aislinn's legs fell to either side of his. *Spread your legs for them piseagan,* he told her, wrapped his arms around her again and began licking and nibbling her neck and ear.

Aislinn blushed beneath her fur and was grateful she had it for the first time. Her stomach fluttered a bit and Cullen hugged her reassuringly. Aislinn closed her eyes and leaned back against him as she parted her knees and spread her legs wide. Everyone could see Cullen lodged firmly inside her. One of Cullen's arms was around her waist, and his fingers twined into the chain of diamonds. The other hand was groping her breast and pinching at a nipple. Aislinn kept her eyes closed, but Cullen watched possessively as the wolves circled them.

Cadifor was the first to approach. The snow white wolf trotted up to the alpha couple, followed by a beautiful black Egyptian looking wolf. Cadifor lowered his nose to their joined sexes and took in their scent. His tongue snaked out and lapped at the inside of Aislinn's thigh first. It was covered with her own juices from their energetic play, and it tasted more of her than Cullen. Cadifor was well aware of the purpose of this part of the ceremony, but he was far more interested in Aislinn's taste than Cullen's.

Aislinn shivered and stifled a moan as Cadifor's tongue slid along her thigh, into the dip along her outer lips, and then along her lips to brush her clit. His tongue was deftly precise as he avoided Cullen's cock. Cullen's gaze bored down into the top of Cadifor's head. He knew what his friend was doing. Cullen wasn't exactly enthused about having the other man's tongue on his cock, but that wasn't the point. Aislinn couldn't help the orgasm that was building already. She whimpered and wiggled in Cullen's arms. His fingers on her nipple twisted, and he held her tighter. The more times she came it was considered good luck. He figured he would talk to Cadifor later about his obvious attention to Aislinn.

Aislinn trembled, her eyes shot open, she looked down at Cadifor, and the moan she'd been holding back finally escaped. The circling wolves howled. Cadifor dragged his tongue purposefully over the base of Cullen's cock and gave one last swipe to Aislinn's clit before lifting his head and licking his muzzle, quite pleased with himself. Makeda nosed him in the rump to get him to move out of the way so she could take her turn. Makeda wasn't as discriminatory as Cadifor had been, but ended up with a similar result.

Aislinn relaxed back into Cullen's arms and surrendered to the sexual onslaught that continued throughout the night. Even when Cullen managed to calm enough, long enough that he could pull away from her and the two of them could move and mingle with the guests again, wolves would approach her, or people would kneel in front of her and lick at her pussy.

By the time they were allowed to retreat to their room alone, Aislinn was exhausted in ways she never thought possible. They showered before getting into bed. Cullen didn't like all the mingled scents that were on her body from the evening. They cuddled together in their bed with the blanket pulled up tightly around them.

"Do I get to tell everyone you're pregnant tomorrow," he asked softly, as his hand drifted to touch her stomach again.

"If you want," she smiled in the darkness.

Cullen hugged her. He could feel that most of her anxiety had passed. They were official now. Jenna and the rest of the mess was Cadifor's problem. From what he could tell, life as he had known it could go back to normal, or as normal as having a litter could be. She smiled and closed his eyes as sunlight began to filter around the curtains on their window. He didn't intend to get out of bed for some time today. He had never been this content in his life. Aislinn began purring, and the two of them fell asleep.

* * * *

When Cullen and Aislinn finally woke up, they cuddled some more before dressing to go downstairs and say good-bye to their guests. There were a few things they needed to do, and then Cullen was taking Aislinn up to a little cabin high in the mountains. It had belonged to his grandfather and wasn't nearly as big, nice, or convenient as the pack cabin. His grandparents hid from the human population and raised his father, aunts, and uncles there. Cullen never took anyone up there before. Even Keith and Sarah didn't know where exactly it was, but that was part of the point. He smirked. *They can't interrupt if they don't know where I am.* He was excited to show Aislinn his secret place. He hadn't told her where they were going yet.

Cullen and Aislinn came down the stairs hand in hand. When they got to the great room, they were inundated with congratulations, hand shaking and smiling. Part of the generally happy and excited atmosphere had to do with the fact that the night had gone so well. Cadifor was already gone. He used the sat-phone earlier that day, and was notified that Jenna had been spotted. As much as Cadifor wanted to stick around and find out what Cullen intended to do to him for playing with Aislinn the way he had the night before, Cadifor had a lost prisoner to recover and was taking the loss more than a little personally.

Aislinn watched Celia and Mack cuddle on the couch. Celia was only a couple weeks ahead of her and was obviously pregnant. She wasn't huge by any means, but her stomach showed a small bulge that couldn't be mistaken for fat. Celia got up and came walking over to them. She smiled warmly at Aislinn. It was such a strange look coming from the woman. When Celia actually leaned in and hugged Aislinn, everyone stared and waited for the punch line.

"Congratulations," Celia said. Then she stepped back from the hug and looked at Aislinn happily. "I was just wondering when you and Lord Arnauk would be back?"

Aislinn shrugged and looked over at Cullen. "I'm kinda just along for the ride. He hasn't even told me where we're going."

Cullen smiled mischievously. "Probably a week. Maybe two. It depends. I originally planned a month alone. But," he looked at Aislinn with a goofy grin that had Celia and the others curious what the secret was, "I don't think that will be a reasonable possibility now."

Celia couldn't help a little jealousy and was momentarily glad her bond with Mack was broken. She had never seen Lord Arnauk look at any woman the way he looked at Aislinn. "I really am happy for you," she said. "I can't help but wonder what the grin is all about."

Cullen didn't answer. He just grinned some more and Aislinn shook her head. There would be no keeping it secret, if he kept looking like that. *Oh well, it's not like I can hide it much longer anyway. You can tell them after I tell Grandma,* she thought at him, then looked at Celia again. "Why were you curious when we'll be back?" Aislinn tried to change the subject.

"Mack and I want to wait to be mated until you both return. So I have to admit that I'm happy it will be sooner," she said and stroked the bulge on her stomach. "I'm going to look ridiculous enough as it is. And it's only going to keep getting worse."

Aislinn grinned. "But you're going to have babies," she said excitedly. "That doesn't look ridiculous. Just consider it extra incentive."

Mack was sitting on the couch listening. He chuckled when Celia groaned.

Keith chimed in at that point. There was no way he could pass up an opportunity like this. "Well, Cel, I guess you shouldn't have been so enthusiastic in your play, if you didn't want to chase little ones around. Speaking of little ones," Keith grinned pointedly at Cullen. He knew how much time the two of them had spent together when Aislinn went into heat. "When are you two going to join the club? I can't have mine growing up without a couple of yours to pick on. All that grinning you're doing and emphatic glances from Aislinn couldn't mean something could it? That was what? About a month ago, I think."

Aislinn blushed deeper crimson with each comment. The people watching her reaction started smiling. Cullen tried to give Keith a hard look to make him stop, but his happiness about the situation precluded seriousness. With a grin bleeding through his hard expression Cullen pushed Aislinn toward the kitchen. "We're going to get something to eat. I want to talk to you later about your mouth," he said to Keith.

The minute Aislinn and Cullen walked away, the excited whispering started. Aislinn sighed, *Okay, so I'm glad he's so happy for you, but is he going to get us into trouble if everyone finds out what we were up to last month?*

Cullen laughed. *There's no way for them to not know what we were up to. Ais, my love, you're going to have the litter way too early for it to have happened after this. Everyone knows that we mated a while ago. It's the worst kept secret in the pack. It doesn't matter. They've all come to accept you at this point. I put on the show for them. It'll be okay. I'll be surprised if anything is ever said about it.*

Cullen and Aislinn headed into the kitchen, intent on finding something to eat. There were tons of great leftovers from last night's banquet. Cullen kept touching her. She couldn't keep his hands off of her, especially her stomach. "Well even if you don't announce it, people are going to figure it out, if you keep this up," she hissed and playfully batted his hands away.

"Then go out there and tell Brinah," he said softly. "Quickly," he added, with a real serious tone.

She knew that he would never be happy with her going into the stone circle where he couldn't get to her. There was something about it that unsettled him.

"When you get back, I'll tell everyone. We're leaving tomorrow morning. I want to deal with saying our good-byes tonight so that we don't have to stop before taking off." He kissed her neck and cuddled her some more.

"Hey now," an older omega said in a grandmotherly tone. "The kitchen is for eating. If you both intend to play some more, then take it into the other room. Pups," she growled in exasperation.

Cullen stayed in the great room to talk to everyone, and Aislinn snuck out the front door. She walked down the path toward the stones. When she got there she was surprised to find Nora. Aislinn was introduced to the ancient druid the night before, but it was brief and hectic.

The older woman watched Aislinn approach. "It's good to see you survived the mating. You certainly are a remarkable young woman. Truly that is to be expected of Brinah's offspring."

Aislinn stared at Nora uncertainly. "I've come to see her."

Nora nodded. "I was told you are capable. Do you realize what a rare gift that is?"

Aislinn shook her head. "I don't know much about that side of myself. Now that the world isn't coming to an end I'm going to spend time with my grandmother here and try and figure it out."

"I'm glad you've decided to embrace that part of yourself. I'm sure it would be easier to continue to ignore it and make your life with the lycans."

"I've never been good at ignoring anything," Aislinn said.

"Still, we make you uncomfortable," Nora said.

Aislinn didn't answer. Of course they made her uncomfortable. She had trouble trusting people. Cullen made her nervous at first.

Nora smiled gently, as if she understood. "Brinah is only capable of so much. You will find that as the length of time since she died increases it will become more difficult to speak to her. When you decide that you are ready and wish to learn more, we'll still be here. I believe I will take my leave of you now." Nora looked around. "This is a beautiful place. I'm glad that one of ours will be watching over it. Too many of our places have been lost to time and what humans call civilization." Nora didn't say good-bye. She just wandered down the path away from the stone circle.

Aislinn took a deep breath. Closing her eyes, she thought of her grandmother. Calm and a sense of change flowed into her with the power from the ley lines. She knew that when she opened her eyes she would be in the still place with her grandmother. There was a strange sense of accomplishment that ran through her, as she realized that she was starting to be able to tell the difference.

Aislinn opened her eyes and saw Brinah standing there. She smiled sadly. She wished she could hug her grandma. But she figured that at least she could see and talk with her. Aislinn didn't like that Nora had said this would get more difficult in the future.

Brinah smiled proudly, walking toward Aislinn. She wished she could have played a role of some kind in her granddaughter's mating the night before. "I'm so happy for you, child."

Aislinn blushed a little. "Did you see what happened last night, Grandma?"

"You didn't think I'd miss it, did you?"

Aislinn's embarrassment increased. "I guess I didn't think about it. You're okay with it?"

"As long as you're happy, I'm happy for you. He certainly seems to make you happy. He appears to be a good man." Brinah's eyes were full of love. Aislinn almost cried. "Is there anything else," Brinah asked in a knowing tone.

Aislinn giggled. Why she thought her grandmother wouldn't know was beyond her. "I'm pregnant Grandma," she said excitedly, and she realized that she really was excited.

Brinah's smile widened. "You'll have to bring them to see me," she said.

"Of course. But I'll have to learn how. I'm still not sure of what to do to bring people here except that Jenna's ring helped with Brennus." Aislinn's smile faded when she thought about that.

"Jenna was holding the ring. That aided you in bringing her along. If you were touching her, however, that would have worked as well."

Aislinn nodded. She could feel Cullen getting nervous already.

"He certainly is protective of you," Brinah said, as if she knew what Aislinn or Cullen was thinking.

"When I brought Jenna here I was hurt. He worries because our connection seems to weaken when I'm here, and he can't get to me."

"Brennus used you," Brinah said with concern. "You have a great deal to learn if you're going to use your abilities Aislinn. You try too much too quickly. It's impressive that you were able, but Brennus took advantage of it. Now he's with Jenna. You are very lucky you survived what he did."

Aislinn felt a terrible feeling run through her. "I don't understand what you mean when you say that he's with Jenna."

Brinah sighed. "Come back to me when you have more time. It's not important now, and your mate paces awaiting your return. Have your time with him. Come back to me when you are able to stay at length." Brinah vanished suddenly, and the trees around the circle came to life.

Aislinn looked around in frustration. She didn't like leaving it at that, but Brinah was right. Cullen was standing against that tree he seemed to like so well. His arms were crossed over his chest, and he was watching for her. Aislinn went to him, concern in marring her features.

"Grandma said something about Brennus being with Jenna. Then she kicked me out because you're being impatient," Aislinn growled.

Cullen's eyebrows raised. "Maybe I like Brinah better than I thought," he said and kissed Aislinn's forehead. "I wouldn't worry about Jenna. Brennus is dead, and Cadifor had a lead. She's his problem now. Besides, Cadifor has the help of the Circle at this point. If Brennus becomes an issue, they can deal with it."

Aislinn sighed. "You never listen to me," she said.

"Ditto," he replied with a smile.

She stuck her tongue out at him. He grabbed her and quickly leaned in to suck on it.

"Hey," she squealed, pushing at him playfully.

"That's what you get for sticking it out," he grinned. Then his tone got more serious. "All right. I'm listening. I leave it to you. I will call Cadifor and tell him what you just said. You decide whether I offer to hand you over, newly mated and pregnant to help him track down and capture a dire lycan who may now have a ghost or something with her, or I warn him and suggest he get help from the Circle, leaving you and I to go away together."

Aislinn growled. "Have it your way, but when we get wherever you're taking me, I get a turn on top," she chided.

Cullen pulled her into his arms and swung her around. "Anything you want."

He made the call as soon as they got back to the cabin. With everything taken care of they went upstairs and got their bags packed. Cullen told her that they would be riding an ATV most of the way, and then doing some hiking, so she only got to take one backpack. "Besides, I intend to keep you naked for most of the time anyway." They decided to tell everyone that she was pregnant when they got back. For now, it was their little piece of happiness and they wanted to keep it like that. The rest of the pack returned to the Madadh-Allaidh Saobhaidh, praying that they would be able to manage for a couple weeks without Lord General Cullen Arnauk, the leader of the pack.

The End

Gaelic Translations

Caoch = Shit

D'anam don diabhal! = May the devil take your soul

Druis = Whore

Eistigi liom = Listen to me

Faigh muin = Get fucked

Galla = Bitch

Madadh-Allaidh Saobhaidh = Wolf den (casino)

Mo gra⸝ = My love

Mo mhúirnín bán= My fair darling

Mo piseagan= My kitten

Móran làithean dhuit is sìth, Le d'mhaitheas is le d'nì
bhi fàs. = May you be blessed with long life and peace.
May you grow old with goodness and riches.

Rach-air-muin = Go fuck yourself

Tá brón orm = I am sorry

Tá grá agam duit = I love you

Tá tú iontach álainn = You are very beautiful

Taigh-O⸜sda = An inn/pub/hotel (name of the
restaurant)

Vae victis = Woe to the defeated

Vaughn = Small one

ABOUT LEIGHANN PHOENIX

It's always the quiet girl. She sits in the back of the class or stands at the bar, while her friends all mingle. She's the one mom always said was a "good girl," and all her friends believe is a prude. Leighann Phoenix has been writing since she was a child. The passion and pain reflected in her writing are little glimpses of what's lurking just beneath the surface. Her publications to date will be left in the dark where they belong. The new incarnation of her writing burns with a fire of it's own.

If you enjoyed <u>LEADER OF THE PACK</u>, you might also enjoy:

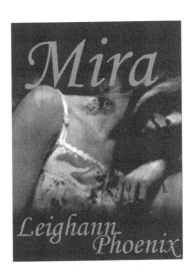

MIRA
By Leighann Phoenix

As a druid sacrifice to a vampiric assassin, Mira is sworn to remain companion to the monster until her death. She never dreamed that she would find anything short of blood and tortured death when she walked blindly into the darkness that he existed in. Finally meeting Rillan, Mira is forced to battle herself and her fears as she attempts to fulfill her vows.

Rillan came to accept his existence as a necessary evil. In a vindictive quest for revenge he committed himself to tormented darkness. He never dared to hope for someone like Mira. Now that the monster has her, the man left in him can't bear to keep her.

Warnings: This title contains graphic language and sex.

Excerpt From <u>MIRA:</u>

Mira stood staring into the darkness of the cave, her white shift blowing slightly in the breeze. Average in all ways, Mira had average brown hair, average brown eyes, average weight, average height, average intelligence, and average bravery. She was just average. She had been dreading this moment since watching the first of her sisters commit to the path. She was the last of this generation. Mira wasn't sure if it was better to have lived a longer life dreading what would come or if it would have been better to have died first and lose what little time she had been given.

The ceremony was almost over. He was inside the cave waiting for her.

She had him pictured as some kind of vicious, desperate creature. The druids had kept him around for centuries and she could hear the lessons that she had been taught since she had joined the order running through her head. Mira had even helped to teach the new generation of girls about him. Now all that was left was for the high priestess to be done with her speech.

Rillan Tiernay was created to protect and serve the circle. He was a guardian, an assassin, and a vampire. Each generation a group of girls was picked to be sacrificed to his thirst. This was his condition for his loyalty. He had come to despise what he was, but his self preservation instinct was too strong for him to kill himself. Each girl given to him was there to feed him until she died or asked him to kill her. Then she was replaced by another. Once she was sent into the caves she could not leave and only came to the gateway to collect the supplies that the druids left nightly. Rillan left only when there was an assignment from the druids. Every girl who entered the cave believes that maybe she will be different. Perhaps she won't want to die. Most last several months. The longest was ten years. The girl who had gone before Mira had lasted three weeks.

When Mira had collected the girl's body from the stone altar just outside the cave entrance it had been a sobering experience. The other times that Mira had performed the duty there had been a feeling of detachment. She rarely even looked at the girls' faces, let alone the rest of their bodies'. But she had never been next in line before. When Mira had collected the last body she had stared at the pasty white skin pulled tight over skeletal features for a long time. She had examined the numerous vicious bite marks that riddled the shoulders and neck of the dead girl. Mira had bathed the body for her burial and had found the bruises on the girl's arms that told how she had been held down. She found the blood along the inside of her thighs. Her body itself had shriveled, drained of blood and starved of food, from the looks of her. Mira had no idea what exactly the girl had suffered over the three weeks that she was inside the cave. She tried to tell herself that anything she could imagine had to be worse than what actually had happened, but was having little success in reassuring herself. He is a good man. Our guardian. The other girls simply weren't strong enough, she told herself.

BUY THIS AND MORE TITLES AT
www.eXcessica.com

eXcessica's <u>BLOG</u>
www.excessica.com/blog

eXcessica's <u>YAHOO GROUP</u>
groups.yahoo.com/group/eXcessica/

Check out both for updates about eXcessica books, as well as chances to win free E-Books!

Made in the USA
Lexington, KY
03 April 2011